Antioxidants & Other Stories

Terry Bennett

Antioxidants & Other Stories

The Toby Press

First Edition 2004

The Toby Press LLC

PO Box 8531, New Milford, CT 06776-8531, USA

& PO Box 2455, London W1A 5WY, England

www.tobypress.com

ISBN 1 59264 084 2

A CIP catalogue record for this title is available from the British Library

Typeset in Garamond by Jerusalem Typesetting

Printed and bound in the United States by
Thomson-Shore Inc., Michigan

Contents

Antioxidants & Other Stories

Terry Bennett

Antioxidants

I carry my mug of coffee down the narrow hallway of our beachside cottage. Liz remains in the rustic living room, reading a magazine. At home, she would read a technical or trade publication, but this is supposed to be a getaway. So perhaps she's brought something of a more personal nature—possibly about rejuvenation, or the power of journaling. I picture my own library at home, with two shelves devoted to the dynamics of effective reasoning, and I'm glad to be holding a coffee mug instead of a book.

To my right, through the small window above the kitchen sink, I see the deep blue, cloudless sky. It rests atop sand dunes, which block my view of the curving beach that greets the tide. I try to imagine the breadth of the ocean, but that slips away as other thoughts intrude. This weekend is supposed to be a reconciliation, something each of our counselors recommended, but nothing seems to be happening. Nothing beyond the little pinpricks of old habits and disagreements rising to the surface.

I turn to the microwave and set down my coffee mug. From a roll of cellophane, I tear off a piece the size of my hand. Carefully, I lay it across the top of my mug and run one finger around the lip and sides, sealing the cellophane—a little trick I learned that retains the moisture, keeps things from burning. I punch a protruding button, which swings open the microwave door, sounding a sharp "*bing!*"

"What are you doing?" Liz calls from the living room.

I picture her, frowning as she looks up from her magazine, marking her place with a finger.

"What's it sound like?" I say. "Reheating my coffee." I set my coffee mug inside and shut the door.

"*Don't,*" she says. "If you drink it fresh, right after it's brewed, you'll get the benefit of its antioxidants. Reheat it, and you're simply distilling the toxins."

Just like our relationship, I think, and close my eyes for a few seconds. Wanting the moment to pass.

When I reach out my hand to program the microwave—an old, battered-looking unit—it starts by itself. Inside a light turns on as its circular glass platter begins to rotate slowly, carrying my coffee mug. The exhaust fan runs with a dull, flat hum, pushing air into my face.

I stare at my finger. It almost reached the "one-minute auto-heat" button, but didn't touch it. Couldn't have, because I didn't feel any resistance or pressure against the tip of my finger.

Puzzled, I watch the digital readout on the microwave tick down. Sixty seconds, then fifty-nine, then fifty-eight. The phone on the kitchen wall, hanging next to the microwave, starts ringing.

I glare at it. No one is supposed to know that we're here—that was one of the ground rules our counselors suggested. This despite the objections of our stockbrokers.

"Now what?" Liz demands, sounding miffed.

Irritated, I grab the phone. "Yes? Who is it?"

A terrible roaring sound assaults my ear—a chorus of screams—like from an amusement park, only these are filled with terror and shredded with static.

I think maybe someone is holding their phone up to a television, next to a video or movie that's playing, when a woman's voice, half-sobbing, blurts out, "Are you there?"

"Who?"

"*Anyone*. My God, we're falling!"

With my other ear, away from the phone, I hear a very faint, far-off whine that is rising in pitch. The same whine, in my phone ear, runs much louder, right behind people who are yelling and weeping.

"The ocean," she gasps. "If we don't hit too hard, maybe we'll have a chance." She starts sobbing as screams overwhelm her voice.

"Who is this?" I insist, hearing another wave of panicked cries and hollering. I wait for an answer, leaning away from the drone of the microwave's fan.

"That realtor," Liz hollers from the living room. "He promised us an unlisted number."

Over my shoulder, I answer, "Hush, Liz."

The screams from the phone continue.

Liz answers, "He'll hear about this."

I cover the phone's mouthpiece and yell, "Be quiet."

I reach out, jabbing the microwave's stop button, without any result.

To my right, through the kitchen window, sunlight glints on a moving speck, high in the sky, catching my attention. Aghast, I realize it's curving downward, aimed at the Pacific.

"Please," cries the woman on the phone. Her voice is muffled. "Oxygen mask," she pants. "I can breathe now."

"Hang on," I say, jabbing harder at the microwave's row of buttons. When I hit "one-minute auto-heat," the microwave stops, and so does the screaming.

"*We're—something's changed*," *she says*. "*We're not falling*." *There's disbelief in her voice*. "*I'm—I'm taking off my mask*."

I see that the microwave is halted, mid-turn, with the cellophane on my coffee mug starting to puff up. There's a wisp of steam visible, but it holds its shape, without rising. And the light inside the microwave has dimmed, but not gone out.

I turn to the kitchen window. The gleaming speck, a little larger now, has arrested itself, an inch lower within the frame of the window.

"No one's moving," she says, *"like in a photograph. But I can reach out and touch them." She sniffs, choking off a sob. "The woman next to me is clutching her daughter."*

"I don't understand." I take a breath to steady myself. "Who are you? How did you call me?"

"When we went into a dive, I grabbed at the seat in front of me, and my cell phone rang. I picked it up."

"You're in a plane?"

"Yes. Headed for Santa Barbara."

This can't be real, I think, then remember the binoculars Liz brought, on the chance we might want to try bird-watching—something from a list of "shared" activities we could explore.

I run to the bedroom. The binoculars are on the dresser in their leather case. I grab them and dash back to the kitchen. As I jerk them from their case, the microwave catches my eye. The platter and coffee mug are still frozen, not moving, but the readout on the one-minute auto-heat is counting down. It's going from 37 seconds, to 36, to—

I aim the binoculars at the gleaming speck and focus. Zoomed to full power at twelve-times magnification, I make out the shape of a plane, hanging in the sky on its side, with one wing pointed down at the ocean. The plane's twisted contrail marks the sweep of its downward trajectory.

Behind me, a *"bing!"* sounds and the screaming resumes. The microwave regains its turning motion, fully lighted, with the cellophane puffing up on my coffee mug.

I press the phone to my ear, trying to concentrate as a man's voice—mechanically distorted—cuts through the screams. "Assume the crash position by bending forward and gripping your ankles. I'm leveling off. Ramps at the exits will inflate, serving as rafts. Please—"

A harsh, thumping vibration interrupts and the screams increase.

My eyes shoot to the window, where the silver speck is moving again, trailing a darker color now.

"I'm afraid," cries the woman, her voice muffled again. "Please, oh please help me."

I look from the plane, back to the microwave and find myself reaching out, pushing the "one-minute auto-heat button." That instantly halts the microwave, and the roaring noise in my phone cuts to silence.

I hear her breathing hard. She says, "We're level now, but I'm going crazy. Everything has stopped again."

"Good," I say. Bewildered, I focus the binoculars, finding the plane frozen in the air. Then, from the corner of my eye, I see the readout on the microwave, counting down from 50 to 49 seconds, and I look back at the sky, saying, "I don't know if this will last."

"It has to," she says. "Doesn't it? I'm too...."

"Too what?"

She giggles hysterically. "Too young to die." She chokes off a full laugh. "God, I sound stupid."

"No," I insist. "You don't. But who are you?" The microwave clicks down to 41 seconds.

"Arlene," she says. "My name is Arlene, and I'm so afraid."

"Don't give up." I blurt it out, wanting to comfort her, but my voice sounds sharp.

She laughs bitterly. "Is that what you call it? Will the headlines read, 'Plane Gives Up,' instead of 'Plane Crashes?'" She begins weeping.

"Please, I didn't mean it that way." The microwave clicks down to 30 seconds, and I rub the tip of my finger against the kitchen counter, getting ready. "Really," I say. "I'm trying to help."

I hear her take a deep breath and let it out. "I believe you," she says. "I'm sure you are. But what can you do?"

Think, I tell myself as the microwave runs down to 25 seconds. Then it comes to me. "Arlene, what did the pilot say? That he was leveling out?"

"Trying to. Wait. I'm looking out the window now, and I can see little specks of white against the blue. Are those waves? Ocean waves?"

The microwave shows 20 seconds.

"Listen," I say. "Reach under your seat. Isn't that where the life vest is? Use this time to get ready, Arlene. Grab your life vest. Then buckle back in."

I hear her grunting. "I can move, but nothing else will budge. Everything but me is stuck—locked in place."

"What about the emergency exits? Are you near one?"

"Bing!" sounds the microwave, and the screaming begins.

"Get off of me," Arlene yells. "This is my life jacket!"

"Hold on," I cry and hit the "one-minute auto-heat" button. The screams are gone.

The microwave stops spinning with the coffee cup near the front of the revolving platter. I look out the window. Without the binoculars, I see the plane is two inches lower in the window.

I punch the one-minute auto-heat button twice, wondering if I can buy her more time, but the readout still counts down from 60 seconds.

"There's smoke now," she says, "but it's just hanging in place."

"Where?"

"Near the back of the plane."

"Wait." I train the binoculars on the plane and see a plume of black, billowing from the engine that's mounted up high, on the plane's tail section. And there's a hint of flame—an orange tint against the tail fin.

"Have you put on your life jacket?" I ask.

"I've—I can't. The damn straps...."

I remember the demonstrations, ones I've seen flight attendants give. "Pull the strap around from behind," I say. "But don't inflate it. Not yet."

"Stop it! Stop telling me what to do. You have no idea...." She takes a shaky breath and lets it out. Softly, she adds, "I know you want to help...but I think it's too late for that."

A tremor runs through my hand, and I readjust my grip on the phone. "Why do you say that?"

"If I look up, toward the tail section, I can see a little patch of sky— where it's starting to separate—where all the smoke is being sucked out. And if I look down, through the window, I can make out individual waves now, even their crests, with sunlight reflecting off them...as if they were etched in glass.

"So beautiful," she adds softly. "If I just knew what to do...how to be with all of this."

I feel helpless, and my eyes begin to tear up. I grip the phone harder. "Is there anything you'd like to tell me? A message for anyone?"

"Tim…well, Tim's moved by now. And I don't think he misses me."

"Parents?" I suggest. "Children?"

"I wanted children, but Tim didn't."

Her silence stretches out, but it feels wrong to interrupt, even with the readout on the microwave counting down to 16 seconds.

Finally, she says, "Your name. What is it?"

"Paul," I answer.

"Where are you, Paul?"

I place my fingertip against the auto-heat button, and try to not look from the microwave to the window. But I can't help myself. I focus the binoculars on the tail section, and can see it's out of line with the fuselage.

"Where are you?" she asks.

"In a little kitchen," I say, "inside a beach house."

"Bing!" sounds the microwave.

I drop the binoculars and jab the button, but not before screams erupt for a split second, followed by a thick silence, as if someone has slammed a huge door—but even in that instant, there's time for the plane to release a ball of flame and lose its tail fin—now frozen in the air, tumbling next to the plane, which looks larger now, and is upside down in the lower half of the window, angled toward me, so that I'm looking down the length of its belly.

In the sheer silence, I hear the rasp of her breathing.

"What is it?" I say, then bite my lip. I imagine passengers becoming projectiles inside a wind tunnel, as the sudden decompression jerks them from their seats and they gain speed, flailing their arms as they accelerate into the open tail section.

"I'm upside down," she says, "but my safety belt is holding me in."

"Look forward," I say. "Only forward."

"Why? What's the matter?" Then she starts laughing, softly at first, but it quickly turns shrill. "What's the matter?" she says, mocking herself. "As if I didn't know."

"Please," I insist, desperate to distract her. "This is your time—these precious seconds. Whatever you do, it can't—well, it can't be wrong, because I'm sure this is for you. These seconds, they have to be." I gulp some air. "Does that make sense?"

She doesn't answer. Then, as I turn to the window, she says, "My parents. It's better if they don't know. Don't tell them how long I had to watch it happen."

"No," I promise, wondering who would believe me trying to explain any part of this. I gape at the window. The shining silver streak of the plane is now separated from the sand dunes by only six inches of glass.

"It's like a painting," she says, "so beautiful, of the ocean, turned on its side. And...lord, I can see birds now—seagulls." She chokes and stops.

"What is it?" I ask.

"The shape of our plane," she says. "Its shadow is on the water."

"Look away," I plead, hoping to lessen her fear. "Look away from the shadow."

She sighs. "There are so many things I wanted to do." She says it in a tone that's more resolved then sad. Measured, instead of rushed.

I imagine myself in her place and can't swallow. Can hardly breathe.

"Paul," she says. "Paul?"

"Yes, Arlene."

"For the rest of the day," she says, "would you please keep looking at things, the same way I'm trying to, right now—taking in the beauty? Will you?"

"I promise, Arlene, I will. For more than today." I can feel the impact coming, rushing up to her, and I have the overwhelming urge to grasp something. Anything. My car keys are on the counter, by the microwave, and I snatch them up.

"Bing!"

I jab the button with my finger, but this time, the microwave starts back up, turning its platter.

Screams rush through the phone, rising in volume.

With my fist, I hammer the microwave.

From the corner of my eye, I see a blossoming line of smoke and fire shoot downward, through the last of the window frame.

The microwave lurches, shuddering as the cellophane on my coffee mug puffs up, lifting higher, fluttering. It bursts as the kitchen window rattles hard, and my mind's eye sees a saltwater geyser shoot eighty feet into the air as her plane plunges through the roof of the ocean, on its way to a sandy floor.

Static. Only static on the phone.

"Bing!" sounds the microwave, no longer turning, as the coffee boils over, running down twisted strips of cellophane.

"...ever use that tone of voice with me," Liz is saying. "Not now, not ever."

I blink, seeing the car keys in my hand.

Liz sticks her head into the hallway. "I will honor your anger, Paul. But I refuse to suffer it. Is that clear?"

Slowly, deliberately, I grip the car keys harder and walk past her.

"Paul?" she says.

I open the front door and breathe deeply, tasting the sharp salt air. Sunshine warms my face.

"Who was that?" Liz asks.

I look at her. Truly look at her, seeing the immobility of her face. Then I gaze outside, up at the curved blue sky that's pressing down on a weathered cypress and the sweep of sand dunes.

"Who was it?" she demands.

It takes me a few seconds, but I find the right words. "Someone whose judgment I trust."

Liz stares at me, and her face seems to pull inward. Frowning, she points at my feet. "You're barefoot."

I smile and flex my toes, thinking, this is how it can be. I open my hand and let the keys fall to the carpet. Feeling lighter, I step onto the porch and close the door behind me.

I take another breath and begin walking, past the car, then up and over the dunes, moving faster, then down to the beach, where wet sands kiss my feet, and I listen to the gulls squawking as they wheel above me.

Soon enough helicopters will crowd the skies, and rescue boats will circle on the water.

But right now there is still time, and so much beauty.

Terry Bennett

Lesson Plan

T oting the binder, Blake entered the cavernous sports bar, grateful for its shadowed warmth. A spill of rowdy arguments greeted him, punctuated by guffaws. He shucked his frayed overcoat, trailing rivulets of rain, then stood in the blue-gray haze and drew a deep breath. Even the swirls of cigarette smoke carried the faint tang of beer and the scent of spiced chicken wings.

Determined not to get sidetracked, Blake worked his way past throngs of younger men in coveralls and windbreakers. Most sat elbow to elbow at sticky plywood tables, caught in the steady glow of neon beer signs or the glimmer of big-screen televisions that showed two black boxers in silk warm-up robes, waiting to be introduced.

Good, thought Blake. The locals don't scream nonstop over the Thursday night fights, the way they do when the Bears kick off, or the Blackhawks take to the ice. Still, he hoped the noise would keep him from nodding off. He hefted his client's three-inch thick personnel manual. At best, he expected a bog of vapid prose, flooded with acronyms and buzzwords.

"*Cumprimentos*, Blake! Greetings!"

Blake spotted Franco behind the bar, wearing a police whistle instead of a tie, and a light brown shirt that matched his cocoa skin. Grinning, Franco pointed to an open table the size of a pizza.

Relieved that Franco was busy, Blake dodged a ponytailed waitress he recognized and grabbed the lone seat. Once he got paid, he would settle his tab.

Coffee he thought. Avoid the beer.

He took a moment, rubbing his knee where it felt like arthritis was setting in. Then he opened the binder. Flipping through its pages, he groaned. Everything was single-spaced, leaving nothing but narrow page margins for comments and rewrites. Shaking his head, he gripped a red pen.

A chilled, amber bottle touched his wrist and he looked up. The ponytailed waitress smiled, handing him a Lone Star. "Your usual."

What the hell, he thought. One won't hurt. He took a sip, crossed his scuffed cowboy boots and glanced at the big screen. Inside a dreary auditorium with bleacher-style seats, tuxedoed commentators introduced the two fighters. Even better, thought Blake—a pair of unknowns. He'd be less tempted to watch.

Gritting his teeth, Blake examined the manual's first page. It stressed how hard the corporation had worked to develop policies that fostered teamwork and mutual respect—but it used six paragraphs of self-serving hype to make that point. With the red pen, Blake crossed out three-quarters of the words. The rest of the page went downhill from there.

As he worked, Blake heard conversations going on around him, then the televised voice of the referee as he cautioned both fighters to obey his commands. By now, Blake had used so much red ink that the first few pages looked like they were bleeding.

The bell sounded, starting the first round, and Blake looked up. The tall fighter worked from a flat-footed stance that showed his age, but threw precise punches that found his opponent. The younger boxer with the buzz cut countered with wide, looping punches, missing with most of them as the older man bobbed and weaved.

Blake pressed ahead. He waded through a slew of policies with prose so lifeless it felt like rigor mortis had set in. He had already missed two deadlines, so he stifled a yawn and kept going, using his pen like a scalpel…until he felt someone watching.

Blake turned toward the nearest table. He met the gaze of a raw-boned man with stark white skin who wore a dark suit. His hair bristled with a silver glint, shorn close to his skull. The man studied him without blinking, from pale gray eyes the color of thick winter ice.

"You are correcting papers?" said the man.

"Sort of." Hearing the man's thick Slavic accent, Blake wondered if he was Russian. Despite the silver hair, Blake judged him to be very fit and about ten years younger than himself. Probably in his mid-forties.

The man cocked his head slightly. "You are a teacher?"

"Used to be. Now I'm an editor." Blake noticed the jeweled stud that anchored the man's tie.

"Ah. An *ed-i-tor*," he said, sounding each syllable. "That is to write?"

Blake shrugged. "Some. Mostly, though, I remove things."

"Re-move." The man said it slowly, as if tasting the word. "But how do you know *what* to remove? Are you familiar? Are these subjects you would write? That you like?"

Blake thought of all the manuals he had suffered through since abandoning his half-written novel that lay in the bottom of his dresser. Nodding at the binder, he said, "This is just information. I'm drawn more to people." He paused, touching his chest. "To their hopes and dreams."

Men at the nearest table clenched their fists and cheered. One slopped beer from his mug.

The pale man pointed a stiff finger at the binder. "So these are not *your* stories?"

Blake shook his head.

"Why not?"

Blake shrugged and raised his Lone Star, taking a sip. "Actually, there was this story I wanted to tell, a few years back. But that didn't work out. So now I just prune things."

The man frowned. "The fruit?"

"No." Blake wagged the red pen and tapped a page he had marked.

"So you *do* teach. You correct. Yes?"

At the next table, a bald man pinched his nose and shouted, "Come on, you bum. Fight back!"

Blake turned to the big-screen as the young fighter caught his taller opponent with powerful hooks that hammered his ribs. The bell clanged, ending the fifth round, and the young fighter raised his arms overhead—as if his victory was assured.

Blake knew he should get back to editing, but the man in the dark suit leaned forward, saying, "Yes? You teach this way?"

As Blake considered how to answer, a waitress came over with a tall dark drink on her tray. It trailed traces of steam as she put a coaster by the man and set the drink on it.

"Nowadays I don't teach," Blake said. "I just edit."

The man offered a stiff smile that made his cheekbones look like they'd been chiseled.

Thinking he hadn't understood, Blake added, "Teaching and editing are different."

"How different?" To the departing waitress, he said, "Also jam, to sweeten my tea."

"Teachers instruct, and if possible, should inspire. As for editors.… " He slashed the air with his pen. "They remove what isn't necessary."

"Ah."

Blake doubted if any of this was getting through, and shifted his attention to the next page of the manual, knowing he had missed all the deadlines he could.

"I am wishing my son had *you* for a teacher."

Blake looked up and spoke slowly. "What I'm trying to tell you, is I gave that up five years ago."

"Teaching?"

Blake nodded, recalling how few of his teenage students had paid attention…even the gifted ones.

"Now," said Blake, "my life is simpler." Simpler, he thought, and poorer, with a modest pension that he couldn't start drawing for another two years.

The waitress returned. She gave Blake a fresh Lone Star, and handed a jar of strawberry jam to the man in the suit. Behind her, three men whistled at the screen, where a blonde in a red bikini and spiked heels held a sign overhead announcing round six.

Ignoring the ruckus, the man stared at Blake. "Why no more teaching?"

Blake recalled impassioned speeches to his students, back when he had believed that desire was a prelude to talent.

"I am asking," the man persisted. "Why not the teaching?"

Blake pictured the amber beauty of whiskey, sitting in a tall crystal glass. "There were too many distractions," he said, tightening his grip on the pen. "Now I just edit."

He studied a paragraph, then crossed out three adverbs and a prepositional phrase. As he turned a page, Blake heard the dull thud of leather on flesh coming from the big screen, as the boxers traded blows.

"But isn't that a lesson for all of us? To remove? To discard whatever lacks necessity?"

Without looking up, Blake realized he was losing interest in the manual, which he had promised to finish by tomorrow. Time to leave, he thought, and work at the apartment, where he wouldn't get sidetracked. Signaling for the waitress, he lost his grip on the pen and it dropped to the floor.

The man leaned forward, pointing at Blake's cowboy boots, which the pen had landed between. "You are not from here?"

Blake glanced at his boots, which had been re-soled and re-heeled so many times that he'd lost count. Even the decorative stitching had pulled loose, reflecting the harsh winters he had encountered in Ontario, before moving to Chicago. Wiggling his feet, Blake said, "I keep these to remind me why I left Texas, twenty-eight years ago."

The pale man answered with a grim smile, tapping his own chest. "*Moscva.* Moscow, to you. But my service ended in Bosnia and Herzegovina." He offered a thin smile. "As a peacekeeper, of course."

"Quit running," yelled a man to their left. "Stand and fight!"

On the big screen Blake saw the old fighter spit blood as he backpedaled, peppering his opponent with jabs. He seemed to find his second wind, and split the young fighter's defense with a double-jab, followed by a right cross that slowed, but didn't halt his opponent's advance.

The waitress arrived, holding Blake's bill, leaning close as she swept back her ponytail.

Smiling, Blake reverted to a Houston drawl, hoping to charm her. "Little Darlin? Just add this to my tab."

She looked doubtful and turned in Franco's direction.

The Russian touched her wrist, saying, "Young lady? Allow me." He passed her a crisp twenty-dollar bill.

"Much obliged," Blake said softly, "but I'm good for it."

The waitress rolled her eyes. She started to speak, but stopped when the Russian rapped the table with his knuckles.

Speaking to Blake, he took her hand and gently closed it on the twenty-dollar bill. "Please. This is my appreciation. As a father whose son has lesson difficulties, I admire your keep-to-it-ness."

Behind the Russian, Franco waved from the bar. Meeting Blake's eyes, he pointed at the Russian and shook his head.

"I shouldn't," Blake said, just as Franco came out from behind the bar, moving in his direction.

The waitress reached into her pocket, pulling out change.

The men at the nearest table roared and Blake turned. The older fighter was backed up against the ropes. He slipped two uppercuts and countered with a solid hook.

The Russian refused any change and the waitress left with a smile.

Blake said, "You didn't need to do that."

In the distance, Franco's progress was hampered by two Portuguese immigrants—friends who had followed him to America.

"This is what I tell you," said the Russian. "I have paid, but we can bet. If your man wins, you don't owe me. If the other wins, you spend an hour with my son. Teaching him." He smiled and raised both hands, palms up, polite as can be.

"But I don't teach anymore."

"Yet you are kindred to it."

"I suppose."

"All right then," said the Russian, nodding at the big-screen. "Which man is yours?"

Blake smiled, then shrugged, enjoying the Russian's persistence. "I'd say the fight's pretty close."

"True. But who is your favorite?"

Blake pointed at the older boxer. "I admire his skill, and what he's done to earn it."

"Good." He clasped Blake's hand. "I see you another time. And, before then, what is your name?"

"Blake," he said, surprised at the strength of the man's grip.

"Alexis," the Russian replied, squeezing harder, then releasing Blake's hand.

Behind Alexis, Franco pushed through the crowed, coming their way.

Blake bent over and grabbed the pen he had dropped. By the time he straightened up, the Russian was gone and Franco was leaning on the table.

"Blake," he demanded, "how can you think of taking money from him?"

Blake blinked, surprised at Franco's tone. "What's the big deal?"

"If it's for your tab, that money can wait."

"*Now* you tell me." Blake said this without admitting he was touched by Franco's loyalty, which he had earned two years ago—tutoring him when he had studied to become a U.S. citizen.

"Your Rooskie pal?" said Franco. "He is a big time street banker."

"A what?" Blake slipped one arm into his overcoat, caught it on the torn lining, and had to try again.

"I have learned, Blake. In this country, he's what you call a loan shark."

Blake grinned. "Except I didn't take his money, Franco. All we did was make a little bet."

"*Please!* Don't joke about it. With a street banker, if you lose, the clock starts ticking."

On the big screen the young fighter threw a wild overhand right that struck his opponent's jaw. Stunned, the tall boxer staggered, and caught the next blow square on his temple. That dropped him to his hands and knees, where he seemed to age another ten years. He made an effort to stand, but lost his balance and landed on his side. The referee caught the glazed look in his eyes and stopped the fight.

"Which fighter did you bet on?" asked Franco.

Blake turned his collar up, wondering if the puddles left by the storm had iced over. "You're pulling my leg. Right?"

"Blake, I shit you not. This Rooskie is what you call the bad news. So settle your bet."

* * *

Two weeks later, Blake sat at Franco's, eating a pepper steak sandwich, feeling flush from the money he had earned on the personnel manual. The late afternoon crowd was thin and subdued, waiting for the next hockey game.

As Blake chewed an onion ring, he sensed someone behind him. He turned to see the Russian standing there, wearing a black suit.

"May I?" the Russian asked, nodding at the empty chair.

"Sure," Blake said, digging out his wallet. "But first, let me square up what I owe you for those beers."

When the Russian sat down, Blake said, "It's Alexis, right?"

"Yes." In the dull light, the bristle on his scalp was barely visible.

Blake held out a twenty-dollar bill.

When the Russian folded his hands on the tabletop, Blake forced himself to smile. "I guess the way you work it, now there's some interest, right? On top of what I borrowed?"

Slowly, the Russian pushed aside the twenty-dollar bill. "Our agreement is not money. It is one hour with my son."

The way the Russian set his jaw reminded Blake of scenes he'd witnessed growing up in Texas, where bare knuckles often had the final say.

"What if your son needs help in a subject I've never taught? Like mathematics?"

Alexis gave him a thin smile and rubbed his index finger against his thumb. "I can teach him the numbers, and what they do." His voice was soft, but held an edge.

Blake nodded, figuring it was best to honor his debt. "Where is your son having difficulties? In what subject?"

Alexis drew himself up, sitting taller. "In the country I am from, there are lessons and stories that tell us which path to take. But my son, Luka, he is confused by America. By its stories."

"Do you mean *reading*, or *writing* them?"

Alexis paused, as if to consider. "Making right choices. That is his problem."

Maybe, Blake thought, his son has trouble expressing himself in English. "How old is he?"

"Six of teen. Nearly seven of teen." For a few seconds, the taut muscles of his face seemed to soften.

"A difficult age." Blake thought back to his high school students—to their indifference and hostility. Still, an hour of that would be safer than arguing with a loan shark. "Where can I meet your son?"

"In the parking lot is a silver car, a Mercedes. My driver will take you to Luka."

Blake saw Alexis incline his head toward the door, and realized he had been dismissed.

Blake nodded, trying to be a good sport about it, and got up, donning his dingy overcoat. He left his half-finished sandwich and coffee sitting on the table.

Outside, the big Mercedes with tinted windshields sat with its engine running. Vapor trailed from its twin exhaust pipes, rising toward a sun that hung low in a bleak gray sky.

Blake approached the Mercedes and its driver got out, opened the back door and stood at attention.

It was Blake's first experience with a chauffeur, but this man seemed out of place in a visored cap and gray wool tunic that couldn't hide his massive shoulders. Something about his rigid posture suggested a military background, and Blake wondered if he had served with Alexis in Bosnia.

As Blake got in, the big man tipped his hat. "Nicolai," he said, then closed Blake's door and sat behind the wheel.

The partition between the front and back seat had been lowered. Blake sat, studying the driver's thick neck. When they pulled into traffic, Blake's thoughts turned to Alexis' son. He tried to imagine the boy's experience of high school in America. As a teacher, Blake had sympathized with his students, because he still remembered how difficult it had been for him in high school, trying to fit in. He imagined it would be that much tougher, coming from another country.

Pulling onto the interstate, Nicolai met his eyes once in the mirror, without displaying any visible emotion. As Nicolai looked away, a motor hummed and a solid partition rose up between the front and back seat.

For an instant, Blake thought he'd been locked in, and his breath caught in his throat. But when he jabbed the button on the leather armrest, he saw the door lock knob pop up. Blake shook his head and scolded himself. This was the kind of reaction his father had scorned and his brother had laughed at during Blake's high school years, back when Blake had joined them working the family oilfields. It had only been a summer job, but he'd been intimidated from the start by all the jostling and rough joking, where bluffs, bets and fistfights were the norm.

Be a man, his father used to yell, whenever Blake complained. *Be a man*. In that moment, that's what Blake told himself to do, instead of worrying as the Mercedes slipped into the fast lane, cruising along with a chauffeur at the wheel who looked like a bodyguard.

Blake reminded himself that Alexis had only asked him to help his son with schoolwork. To spend an hour with him. And the boy having language difficulties made sense, after hearing the father's broken English.

As Blake reassured himself, early commuters began to thicken the flow of traffic, some with their parking lights on. Blake felt the Mercedes angle downward as Nicolai took an off-ramp from the interstate. The street he turned onto looped around, beneath the interstate, until it reached the parking lot of the Tri-Corner Mall.

The Mercedes came to a halt near the south entrance, where a tall, pulsing water fountain caught Blake's attention.

It was surrounded by concrete benches and clusters of teenagers who wore mostly dark colors in long pants and thick jackets or sweaters—loose on the boys and tight on the girls—with the occasional splash of red or gold from scarves or knit stocking caps. Further away, more teens sat on rows of steps that ran across the front of the mall, keeping their hands in their pockets, acting like they weren't cold.

Nicolai opened the passenger door and stood at attention.

"Which one is Luka?"

Nicolai extended his arm.

At the far corner of the mall's entrance, sitting on the steps, Blake saw a long-limbed boy wearing baggy pants, fancy gym shoes and a bulky gray sweater. He was smiling as he talked to a girl in a black parka who snuggled against him. Blake noticed that the boy's blond hair was spiked, like hers. They did a good job of facing in another direction, once they saw Nicolai.

Blake sighed, thinking Luka had to be embarrassed. "Could you wait here?" he asked Nicolai.

Without comment, the chauffeur backed up, taking a position near the front of the car, facing in Luka's direction.

Blake started toward Luka and the girl, sorry to intrude. When he was halfway there, Luka whispered to the girl. She hugged him, got to her feet and walked away.

Luka sat, keeping his pose, and didn't budge when Blake reached his side.

Blake wasn't sure what to say and stood there for a moment. He noticed that gel had been used to spike the boy's hair, which wasn't overly long or short. Despite rings on several fingers, Luka didn't wear any jewelry that pierced his ears, nose, lips or eyebrows.

Finally, Luka said, "My father sent you." It was an accusation, delivered without a Russian accent.

"Look," Blake said, pulling his collar up against the wind. "I'm sorry to butt in like this, but I had to."

"Why?"

"I owe your father something."

Luka gave him a look of disdain. "Too bad for you."

Blake held his temper, remembering the futility of arguing with teenagers. "Maybe so," he admitted. "But I promised I'd talk to you."

Luka's shoulders seemed to tense. "About what?"

"School, and the problems you're having."

Luka's eyebrows arched. "Problems?"

Blake blew on his hands, trying to keep warm. "It's been five years, but I used to teach. Maybe I can help."

Luka gave him a crooked smile, then laughed. Tapping his temple, he said, "I'm Dean's list all the way. Second in my class."

Blake frowned, realizing how articulate the boy was. "But your father said..." He tried to remember his words. "*Stories* is what he said. That you needed help with them, and with choices. Maybe expressing yourself?"

"Coming from him," Luka said, "that's almost funny." He stood, and Blake found himself looking up, then took a step back, nearly tripping on a green daypack.

Luka bent over and scooped up the daypack. "What's with the bullshit? What kind of game are you playing?"

Blake raised both hands in a calming motion. "My name's Patterson. Blake Patterson. I'm an editor now, not a teacher."

"Convince me. What do you edit? Books? Magazines?"

Blake shook his head, less worried now by the boy's size. As a teacher, he'd discovered that the ones who tried to sound tough hadn't reached the point of no return.

"I edit manuals, Luka. Manuals that bore me to tears, written by companies that claim to be cutting edge."

"Are they?"

Blake raised one hand and slowly traced a downward arc across the sky. "Imagine a model of pure mediocrity, fueled by the latest technology."

Luka laughed and slung the green daypack over his shoulder.

"Mostly," Blake added, "their chief talent is spawning a mongrel language—the bastard offspring of engineers and bureaucrats."

"That sounds nasty enough to be true."

"What about you? Is that a load of crap, about you being the star pupil?

Luka grinned, and pointed upward, like Blake had. "Bright and shining, I assure you."

"*Touché.*"

Luka adjusted the shoulder straps of the daypack. "Now what?"

Blake shrugged.

Luka glanced toward Nicolai, then looked at him. "You really think you're going to teach me something?"

Blake pursed his lips and used the toe of his cowboy boot, kicking softly at one of the steps. "It doesn't make sense, but your father said you were in school and needed lessons, or some kind of help."

"Ahhh." Luka adjusted a strap on his daypack. "With my father, lessons and school are not the same. If lessons came up, it wasn't school he was talking about."

Blake smiled. "Well, then. Since you're the star pupil, and I'm on the hook with your father, how about explaining what he meant?"

"Only if we ditch dad's driver." He nodded at Nicolai, who stood by the Mercedes.

Blake stomped his feet softly, feeling the chill in the breeze. "He's not going to come after us, is he?"

"Nah. I expect he'd like to, but he always stays with the car."

Luka set out with long strides, turning the corner of a building that was flushed with golden light from the setting sun. Blake hurried, falling behind Luka, entering an alley where blue Dumpsters were parked at intervals near reinforced metal doors that allowed deliveries to shops in the mall.

Blake called out, "Slow down."

Luka stepped up onto a small crate, then climbed to the top of a Dumpster and offered Blake a hand up. Blake took hold and was lifted up as Luka said, "Over the wall."

Blake looked over the brick wall, thinking it would be a ten-foot drop, but there was a Dumpster on the other side. Its lid didn't shut where it overflowed with rotten produce and empty cans.

Luka jumped, landing with a thump on its lid, then hopped to the ground. Blake followed, feeling the impact in his knees and ankles.

"Where are we going?" Blake asked, brushing wilted lettuce from his frayed overcoat.

"Follow me and find out."

Luka started down an alley bordered by tall buildings that blocked much of the late afternoon light. Many had broken or boarded up windows.

Blake followed, figuring they had another half hour to an hour before it started turning dark. He shook his head, reminded of his own teenage years. Of his failed attempts at passing muster with his brother and the crowd he ran with—boys who loved to swagger and curse as they drank, rutted and fought their way through adolescence.

34

Luka and Blake passed a gray cinderblock building that housed a radiator repair shop. In the alley, its east wall had been tagged with purple and gold paint, portraying a fierce, yellow-eyed wolf. It sat on its haunches, howling upward at a broken moon that had purple tears falling from its eyes.

Blake trailed after Luka through a labyrinth of alleys, side-stepping broken glass and the occasional syringe as they passed gutted apartments and warehouses.

Luka stopped beneath the rusted fire escape of an abandoned brick hotel. Soot marks streaked upward from its bottom row of windows where a blaze had flushed smoke and cinders into the alley. Luka jumped, grabbing the overhead ladder. It clattered down its rails, coming to rest a foot above the ground.

"Can you make it?" Luka asked, pointing to the top.

Blake nodded, but wondered.

They started up, with Luka in the lead. Blake counted each story they passed as they climbed the ladder. He was breathing hard before they reached the top and stepped over a low parapet, onto a flat, gravel-bed roof.

Wheezing, Blake walked over to three mismatched folding chairs and a small wooden table. The table pressed up against a broken sheet metal structure that, at one time, must have housed an air conditioner. Blake sat in one of the chairs and pulled his overcoat tighter, catching his breath.

Luka smiled, stripped off his daypack and joined him at the table. "Check out the view."

Blake found the energy to stand. They were high enough that he could see other, similar rooftops against a gray sky that was taking on a reddish tint, with streaks of gold. Further west, he saw the mall they had come from, with the fountain and concrete benches marking its entrance.

Somewhere below Blake heard a few fumbling notes from an electric guitar, which faded to silence. Then muted laughter.

"Other friends of mine," Luka volunteered. "This is pretty much our building. Dancing, drinking…you name it." His tone was a mixture of pride and defiance.

Blake nodded. "It's nice of you to share this, Luka. But why?"

Luka pulled a pack of cigarettes and a lighter from his pocket. As he lit up, Blake realized that Luka's hair—without the gel—would comb back evenly, without any gaps, and he figured that's how Luka wore it at home.

"Here's the deal," Luka said. "It was bad luck, you getting tangled with my father, but there isn't much I can do about that."

Blake shrugged, keeping his hands in his pockets. "All he expects is for me to spend an hour with you, talking about school. Giving you a hand with some stories, he said."

Luka leaned back in his chair. "You think it's that simple, dealing with my father?"

"Look, all I want is to get through this without any hassles. For you or for me."

Luka smiled as a gust of wind cut across the roof, tearing the ash from his cigarette. "Convincing my father is the key. And my father can be difficult."

"Just tell him we talked about school."

Luka grinned and took a pull on his cigarette. "That won't cut it. Not with my father."

"What do you mean?"

"He won't just check with me. He'll find you and ask how it went. He'll want you to spell out everything we did. Like, *this* happened, then *that* happened...."

"Okay. So it wasn't just school we talked about, but stories."

Luka scooped up his daypack, unzipped it and spilled schoolbooks onto the table. "Stories, or 'some' story isn't enough. You'll have to name it. So tell him it was..." He paused, holding up an anthology of short stories as the wind fanned its pages. "Tell him it was 'The Killers,' by Hemingway, and that you explained it to me."

"Why that story?"

Luka gave him a thin, hard smile. "It's one my father would enjoy."

Blake thought he'd read it in college. Vaguely, he recalled it being about this guy who was in trouble, and had the chance to run, but didn't.

"Okay," said Blake, "but now you've got me wondering. What kind of story would *you* like?"

Luka regarded him carefully. "First, let's have a drink."

Luka knelt by the broken sheet metal housing. From it, he removed another daypack, like the one he had brought with him. He unzipped it and produced a metal hip flask. "Brandy," he said.

It reminded Blake of the way his brother had taught him to drink, first snatching Lone Stars from the cases his father brought home, then buying him a flask and showing him how to tuck it into his boot, so their mother wouldn't see it outlined in the back pocket of his jeans.

Luka took a swig, then passed it to Blake, whose hands had begun to ache from the bite of the wind.

"Thanks." Blake put the flask to his lips and swallowed, grateful for the trail of warmth that passed down his throat. He felt the chill sharpen around him as the sun dropped low enough to touch the horizon. He closed his eyes and took another drink. The brandy's soothing warmth resurrected memories of his old love affair with hard liquor, and what it had cost him. Whiskey had given him the courage to put aside his short stories and start a novel, then trapped him between writing that stalled, and red-eyed outbursts that eventually cost him his job as a teacher. First in Canada, then in Chicago.

"Blake?"

"What?" He opened his eyes.

Luka regarded him closely. "Do stories interest you?"

Blake smiled and gave the flask to Luka. Even the boy's curiosity was guarded. But he'd taken a chance, asking a question, so he deserved an answer.

"Actually, Luka, that was the part of teaching I liked, exploring what stories offer. And for a while, I even aspired to write them." He shrugged. "But few people appreciate what it takes. You bust your ass, getting it down on paper, and it's still a hit or miss proposition. You see it clearly, or *think* you do, but what if the reader doesn't? Then you've got to start over."

Luka nodded, hunched up against the cold. "Even friends who like my stories, sometimes they don't get what I mean."

Blake wondered what his stories were about.

Luka added, "Sometimes that bothers me."

"Maybe they think they know you, but they don't. Not really."

Luka flicked his cigarette over the parapet. "Even my father wouldn't understand my stories. Not that I'd ever share them with him."

"Have you tried?"

Luka scowled. "He thinks they're a waste of time."

"Is that because English is hard for him?"

"My stories aren't in words."

"You've lost me."

Luka opened the second daypack and dug out a camera, then three eight-by-ten photos, each mounted on poster board.

Blake caught a flicker of doubt in Luka's eyes, and saw how closely the young man held the photos to his chest.

"*These* are my stories." Hesitantly, he reached out, passing them to Blake, who used his back to shield them from the wind.

The daylight was fading fast, but Blake could still see the photos.

The first was of a brick apartment building, shot from a low angle, as if Luka had taken it from the sidewalk while lying on his back. The view followed the upward zigzag of a rusty fire escape, past a streaked and dirty window with a crumbling brick sill, then another window and another, until it reached the youth who stood at the fire escape's peak with outstretched arms, flying a ruby-red box kite that challenged a flat blue sky.

The second photo had been shot from above. It framed the narrow paved alley between two tall buildings, and the brilliant explosion of lime, fuchsia, yellow and powder-blue chalk-lines that began as hopscotch squares, then fanned out into more intricate patterns once they emerged from the alley, blooming into vines and flowers that reached into the parking lot, where a teenage girl with curly hair knelt, gripping a fistful of chalk as she filled in the petals of a pink rose.

The last shot had been photographed from the side. It captured the silhouette of a long-haired boy at dusk, in baggy pants, as he plunged down the metal railing of a steep stairway, riding a skateboard that threw a long trail of sparks from its underside.

As Blake took in the raw beauty of Luka's photos, he was gripped by a sense of freedom he hadn't felt in years. "These are outstanding."

Luka looked doubtful. "You're not just saying that?"

"No, I mean it. These photographs are wonderful."

Luka smiled shyly.

"I hope you keep doing this."

Luka's smile broadened. "It's what I want to do with my life, catching…" He paused, putting his thumb and index finger close together. "Catching little slices of time, where you see the truth." His voice was soft now, with none of the false bravado.

Blake nodded. "With more of these, you could put together a show."

Luka pulled back. "Don't jerk me around."

Blake tapped the photos. "I'm *not*. Your photos are excellent. And lots of places exhibit photographs, especially when they follow a theme."

Luka picked up his camera and aimed it at Blake. "Taking photos is easy," he said, looking through the viewfinder. "I mean, this feels natural to me. But finding some theme…" His voice faltered as he lowered the camera.

Blake tapped the photos. "To me, you've already done that, the way these go together."

"How? Tell me what you see."

Blake took another look at each shot. "Somehow, what you've done is to capture this moment of courage, where people are out to change themselves—or the world around them."

"Really? You can see that?"

"You could even caption them." He pointed at the photo of the soaring kite. "Touching the sky." He nodded at the photograph with the bloom of chalk lines, emerging from the alley. "Finding a path." He touched the shot of the skateboarder, trailing a stream of sparks. "Lighting the way."

Luka nodded, hefting his camera. "You've got me thinking about other photos I've shot."

Blake smiled. "Having a show…maybe that's your next step." He handed the photos back to Luka.

Luka started to speak, then shook his head. "My father wouldn't stand for it. He thinks anything like this is a waste of time. Worse than school."

Blake could see the boy's frustration as he knelt and put his camera inside the daypack, then gripped his photographs and stared at them.

The boy was gifted, but having a father like that…. Blake tried to imagine being Luka's age and having Alexis for a father. For a moment, it reminded him of the first short stories he had scrawled in longhand, then hidden from his own father, whose notion of a story was something you told in a bar, over shots of whiskey.

The wind picked up and Blake noticed that the sunset sky had faded from red to purple. His hands ached, and his ears and nose had begun to sting. He rubbed his hands and said, "What if you did a show under another name? Maybe got a friend to front it for you?"

Luka pursed his lips and nodded. "That might work…with captions, of course."

He said the last part looking at Blake, who smiled as Luka put the photographs away, then picked up the flask.

"It's getting late, Luka." Above the horizon, Blake could see the first star of the evening.

Luka took a hit of brandy, and then passed it to Blake. "There's only a little bit left."

Blake drained the flask, feeling a warm glow as it went down. "I'll need help finding my way back to your father's driver."

Luka looked across the darkened rooftops, toward the mall, where outdoor lights criss-crossed its entrance. "Tomorrow's soon enough for my father. But I'll get us out of here."

"In that case, I'll take a bus instead of riding with Nicolai. Tell your father I'll be at Franco's tomorrow, for lunch." Shivering, he started for the fire escape.

Behind him, Luka called out, "Just stick to our story, all right? About me reading 'The Killers,' and you explaining it to me?"

Blake looked back as Luka shoved the daypack inside the sheet metal housing. "Relax, Luka. I won't forget."

"Promise?"

Blake nodded, wondering how difficult it would be, going down the fire escape in the dark.

Luka pulled out another hip flask. "Let's finish this one before we leave."

Blake had the urge to warn him. To tell him where alcohol could lead. But he found himself licking his lips, remembering the flood of dreams it could bring, and that fleeting sense of courage.

∗ ∗ ∗

When Blake reached his apartment building, he still felt a buzz from all the brandy he'd consumed. He walked though the entrance, passed by the broken elevator and made it to his door. He slipped the key in on the second try and opened the door.

Swaying, he gripped the bookcase and shut the door. Carefully, he sloughed off his overcoat and stood there, listening to the drip of the kitchen sink. He felt light-headed from hunger, but was too tired to eat. That's when he noticed the blinking red light on the message machine.

It occurred to him that Luka's father might have wanted his report tonight, despite what Luka had said about tomorrow being soon enough.

Blake steadied himself and walked to the machine. Three messages were waiting. He only listened to the beginning of each message, then skipped ahead. They were all from his only client.

Relieved that Alexis hadn't called, he decided the messages could wait and didn't play them back. Instead, he stripped off his clothes, took a hot bath in the rust-stained tub, and crawled into bed. Soon he was dreaming of wandering through glass-strewn alleyways and the rubble of brick buildings, seeking a pathway to the sky.

* * *

Sitting at a table in Franco's, Blake felt the soft brush of air from the overhead fan and was grateful for the dim interior. Ignoring his headache, he finished his ham and cheese sandwich. Slowly, he sipped at his second cup of coffee, feeling better than he had when he'd gotten up, still dull-witted from the previous night's brandy.

The nearest big-screen televisions in the bar carried a sports center show, with an announcer reviewing last night's basketball scores. Blake counted up how little was left in his wallet. He'd given half of his savings to Franco's day manager, to pay off his tab. What remained wouldn't cover the rest of his bills. He thought of the work he had done on the personnel manual, and hoped his client had another job for him. Maybe that's why he'd left the messages Blake had found last night, but he still hadn't played them all the way through. He'd be sure to listen to them when he got home.

The noon crowd was thinning out, and Franco didn't start his Friday shift for another hour, so Blake nursed his coffee and started in on the last of his French fries. To make them last, he broke each one into smaller pieces. Maybe Franco could give him some advice before he talked to the Russian.

Half the big screens carried a bowling tournament, while the others ran clips from last night's NBA games. Blake hoped for a few boxing highlights, but none were being broadcast.

As he started his third cup of coffee, Luka's father showed up, wearing a wool greatcoat that fit him well enough to be tailored. Its bulk and slate color reminded Blake of Nicolai, who was probably waiting with the silver Mercedes.

Alexis shed the greatcoat and sat across from him. With a smile, Alexis studied him carefully.

Blake gripped his coffee cup, wondering if the man's smile was genuine, or simply his way of letting him twist in the wind.

"My driver told me you were kidnapped. That my son, he pulled you over a wall."

Gingerly, Blake said, "I suppose Luka doesn't like being watched."

Alexis gave an elaborate shrug. "Teenagers, yes?"

His tone was pleasant, so Blake nodded.

"So what happened, after you left with Luka?"

Blake took a sip of coffee, remembering his promise. "I asked about school, and he told me his grades were good."

When Alexis didn't respond, Blake said, "But he did show me a story he had read. One he had questions about."

"What story?"

"One by Hemingway."

"Whose way?"

"*Hemingway.* That's the man who wrote it."

Alexis leaned forward. "So tell me this story."

Blake ate a French fry, buying some time. It had been thirty-something years since he'd read it. What if that showed?

Alexis sat there, waiting.

"The heart of the story? It describes one man's troubles. Dangerous men are angry with him, over something he has done. They want to kill him."

"What happens to this man?"

Blake raised his hands, palms up. "It's left for the reader to decide."

Alexis paused, rubbing his chin. "The story doesn't finish? You have to figure the ending?"

"You only know that the man has decided not to run. That he's made his choice."

Alexis steepled his hands. "What choice? To fight them?"

Blake gave a slow shrug. "He's hiding when the story ends, but he's thinking about facing them."

"Does he?"

"We don't know. But this man thinks it won't work, trying to escape, so he has to decide. Neither choice is good—hiding or facing them. But he has to choose."

Alexis smiled. "Good. A better story than most, because of its truth. That nothing is easy."

Blake wondered if he had said enough, or too much.

Alexis gave the table a soft rap with his knuckles. "I like this story. How it speaks to hardship. That the world is tough and doesn't care about you. That you must make your own way." His smile broadened. "You agree? Pain, but the hope of no suffering?"

"Pardon?"

Alexis leaned forward, making a fist. "It is my belief that you cannot escape the pain. Always there are hard choices and there is pain. But if you are strong, instead of weak, it happens quick, whether you win or lose. Then there is no suffering."

It occurred to Blake that Alexis might borrow the story from Luka and struggle to read it. Then want to discuss it in depth. Probably he wouldn't, but Blake decided he would get the story from the library and read it again. Just in case.

"Excuse."

Blake turned and saw Nicolai standing off to the side, next to a bearded man in coveralls and work boots, who stiffened when Nicolai nudged him, urging him forward.

"My apologies," said Alexis, looking at Blake. "Business."

Blake picked up his plate of fries and started to leave, but Alexis held up a hand, saying, "This will take only a moment."

The bearded man bowed his head as Alexis narrowed his eyes and spoke softly. "Which is it? You *can't* pay, or you *won't?*"

"My next paycheck," the man said, and began to tremble. "I promise."

"Yet," said Alexis, "you told me this same thing last week."

The man bit his lip. "I know. But I didn't get to pull over-time, and I've got a family to feed."

Alexis pondered that a moment, then said. "Remind me. What is it you do for a living?"

The man swallowed. "I'm a mason, working bricks and concrete."

Alexis raised his eyebrows. "So you need both hands."

The man blanched and nodded.

"This, it is small money," said Alexis. "So I will give you one more chance."

"Thank you," the man said, sagging with relief.

"But," said Alexis, lowering his voice, "you need a reminder. Something to tell you what a promise means when you make it." He inclined his head toward Nicolai, then pointed at the man's feet. "One toe."

The man clasped his hands and began to beg. "I swear, next week. *All of it.*"

Nicolai clamped a hand on the man's shoulder and spun him around, toward the exit.

Dry-mouthed, Blake watched the man leave, held firmly in Nicolai's grasp.

"Black tea," Alexis called to a passing waitress. "Hot, please, in a tall glass."

He turned to Blake, as if nothing had happened. "So, you were telling me?"

Blake swallowed. "Luka showed me the story. We talked, and I made sure that he understood it." Blake held his breath, hoping that would satisfy Alexis.

Smiling, Alexis extended his hand, and Blake shook it, flinching as Alexis strengthened his grip.

"Thank you, Blake, for honoring your debt. We are square now."

"Good." Blake swallowed, managed to nod, then left, having no appetite for the rest of his fries.

* * *

Walking home in the brisk afternoon air, Blake felt his innards twist at the thought of the punishment Alexis had ordered for the bearded man. But he also felt weak-kneed with relief. At most, he had hoped to bluff Alexis and settle his debt. But the man had actually seemed pleased.

By the time Blake passed the donut shop with its grimy windows, he was experiencing a strange sense of elation…a lightness that centered in his chest, from knowing that this business with Alexis was behind him.

Smiling, he began to imagine how he would tell Franco what had happened. How he had stood up to the Russian. How he had pulled it off. It was the kind of escapade Franco would enjoy. Blake expected he could stretch it out, saying, stand me another drink and I'll tell you the rest. But as he walked along, rehearsing for Franco, he became aware of his toes, riding snug in his cowboy boots, and couldn't help thinking of the bearded man who hadn't paid Alexis.

When Blake reached his apartment, there were two sheets of paper tacked to his door, easily seen by anyone entering the building. One was an overdue rent notice. The other detailed the eviction process that would ensue if he didn't pay last month's rent, and this month's—already ten days past due.

The way the notice was posted galled Blake. Why couldn't the landlord have shoved it under the door? Fortunately, the rest of his money would cover one month's rent. That, and his utilities. He tore the notice from the door and shoved it into his pocket.

Because he hadn't left the heat on, when he opened the door it was frigid inside, so he didn't remove his overcoat. Still, he felt the urge for a beer and took one of the Lone Stars from the refrigerator.

Drinking it, he played back the messages he had passed over last night. All three were from his client. The first two mentioned another project. One that couldn't wait. Would he please call immediately? In the third message, his client said they had hired another editor, and would no longer need his services. Not for this or any other project.

Blake pulled the rent notice from his pocket and his stomach began to churn.

He knew he should call his landlord and work something out. At least explain that all he could do, for now, was narrow the gap on what he owed. But he put off phoning, because he had argued in the past over repairs that the landlord had refused to make. Gripping the rent notice, Blake finished his beer, knowing he had nothing left to pawn. All that remained of his better days were the books that filled his shelves.

Blake closed his eyes and couldn't help thinking of the pint of Johnny Walker that he'd tucked away behind the kitchen breadbox, promising himself that his brown-bag days were over. Shivering, he found a blanket in the closet and wrapped himself in it as he stood there, without taking off his overcoat.

Then he walked to the kitchen and pushed aside the breadbox, telling himself that all he needed was one nip. Just to cut the chill he felt.

* * *

It was dark when Blake awoke on the couch. Fumbling, he turned on the floor lamp. His head ached and he could see the vapor of his breath rising inside the cold room. Wrapped in the blanket, he shuffled to the kitchen. The round wall clock above the fallen breadbox read fifteen minutes past five, which meant he had slept straight through the night.

He picked up the breadbox. Inside it, he found a quarter-loaf of bread. It was stale, like a giant crouton, but he removed a slice and felt better biting into it. Today's headache wasn't as bad as the one he'd suffered following his rooftop drinking with Luka.

He decided to go for a walk. Fresh air, he thought, would raise his spirits. Plus, he could buy a paper and skim the want ads. Find some possibilities and get presentable for an interview. That was the thing to do. Definitely the thing to do…but it had been a while since he'd had to convince anyone to hire him. And now the economy was dragging, so lots of people would be chasing the same jobs.

As he chewed on the dry bread, he noticed the tremor in his hands—something he hadn't suffered from since his last serious bout with hard liquor, almost two years ago.

Staring at his hands, it dawned on him that he had nearly reached the end of his rope. That he'd better do more than skim the want ads, thinking he'd land, then hold onto some new writing job without burning his bridges. Flat-out, he decided he'd better find a new line of work.

That's when he saw the large manila envelope that had been slipped in beneath his door.

"From Luka," was printed on the outside in large block letters. Below that, more neat printing: "You were the only Blake Patterson in the phone book. I came by to thank you, because my dad has really backed off. But it was late. I didn't want to wake you, so I left this instead. Please accept it as my thank you."

Inside the envelope, mounted on poster board, Blake found an eight-by-ten-inch color photograph. It was a close-up, shot with a telephoto lens from above and off to the side, catching a pale gray pigeon with startling green eyes, poised on the window ledge of a high-rise, while it cocked its head and gazed at the street far below. The compression effect from the telephoto lens seemed to sharpen the blue sky surrounding the bird as it arched its wings and leaned forward…reaching the exact point of no return. And with a speck of sunlight reflected in the bird's eye, there was even the feeling that it knew what would happen in the next instant, when it embraced the downward pull of gravity, with the air rushing past.

A caption came to mind. "Ready for freedom."

Blake held the photo at arm's length. It deserved a spot where it could be displayed and appreciated.

He considered the narrow hallway to the bath and bedroom, but that was crowded with copies of old manuals he had revised and then stacked along the wall, beneath several snapshots of his brother Neal. The row of photos traced Neal's brutal but brief ascent as a middleweight boxer, cut short in 1968 by a one-way trip to the Mekong Delta.

In each photo, Neal was filled with raw determination, of the sort Blake had suffered first-hand, growing up with him, whenever their father had found them tussling or arguing, and "helped them along" as he liked to put it. First by dragging them outdoors and drawing a circle in the dirt about ten foot across, using the heel of his boot. Then by telling them to get inside it and start fighting, while he stood and watched, until only one of them was left standing. At which point, their father would beat the tar out of the victor, then instruct both of them "to always finish what you start."

In ten years of fighting with his brother, Blake had never had the courage to win, and face his father. Or after high school, to wait for his draft number to be called up the way his brother had. So twenty-eight years ago, he had retrieved all the stories he had penned from his hiding place, then ridden a train to Chicago, and hitchhiked his way through Michigan and across the border at Sault St. Marie, to take refuge in Ontario, where he tried to find his way as a writer, then as a teacher…staying there until 1977, when amnesty was granted.

Facing the ringside snapshots of his brother, bleeding but victorious, Blake decided that Luka's photograph deserved a spot of its own.

Without walking down the hall, he knew the bathroom wouldn't do, with its mold and peeling wallpaper. At the very least, Luka's photo deserved a clean backdrop that lacked clutter and invited contemplation.

He went to his bedroom. There was plenty of open space above the dresser, but it felt wrong, the notion of hanging Luka's photo above his own unfinished novel—as if that might jinx the boy's creative spirit.

Finally, he placed it in the kitchen, inside an alcove meant for a telephone, where a small, recessed light bulb cast a soft glow around the photograph. He smiled as he backed up, getting the total effect. Nested in the alcove and surrounded by light, the image of the bird seemed like a passageway to something beyond. He savored that for a moment, then took in the other side of the kitchen, with its dripping faucet and the dented refrigerator.

It was time to get the *Tribune's* late edition and check the want ads. Hopefully, he could find part-time work within walking distance of his apartment. Anything really. Any job that was available. But what he hoped for was employment in a bookstore, where he pictured himself having a good time shelving books as he chatted with customers, then taking his breaks with a cup of coffee while thumbing through a volume of poems. Or maybe he could fall back on his teaching skills and find a few parents seeking tutors for their children.

He took another slice of bread to bolster himself and left his apartment, wanting to believe in himself.

* * *

Blake walked slowly going back to his apartment. The slick soles of his cowboy boots gripped poorly on the sidewalk, iced over from last night's rain. He carried the want ads, with only two jobs circled. An entry-level position at a warehouse—probably hefting boxes, and an opening for a dishwasher at LeeAnne's Diner. But if it came to that, maybe Franco would let him fill in, bussing or washing dishes. At least that way he could catch a few fights on the big-screen.

Inside his apartment building, Blake found another note from the landlord, tacked to his door. He dropped it on the kitchen table, thinking he should call and tell him he was looking for work.

The phone rang and he backed up a step. He let the answering machine engage, to hear who it was.

He recognized Luka, saying, "Blake? Are you there? Did you find the photo I left?"

He picked up, saying, "Yes, Luka. It was a great surprise."

"So, I…well, what do you think of it?"

Blake smiled, pleased that his opinion mattered to someone. "It's a powerful image. Extraordinary, really."

He heard the boy swallow, then clear his throat softly. "Blake, I've decided. I…I want my photos to be shown."

"Good for you."

"So, I was wondering," he said, rushing the words, "could you help me caption the photos I've mounted?"

He started to say, I'm sure you can do it. Then he considered how difficult it might have been for the boy, asking for help. "Sure," he said. "Let's look them over."

"Now?"

Blake smiled to himself. "Why not? I'm between things at the moment."

"Can you meet me for coffee at Paulo's? It's this funky little sandwich shop, out by the Tri-Point Mall. Right now, it's my best shot."

"You've lost me."

"One of my buddies showed three of my photos to the guy who manages the place, and he wants to see more. Said he'd display them if the other shots live up to the ones he's seen."

Blake thought of cab fare to the mall, or even bus fare, and how little money he had. "How about meeting at my place instead?"

* * *

Drinking the instant coffee that Blake scrounged up, he and Luka started in on the stack of eight-by-ten photographs. It went slowly, because Blake needed to absorb each image. Then he wanted to find words for each caption that felt right to Luka. So they took their time, sitting, standing, or pacing about as they discussed each shot.

Occasionally, Blake would look up from an eight-by-ten and see Luka examining the books on his shelves, or taking in his apartment's shabby interior. But Luka only spoke about the photos, with both of them tossing out captions whenever they came to mind.

As they kept at it, Blake had Luka record each caption in a tattered spiral notebook. He wanted Luka to get in the habit of writing out captions, so that it would feel more natural to him the next time around.

Watching him, Blake could see the boy settling into the process, gaining confidence. The ease with which he expanded his sensibilities, from images to words, made Blake wonder. How much talent did he have?

If anything, Blake found these new photographs even more stunning than the three Luka had shown him atop the windswept building. Using the kitchen table, Blake began to lay out the ones yet to be captioned.

The first photo caught three wild-eyed teenage boys playing chicken, wearing baggy pants that begged them to trip as they dodged cars on a busy street.

The next shot showed a freckled girl hanging upside down by her knees from a playground's chin-up bar, as she kissed a boy who stood on tiptoe, his hair beaded in cornrows.

Then a photo of three schoolgirls in matching white blouses and navy-blue skirts from St. Mary's, hurling rolls of toilet paper upward, unfurling long streamers that crisscrossed an Army recruiting billboard.

That was followed by a shot of two boys, bent over with their pants at half-mast, mooning a line of people who had queued up at the museum, alongside an austere sign that promoted its neo-realist exhibition....

By early afternoon, they were finished, with forty captioned photos.

It should have been a moment of satisfaction, but Blake found himself thirsting for a drink, which he had been for the last hour, to the point where he found himself rocking back in his chair as he rubbed his thighs with his palms.

Luka noticed his discomfort and said, "I'd better get going. But I'll call you, once I hear, you know? I mean, whether they'll exhibit my stuff."

"Great. But don't give up if they say no."

Luka nodded and they walked to the door. Hesitantly, Luka extended his hand and Blake shook it, wishing him luck.

Blake watched Luka depart, then stood there for a moment which felt like an hour. Wetting his lips, he grabbed his overcoat, locked up and headed for Franco's. It was a dozen blocks to get there, but a drink seemed in order, to celebrate Luka's victory.

* * *

Franco called him to the counter, saying, "We need to talk."

Impatiently, Blake shucked off his overcoat. "Run a new tab and I'll listen."

Franco produced a chilled Lone Star and used a bottle opener, popping its cap. "Paying me is the smallest of your worries."

"Meaning?" Blake gripped the beer and took a long swallow, savoring its taste. Then another swallow.

"You just missed Alexis. He was asking about you. Asking while he collected money people owed him."

"So?"

"Did you clear your debt with the man?"

Blake took another swig, then nodded. "One hour with his kid was the deal. Afterwards, Alexis seemed happy."

"You're sure?"

Blake thought of Alexis, pointing to the mason's foot and saying *one toe*. "Hell, Franco. He said he was satisfied."

Franco pursed his lips. "Well something's up, so be watching your step. And your back." He moved down the counter and poured a round of drinks for a cocktail waitress.

Blake took another pull on the Lone Star. That emptied the bottle. He got a fresh bottle from Franco, then sat near the pretzel cart. He watched the Lakers whip the Trail Blazers, 118 to 92. When the game ended, he realized he hadn't asked Franco about part-time work. He turned and saw Franco, up to his elbows in drinks and customers. Tomorrow then. Tomorrow he would ask him.

He studied the few broken pretzels lined up in front of him on the table, next to shot glasses and beer mugs. He didn't remember switching to drinking shots with beer chasers. Staring at the nearest shot glass, he tried to think of other jobs he could do, but everything he thought of—from painting houses to driving a taxi—seemed overwhelming, because he had lost the kind of concentration those jobs demanded. As he sat there, even the simplest tasks seemed overwhelming.

He began to drift...thinking of the bird that Luka had photographed, perched on the ledge, finding its point of no return.

* * *

Blake awoke in near-darkness on a canvas cot he didn't recognize. He sat up with a start and looked around. He found himself in a small storeroom, crowded with rows of shelves that formed aisles. The only illumination came from a single light bulb, hanging in the far corner. He saw that a blanket had been thrown over him and that he was still wearing his clothes.

Next to the cot he found his cowboy boots, with a note on top. In a large, looping cursive script, it said, "You were out of it, is why I put you in the storeroom. The back door self-locks, so let yourself out. Franco."

Groaning, he pulled his boots on, and stood up. Feeling queasy, he opened the back door. Immediately, he felt the chilly bite of the wind and shielded himself from the glare of the sun, pushing through a layer of clouds.

After a moment breathing fresh air, he felt better. He ran his palm across the stubble on his face, then did a few knee bends to get the stiffness out of his joints. Satisfied that he could walk, even though he felt weak, he stepped outside and locked the door behind him.

He started walking, even though his head ached and the inside of his mouth felt gritty and raw.

Halfway home, he thought about the stale bread in his kitchen. He should have filched a can of olives or maraschino cherries from the storeroom, and left Franco a note.

When he entered the apartment building, he was stunned to see his door off its hinges and resting on sawhorses in the hallway, with two carpenters at work. The one in the hallway was bent over, painting the door, which had been sanded down through several layers of blistered paint to its wood grain. The other carpenter was on a ladder in the living room, patching cracks in the plaster that surfaced the ceiling. On the floor, open packing boxes held Blake's books and clothes.

Blake's stomach clenched as his heavyset landlord stepped into the hall, gripping his suspenders.

"At last," said the landlord. "You're here."

Beads of sweat dotted the landlord's forehead and stained the collar of his shirt. He half-bowed, saying, "I assure you, everything will be taken care of. Your rent is prepaid and a full crew of carpenters will finish the repairs. They'll also paint your apartment." Again, he bowed. "I apologize profusely for any past misunderstandings."

Blake tried to make sense of what he was hearing and seeing. He started to enter his apartment, when a thought struck him—a suspicion, actually. Ignoring the landlord, he went back outside the building and looked for a silver Mercedes.

There, at the end of the block, he spotted it. Nicolai stood in its shadow on the sidewalk, smoking a cigarette.

Blake walked to the Mercedes, confused and concerned by his landlord's comments.

Nicolai opened the door, revealing Alexis in the back seat.

"Please," said Alexis. "Will you join me?" His tone was soft, but his hard gray eyes seemed to be taking Blake's measure.

Blake could feel the sweat forming on his brow, even as the vapor from his breath dissolved in the frigid air that had kept ice on the sidewalks. He glanced at Nicolai, then got in, and the door closed. A moment later, the car pulled away from the curb and Nicolai raised the partition, giving them privacy.

Still flustered, Blake said, "I didn't ask for this."

Alexis nodded. "Of course not."

"Then why do it?"

"For my son."

Stunned, Blake said, "Luka asked?"

Alexis made a vague motion with one hand.

"Well *I* didn't ask, and *I'm* the one who lives there."

Alexis faced him. "Do you wish me to send the workers away? To take back the rent money?"

Blake swallowed, knowing how close he had been to living on the street. Outside his window, slower cars were passed with ease and quickly fell behind.

"I take that for a 'no,'" said Alexis.

"But I can't afford this, and I stand little to no chance of paying you back. Especially if you charge interest." He screwed up his courage. "Or is this free?"

Alexis smiled slowly, without blinking his eyes. "*Nothing* is free. But for you, the price is not money. Just time with my son, to help him."

Thinking of how easy that could be, Blake was tempted. "But I want to know," he said. "Was Luka telling the truth, about having good grades?"

"Yes. But there are other, more important things to learn."

Without looking down, Blake could feel the tremor in his hands. "And I'm supposed to teach him?"

Alexis tapped his wristwatch. "Just spend time with my son. Five hours a week. Yes or no? That is the deal."

Blake looked out through the window as Nicolai drove the Mercedes through a sharp turn, then sped along the lakefront, where the wind scoured Lake Michigan, clipping the tops off rows of whitecaps.

"What if Luka isn't willing?"

"Okay. Only if he wants. But if he *does*, five hours a week."

Blake's felt trapped. "For how long?"

Alexis looked out the window at a flock of birds rising into the sky, then turned to him. "For the three months your rent is paid." He held out a one hundred-dollar bill. "Get a room for tonight, while the paint dries in your apartment."

* * *

Late the next morning, after a motel breakfast that settled his stomach, Blake entered his apartment and looked around. He was amazed at how bright and cheery the place looked. The walls and carpet were shades lighter than they had been. He approached the bookcase and saw that everything had been dusted, then put back in order. On the kitchen counter, which was covered with new Formica, he found the dishes washed, sitting in a drying rack. His open pantry had been stocked with canned food. Inside the replacement refrigerator he found fresh fruit and vegetables, plus two six-packs of Lone Star beer.

He looked at the kitchen alcove and blinked. Luka's photo of the bird was missing. He wondered if Alexis had taken it. Blake knew he hadn't mentioned the photograph to Alexis, so how could Alexis have known it was Luka's? Or had Luka revealed that it was, in return for his father helping him? Was that the price? Was this part of the lesson Alexis had planned for Luka?

He considered the consequences of asking either one of them, father or son, if Alexis had taken the photo. He realized that could make things worse. Asking Luka would send him to his father. And Blake didn't trust Alexis to tell the truth to Luka, or to him if he should ask. Besides which, Luka didn't deserve more problems with his father.

Blake sat on the reupholstered couch and tried to think through the situation he was in. He realized that Alexis hadn't threatened him, but he had certainly tied him to a leash made of money. Already, Blake could feel its tug. And in three months, when his rent was used up, it would be worse. That, more than anything, convinced him that he had to make changes in his life. And had to complete them before time ran out. Before Alexis or the liquor took over his life.

Leaning against the counter, he had to admit that it might take more than a new job. He might have to move, out of town or even out of state. But the good news in all of this was that *now* was the perfect time to plan a new beginning. Now, while he had money in his pocket, food in his stomach and no one hounding him to pay bills.

Determined, he set out for the corner to buy both a *Tribune* and the *Sun-Times*, to check the classifieds for jobs and apartments outside the city.

He came back thirty minutes later, carrying the Sunday papers and two cartons of Chinese takeout—potstickers and tomato beef chow mein.

When he saw the blinking light on the message machine, his appetite faded. Praying that it wasn't Alexis who had called, he pressed the replay button.

"If you can, come to the mall entrance this afternoon, about one. The same spot."

Blake recognized Luka's voice and sagged with relief. Then thought again. He had to be careful. He had to find out where he stood, without making things worse for him or the boy.

* * *

Blake used the change from the hundred-dollar bill Alexis had given him and took a cab. He had the driver drop him off across from the mall, which was filled to capacity with weekend shoppers, despite icy winds. He climbed up on a Dumpster and took ten minutes, studying the mall's parking lot. He didn't see any sign of the silver Mercedes, or Nicolai or Alexis, and decided it was safe.

He crossed the street and looked for Luka. He spotted him almost hidden by a cluster of teenagers. He sat on the mall steps, bundled up, wearing headphones as he bobbed his head and snapped his fingers.

Seeing him, Luka slipped off the headphones and stood up, grinning. "My photos are going to be shown, under my friend's name."

"That's great."

"But they can only use twenty of the forty we captioned. Will you help me pick the best twenty?"

Happy for him, Blake said, "I'm used to editing words, not photographs."

"Yeah, but I trust you." He stuffed the headphones and CD player into his daypack.

Blake hesitated, then decided it was better to ask now, and get it over with. "Look, speaking of trust, I need to know. What did you say to your father, about my money situation?"

Luka cheeks turned crimson. "I asked...I asked why he couldn't pay you for the lesson."

"Pay me?"

"Instead of just canceling your debt."

"Pay me how much?"

"I didn't say." The blush spread downward to his neck. "I don't know what teachers earn. Or editors."

"When did you ask for his help?"

"Saturday, when I left your apartment. Right after we captioned my photos."

Blake took that for the truth and didn't press further.

A gust of wind pulled at Blake as Luka bit his lip. "Did he pay you enough?"

Blake raised both hands, sorry that he'd asked. "More than enough."

Hesitantly, Luka asked, "Did I do something wrong?"

Blake felt bad for asking, seeing Luka's discomfort. "It's nothing to get upset about. I was just curious, is all."

Luka nodded, but didn't look convinced.

"So where are your photos?"

Luka hefted his daypack and glanced around the parking lot.

"Luka, I came by myself."

"Sorry. Watching my back has become a habit."

He led Blake inside the mall. They went up an escalator, then into a narrow pizza parlor where wire baskets that were trimmed with garlic and filled with bell peppers hung above the counter.

Blake felt chilled and fatigued, despite getting a good night's sleep and starting his day with a decent breakfast. He bought two coffees and followed Luka to a booth in the back.

Luka shrugged off his daypack, opened it and removed the box that held his photographs.

Blake took a few sips of coffee, then set both cups off to the side, while Luka used the whole table, spreading out the photos they had captioned.

Looking from the photos to Blake, Luka said, "How do I choose?"

To put him at ease, Blake said, "All of them are good enough to exhibit."

"Maybe so, but the manager said twenty shots. And I want them to be my best photos. Truly my best."

Blake thought of the photograph of the pigeon, missing from his apartment.

Luka gestured at the photos. "What should I do?"

The concern on his face seemed genuine, and that helped Blake view this as a chance to move forward and make some progress. Even if it was with someone else's life, instead of his own. Nodding as much to himself as to Luka, he said, "You can approach it from two directions. Either try to pick your best shots as the ones to keep, or try and spot those with a little flaw or weakness and remove them."

Luka's face pinched with worry. "Which way's better?"

"Neither. But spotting a weakness can be easier than choosing your best work."

"How come?"

Blake took a sip of coffee. "Because when something doesn't quite fit, it catches your eye."

"Okay. Let's sort them into weak and strong."

"Before we start, do you have two pens and some paper?"

Luka nodded and dug through his daypack, coming up with a tablet and two ballpoints.

Blake took one pen. "We each need a sheet of paper. On it, for each photo, we'll write down anything that bothers us. But we won't compare notes. Not until we've gone through all the photos."

Luka smiled. "Independent thinking. I like that."

It took forty-five minutes, but in the end, they were surprisingly close in the shots they had chosen and the flaws they had spotted.

Blake was pleased. To him, it seemed they preferred the same type of photograph—ones that seized your imagination and wouldn't let go.

Luka, thanked him several times as they walked to the front of the mall, then waited with him until he hailed a cab. Awkwardly, the boy extended his hand, and Blake shook it, telling him to call when his show opened.

Blake climbed inside the cab and gave his address. When the cab pulled away, he caught a glimpse of Luka, smiling as he worked his way through a crowd of teenagers.

Blake shared the boy's smile, pleased with everything they had accomplished.

* * *

In front of his apartment building, Blake watched the cab depart, then looked at the afternoon sky. Windswept and cloudless, its blue expanse seemed cold and empty. It reminded him of the Texas skies he had abandoned in his flight to Canada.

He shook off that feeling and entered his apartment. He walked to the refrigerator and opened it. As he popped the cap on a Lone Star, he happened to look at the alcove. The photograph was back—Luka's shot of the gray pigeon, ready to plunge from the ledge.

Shaken, Blake realized that Alexis had a key to his apartment.

That's the message, he figured. Or was there something else waiting to be discovered?

Cautiously, he examined his bookcase. Then walked to his bedroom, opened the closet and flipped through the few pants and shirts that hung from the rail. Then he had a sudden realization and cursed himself for being so slow. Alexis had *already* scrutinized every detail of his life, back when all of his belongings had been boxed up and moved, to paint his apartment.

He stared at the dresser, then removed his unfinished novel from the bottom drawer. He clenched his jaw in a rush of shame that turned to anger. The story he had struggled to finish and ended up ruining his life over had been laid bare—viewed by the man he was indentured to like a slave. Blake's hands shook, gripping the manuscript, until it came to him that none of it would make sense to Alexis. The way the man struggled to hold a conversation, reading a simple newspaper was probably beyond him.

Still, Blake's emotions wouldn't subside, so he carried the novel's manuscript into the kitchen and sat down, putting it on the table.

Maybe now he could finish it. This, he realized, could be the perfect opportunity, with three months rent paid in advance. He took a deep breath, wanting to convince himself, and looked past the table, into the alcove, where the bird—poised in Luka's photograph—seemed to stare at him.

Find your own way, he told himself. Quit making excuses. Be like Luka. Show some courage.

He faced the stack of typewritten pages and began to read. It had been his grand attempt. Written in Canada, then in Chicago, but set in Texas, his novel bore witness to the friends and family he had known, driven by the dreams and demons that had torn them apart.

By the time he'd reached the end of the first chapter, he rediscovered what had made him quit. The words. The very words he had written. They were descriptive, and the prose was polished, but none of it compelled him to keep reading. The words on the pages didn't fill him with any burning need to follow the lives he had written about, or to discover the fates that awaited them.

For a long moment, he held the remaining pages—not reading them—as the extent of his failure sunk in. When he looked up, facing Luka's photograph in the alcove, the truth of it pained him.

His novel lacked the striking clarity of the bird on the ledge, with its ability to evoke a wealth of emotion.

He stared at the photograph and felt himself drawn into it, deeper and deeper, until he gained a penetrating awareness of what it must feel like to abandon that precipice and plunge to freedom.

Shaken, he finished his beer. Then, not bothering to put away his manuscript, he stared at his hands and thought about buying a fifth of Johnny Walker. Enough to help him slide into a haze. It tempted him, but even that, he realized, offered little solace now. Not after having seen himself so clearly.

After a moment, he felt something change inside him, and his anxiety lessened. Not from anything improving in his life, because it hadn't. But he began at least to feel a sense of acceptance, and that allowed his thoughts to shift from himself and his situation, to Luka, and how determined Alexis seemed to shape his boy's life.

Blake realized it had to be Alexis who had returned Luka's photograph of the bird. But what was the father's intent? It was hard to believe that Alexis would go to such lengths to monitor his son's interest in photography. Still, Luka's secrecy suggested fear on his part. That, and knowing that his father opposed his dreams.

None of this told Blake exactly what Alexis wanted. But for Luka's sake, and probably for his own, Blake knew that he had to break free. Absolutely had to if he was going to make a fresh start in his own life, instead of backsliding into booze and oblivion.

He glanced at the round wall clock in the kitchen. A little past three. Then he noticed the shape of the clock. Round. Like a circle, drawn in the dirt with the heel of a boot.

Now, he thought. If I don't do it now, I'll never do it.

* * *

Inside Franco's, Blake passed a big-screen television. On it, a pair of Mexican fighters hammered each other in the corner of the ring, spattering their chests and trunks with blood.

Blake kept walking until he found Alexis at a small table, sitting in a dark corner.

"Join me," said Alexis.

Facing him, Blake felt a tremor in his legs, but sat down.

"What brings you?" said Alexis.

Blake glanced at the televised fight in progress. As the boxers clinched, a graphic popped up in the corner of the screen, indicating that it was the twelfth and final round.

"I want to make a bet," Blake said, "on the next fight."

Alexis took a sip of tea. "On the main event?"

"Yes." Blake caught the attention of a passing waitress and said, "Johnny Walker. Straight up."

Alexis raised his eyebrows. "What kind of bet?"

Blake edged forward in his seat. "For my freedom."

Alexis gave him a dark smile. "Ease yourself. All you owe me is time with my son."

"I want it back. All of my time."

Alexis kept smiling, but his eyes seemed to harden. "In that case, you owe me three month's rent. And the repairs. Plus interest."

Beneath the table, Blake clasped his hands, so they wouldn't shake. "That's the amount I wish to bet."

Alexis set aside his tea and leaned toward him. "Think very carefully. For you, this is big money, not small money. When the fight ends the bet is due. And there are but three ways it can go." He raised one finger. "A draw is a draw." He raised another finger. "If your man wins, you are free, with no more duties to my son and can keep the rent, the repairs, and even the interest." He raised a third finger. "But if my man wins, you must put the money in my hand." He paused, using three fingers to tap the palm of his other hand. "Right then you must pay. At that moment."

Blake forced himself to nod.

"So now I ask you. Do you have that kind of money?"

Blake thought of his brother enlisting while he hitchhiked to Canada.

"Do you have it?" said Alexis.

"No. I don't."

"Do you understand," said Alexis, lowering his voice, "what happens to someone—to *anyone* who does not pay me?"

Blake felt the urge to run, but gripped the table leg instead. He looked Alexis in the eyes and nodded.

The waitress brought Blake's whiskey, and Alexis handed her his half-finished tea. "Bring me a vodka," he said, "on rocks of ice."

On the big screen, a pair of tuxedo-clad commentators finished their post-fight interview. Then, as the bloodied winner walked away, the commentators began their preview of the main event, gesturing at two robed fighters entering the ring.

Blake swallowed half his shot of whiskey, feeling the burn.

"Which is your man?" asked Alexis.

"Give me a moment."

Blake studied the graphic that flashed up on the screen, pro-filing each boxer. They were welterweights. One fighter he hadn't heard of, from London. He recognized the name of the American, but had never seen him fight.

In the photo shown above his fight record, the Londoner was pale as the belly of a fish and looked whipcord thin, but had won most of his fights, usually by decision. In his photograph, the American was shorter, but bigger through the shoulders, and his record had him winning two-thirds of his bouts, mostly by knock-outs.

"Make your choice," said Alexis, "before the first punch."

Blake felt the Brit's advantage was in the total rounds he had boxed. Both fighters were the same age and had fought an equal number of fights, but more often than not, the Brit had gone the distance to win by decision. So his endurance was proven. And he may have learned a few tricks, surviving all those rounds. On the other hand, the American had power, and was eager to use it. The commentator had said his knockouts always came in the first three rounds.

The waitress came by and gave Alexis his vodka.

The fighters' robes were removed and they jogged in place, trying not to lose their sweat. The Englishman looked stiff and tense. Not good against a brawler.

"The American," Blake said, praying that he was right.

"Done," said Alexis and raised his vodka.

They touched glasses. Blake had a sip. Alexis swallowed his vodka in a single gulp.

The bell sounded and the fighters met in the center of the ring. The Brit got his jab going, but had to backpedal as the Ameri-can pressed forward, catching more punches than he threw.

The Brit got cornered and connected with a left-right com-bination, but the American hunched over and burrowed in, throw-ing uppercuts. They missed. But in the course of the exchange, he headbutted the Brit, who immediately clinched, with blood drip-ping from his forehead.

The referee forced them apart and the Brit complained, but the referee ignored him.

A few tables over, a man with a mustache yelled, "It's not a damn waltz! C'mon. Mix it up!"

The round ended with the Brit landing a straight right that jarred the American.

Blake scored the round even for both fighters and finished his whiskey, not feeling the burn this time.

Alexis said, "On me," and signaled the waitress for drinks.

In the second round, at the urging of his corner, the Brit threw more punches. He also circled to his right, like a southpaw, which seemed to baffle the American. But the Brit's bleeding worsened, and he began using his glove, wiping at his eye. Whenever he slowed down, his corner screamed, "Bloody 'ell, stick and move!"

The American scowled and pressed forward, but the Brit kept circling to his right. That prevented the American from setting up properly, to throw his punches. Despite that, in the round's final seconds, the American landed two hooks to the ribs that buckled the Brit's knees, nearly putting him down.

"He's a tough bastard," Alexis said, nodding at the Brit.

It was a twelve-rounder, and Blake found himself willing the American to headbutt his opponent. Do whatever it takes, he thought. Just finish the Brit!

The bell sounded, starting round three, and the Brit circled to his right. As he cut across the ring between the American and the referee, the brawler threw a low blow at him. Wincing, the Brit backpedaled as the American lunged, throwing a wild overhand right. The Brit dodged it and bounced off the ropes, avoiding further damage.

Passing the referee, the Brit complained and his cornermen screamed for a foul.

"Pussy," yelled a ruddy-faced man to Blake's right. "Quit running!"

Both fighters moved in suddenly, exchanging hooks and body shots, then clinched.

Wrapping one arm around the Brit, the American rabbit-punched him to the back of the neck. This time the referee saw it, but only issued a warning.

"Come on," growled Blake, clenching his shot glass. "Corner the Limey bastard and hammer his body."

And that's what the American did, throwing a vicious hook to the ribs. That folded the Brit over, saving him as the American fired a right cross where his chin had been.

Sensing his advantage, the brawler pressed forward and double-jabbed the Brit's forehead, finding the cut above his eye.

The Brit managed a quick pivot, getting out of the corner, planted his feet and threw a ripping uppercut as the American rushed in, catching him square on the chin. The force of the punch snapped his head back as it jerked him up, onto his toes.

Blake winced as the American wobbled, keeping his balance for a second, then fell with his eyes rolled back, as his shoulders and head hit the canvas.

Blake's stomach churned and a tremor shot through his legs.

The referee got to three in the ten-count when the American's cornermen threw in their towel, ending the count.

They went to their fallen man, knowing he was finished.

The lighting inside Franco's was dim, and seemed to darken further as Blake gripped his whiskey glass. He took the last sip of whiskey and tried to compose himself. To at least maintain his dignity.

Turning to Alexis, he managed to speak in a level voice. "What happens now?"

Alexis looked him in the eye. "Luka will learn the lesson I planned."

Blake bit his lip. "What do you mean?"

Alexis stood. "Come. Let us walk to the door."

Blake found the strength to get up, and they wove their way through the crowd, with Blake scarcely hearing bits of conversation and the occasional laugh.

Standing in the entryway, Alexis paused to unbutton and briefly open his coat. Riding high on his hip, in black holster, was a snub-nosed revolver.

Blake sucked in his breath and Alexis put a gentle arm around his shoulder, the way a friend might, to steady him.

"Usually," said Alexis, "it is Nicolai who handles such matters. But not with you."

Blake blinked, feeling lightheaded.

In a soft voice, Alexis said, "I will tell Luka this choice is *his*. That there will be pain, but there needn't be suffering."

Blake felt himself sway and gripped the doorknob. Setting his jaw, he opened the door to sunlight and tasted the crisp, afternoon air. Still holding the door, he took a deep breath, and that helped.

Alexis leaned close and whispered. "Luka is the one who must decide…how it will go. Slowly or quickly."

Balanced on the doorstep, Blake looked up. He saw the stunning blue sky and thought of the photo Luka had given him. Of the bird, poised on the precipice.

Terry Bennett

All the Same

H

e held her hand as they slipped outside, beneath the moonlit shadow of the hotel canopy.

The night air held a lazy warmth and a pungent sweetness, like a lei of white ginger. To either side of them, streams of subdued light filtered through the etched glass of sculpted tiki torches.

It was late, and the few voices he heard fell away as they crossed the stone terrace.

He took in the weight of the full moon above, against an immense blanket of stars. Then the iridescent blue of the swimming pool distracted him, casting its glow, edging the fronds on the nearest palm trees.

"*Beach villas, this way*" read the sign, just beyond the lounge chairs where the shadows deepened.

As they passed the pool, he could see, even in the dark, the paths of crushed oyster shells. Sun-bleached by day, they were luminous in the moonlight.

She pointed to the widest path, and they took it, veering to their left.

As they walked, holding hands, he took note of every detail—not knowing what he would record in his journal until afterward, when it truly began…the wonderful counterpoint of memory and imagination.

He paused. Overhead, the tangle of stars seemed to sharpen and expand.

"Don't worry," Mona said. "I know the way."

He almost smiled. For many cultures, "the way" meant a path to enlightenment. He thought of Lao Tzu and the *Tao Te Ching.*

"Ready?" she asked.

With a slight bow, he said, "Of course." Then, thinking that it suited the moment, he raised up her hand and kissed it.

Mona smiled, then stepped ahead of him, where the path narrowed to shoulder-width.

He felt the slight give of pulverized shells crunching beneath his feet as he followed in the wake of her perfume. She smelled exotic to him—stronger than the plumeria that had graced the lobby.

Her stride lengthened, and he thought she was humming softly, though it was hard to tell against the soft hiss of the rising sea breeze.

"We're almost there," she said.

From behind, her halter-top exposed the delicate cleft between her shoulder blades. For some reason, that eased his apprehension. Certainly, embracing the flesh had transformed others, so why not him?

The path sloped downward. He focused on the gentle sway of Mona's hips beneath her wraparound skirt until they reached the "villas." Up close, they seemed more like a row of cottages shoved together, surrounded by garden lights that reflected off corrugated tin roofs. Nearby, he heard waves cresting, but couldn't see them with the cottages blocking his view. Good, he thought. I'm tired of images that belong on postcards.

Mona stopped at the second cottage, next to a small, lighted sconce. Its glow caught her auburn hair as she pulled a ring of keys from her purse.

Two cottages down, he glimpsed a thick-bodied black man wearing light shorts and a dark T-shirt, sitting peacefully on a bench with his head bowed. Sleeping, perhaps, his eyes hidden by a spill of dreadlocks. Mona seemed to sense the man's presence and glanced his way, then faced the cottage door. She unlocked it as he stood at her side, then gave him the same lingering look that she had when he first approached her. She'd been sipping one of those specialty drinks with gold and green layers as she sat in the hotel bar, near a brass leopard's head that trickled water into a bowl of coins. When he had walked closer, she had looked up at him with stunning green eyes, flecked with gold.

"I'll bet it's my drink you're wondering about," she had teased, then raised her glass for his inspection. "It's a Frozen Matador, made with gold tequila, pineapple juice and lime juice, topped off with a slice of fruit; lime for the locals...passion fruit for me."

"A matador that's frozen," he'd said, wondering if this was synchronicity...her sensuality, drawn to his intelligence.

"But *you* aren't frozen," she'd added with a wink.

That's when he had realized it was meant to be.

Now, as Mona swung open the cottage door, she smiled, put her hands on his shoulders and turned him toward the bed. It had a modest headboard with vertical slats and a beige bedspread. To the left was a door made of lashed bamboo, then a chair and a rattan dresser with a single lamp.

"Take off your sandals," she said, "and get comfy."

He smiled. "I intend to."

He approached the bed, intrigued by its pale bedspread. Everything else on the island was bathed in blues and greens, or basked in pinks and oranges. Later on, he might take satisfaction in mentioning that the bed had seemed a bit stark...then suggest that even this tiny lapse in paradise had played its part in his transformation.

He sat on the bed and heard a click as Mona locked the door. Then came a softer click, like a faint echo.

He watched Mona set her keys and purse on the dresser, by a small digital clock.

Sitting on the bed, he noted how the lamp cast his shadow on the wall. Excellent, he thought. The duality begins—self and the awareness of self.

As he debated whether to remove his glasses, Mona picked up the digital clock. He looked again and realized it was a timer when she pushed a button and numbered red seconds flickered into existence.

"Are you going *a la carte*," she asked, "or do you want the seven-course extravaganza, with dessert at the end?"

Her accent was more clipped now than in the bar, and he thought of New York, despite her gorgeous tan. In fact, her tone grated a bit. It interfered with the natural grace of their elemental setting.

"We can do whatever you want," she added, then laughed. "Within reason."

"That's good to know." He began unbuttoning his shirt.

Above the dresser he saw a faded print that portrayed dark-skinned natives, paddling outriggers. At least in the lobby, the Gauguin print had been in the shadows, where he could pretend it was an original, capturing a sumptuous island woman as she knelt before a fiery sunset that all but consumed her.

Mona stepped closer. "While you get ready, there's a down payment. My minimum."

He fumbled, half-rising from the bed, enough to pull his wallet from his trousers. Sitting on the edge of the bed, he opened his wallet to display an abundance of French Pacific Francs.

"Oh no, honey. Strictly American. Ben Franklins if you can, because twenties get so bulky."

He frowned and raised a narrow flap inside the wallet, where five one-hundred dollar bills were concealed.

"How much," he asked, "for conversation?"

That drew a blank look. Then, "You mean talking dirty?"

"No, no. What I—"

"One hundred's my minimum."

Nodding, he removed a bill.

She took it and walked to the dresser, where she held it up to the lamp and examined it. "Have you got a script? Because I've done that before. Long as it's twenty minutes, tops."

"There isn't any script." If she kept interrupting he realized it would be difficult, explaining what he wished to do.

Mona pointed at the timer. "Your hundred buys twenty minutes, but some things run extra."

He saw the timer—now up to two minutes ten seconds, and counting.

"I meant talk, as in...well, 'visiting' is too prosaic."

"It's up to you," she said. "We don't have to visit." She folded his money and set the lamp to one side, revealing a slot in the wall. She inserted the money, which disappeared.

"What are you doing?" he asked.

She smiled, then crossed the small room and sat next to him, touching her knees to his. "Relax, honey. I always make deposits with my banker."

"Your bank's in this hotel?"

She shook her head. "No, darling. My banker." She inclined her head toward the bamboo door, next to the dresser.

He blinked as it sunk in. "I expected privacy."

Mona laughed softly and stretched out on the bed. "Minarii doesn't look. Not unless you want him to."

Offended, he stood up, and was surprised when she reached out, touching his groin.

"Come on," she coaxed, rubbing him lightly. "Minarii's only here for my safety."

"This... this isn't what I envisioned." Still, he couldn't make himself pull back from her hand.

"Where's the fun," she said, "if there's no surprise?"

"Truly, I came here—"

She gave him a firm squeeze that took his breath away.

She let go, then nodded at the timer. "Tell me what you want."

Before he could answer, she took his hand and pulled him closer, until he was lying beside her.

"Actually," he said, feeling a bit rushed, "there's a certain primal exchange I'm seeking. It begins with words, but should lead—"

She scooted closer and ran a fingernail down his sternum.

That undermined his concentration, which bothered him. This was supposed to be *his* moment. *His* awakening.

"About your 'menu,'" he said, drawing back. "I don't suppose it caters to nuance."

"Should it?" She pursed her lips, as if reappraising him, then reached back to the headboard. Hooking her hands though its slats, she arched her back. That drew his gaze to the pitch of her breasts, straining against her halter-top.

"Shades of meaning," she whispered, then stopped. She squeezed her eyes shut and wrinkled her brow. "Shades of...."

Puzzled, he waited.

She opened her eyes and recited quickly, "Shades of meaning form the labyrinth of art."

He blinked. "Where did that come from?"

"A humanities class." With a grin, she held onto the headboard and canted her hips from side to side. "One that I took at Brown."

"In that case," he said, "I suppose it can't be helped."

"What can't?"

"Your urge to parrot the first metaphor that comes to mind."

She lost the sultry look and sat up, frowning. "If there's no script, what's with the put-down?"

"All I'm saying—"

"Am I supposed to zip my lips? Is *that* the deal? Because I've got things to say, mister, like anyone else."

He raised a hand to calm her down. "My concern, Mona, is that what lies before us is of greater consequence."

She took a moment, as if making up her mind, then brushed her hair back. "Fine," she said, not sounding like she meant it. "But you're *acting* like there's a script, even when you say there isn't."

He took a breath and blew it out. "I prefer to think of it as a template."

She gave him a blank look.

"A template for transformation."

She sighed. "Whatever."

He set his jaw. "Do not dismiss—"

"Enough with the lecture," she said, and lay on her back, plopping her head on a pillow. "It's been a long day and we really need to move things along."

"Meaning?"

She sighed, then tugged at her halter-top, showing a little cleavage. "Meaning, I'm ready if you are."

He rolled his eyes. "Of *course* I'm ready. That's why I left the States. To escape petty minds."

"This isn't...." She raised herself up on one elbow. "You aren't on vacation?"

He thought of the sacrifices he had made, developing his thesis, only to have it belittled by a committee of reactionaries.

"Mona, this is hardly the Hilton. It's second-class, at best."

She sat up and leaned forward. "Are you saying that I'm—"

"No, no, no. *Listen.* My presence is self-imposed. *That's* what I'm telling you. That I'm here in exile."

She gave him another blank look.

"Like Gauguin. Except I'm a critic, not a painter."

A small furrow appeared in her brow. "A critic of what?"

"Contemporary literature."

Her shoulders sagged. Briefly, she seemed to consider responding. Then she glanced at the timer and her expression changed. Smiling brightly, she touched one of her earrings.

"Tell me," she cooed. "Are you a nibbler?"

He frowned. "Didn't you hear me?"

Her smile grew tighter as she tapped her earring. "If you are, I can take these off."

"Voluntary exile," he said, drawing it out. "That's the price of intellectual freedom."

Removing an earring, she said, "How about an appetizer?"

"Mona?" He took the earring from her hand and tossed it aside. "This menu business isn't working. Forget *a la carte*. The same for the *hors d'oeuvres*, if that's what your earlobes are."

She leaned back against the headboard, crossing her arms, and glared at him. But that didn't matter. Finally, she was listening instead of talking.

"It's vital, Mona, that you understand what I'm about. Because what I'm seeking exceeds mere physical appetite. If you will, there's a threshold I need to cross."

"Ooooo," she said, rolling her eyes. "A fucking *threshhhhold*."

Irritated, he said, "Is that beyond you? The concept of a threshold?"

"Try me, Einstein."

"Look, there's no need to—"

She snapped her fingers, leaning forward as she spoke. "A threshold, as in...as in—"

"As in *what*?"

She clapped her hands and smiled triumphantly. "A threshold, as in, 'Do I dare to eat a peach?'"

His skepticism must have shown, because she raised her chin and added, "T.S. Eliot, right?"

"I'm afraid so." Admitting that, he lost momentum, then felt a little exposed. Not to mention irked by her unsolicited comments. Reluctantly, he said, "When you mentioned a class at Brown—"

"Brown University," she said with a hint of pride. "Rhode Island's finest." She smiled and reached down, slipping off her sandals.

Her mention of a university made him scowl. He couldn't help recalling the insufferable committee of tenured professors refuting his thesis. As if they couldn't grasp his brilliance in mapping contrapuntal harmonics within metafiction.

"Those were the days," she said wistfully.

He frowned, remembering the myopic judgment of the review committee.

She sighed and rolled onto her side, with her knees tucked up, giving him this pensive look. "In my sophomore year," she said, "I met someone from Jamaica. He really...changed my life and...well...after a while, I had to drop out." She shrugged, offering a melancholy smile. "Then I moved."

He closed his eyes, vexed by the petty details of her life.

"First we traveled to Jamaica. Then here."

He wished that she hadn't said a word. Or that she'd at least stop talking. Then he could test his supposition, that a searing sensual encounter would—

"Where are you from?" she asked, and he felt her hand settle on his thigh.

He opened his eyes and made himself smile. Be patient, he told himself. It's a matter of turning her curiosity in the proper direction.

"Right now," he said, enunciating each word, "it's the *journey* that concerns me. Not the point of departure."

She seemed to think about it. "In that case, maybe I should give you a ride. One you won't forget." She grinned and stretched out on her back, then raised her hips.

He bit his lip, pained by her ability to reduce elegant concepts to insipid chatter.

For a second, he thought he heard a faint creak coming from the wall, behind the rattan dresser.

"Hey, cowboy," she said, with a little buck of her hips. "Ready to saddle up?"

Reluctantly, he looked at her. Truly, she was beautiful. But the prospect of simplifying his theory to the point where even *she* could understand it, made him gnash his teeth. Still, what choice did he have? If his supposition was correct, she was the instrument he needed. She was his gateway to heightened awareness.

Forcing a smile, he scooted to the side and slipped a pillow between his back and the headboard. When she settled back down, looking puzzled, he steepled his hands, feeling like a weary parent, obligated to tell a bedtime story.

"What I'm saying, Mona...what I'm trying to express—"

"You want it with the lights on, or off?"

"*Damn it all!* Will you let me explain?"

A sharp thump rattled the wall, near the money slot.

Startled, he sat up, staring at the wall.

She waved away his concern. "Minarii's just checking. Making sure that I'm all right." Quickly, she sat up, lifted her hand to the wall and tapped out a brief but intricate rhythm.

Flustered, he pressed his palms to his temples. "Can't you just stop for one minute? Stop what you're doing and listen?"

She compressed her lips into a thin line, then brushed her hair back. "Fine," she said. "You talk and I'll listen."

"Well, then." He took a breath, waiting for his anger to subside.

"You need to understand," he said, lowering his voice, "that a physical coupling isn't the *only* thing I'm after. There's also…well, what I'm trying to get at—"

"Yes?" said Mona, retrieving a pack of cigarettes from her purse. Deftly, she tucked one between her lips.

"Please don't," he said, apologetically.

She rolled her eyes, dug out a lighter, flicked it and lit up, taking a long pull on the cigarette.

"What I'm trying to explain—"

"End of a relationship," she said. "That's my guess."

"Pardon?"

"You got dumped." She blew out a long stream of smoke. "Nine times out of ten, that leaves a man in limbo."

He frowned. "I'm hardly in limbo."

She eyed his groin. "When I touched you, a while ago, it was pop-goes-the-weasel."

"So?"

"Now I say the 'R' word, and Mister Weasel takes a powder."

Feeling the heat of his blush, he glanced at his crotch, then at the timer, which was up to 16 minutes.

"Who's to say it wasn't *me*?" he said, speaking more quickly. "*Me* wanting to free myself from a relationship that's dying. To admit to the possibility of new partners. To new horizons and perceptions—without, if you will, any strings attached?"

She smiled. "Well, then. Here's to no strings."

She reached behind her neck and pulled at the strand that secured her halter-top.

"Wait!"

The halter-top slid down, revealing her breasts.

"Christ," he said, squeezing his eyes shut, then popped them open and stared, amazed by the perfect areolas of her nipples.

She tossed the halter-top aside. "Something *a la carte*?"

He wanted to rebuke her, but couldn't ignore the rising bulge in his trousers. "I...I..."

Glancing over her shoulder, she said. "Sorry. But you had your chance."

"Pardon?" he managed.

"Your twenty minutes are up." She pointed at the timer, then reached for her halter-top.

He grabbed it and held it behind his back. "*That's it*? That's how this goes? You keep interrupting, until my time's up?"

She met his gaze. "It wasn't *me* who couldn't get started."

"Oh," he said. "I see. As if you're beyond reproach?"

A faint shuffling sound came from the wall, just as she said, "I don't get many complaints because...."

She paused, giving her shoulders a sharp twist, then acted bored, studying the effect of the movement on her breasts, which swung left and right, finding their equilibrium.

"Because with me," she said, "most everyone gets off."

She reached for her halter top, which he held at arm's length behind him.

"But I didn't have my say!"

"Your *say*?"

"Damn it, the chance to articulate what I'm seeking!"

"'Tis true," came a deep voice from the other side of the wall. "You kept interruptin', Mona."

Surprised, he shook his head, losing his train of thought.

"Well, then, Mister fair-and-square," Mona said to the wall. "He can pony up another Ben Franklin, and we'll give it another go."

She covered her breasts and turned from the wall to him, adopting a look of mock innocence. "Sound like a plan?"

He felt himself harden and struggled to regain his composure.

She parted her lips with her tongue, then used her thumbs and fingertips to massage her nipples. "It's now or never, Mister Weasel."

He clenched his jaw. "Only if you listen. *Truly listen.*"

She nodded and dropped her hands to her lap. "Fine by me. How about you, Minarii?"

"By all means… satisfy da customah."

He dug his wallet out and forked over another hundred. She stood and pushed it through the wall slot, then restarted the timer.

Beaming, she sat on the bed and cupped a hand to one ear.

He grabbed her wrist, pulling her hand down. "Can't you be serious? Must you treat our exchange like a parody?"

"Of what?" she said.

"Isn't that obvious? The *template* I'm striving to create."

She smiled. "Just you? Or will this take both of us?"

"If you'd bother to listen, you'd understand."

"Understand *what*?"

"The transmutation we're about to consummate."

Her shoulders slumped, and she eyed the timer, as if willing it to go faster.

Annoyed, he shifted his position, blocking her view of the flickering digits. "Can't you see the inherent possibilities? The portal that awaits us?"

Her eyes seemed to glaze over, but a soft tapping on the wall revived her. She peeked at the timer, then spoke to the wall. "He's got fifteen minutes."

"Dat isn't da point," Minarii answered in a gentle baritone. "Ess allegory dat he wants, not da actual sexin'."

My God, he thought, literacy among pimps.

"Isn't dat da truth, mon? Whatchu be getting at?"

He reached past her and rapped on the wall. "Hey, Minarii—if that's really your name."

"Yeah, mon?"

"If you keep interrupting, it's time off the clock."

"Well—"

"*Great*," said Mona. "I could've been done by now."

"Mon, as a mattah of honor, I agree wit you. Yes, cuz I broke da silence—but wi da best of intentions. Plus, you haf ma sympati."

He reached past her and thumped the wall. "Who cares about your intentions?"

"Oh jeez," said Mona, shaking her head. "Here we go."

"But you an' me, we're brudders of a sort, bein' in exile. An' what I'm sayin', mon, is dat she'll never get it—whatchu be seekin'."

Mona extended her middle finger, aiming it at the wall. "Says who?"

"Innar Lit class, Monique, who wrote da papers? Who crafted da words for our professar?"

"What do you mean," he demanded, "that we're brothers? In what sense?"

"*Fine*," she huffed. "But tell him, Minarii. Who memorized the damn quotes?"

"*You*, Monique. Den, too late, we discover da professar loved da footnotes more dan da quotes. A man of minutiae, if you will."

"Yeah? Well who screwed his brains out to improve our grades?"

He reached past her, banging on the wall with his fist, hard enough that the bed shook. "I don't give a shit about that!"

"*About which?*" she demanded, grabbing his arm. "His version or mine?"

"Christ," he muttered, trying to pull his arm free. "How could a pimp be in exile?"

"Jamaica," she whispered, tightening her grip, "was very sweet." She pulled him closer, then glanced at the wall. "But it soured when Minarii got into it with the *Gendarmes*. Instead of slipping them a few francs, he had to call himself a champion of free enterprise."

"*Enough*," he exclaimed. "Both of you!"

She released his arm and glared at him, while Minarii said, "Sorry, mon. Jus tryin' to harmonize with a brudder in exile. To give you da true island hospitality."

"As if…" she yelled at the wall, "as if you had a clue, back in Jamaica, about the trouble your mouth would cause."

Tired of their bickering, he grabbed her hand and put it on his crotch.

She gave him a weary look, raising her eyebrows. "Back on track?"

"Indeed," he said, thrusting his pelvis forward. "That is my fervent wish."

She gave a squeeze, which produced no rise or resistance.

In a funk, he hunched forward on the bed, resting his elbows on his knees.

"Shit," he said. "Shit, shit, shit."

"Hey. It's all right," she said softly. "Sometimes that happens."

He shook his head. "The tragedy, Mona, is what this could have been."

"Yeah?" She put her hand on his knee.

He held up his thumb and index finger, with a small gap between them. "We were this close to an epiphany."

A look of faint recognition crossed her face. Suddenly she brightened, saying, "Oh, wow. *Now* I get it. Instead of a fuck, you wanted a metaphor."

"*Der!*" Minarii exclaimed through the wall. "You see? You see? I was *right*. Just like Ernest damn Hemmingway. Cuz his perfect day was Mass in da mornin', bullfight in da afternoon, wid da ho' in da evenin.'"

He shook his head, covering his ears. "*Idiot!* That wasn't Hemmingway. It was Pablo Picasso, speaking to Andre Maraux. And what he said was, '…for us Spaniards it is Mass in the morning, the bullfight in the afternoon and the brothel in the evening.'"

"Oooo," she said, excited now as she bounced on the bed. "And I helped, didn't I, with the bullfight part. You know, with my drink—the frozen matador!"

He groaned in disbelief.

"And now...." She spread her arms triumphantly and gave a shake of her breasts.

"Do *this*," he told her through clenched teeth.

"What?"

He gestured for her to kneel, then tapped his crotch.

"I'm supposed to blow you?"

"Damn right, if it'll keep you from saying another word."

With a spiteful look, she got off the bed and sank to her knees. Grabbing his zipper, she yanked it open.

"Hey, mon!" called Minarii. "She meant no harm. Truly, she jus be joinin' you."

"In what?"

"In da cozy circle-jerk we all be havin'. Cuz, you know, it's all da same. Yankin' da crank, tweakin' da twat, or mouthin' off wi dis college stuff."

"College stuff?"

"Yeah, mon. Masturbation of da intellect."

He wanted to say, *fuck you, Minarii,* but Mona's mouth had found him, and the whole room seemed to tremble as every word disappeared.

Terry Bennett

Blind Faith

E lita strides up Ocean Street on slim legs, warmed by morning sunlight that angles down. Not quite frowning, she talks beneath her breath. "For *you*," she tells herself of her weekend getaway. "Just for you."

She breathes deeply, trying to lose herself in the fresh salt air of Santa Cruz, beneath a spring sky that's sapphire blue. She passes tourists who clutch shopping bags and sidesteps college students, easily identified by their long hair, recycled clothing and scuffed leather sandals. They're so relaxed, she thinks...like Tom.

She feels a pang of loss, lowers her head and walks faster.

As she walks, to relieve the growing tension in her neck, she tries gazing at the sidewalk vendors. They seem so at ease, basking in the sun, sitting at card tables that are spaced out between little shops with brick or stucco facing. Each vendor's wares are hand-crafted, ranging from purple and yellow tie-dye scarves and T-shirts to musical instruments made of polished gourds, filled with seeds.

A block later she eases her pace. Just ahead of her, between the sidewalk and a bookstore, a man catches her eye. He sits, slouched in a gray lawn chair with his feet propped up on a crate, next to another lawn chair. He seems older than the college students—but not by much. He has weathered skin and a lanky body, clothed in worn Levi's and a faded yellow T-shirt. His hair is dark brown, tinted gold on top—from the sun, she expects. Not something in a bottle.

Next to his feet, up on the crate, is a sign. She stops to read it, but can't because it's angled off to the side.

He turns in her direction. He's sipping from a stoneware coffee mug, wearing slate-colored sunglasses. Dark enough that she can't see his eyes.

Beneath his chair she notices a polished wooden box.

Elita lets two women with baby strollers go by, then steps around, getting in front of him. The wooden sign, neatly painted in black, reads "Blind Photography, $5 a shot." Next to the sign, she sees an upturned baseball cap that holds several one and five-dollar bills—all of them fluttering in the breeze, weighted down by a roll of quarters.

The Polaroid camera in his lap completes the joke, like a punch line, and she grins. Then she spots the collapsible white cane, lying alongside the other canvas chair. She squints, trying to see through his sunglasses.

"Blind photography?" she says to him. "You're a comedian, right?"

He cocks his head in her direction, so that one ear is tilted her way. "It's not a joke," he says, smiling.

Crossing her arms, she doubts him.

"Come closer," he says.

He encourages her with a small gesture, and she toes the edge of his crate.

He leans forward, lifting his opaque sunglasses, revealing eyelids that are sewn shut.

She recoils, then stops herself, putting a hand to her chest. "The—the photography is what I meant," she stammers. "I wasn't kidding about…not about—"

"My sightless condition?" he offers, still smiling.

"Yes." She almost swallows the word.

She realizes it's scar tissue holding his eyelids closed. From stitches, she thinks, that must have dissolved as scar tissue formed.

As he slips his sunglasses back on, she adds, "I didn't mean to offend you."

"Believe me, you didn't." He pats the Polaroid camera in his lap. "I've been doing this for a long time."

She takes half a breath, a little relieved, but is still worried about making another comment.

"Blind since age seven," he adds, hefting the camera. "But I earn my living taking photos."

This has to be a prank, she thinks. But he sounds *so sincere*, so matter-of-fact about it.

"The way it works," he says, "is I hold the camera, and you tell me where you're sitting or standing. That points me in the right direction."

She smiles uncertainly. "You make it sound…simple."

"It is."

He takes his feet off the crate, puts the camera down, then reaches beneath his chair and picks up the box, which is made of rosewood and is large enough to hold a pair of shoes. He sets it on his lap and raises the hinged lid. Inside, she sees a colored jumble of Polaroid shots, with the tip of something sticking out from beneath them, glinting in the sun.

"I always take two shots," he says. "The client gets one and I keep the other."

The Polaroid Elita sees on top is of a blonde woman, about her age, wearing an aquamarine V-necked blouse. She's struck an exaggerated pose with her head thrown back and hands on her hips. The way she has pursed her lips, it seems like she's clowning, instead of flirting.

Elita taps the blonde's photo. "Who picks the pose?"

"They do. Or you do…whoever I photograph."

She pictures herself in a smiling pose, but in that instant, the notion feels phony. Still, she imagines looking back on this weekend…maybe talking with her best friend, holding up her Polaroid and saying, *See, Carrie? I did have a good time.* But for that to work, she would have to smile when he tripped the shutter.

"Care to try it?" he asks.

He's so at ease, and she's grateful for the distraction. "Do you guarantee your photos?"

"You mean, whether they turn out?"

She nods, then catches herself. "Yes."

He shrugs, looking relaxed. "Polaroids are pretty reliable."

"No, no," she says. "I mean the *pose*...how they look."

"Well," he says, "of course I always ask. Are they satisfied? And if they are, I ask why. Otherwise, how would I know?"

"Whether it turned out?"

"Yes. And what it reveals."

"*Reveals?*" She cranes her neck, looking at the slew of Polaroids inside the box.

He tips back in his chair, smiling at her skeptical tone.

"Aside," she says, "from whether your photo's in focus, what can they tell you—your subjects, I mean—about their photo? Or themselves?"

His smile broadens. "You'd be surprised."

He's so full of it, she thinks.

"Only five bucks," he says.

She imagines herself posed against the brick wall behind him, standing by the spill of ruby red bougainvillea from the long wooden planter. She considers the avocado green wraparound skirt she's wearing, and the honey-gold blouse that shows off her caramel-colored skin and black hair. Not the real me, she thinks. Too festive.

"Come on," he says. "It's just five bucks."

"What if I'm disappointed?"

He jiggles the box of Polaroids. "What if it's a masterpiece?"

His serious tone mimics hers, but comes across as good-natured teasing. She finds him hard to ignore. Almost appealing.

"Next thing I know," she says, "you'll be *paying* me, just to give it a try."

He laughs. "Forget about the money, okay?" He pats the canvas chair beside him. "Look through my photos and tell me what you see."

"What'll that prove?"

He smiles as if they're sharing a joke. "Give it a chance."

She hesitates, feeling the edge of her loneliness. Not quite trusting herself.

He gently shakes the rosewood box. She knows that he's charming her, but decides to play along.

"All right, Mister Photographer." She sits beside him, glad that she didn't stay in Sacramento, moping about Tom.

"By the way," he says, "I'm Chris. Christopher, actually."

He offers his right hand and she notices a series of scars on his fingers.

"Elita," she says, taking his hand. She's surprised by the self-assurance his grip conveys.

"Thanks for lending me your eyes," he says.

"Pardon?"

He laughs. "For saying you'll look at my photos. Here…." He holds up the rosewood box.

Curious now, she accepts it and sets it on her lap. She sees that it contains maybe three-dozen Polaroids.

"When you look," he adds in a confidential whisper, "there's just one condition."

She leans back, deciding to enjoy herself. "Ahhh. Nothing predictable, I hope."

"All I want," he says, "is for you to tell me what you see."

He sounds serious and her self-confidence fades. "What I see?"

"Right. Not the pose or anything that obvious. I'm talking about…the *other* stuff."

"Of course," she answers, regaining her confidence. "You must mean the souls you have captured."

Softly, he applauds.

"All right, Chris. Let's see what spells you've cast." She starts sifting through the Polaroids.

"Just the photos that grab you," he adds.

She examines the Polaroid she has moved to the top. It's of a young woman with short, copper-tinted hair, wearing a halter-top that barely contains her. Elita trades it for one of a pale, redheaded teenage boy holding a skateboard. He's wearing super-baggy pants that fall to mid-calf, with black, laced-up combat boots and a sleeveless T-shirt that reveals several tattoos on his skinny forearms, mostly of snakes and dragons biting each other and drawing blood. His ears hold several earrings and his hair—shaved close—still has a red cast to it, natural or dyed, she isn't sure. But his grin is genuine, with his head tilted back as he laughs, bunching up cheeks that are peppered with freckles.

"I see…innocence," she says, "…a sort of happiness he still has. You caught that and let him show it, despite his tough exterior."

He inclines his head. "Who's that you're talking about?"

She feels the heat of a blush, rising through her cheeks. "Sorry. The skateboarder, wearing combat boots."

He nods knowingly. "Next?"

She shuffles the Polaroids, bypassing three shots of smiling young women, each wearing shorts and a tied off blouse or tube top, displaying slim midriffs. The next photo tugs at her.

"It's a close-up," she says, "of a gray-haired, black-eyed woman, holding one finger to her lips." My mother's age, she thinks, noticing the accumulation of wrinkles where the woman's cheeks have sagged, and the beginnings of a double chin. "There's something about her eyes," she adds. "Mischievous…almost like she's just told you something. Maybe a secret."

She recalls visiting with her mother last week at the garment shop, being treated like a child. Her mother, while stitching a cotton dress, addressing her as "poquita" Elita. Then chastising her "independence," treating it as a sign of disrespect.

"What kind of secret?" Chris asks.

She purses her lips and turns the Polaroid face down. "How to be the perfect daughter."

"Indeed," he says, with mock reverence, bowing his head for a second. "Clearly a secret."

"More like a mystery," she mutters, and digs to the bottom of the photos, where she feels a lump. Pushing the Polaroids aside, she sees what glinted in the sun before. A pearl-handled switchblade.

Surprised, she says, "What's with the knife?"

He shrugs, giving her a big smile. "I use it to peel oranges."

She starts to say, "Why joke about it?" But then she notices an orange rind in the gutter.

"Pick another photo," he urges.

For a second she stares at the knife. Then she selects another Polaroid. It frames a tall, attractive fellow, probably in his thirties, astride a cross-country bicycle. Gripping the handlebars, he flashes an uneasy smile.

"A tall, good looking guy," she says, "who seems...I don't know...a bit self-conscious? Not too happy?" My type, she thinks. The kind I usually end up with. Handsome, but so self-centered...like Tom. Pained by their breakup, she tucks the photo in with the others.

"What's he doing?" Chris asks.

Reluctantly, she retrieves the photo. "Looking like he'd rather be someplace else."

In her mind, she substitutes Tom's thinner body, adding the crystal necklace he always wears. Bitter now, she pinches the photo between her fingers, thinking of Tom, stuck in his endless routines, performing little rituals for everything you can imagine—right down to brushing his teeth.

She drops the Polaroid into the box and shuts the lid. "I'm convinced," she admits. "You've got a gift for getting people to reveal their inner selves." She sighs, wishing she could forget about Tom.

Facing her, Chris says, "You don't seem too happy about it."

She brushes the rosewood box with her fingertips. "Sometimes things are best forgotten."

He nods once. Quietly, he says, "I couldn't agree more."

Surprised, but relieved by his answer, she leans back in the chair. "Wouldn't that be nice? Zip-zap-zip and it's gone, whatever you need to forget."

"Like a chain reaction," he says, arching his eyebrows. "I forget, you forget, then someone else forgets."

Intrigued, she says, "How would it work?"

He raises both hands, fingers outstretched, as though casting a spell. "Focus," he intones, "on the memories you wish to erase."

She grins, recalling her last argument with her two older sisters, Consuela and Anita, broader-hipped versions of herself who also failed to marry. They complained about Elita not spending enough time with her parents, who are counting on her for their family's "last chance" for respectability, or grandchildren—which, for them, amounts to the same thing.

"Blanking out the bad times is so tempting," she tells Chris, "but too involved." She sighs. "Besides, you can't have it both ways."

"What do you mean?"

She taps the rosewood box. "All these photos. They're the opposite of forgetting."

Carefully, he reaches out, finds the box in her lap and sets it on the ground. "You sound upset."

"I suppose."

"Maybe what you need is to get away from it all. To sit outdoors in the sunshine and watch the world go by." Smiling, he makes a slow, sweeping gesture that takes in the locals and tourists walking past.

She can't help laughing, because that's why she came to Santa Cruz.

"Thank you," she says. "I needed that."

"And," he says, leaning closer, "maybe a latte or a cappuccino?"

Is he that considerate, she wonders, or just a smooth talker?

"I know a coffee house," he says, "with sidewalk seating and pastries that melt in your mouth."

"Well," she says, "if it's not too much trouble...."

Chris reaches out, finding his "Blind Photography" sign. She watches his fingertips locate a pair of notches, marking its front side. He turns it over, so that it reads, "Back in a Bit." Then he reaches down and finds his collapsed white cane. Pulling on both ends, he doubles its length.

"Just like that?" she asks. "You can pick up and leave?"

He grins. "Just like that."

He finds his baseball cap, centered on the crate, and pockets the money it holds. With smooth movements, he stows his camera beneath the crate, along with his box of Polaroids. Inclining his head, he turns toward the nearest street vendor, a skinny black woman in a pink sarong who's selling beaded ceramic jewelry in different shades of blue.

"Mary," he calls out, "will you watch my stuff?"

"Hang on," Mary answers. She raises both hands, palms up and gives Elita a questioning look.

Elita wonders what Mary is trying to convey and glances from her to Chris, then back to her.

"Is this a good idea?" Elita says it to Chris, but looks at the woman. "I mean, you could miss some customers."

"Forget about that," says Chris. "You're going to love this place."

Silently, Mary mouths, *It's up to you.*

"Do you mind?" Elita asks, wondering what's going on. Has Mary been bothered one time too many? Or is she simply protective of Chris?

"Got you covered," Mary answers. "Take your time."

As she and Chris stand up, he looks so happy that Elita feels her hesitance begin to fade. "How far is it," she asks, "to this coffee house?"

"Five blocks and twelve steps." He smiles and taps the sidewalk with his cane. "Take my arm and I'll show you."

Mary nods at her, and Elita feels she must have misunderstood Mary's silent communication. Besides, she tells herself, it's only a cup of coffee.

She hooks her elbow with his, and they start up the street. At first she tries too hard to match her movements to his. Then she sees how relaxed he is with her walking at his side. Smiling, she falls into the soft but steady rhythm of his stride, punctuated by the sweep of his cane.

"It feels good," he says, "to get out and about."

"I'm glad."

The crowds have thinned, and Chris reels off the names of the stores and their owners as they pass a sporting goods shop with day-glo orange surfboards stacked in its window, then a sunglasses boutique, followed by a few tiny "kiosk" shops, like the Ali Baba Cafe. Five blocks later, he guides her across the street to the Espresso Royale.

They sit outdoors, at a tiny wrought-iron table placed next to a marble planter, where a skinny young man with braces on his teeth takes their order.

Though the open French doors, she sees a mostly jeans and T-shirts crowd whose conversations compete with a jazz trio that's on the sound system, with a saxophone taking the lead.

"This place," says Chris, "do you like it?"

"Yes. Especially being out here in the sun."

Their server returns with their drinks, and Chris hands him money before she can get her purse open.

"I can pay for mine," she offers.

"My treat," he insists.

"Well, okay." She sets her purse down as he turns his head slightly, facing into a breeze that ruffles her skirt and eases the warmth of the sun. Relaxing, she says, "This is so cozy, compared to Sacramento. I love all the little shops you have here."

He sips at his cappuccino. "I like the people who pass through."

She blushes, certain that he's referring to her because of his smile, and the way he leaned closer, saying it.

"You have a way with people," she admits. Then adds in a teasing voice, "But sometimes you're so smooth, it feels…well, a little bit rehearsed."

When he doesn't answer, she says, "Did I offend you?"

He shakes his head. "To tell you the truth," he says, lowering his voice, "I even get tired of myself, being the happy tour guide. But people feel threatened by handicaps, so I compensate."

"We all do," she says. "Otherwise it gets too scary, don't you think? You know, wondering if people will put up with us, warts and all?"

"Exactly." He raises his coffee cup toward her and she taps it with hers. "So here's to us compensators."

"Maybe you're right," she says, and feels more at ease than she has in days.

He's quiet for a moment, then speaks as the couple behind him get up and leave. "So, Elita," he says. "Now that I don't have to keep trying for suave and debonair, what color are your eyes?"

She laughs, starts to answer, then says, "Do you remember colors?"

"Sometimes. I recall things from my childhood, when I could still see—like Mickey, my tan-and-white collie. Or this red Schwinn bicycle I had, with black balloon tires, that had a set of training wheels attached."

She tries to imagine all the things he has lost, being blind. "My eyes," she says, "are light brown…like coffee with a dollop of cream."

He nods. "Mine were blue. I remember standing on a chair and watching myself in the mirror, noticing their color." He pauses, as if recalling his childhood, then lowers his head.

She feels bad for him, but doesn't want to interrupt, or say something just to lessen her own discomfort.

He reaches out, finds his cappuccino and turns it slowly.

"It was a car accident," he says, "when I was in the second grade. I remember seeing this big station wagon skidding sideways, coming right at us. Then…nothing, until I woke up, blind."

He goes so still, talking about it, that she wants to reassure him by touching his hand. But she stops, thinking, what if he's sick of pity? Maybe he got too much of that as a child—which makes her wonder how his parents dealt with his loss.

He takes a breath and looks up, saying, "For fun, Elita, what do you do? For a good time, I mean."

Relieved to see him smile, she says, "Sometimes I go to a bookstore. Usually one with overstuffed chairs and a coffee bar, where I can curl up and people-watch from behind a book."

He chuckles and nods. "Me too. Except I check out the latest music at the listening stations, and eavesdrop on whoever I can."

"How perfect," she says. "I do that too, listening in on people." She thinks, again, of her best friend, Carrie, and all the gossip they share—mostly about Carrie having her way with men.

"Elita," he says. "May I...may I read your face?" He runs a hand over his forehead, demonstrating as his fingers trail shadows in the bright sunlight.

Remembering his handshake—how reassuring it felt—she takes his hand and raises it to her face.

He starts with the crown of her head. Using both hands, he moves slowly downward. His touch is smooth and she finds herself closing her eyes. She concentrates on the warmth from his fingertips as they follow her forehead, then her cheeks, like a lingering caress.

As he traces her eyelids, he says in a gentle voice, "You're holding your breath."

She laughs, embarrassed.

He smiles, finding the sides and tip of her nose. Next, he traces her lips, which gives her a tingling sensation.

When he finishes at her chin, he says, "I trust your face, Elita. It goes with your voice."

That surprises her. She expected some comment on her facial features—like her nose, which she considers too narrow, or her cheekbones, too high for her liking. "What do you mean?" she says.

"Your voice and your face, they're both kind...and open."

She glances at her hands, pressed together in her lap. "Do you say that to all the women?"

"What I try to do," he says softly, "is tell the truth. At least when I'm brave enough to quit being the happy tour guide."

She wants to ask more questions, but two motorcyclists wearing leather pants and jackets pull up to the curb with a loud rumble, and leave their bikes running.

Chris sets a dollar tip beneath his cup and stands up, extending his cane. Raising his voice above the idling motorcycles, he smiles and motions to her. "Come on. Let's finish the neighborhood tour."

Once more she hooks an arm through his, while his other hand works the cane, leading the way.

As they walk, he identifies each restaurant by smell. One carries the aroma of cilantro and roasting chicken. Another is more pungent, thick with the fragrance of tomato sauce and garlic. He pauses, telling her about Art Green, who owns The Bella Luna. "He runs it under the name of Arturo Verde, acting like a Wop prima donna, and all the tourists buy into it. But the taste of his *vitello bellagio* is worth it."

She thinks of her own neighborhood with its ancient stuccoed buildings, off Del Paso Boulevard, where she lives in a small apartment behind a boxing gym.

Just ahead of them she sees a silver-haired man, sitting on a folding chair. He is playing a nylon-stringed guitar with nicotine-stained fingers while singing an Irish folk song in a strained tenor.

Chris leads her past him without slowing down, but a block later he stops by another seated musician. This one's bearded and pale, wearing a Panama hat. In his lap he cradles a steel-faced National guitar that glistens in the sun as he plays it bottleneck style, releasing a mournful melody that seems to shimmer and whine.

"Hey Chris," says the guitarist. "How you doing?"

"Good, Carson. And you?"

"Can't complain." Carson ends his tune with a flourish, picking three notes that hang in the air.

"Still got the touch," says Chris.

Carson smiles. "The way you travel, I didn't expect to cross paths this soon."

Elita wonders about that, but Chris only nods.

"Who's your friend?" asks Carson.

"Elita," Chris says and squeezes her hand.

Carson touches the brim of his straw hat, half-bowing to Elita. "It's a fine afternoon for a stroll."

"It is," she answers, looking from Carson to Chris, who treat each other like old friends.

"Be seeing you," Chris says, and they start up the sidewalk, with her giving a little wave to Carson.

She starts to ask Chris about his travels, but is distracted when—behind them—Carson hammers out a set of chords that seem to twist and moan as he calls out, "Delta Blues, here I come."

"He's talented," she says.

"Forget Carson," says Chris. "It's *you* I want to know about."

She looks at him. "You mean what I like? Or what I do for a living?"

He smiles as they keep walking. "You decide. But if I can't hide by playing tour guide, neither can you."

"Well," she says good-naturedly, "so much for telling you about my job at the university bookstore back in Sacramento, where I'm an assistant administrator."

He nods. "So much for that."

They keep walking.

After a minute, she says, "What the hell. I'm twenty-five, single, recently dumped, fond of Salsa music, and..." she sighs. "And really struggling to figure out my life."

"At least you're trying," he says, slowing his pace.

Trying, she thinks, *but not succeeding*. That's what she hears every Sunday, when she and her sisters get together with their parents. Still, she takes comfort in the personal disasters of her sisters. Between Consuela—her oldest sister, a hysterical waitress just turned lesbian, and Anita—her middle sister, so argumentative that she's suspended once a year from her job as a paralegal, Elita knows her parents are too distracted to concentrate on her shortcomings.

She bites her lip, suddenly aware that her thoughts were drifting, and wonders if Chris noticed. "Could you repeat that?" she says, worried that she's missed something.

"I said, at least you're trying to figure things out."

"And getting nowhere most of the time."

Chris half-smiles. "Well, some things *none* of us can figure out."

As they cross the street to the next block, she says, "When that happens, what can you do?"

She waits for his answer as they move forward, arm in arm, with his cane brushing the sidewalk.

He shrugs, leaning closer. "That's when you have to let go."

She lowers her arm that's looped through his, finds his hand, and gives it a squeeze.

He squeezes back, not slowing his stride or missing a beat with his cane.

"I have to admit, Elita. You've shared more than a photo would've told me."

She turns to him, feeling a twinge of anxiety as she watches his expression. "What do you mean?"

"You could've held back about your life and what you're feeling."

For a second she's flattered. Then miffed with herself as she thinks, don't be naïve. Chris is polite and a good listener—maybe even grateful for someone who's honest. But you want it to be more.

All at once, she realizes how badly she wants to get over Tom.

"I mean that," he says. "You've taken a chance by sharing."

Now isn't the time, she warns herself. Not when you're trying to bounce back.

She hears barking and sees a golden retriever loping toward them. Quickly, she puts an arm around Chris, helping him sidestep the dog.

"Close call," he says. "Thanks."

Feeling self-conscious, she removes her arm. "What about your life?" she asks.

He smiles, then mocks a deep announcer's voice, intoning, "Christopher Monroe, Santa Cruz celebrity. World-class photographer. Capturer of souls."

"Are you now?" she asks, relieved that he's less serious.

"I will confess *all*," he says, continuing in the announcer's voice, "every last detail—starting with my first job." He stops and turns to her, speaking into his cane as if it were a microphone. "Are you prepared for this?"

She laughs. "By all means, *do* confess."

"Well, then." He extends his cane, and they resume walking. "My first job was as a mechanic." He shrugs, adopting his normal voice again. "Mostly I serviced conveyor belts in this factory…endless strips of rubber and chain mail, driven by cogs and gears, with splines and shafts that kept it all moving. I got the job, as you'd expect, because I could do it strictly by feel."

"Were your parents pleased, about your job?"

He lets go of her hand and stops, resting his cane against the sidewalk.

"What is it?" she asks. She steps closer, trying to read the expression on his face, but he has gone so still, that she's suddenly unsure of herself. "Are you all right?" she asks.

"My parents, Elita…I lost them as a child, in the car accident that took my sight."

"Oh, Chris," she says, raising a hand to her mouth. "I'm so sorry."

"There's no way you could have known." He manages a faint smile, but he suddenly seems distant, as if memories have pulled him away.

Trying to recover, she says, "It must have been hard."

He cants his head and adjusts how he grips his cane. "My first job? Not really."

"No—"

"I was good at it, no doubt. But it cost me." He shows the back of his hands, crisscrossed with thin white scars, mostly at the knuckles.

She wants to comfort him, but he keeps talking, saying, "Mostly it got damn lonely, because everything was serviced after-hours. So it was just me and one other mechanic, usually working on separate floors or in different buildings—which is how I got hung up on a conveyor belt."

Her own troubles seem to shrink as she listens. She reaches out, gently taking his hand.

She sees the tension leave his shoulders, and he gives her hand a gentle tug.

They start walking again, silent except for the tapping of his cane.

"After that," he says, "I got a job with this software corporation, as a telephone receptionist." He smirks. "If all else failed, when callers got confused by the endless phone tree, or refused to use voice mail, they got shunted to me. By then, they were pretty ticked off."

"That would be tough."

Off to their side, a toddler in coveralls and pigtails cries, wanting to be held, and her mother bends down, scooping her up.

"I could deal with the angry callers," Chris says, "and I wasn't isolated, like at the factory. But my employers sucked. I could tell they were just filling quotas—using the handicapped to qualify for government contracts. So I left them a nasty voice mail about their platitudes and attitudes."

"Really? You actually did that?"

"Sent it straight to Mister Big, the CEO."

She hears the anger in his voice, but can't imagine taking that kind of chance. "Did he answer?"

"Oh yeah." His cane hits an empty paper bag and he steps over it.

"The head of personnel gave me severance pay and walked me out the door." He laughs. "They even had one of their legal-eagles warn me off, like they were expecting some kind of discrimination suit." He shakes his head, and they keep walking. "As if I'd waste my time on their sorry-assed bullshit."

She tries to imagine striking out in anger. "That took guts."

"I don't regret it," he says. "But maybe I should think twice about casting the first stone."

"Why do you say that?"

He stops and strikes an exaggerated pose, looking left, then right, like a fugitive on the run. "All right," he says in a theatrical whisper. "*I confess.* I'm not the prince you think I am. Before becoming a world-class photographer, I made ends meet by telemarketing. That's right," he says, drawing it out like a dirty word, "*tel-e-mar-ket-ing.*"

"Selling what?"

Ahead of them on the sidewalk, two women with shopping bags share a boisterous laugh, then enter a pottery shop.

"I pushed second mortgages to people with bad credit. Borrow from us, I'd say, to pay off those bills. Your freedom, for one payment a month. La dee da, la dee da. All of it from little scripts they read to me, until I memorized every line."

She feels his anger, like a sharp edge, cutting through his humor. "How long did that last?"

He smiles. "Until I built up a bank roll, and started fooling around with this Polaroid camera at a party—getting people to pose while I snapped pictures. It was a blast, and everyone kept telling me what a natural I was…so, I figured I'd give it a try."

Ahead of them, she spots a crowd of college-age picketers, gathered in front of a trendy shoe store. The picketers appear agitated, thrusting placards overhead as they chant, blocking the display windows.

"There's a disturbance," she says. "Should we cross the street?"

"Then how would I eavesdrop?" He says it with a hint of mischief and pulls her forward. "Come on," he says, inclining his head toward the crowd.

She's concerned that he might get tangled up and trip. She grips his arm more tightly, but he narrows the sweep of his cane and moves ahead, plunging into the crowd.

A blonde, frizzy-haired teenager in a purple tube top, khaki pants and platform shoes tries to hand her a flier. Elita ignores her, staring straight ahead, not speaking as she and Chris plow through the crowd. Between the chants and counter-chants, she finds it difficult to understand what people are saying.

"Fascinating," Chris says as they clear the crowd and slow down, crossing to the next block. "They're save-the-earth types, trying to outdo each other. One group's in a huff," he says, "over leather shoes causing the needless slaughter of innocent animals. The other side thinks it's a worse sin to wear synthetic shoes, made out of plastic that will never biodegrade."

"You could make out all of that?"

He laughs. "Yesterday a street vendor gave me the gist of it. But I like hearing it firsthand."

"They're all so worked up."

"True," he says, and turns back, facing the picketers for a moment. "But anger can be seductive."

She studies his face, to see if he's being sarcastic, but can't decipher his expression. Still, she is beginning to grasp what's hidden by his happy-photographer-and-tour-guide routine. Bad memories and anger. But could she do any better, she wonders, with a past like his?

"You seem happy now," she says, "doing your photography. Are you?"

"*Happy?*" He seems to think about it. "Well, at least photography lets me stay open to the world, and I'm grateful for that."

She thinks about Sacramento, where she feels so confined… penned in by her job, her parents, her sisters, and the collapse of her relationship with Tom. She imagines leaving Sacramento. Disappearing—then traveling until she finds something better. That makes her think of the musician in the straw hat, mentioning how much Chris travels.

"What did your friend the guitar player mean," she asks, "about not expecting to see you this soon?"

"Carson?" Chris smiles. "He and I cross paths, usually in the summer, on this circuit we follow. Basically, we work college towns, mostly along the coast."

A bicyclist rides past, hugging the curb as she and Chris pass a bakery with rows of croissants in its windows.

"Why not stay in one town?"

He takes a moment, then says, "After I lost my parents, I was raised in institutions for the blind. Eleven years' worth. Once I got out, I swore I'd never live like that."

"Like what?"

"Stuck in one place."

"So you keep moving?"

"With street photography, spring and summer are good, fall's so-so, then it tapers off fast, heading into winter. That's when I take my trips."

"Move, you mean? To another college town?"

"No." His cane hits a dip in the sidewalk and he detours slightly. "There's no strict schedule for moving, and it's pretty much the same towns on the circuit, from one year to the next. I spend several months in each town."

"So there's no schedule, but kind of a pattern?"

"My trips are separate from that."

"How?"

"I pick a city I've heard about, but never visited. Then buy a round-trip ticket on the Big Dog."

"The big what?"

"Greyhound. It's cheap, with plenty of eavesdropping."

She laughs. "Do you go with friends?"

He shakes his head, looking quite serious. "Solo."

She can't imagine being blind and traveling by herself. "Why not with someone you know?"

He stops, just past a sidewalk bench. "It's something I force myself to do. Otherwise, I'm afraid I'll settle down, you know?

Then fall into a routine...until all my tomorrows are the same as yesterday."

She flinches, thinking of the unhappy life she leads, shuttling back and forth between her boring job, critical parents and sisters, and the loser boyfriends she seems to choose.

He finds her foot with his cane and taps it softly. "Know what I mean?"

"But it seems risky," she says, "traveling alone." She recalls how hard she found it, just driving from Sacramento to Santa Cruz. She wanted to do it, but kept having her doubts, until Carrie coaxed her into going.

"The risk," he says, "is worth it. Each time I find something new, so it feels like a gift. Hard-earned, but a gift."

They start walking again, and she tries to imagine traveling with Chris on a Greyhound bus. With his sense of adventure, she wonders, would he find her too tame? Too timid and safe?

She can't help thinking of her friend Carrie—or someone like her—having more appeal for him. Someone who thrives on taking chances. Like the time Carrie accepted a dare, joining up with a bronco rider when a rodeo came through town, then flying home three days later, laughing at the rowdy times they had.

"Here we are," he says.

"Where?"

He stops and raises his cane, pointing across the street at his crate and pair of canvas chairs. "We've made the full tour."

She looks around, amazed that he's so precise, knowing where they are.

He turns to her and smiles. "Well..." He says it with a lift of his shoulders.

She realizes they're about to part, and feels a sense of loss. He's been so attentive and open...even with things that have hurt him. Now she'll be alone again. That reminds her of Tom and their last conversation, when he told her how sorry he was that they weren't meant to share the same path.

Facing Chris, she forces herself to smile. "I've enjoyed myself," she says. "And you."

He raises his face to the afternoon sun, judging its position, she supposes, by its warmth.

"I've got a few hours left," he says, "before the light's too weak to take good photos. After that, maybe you could drop by for a glass of wine."

"Where?"

He digs a business card out of his back pocket, with a phone number and address next to his name.

"It's a duplex, four blocks from here." He seems to check his bearings somehow, and then points east, to where she sees a series of cottages and bungalows on a small hill. "Up that incline," he says. "I'm in unit B. Think you can find it?"

She takes his card and holds it tightly. Acutely aware of him standing there, expecting her answer, she starts flicking the business card. Then stops, irked with herself for being such a coward.

"What time were you thinking?"

"Six-thirty." He traces a small pattern on the sidewalk with the tip of his cane.

She bites her lip, trying to decide. He's been so considerate, but how much does she really know about him? She looks across the street at the black woman who sells jewelry next to Chris, and recalls the questioning look she gave her.

Normally she takes a friend like Carrie along on a first date. But Chris seems so insightful, and kind.

"All right," she says. "I'll come by at six-thirty."

* * *

For nearly an hour, Elita tries choosing between different outfits laid out on her motel bed. It's stupid, she knows, feeling so indecisive when Chris won't even see what she wears. But she keeps trying on her pedal pushers and two skirts with different tops, hoping to settle her nerves. Wanting to feel attractive.

"Damn it." She stands at the foot of her bed, holding up a denim vest. "Relax!" she tells herself. "*He's* the one who asked you over."

She considers phoning Carrie for advice. With an effort, she doesn't, knowing she's too dependent on her. Besides, she and Carrie seldom see things the same way, especially when it comes to men. Carrie likes to challenge them with her good looks—just short of flaunting herself. On top of which, Carrie doesn't believe in relationships…only personal satisfaction. So whatever Carrie suggested would be too much. At least for her, it would be.

Finally, Elita decides. She chooses the black pedal pushers with an ivory colored scoop-necked blouse, and black flats. She considers the perfumes Carrie loaned her—*Obsession* and *Fire and Ice*, but decides they're too bold. Instead, she touches a few drops of lavender-scented oil to the base of her throat and behind her ears. Drawing a deep breath, she looks in the bathroom mirror. You're ready, she thinks.

She leaves her motel room, noticing the sun. It's dropping toward the horizon, and the sky is turning pink. She gets into her Geo Metro and drives north, finding the hill Chris pointed out from Ocean Street. Driving up the narrow lane, past ivy-covered picket fences, she looks for the address on his business card. She slows down as she comes to a blue-gray bungalow. She likes its broad gables, supported by white columns that frame a wide porch with an entrance at each end.

She sees it's the right address.

Still, she bites her lip and drives past. She felt fine earlier in the day spending time with him, but now her mouth is dry, and her stomach feels like a tight fist.

She takes a deep breath and circles the block, chiding herself for being so nervous. Carefully, she parks between a maroon truck and a black motorcycle, then gets out, reminding herself to relax. She grips her purse and opens a creaking, wrought iron gate, then takes a brick walkway across the lawn, admiring the yellow gladioli that border the walkway.

As she steps up to the porch, she sees a wind chime of hollow metal cylinders hanging from the eaves, ready to sound if the breeze picks up. The brass address plate indicates that Chris lives in the duplex to her left.

Through the screen door, she sees him, wearing the same faded Levi's and sunglasses, but a different T-shirt. This one is a soft chestnut brown and he's barefoot. His back is to her as he reaches inside a kitchen cabinet, putting a dish away.

He turns in her direction, lifting his chin.

"Did you hear me?" she asks.

"Smelled your perfume," he says. "Except it's not what you had on this morning."

Despite the soft breeze, she feels the flush of warmth in her cheeks.

He walks to the screen door and pushes it open. "Come in, come in." He bows deeply, sweeping one hand below his waist.

Behind him, she hears a soft string of notes from a jazz piano, surrounded by the steady thrum of a bass and the silken caress of brushes on a snare drum. She's soothed by these sounds. They're such a relief from the unrelenting Tibetan chants and drumming that Tom played over and over from recordings of monks in monasteries.

She enters the bungalow, letting the screen door creak shut as she glances around. The kitchen is crowded with a wooden table painted mustard-yellow and four chairs, a corner stove and a small refrigerator, near a sink that's flanked by grey Formica counters. Above the counters are white cabinets, painted unevenly.

"Have a seat," he offers.

She sits down and notices that the walls match the white cabinets, with long snaking dribbles that dried on their way to the floor. She thinks he must have painted the kitchen.

"Is red wine okay?" he asks. "A Merlot?"

"Sure." If he buys more than one kind of wine, she wonders how he tells them apart once they're in the refrigerator. From the shape of the bottles?

He takes two goblets from a cabinet and sets them on the table.

He removes a dark bottle from the refrigerator and peels off its foil seal.

"Any trouble finding the place?"

"No. But parking was tough."

He chuckles. "Around here," he says, "you could retire on the money it takes to feed a parking meter."

She laughs, to be polite.

As he works smoothly with a corkscrew, opening the bottle, she looks around. She's surprised that the kitchen walls are bare. She recalls his photographs and tries to imagine a few on the walls, enlarged and framed, or something tactile, like wall hangings or relief sculptures.

He grips the stem of her goblet and guides the neck of the bottle to its rim, then pours. "Here you go."

As he pours his glass of wine, she looks into the living room. It holds a dark couch, an easy chair with faded floral upholstery, and a row of cardboard boxes lined up between a picture window and a coffee table that holds two lit candles. A few tin sconces are on the walls, with something multi-colored hanging near each of them. She can't see any speakers, but hears the music coming from that direction.

He takes both goblets to the kitchen table and sets them down. When they're both seated, he uses both hands, holding out her glass. She accepts it, and begins to feel less anxious.

"Cheers," she says, and he responds, raising his glass, which she clinks with hers.

She takes a sip of wine, wanting to say something personal, but her mind goes blank, like the kitchen walls behind him.

From the porch, she hears the gentle ching of the wind chimes, almost in tune with the soft jazz from the stereo.

"Thanks for accepting my invitation," he says.

"I enjoy older homes," she says, "like this bungalow. It has such character."

He nods, then says, "You know, it's more comfortable in there. Warm, from the setting sun." He tips his head toward the living room, which has a soft tint of peach-colored light that's spilling through the window, past the flickering candles on the coffee table.

She hesitates, then says, "All right," hoping to regain the sense of connection she felt when they walked about town.

He gets up and she follows him, noticing that he walks differently without the cane, taking shorter steps.

It's not a big room, but he goes to the far end and chooses the easy chair, next to the low, glass-topped coffee table. Beneath the table are two speakers that radiate the low vibration of a string bass, thrumming out a soft progression of chords.

She sits on the sagging sofa, close to him. Through the picture window she sees a small yard. It's mostly lawn and a gray, weathered fence, with one small orange tree—beneath a horizon that's turning pink, with hints of purple. Below the window, against the wall, she notices that the row of cardboard boxes are all closed, precisely aligned and without labels. Sitting atop the last box is his camera, his "Blind Photography" sign, and the rosewood container full of Polaroids.

"This is nice," she says, tapping an armrest.

He smiles. "Just short of worn out."

"Comfy," she insists.

Her eyes are drawn to the flame of the two candles on the coffee table. Both candles are tapered, with layers of orange. They provide the room's only illumination, beside the fading sunset. She bends forward and inhales. "Your candles," she asks, "are they scented with persimmon?"

"And tangerine. Do you like them?"

She nods, then catches herself. "Yes."

She tries to imagine lighting candles that she couldn't see, and knows she'd worry about starting a fire. Turning, she considers the two doors at the end of the room. The open one, she sees, leads to a bedroom with more lighted candles. She wonders, is that the next step? Is that what I want?

Near the bed, she catches the glint of a mirror and sees a nightstand, holding what she expects is a CD player. On the bedroom carpet she spots a pair of small, black boxes with a shiny finish.

"More wine?" he asks.

"I'm doing okay." Seeing the other closed door, it occurs to her that he might not live alone. She looks for anything that will tell her, one way or the other.

She views the rest of the living room, which has nothing on its walls except three circular lighting sconces made of tin, each shaped like the sun, with smiling faces surrounded by pleated spikes of tin, suggesting rays of sunshine. No lights are turned on behind them and each sun's face is tilted sideways, which makes her think he put them up by himself.

Next to each sconce, hung from the ceiling, are flat diamond-shaped designs of brightly colored yarn—mostly blues, greens and yellows—each with a simple wooden cross as its center. Caught in the candlelight and sunset, they cast soft shadows in two directions.

"Those hanging yarn pieces," she asks, "what are they?"

"Indian artwork," he says. "Those are Navajo pieces, but earlier ones were made by the Huichol Indians of Jalisco, Mexico."

"What are they called?"

"*Ojo de Dios,*" he says, "meaning God's eye." He smiles. "It's a little joke, about my sense of a religious vision."

His tone makes her uneasy and she glances about, looking for a crucifix or other religious icons. Seeing none, she says, "What's the joke, exactly?"

He shrugs, then sips at his wine. "I'm still awaiting God's divine plan, after taking my sight and my parents at age seven."

Uncomfortable now, she takes a drink of wine, then fixes her gaze on the row of cardboard boxes lined up by the window, bathed in a magenta tint as the sun sinks lower. From the porch, she hears three distinct notes as the wind chime sounds.

"Why so many cardboard boxes? Are you still unpacking?"

He shakes his head. "Wherever I live, I never unpack. Not completely."

She looks around. "But you've got enough room."

"I don't like to get too settled. For me, that gets claustrophobic. That's why I keep to my routine, moving from town to town."

She thinks of her own apartment. When her life's been good, she has enjoyed decorating it, filling it with stoneware pottery and colorful posters of Cuban art. Now though, it seems too cluttered with reminders of Tom.

"How long do you live someplace before you move?"

"I don't have an exact timetable or schedule. It's just…I reach this point and know it's time to leave."

She considers the row of cardboard boxes, trying to understand his cycle of travels and moving.

He shifts in his chair and sips his wine.

When they were touring the town, she thinks, conversation was so much easier.

He edges forward, resting his elbows on his knees. "I'm glad you came by, Elita. It's nice meeting someone new."

She smiles, wondering if this is a line he's feeding her—whether he's back to being the pleasant tour guide.

"Judging by all the Polaroids you showed me, you meet a lot of people."

"Well…." He swirls the wine in his glass. "We can all do *that*, can't we? Meet people?" He faces her, with the fading purple sky reflected in his sunglasses.

"I suppose," she says, wanting this moment to be genuine…and to forget how bad she feels about the rest of her life.

"But," he adds, lowering his voice, "how often do we encounter someone who's *truly* open? Or honest?"

"Seldom," she admits.

"Exactly." He raises his wineglass. "That's why it's such a pleasure discovering you, Elita."

She feels the heat creeping up her neck and knows that she's blushing at his words, just as everything within the room seems to change.

The music is so clear—a run of lilting notes from the piano, and she savors the failing light, spilling through the window as dusk turns to evening, brightening the flames of the candles. In that instant, she finds a delicate precision in every detail.

Softly, she asks, "How long have you lived here?"

"Six months. In Santa Cruz, that is."

"But not in this house?"

He shrugs. "I started out with a studio apartment. It was so close to the Boardwalk that I could hear riders screaming on the roller coaster. Then I moved here, starting off with a roommate. But that didn't last."

She wonders if it was a man or a woman, and her anxiety begins to return. For the first time, it occurs to her that maybe he's gay, and she can't help studying his ears to see if they're pierced. Then she scolds herself, knowing nothing's that straightforward any more.

She sips her wine and tries to settle down—to quit holding her breath. Just be yourself, she thinks. Without wanting to, she recalls the last time she saw Tom. He gave her a dozen reasons why she was holding him back. Keeping him from whatever "next step" he was supposed to "attain" in his karmic progress.

"Elita," Chris says. "What sort of music do you like?"

"Pardon?"

"Music. Do you have any favorites? Artists or songs?"

Embarrassed, she realizes she's been drifting. "Whatever's playing is fine."

"Okay, but if you were at home, what music would you play?"

She puts her wineglass down and looks at Chris. Truly looks at him, wanting to pay attention. Wanting to connect with him. "*You* guess," she says, taking a chance. "Tell me what I like."

"A challenge," he says, then smiles, sitting up straighter. "I like that. Just give me a minute."

He sets his wineglass on the coffee table, then rubs his forehead, nudging his sunglasses. He adopts an expression that suggests deep concentration, and she gets the sense that he's enjoying himself. He holds that pose for a few seconds, before giving her an expectant look.

"How about Santana?" he says. "Isn't he making a come back?"

She laughs. "No way. You might as well have picked Linda Ronstadt."

"Soooo," he says, raising a finger. "Carlos is history. And Linda is out."

"He's too old and she's too sentimental, besides being my mother's favorite."

"Ahhh. And yours?"

She thinks about it, realizing her taste in music has shifted with the men she has known. "My first tapes and CDs," she says, "were of Gloria Estefan."

Chris smiles. "With all that percussion, she's great for dancing."

"True. But after a while, her lyrics seemed too adolescent, always falling hard for some guy, or struggling to keep him." Just like high school, she thinks, where she suffered such heartache, fighting her parents over each and every boy that she dated.

"Any favorites," he asks, "who have stood the test of time?"

For an instant, she recalls her childhood—with her father playing records of the rumba music that he loved, as though he still lived in Cuba, and how he taught her to dance while she stood on his shoes, reaching up to hold hands with him.

"None?" says Chris.

"Sometimes I like the new Salsa artists. But lately, my favorite is Mary Chapin Carpenter."

"Really?" He pauses, then nods at his bedroom. "I've got two of her CDs. Will you help me find them?"

She knows his question is an invitation to more than music, but she hesitates. Holds back, despite the longing she feels. Then, looking at him, she recalls the box of Polaroids he shared with her, and the gift he seems to have for letting people be themselves.

"All right," she says and stands up, leaving her purse on the couch.

As he leads her into the glow of his candle-lit bedroom, she takes a deep breath, then looks at the bed, covered with a gray comforter. At the foot of the bed, two tall mirrors stand in the corner, like an open book.

He sits on the bed. She joins him, and their silhouettes merge behind the quiet flutter of two candles, casting a single shadow that angles across the flat headboard and up the wall.

He's closest to the CD player and picks up a black lacquered box, full of CDs, which he sets on his lap. She notices the clock radio, reading 7:22 p.m., with raised numbers that flip over, and no glass face. Next to the clock rests a plastic CD case that has a cover showing Wynton Marsalis holding a trumpet.

Chris scoots closer, so that their thighs touch. She can feel his warmth. She also smells his after-shave and the scent of soap.

"Can you find it?" he says, shifting the box so that it's sitting on both of their thighs.

For some reason, the weight of the box helps her relax, and her concentration returns. She realizes the CDs aren't in alphabetical order. Nor do they seem marked with Braille. Several aren't pointed or facing in the same direction. She leans over, so that their shoulders make contact as she flips through the CDs. It takes her a moment, but she finds Mary Chapin Carpenter's *Stones in the Road*.

"Here's one." She removes the CD from its case, gripping its edges while he reaches over, pushing buttons on his CD player.

The jazz piano stops and a CD ejects. As he slips that CD into its case, his hand brushes hers, sending a slight shiver up her arm.

"Ready?" he asks. He takes the CD from her and slips it into the player.

Seconds later, they hear a strumming guitar. Then Mary Chapin Carpenter sings about pain and trouble in a voice that carries hope.

They sit there for a while, listening to that song, then the start of another. The whole while, she's leaning against his shoulder, wanting him to kiss her.

Without speaking, he takes the box of CDs and sets it aside, then holds her hand. She feels her heart beating. As they turn toward each other, she catches their reflection in the pair of tall mirrors. For an instant, she feels as though she's watching another couple, but his touch brings her back, drawing her closer as he fits his hand to the small of her back. She sighs, almost closing her eyes and faces him, glad that this is happening.

Their lips meet. His kiss is soft and sure. Surprised by his tenderness, she cups her hands to his shoulders and pulls him closer.

As they settle into each other's arms, Mary Chapin-Carpenter sings *a cappella*:

"Why take when you could be giving,
Why watch as the world goes by… "

In their embrace, Elita finds herself falling into the song as they kiss.

He shifts the angle of his head and nibbles at her lip. Ever so gently, his free hand finds the base of her throat, then his fingertips slide lower, tracing the yoke of her scoop-necked blouse.

She returns his kiss, then inhales sharply as his hand slips inside her blouse, finding her breast.

She feels his thumb and index finger on the sheer fabric of her bra, teasing her nipple.

She leans back, whispering, "More."

He responds, shifting to her other breast with a tender caress.

"Mmm," she says, savoring his touch.

Lush with warmth, she undoes the buttons on her blouse, helping him along. She unhooks her bra where it joins in front, then stops—remembering. The door to the porch was open when she first saw Chris, through the screen door.

"What is it?" he asks.

Looking up, she realizes the porch doesn't face into the bedroom and laughs at herself. "Nothing," she says, and kisses his earlobe.

She wants to see more of him and starts with his shirt. She untucks, then unbuttons it, revealing a shallow chest with hardly any hair and two parallel scars the width of her hand, running below his left nipple. In the wavering candlelight, the scars seem to shift slightly, as if they're floating on his skin.

"Are these from the car accident?" she asks, barely touching them.

"Yes," he answers in a hoarse whisper, then angles his head to find hers, kissing her deeply.

It goes so smoothly—their undressing—that it feels like they're longtime lovers, and she abandons the rest of her doubts, knowing she needs this.

The last thing to go is his sunglasses, which he sets on the nightstand. When he faces her—with the trembling candlelight playing across his face—the scars where his eyelids are joined cast a small web of vibrating shadows. Somehow, that makes her realize how fragile and precious life is, and she feels a sudden tenderness toward him for trusting her. For revealing himself so fully.

Eager for him, she shoves their clothes off the bed and they stretch out, pressed up against each other, trapping the heat of their bodies. His erection pushes against her thigh, and she feels a soft ring of warmth, growing within her.

Mary Chapin Carpenter is singing, but Elita barely hears the music as Chris touches her. He traces the edge of her shoulder, while his other hand slides down her spine, making her shiver as she arches her back.

He turns her onto her side and she blinks, surprised by the nude couple in the pair of mirrors. *Them*, she thinks. No. *Us*. A pair of lovers, seen in the mirror by flickering candlelight. They seem so remote, compared to the pulse in her ears and the slow rise of pleasure that she feels within.

She closes her eyes, savoring the exquisite sensation at each and every spot their bodies are touching. Thighs. Hips. Breasts. Arms. Lips.

Nothing is rushed as they both find time to touch and caress, and that makes her thirst for more.

As her eyes drift open, she asks herself—if he could see, would he like this any better? Then she feels his hands, gentling urging her to roll over, onto her back, and she realizes that he *does* see. By touch.

She turns onto her back, catching a glimpse of the mirror. *Us* and *them*, she thinks—a pale-chested man, caressing a brown-skinned woman.

All at once, Elita wonders, how does she compare to the other women his hands have seen? A wave of pleasure interrupts, washing over her as he cups her breast and sucks at her nipple. She moans as he straddles her and flicks her hardened nipple with his tongue.

She reaches up and begins to stroke him lightly, then wants to ask. To at least say something about protection. But she can't find the words.

"That feels so good," he says, responding to her hand sliding up and down.

After a moment, he says, "Don't stop," and reaches across her, to the nightstand, and opens a drawer.

She raises her head and sees an orderly row of socks in the drawer, then his hand retrieving a small foil pack.

He uses his teeth, peeling open the pack, and removes the condom.

She hesitates, still gripping him. "Want me to help?"

Chris smiles. "That would be nice."

He stretches out alongside her, leaning back on his elbows, and she strokes a little harder, watching him stiffen in her hand. She slips the condom onto him, using both hands to secure it.

He reaches for her and finds her waist, saying, "Don't make me wait."

She swings her leg across, getting on top, and he draws his knees up, so that she can brace herself, getting her back against his thighs.

She eases downward as he begins a gentle thrusting, finding her.

Guiding him, she helps, until he begins to enter her. She shudders, feeling a delicious bloom of heat as she takes him by gradually seating herself.

She responds to his hands, which are pulling her forward by her hips. He penetrates more deeply, rocking against her. She places her hands on his chest for balance, and he keeps both hands on her hips, giving her a rhythm by pushing and pulling, urging her to move faster.

As she picks up the pace, he whispers hoarsely, saying, "Yes. Oh god. *Keep going.*"

Wanting it to last, she alters her rhythm, catching her breath and slowing for a bit, then rocking hard for a few seconds. He answers each shift in her rhythm and—together—they begin to gasp in each other's arms.

Soon they have joined in a duet of moans and shudders, and she no longer wants to hold back. The honeyed throbbing deepens at her center, pulsing with exquisite sensation as it rolls outward, engulfing her. She begins to quiver and bites down on her lip, not wanting it to end.

Finally, she arches her back, feeling herself come, and grips his shoulders, wanting to prolong the rippling seizure as it turns incandescent. She cries out twice, clenching at him with her thighs, then goes rigid, no longer rocking—too flooded with pleasure to move.

Lightheaded, she wants to wilt, but he begins bucking beneath her. Grasping her hips with both hands, he pumps harder and deeper, until her body responds. Possessed by a sudden lust that borders on pain, she churns her hips, rocking back and forth.

Wide-eyed, she watches him gasp, then arch his back, thrusting faster and deeper, until she feels drunk with power.

She begins grinding her hips, then uses her whole body. She matches his frantic thumping and slamming with a ragged frenzy of her own. She finds their reflection in the mirror and that makes her go faster, seeing the rapture that's taken hold of her.

This, she thinks, shocking herself. *This* is what I want a Polaroid of.

In her mind, glancing at the mirror, she captures the image, the blurred movement and wild abandon that illuminate their passion.

He grunts hard, catching her attention and his expression tightens. He grunts twice more, then cries out, pumping fiercely.

Suddenly, he clasps his arms around her and arches his back, hanging on as she feels him pulse within her.

Then he shudders and lets go, slowly collapsing into the comforter and bed, with her still straddling him.

His breathing, like hers, is labored, but she sees that his face carries a look of stunned satisfaction, and that pleases her immensely.

Smiling, she closes her eyes and bends forward from her waist, resting her cheek on his collarbone. There, she enjoys the rise and fall of his chest as his breathing slows, and she feels the beating of his heart.

"That," he whispers, "was marvelous."

She squeezes his arm and snuggles closer. The candle-lit room smells of scented wax and sex as she breathes it all in, feeling safe and drowsy. "Yes," she says, "it was."

They lie there for a moment, his fingertips tracing the crown of her shoulder.

She turns her head toward the living room, which is illuminated only by candlelight, and sees the row of cardboard boxes with his camera on top.

As she savors the warmth of his chest pressed to hers, she can't help whispering, "Would it be that bad, living in one place? One town?"

He shifts beneath her, removing his hand from her shoulder. "For me?" he says, "Or for you?"

Heat rises in her cheeks, and she's glad that he can't witness her blush.

"I don't know," she answers, sitting upright. But she *does* know, and is angry with herself over wanting him not to travel, on the chance they could spend time together...or at least share their weekends.

"Instead of being tied down," he says, "what if you could visit new places? Discover new things. Wouldn't that be great?"

"I suppose," she says, trying to sound lighthearted. Then her stomach growls, adding to her embarrassment.

He chuckles and rubs her thigh, saying, "If you like I can fix us an omelet."

She laughs, relieved that he's so down-to-earth, and that the subject has been changed. "That sounds good," she says.

She slips off of him, moving to the side, and he reaches down over the edge of the bed, finding their jumble of clothing.

"Here," she says. "Let me help."

He grips his Levi's. "These are all I need."

He gets up, carrying his jeans, and opens a narrow door by the bed's headboard. "If you need it," he says, "the bathroom's in here." He steps inside.

A moment later, she hears a toilet flush, then water runs for a moment. He comes out wearing his Levi's and walks through the bedroom, then the living room, heading for the kitchen.

She enters the bathroom and uses it, shutting the door so he won't hear her pee.

His bathroom is clean, but practically bare, with a bar of soap, one washcloth, two mismatched towels and a stick of incense tucked into a nub of clay atop the windowsill. She thinks of her own bathroom with its color-coordinated towels, small ceramic dish that's filled with perfumed soap balls, and the miniature glass pyramid that Tom gave her—to improve her karma.

At least in this bathroom she doesn't see toiletries that suggest a roommate, or regular visitors.

She returns to the bedroom, wondering if it holds any secrets.

From the kitchen, she hears the refrigerator open, then shut. Quickly, she peeks inside his closet. On plastic hangers is a modest selection of casual shirts and pants, next to a small dresser. It's the opposite of her apartment bedroom, which holds more clothes than she needs, divided between her closet, two bureaus and a series of plastic tubs she keeps in her parents' garage, storing whatever's out of season, or won't fit in her bedroom.

She shuts his closet and approaches the nightstand, with its half-open top drawer. Inside it she sees three more rubbers in foil packs, along with the row of socks. Unlike his CDs, she realizes the socks are neatly sorted and paired. She wonders whether someone did that for him.

"Do you like mushrooms?" he calls from the kitchen.

"A few would be good." She starts to say, chopped, then wonders how well he uses a knife.

"How about tomatoes?" he asks.

"Sure."

"Cheddar or Jack cheese?"

"Both?"

"No problem."

Still naked, she turns to the pair of mirrors in the bedroom's corner.

Despite the delicious feeling she still carries from their lovemaking, she doesn't like what she sees. Her figure is compact without being fat, but she can't help comparing herself to what she sees in the magazines—fashion models with figures to die for. Her legs are too thin, her hips are too wide, and her breasts are uneven, with one turned slightly outward. She sighs and pivots. Looking over her shoulder, she runs her hand across the swell of her bottom. Feeling her own hand touching her skin, she's grateful that Chris can't see all the magazines, filled with perfect women. Then she wonders when he sees her by touch, whether he thinks she's pretty.

She hears the sizzle of something cooking in the kitchen and realizes Mary Chapin Carpenter has stopped singing. The aroma of frying bacon reaches her.

"Hope you don't mind a little grease," he calls to her. "That's how I oil up the skillet."

She hears a staccato chopping sound. Then something more gentle, with a steady rhythm at a lighter, higher pitch. A whisk, she thinks, mixing the eggs.

"Almost ready," he says.

The smell of bacon is stronger now, and she debates what clothes to put on. She hopes, from Chris putting on only his jeans, that they aren't through for the night.

She thinks of Carrie. What would Carrie do? Something bold. Smiling, Elita moves to his closet, selects a blue, long-sleeved work shirt, and slips it on. It comes to the middle of her thigh, and her hands are lost in its sleeves. She rolls the sleeves up. Thinking like Carrie, she buttons only the bottom half of the shirt.

* * *

At the kitchen table, she eats her omelet with relish. "This is delicious."

He answers while chewing. "Glad you like it."

He hasn't turned the lights on, but she can make out the kitchen in the golden light cast by the living room candles. The only clutter is from the skillet and utensils he just used. "You seem well organized," she says, "the way you keep your duplex."

He nods. "Most of the time. And you?"

She thinks back through different makeovers her apartment has endured, one for each of the men she has loved since leaving her parents' home. For Tom, she decorated with plants and crystals. But those would go, now that he had dumped her. For Marc, it was photos of the mountains he climbed. For Isaac, a teaching assistant at the university, she proudly displayed the books he had given her—which she thought he had personally selected, just for her, until she discovered they were the exact textbooks required of his students.

In front of her, Chris stops eating, halfway through his omelet. "Silence is hard for me to read," he says. "Did my question bother you?"

She shrugs. "It brought back memories. Things I'd rather forget."

He sets his fork down and regards her quietly. "Are you okay?"

"Yes," she says, determined to enjoy herself. "How could I not be, the way you're spoiling me?"

"In that case," he says softly, "how about something to drink? Coffee? Orange juice?" Smiling, he adds, "And of course there's wine."

She takes in his smile, which overpowers the scar tissue where his eyelids are sealed. "Yes," she says, feeling better. "Wine. I can get it."

"Half a glass for me," he says.

She pours, and they sip wine with the rest of their omelet.

When they finish, she carries their silverware and plates to the sink and begins washing them. Running the hot water, she thinks of her own apartment, with its empty refrigerator. She hasn't shopped for groceries. Not since Tom broke off with her.

She hears Chris humming as he walks up behind her, then gently squeezes her shoulders. "Forget the dishes," he whispers.

She hesitates, until he reaches around to cup her breasts.

She leans back, closing her eyes, glad to be held.

They walk to the bedroom and he steps out of his Levi's as he stands near the candles, which have burned way down. The candles flutter, close to going out.

She unbuttons the shirt she's wearing, facing the half-opened drawer with its perfect row of socks.

"Your socks," she says, "are all different colors. How do you sort them if you can't see?"

He smiles and helps her out of the shirt. "There are other ways to recognize things."

"Such as?" She takes his hand, guiding him, and they stretch out on the bed.

"Shape," he offers, cupping her breast. "Or texture," he adds, tracing her nipple with his fingertips.

"Or," she says, nuzzling his neck, "by smell."

"Of course." He brushes her lips with his. "Or taste."

She lays a string of kisses along his chest. "No wonder your socks are in order."

"Top to bottom, or left to right. Whichever your prefer." He brushes the side of her neck with his lips.

She likes that they're going slowly. Gently, she runs her thumb along his collarbone, then down his arm to the crook of his elbow. "If your socks are in order," she says, "why not unpack the boxes in your living room? I could help, you know."

He draws back from her and sits up. "I told you, I never unpack. Not completely."

She sees the rigid set of his shoulders. "It was just a thought, Chris. That's all."

For a few seconds, she thinks he's going to get up and leave, then he speaks, just above a whisper.

"When I lost my parents, Elita, I had no other family. No one. So the state sent me to this institution that worked with the blind. They gave us room, board and special schooling—training us to live independently, you know? How to organize our clothes so that our socks would match when we dressed ourselves. How to count money so we wouldn't get screwed when someone made change for us. How to cook without causing a fire."

"Was it that bad?"

Sitting there, he draws one knee to his chest and regards her carefully. *"Everything in its place,"* he said. "That was the key to their system."

His answer makes her uneasy. "Wasn't there anyone nice?" she asks. "Other kids you got to know?"

"Go along to get along," he says. "That's what we learned. Like they teach in the military. Or prison."

Lying next to him, she reaches up, touching his hand. "The last thing I wanted," she says, "was to upset you."

When he doesn't answer, she feels like he's waiting, expecting her to make it worse by saying the wrong thing.

"You've got your own life now," she says. "And you're a success with your photography."

"A *success?*" His tone is bitter. "Waiting for people to throw down five bucks, because they're curious? Or if they pity me?"

Desperate to turn things around, she says, "You're a great lover. Isn't that a gift? I mean, the way you touch...doesn't that comes from being blind?"

"For god's sake," he says, raising his voice. "As if that makes up for the rest of it."

On the verge of tears, she sits up, saying, "Please, Chris. I didn't mean it that way."

"Didn't you?" He straightens his back, drawing his knees to his chest, then wraps his arms around them.

"Wait," she pleads, wanting him to understand—to realize that she means well. "Instead of just—you know, popping off—saying things that offend you, what if I found out first?"

He cants his head. "Found out what?"

"What it's like for you, being blind."

"Of course," he says sarcastically, resting his chin on his knees. "That should be easy."

Irked by his tone, she says, "*Fine.* While you're doubting me, I'll blindfold myself." She reaches over to the nightstand and jerks open the top drawer. She grabs a dark pair of socks and knots them together. She stretches them across her eyes, blocking her vision, and ties them behind her head, cinching down as she makes the knot.

The pressure against her face bothers her, but she's still irritated and says, "There! See—well, I mean…feel for yourself." She reaches out, trying to find him and pokes him with her fingernails, catching what feels like a leg.

"Ow!"

"Sorry." She jerks her hand back, then rises up on her knees. Balancing on the bed, she leans in, trying to find him and cracks her head against something hard.

"Jesus!" She recoils—gripping her head with both hands—and lands on her rear end, bouncing on the mattress.

"You hurt me," he says, and she realizes they've cracked heads.

Now he's laughing softly, saying, "Uncover your eyes—*please*—before you kill us. Really, if this is the flip side, I'd rather be misunderstood."

"Me too." She groans, then laughs, pulling off her makeshift blindfold, and blinks, recovering her sight.

The dim glow of the candles sculpts his body, bathing him in shadows.

Smiling, they both lie down, then reach out carefully, finding each other. She rubs her forehead, which is hurting less. Then they snuggle in silence.

After a while, he says, "I'm really tired. Are you?"

She giggles. "I guess so, between the wine and cracking our heads."

"Let's get under the covers."

They do, and move back together, working out how to put their arms around each other as they settle in.

After a while, he falls asleep, snoring gently.

She knows it's late, but wishes that morning wouldn't come. Still, she can't help wondering how it will be, going back home, telling Carrie about her unexpected weekend.

A blind photographer, Carrie will say. You're making it up. But Elita knows she'll convince her, describing where she met him on Ocean Street, next to a wooden planter filled with red bougainvillea. Telling Carrie where they shared coffee on the patio of the Espresso Royale. Then explaining how his duplex is decorated— sparsely, with scented candles and a row of never-to-be-unpacked boxes, which Carrie won't understand. And in bed? Carrie will press—eager for all the details, since she's never flustered about providing her own. But as Elita thinks about it, she realizes that words won't do it. Won't convey the safety and freedom she felt, or the exquisite kissing and touching that swept away her depression and awakened her passion. No, it didn't work the second time around, she'll admit. But it was a real adventure and made her happy. At least for a little while.

As she lies there, Elita tries to picture herself and Chris, living together, or riding somewhere on a bus. But she knows it wouldn't work. He has his own pain, she realizes, from things she could never change. That saddens her. But in a way, it's also a relief, because usually she blames herself when her lovers are unhappy—thinking that *she* should change, instead of being who she is.

Now, lying in bed, Chris turns away from her in his sleep, bumping her hip with his. She smiles, taking comfort in his company. Slowly, she shifts in bed, easing onto her side and inches forward, curling up to his backside. Then she presses closer, until she feels the slight expansion of his back each time he breathes in, matched by the rhythmic lift and fall of his shoulders.

She closes her eyes and drifts off.

* * *

In her dream, she and Chris have company. It's the black woman in the pink sarong—the one who sells jewelry from a sidewalk table, next to Chris. Now, without speaking aloud, she stands at the foot of the bed, and mouths the words, *Are you sure?*

Feeling anxious, Elita gestures for her to come closer.

Instead, the black woman turns her back on Elita and sits on the end of the bed. Immediately, her shape wavers, and she becomes Elita's father.

His serene posture conveys that he's unaware of her presence and that of her lover, stretched out beside her.

As always, her father is precisely dressed, wearing trousers with a knife-sharp crease and a starched white shirt. Despite having his back to her, she knows that he's wearing a faded, hand-painted tie from his native Cuba, capturing a line of people in the marketplace, joyously performing the rumba, like he used to do with her when she was a little girl.

Strangely, instead of being unnerved by her father's presence, she wants him to bless her moment of happiness. Yet she's afraid that waking Chris would change everything, cause a horrendous quarrel. So she holds still, pained by her own silence.

Watching her father, she feels like a child and a woman at the same time, both younger and older. Now a sense of panic invades her, because she's certain that her father won't understand.

Slowly, her father stands up with his back to her and checks the crease of his trousers. Keeping his shoulders level, he leaves the room, moving with a quiet dignity, never once looking her way.

In her dream, Chris begins to stir and she looks down at him. His eyes are closed, still sewn shut, and she remembers him describing them as blue. But as she recalls the journeys he keeps making to distant places, something changes. She's certain that his eyes are filled with brilliance, like a pair of fiery opals.

* * *

When she awakens, Elita feels out of place and lost. Then, seeing Chris, barely visible by the glow of the digital clock, she sits up, recalling the entire evening.

Her motion awakens him, and he cautiously says, "Hello?"

"Here," she answers and reaches out, squeezing his shoulder. With both candles extinguished, the bedroom is dark except for the faint light of his clock.

He yawns, then sits up and scoots sideways. Carefully, he puts one arm around her waist. With his other hand, he lightly touches her face. And keeps touching, finding her features.

Suddenly she wonders, does he remember who I am?

"What time is it?" he asks in a voice thick with sleep.

She reaches over, turning on a small lamp next to his clock. "Almost six a.m."

"Mmmm," he says. "In another few of hours, I'll be hard at work."

She thinks of all the Polaroids he has taken, especially those he had her sort through. Most of them women, she recalls, in their early or mid-twenties. Some men and a few children, or older women, but not many. In fact, most of the women were young enough for college. Then she feels herself blush, recalling last night and the photos she took in her mind, catching herself in the mirror as they made love.

"How about you?" he says.

"Pardon?"

"When do you go back to work?"

"Not until Monday." She sighs and thinks of her job at the university bookstore. Not that different from his surroundings, she expects, living in a college community. Except he's not stuck inside a building, and he reaches out...does something to meet people.

"Excuse me," he says. He gets up and walks to the bathroom.

He shuts the door, but she hears his stream of urine, hitting the water inside the toilet bowl.

She lies back with a thump. Not wanting to think about her life in Sacramento, she pulls the covers to her chest. Why, she thinks, does this have to end so quickly?

The toilet flushes and water runs briefly. He comes back and sits on the edge of the bed.

"You could join me, Elita, on the sidewalk. Or rest here if you're tired." His voice is soft. "I'm usually home by early evening."

She touches his shoulder, grateful that he remembers her name.

Gently, he holds her hand, then traces each finger with one of his. "Would you like to spend another day?"

She wants to answer, but can't. She's thinking of the loss she'll feel, leaving Santa Cruz. Another day with Chris, she thinks, would make the loss deeper. She looks at the mirror, finding the two of them on the bed, but it seems like she's seeing herself from a great distance. She feels a hollow spot forming in her chest. Still, she resists the urge to pull him closer.

"Why don't you think about it," he says, "while I take a shower?"

As he gets off the bed, she sees the ease in his movements, and knows that whatever happened between them won't hold him back. Won't create any lingering sense of obligation.

"If you like," he adds, "we could shower together."

"No thanks." His being so considerate makes her both grateful and sad. "I need a few minutes to myself."

He nods and closes the door, leaving her in bed.

She hears the drizzle of the shower and turns on her side, then thinks of going home. Thinks of Tom's absence. Then of the comfort Carrie will offer, coming over to visit so she won't be alone.

Carrie, undoubtedly, has been invited to a few parties and will let her tag along if she asks, or even hints. But it would feel too jarring, she thinks…too loud…after this.

She looks around the sparse bedroom. She considers putting on another CD, but doesn't. In the silence, it's easier to hold onto herself. To know her own feelings. To struggle for some new beginning that centers on *her*, instead of on someone else.

A metal squeak sounds from the bathroom as the shower water stops running. Then she hears the soft pop of the shower door opening.

Still lying on her side, she throws off the covers. The morning air is chilly as she inhales the scent of the extinguished candles, mixed with the odor of their sex, still on her skin. She breathes deeply, wanting to savor and remember it all.

Turning her head, she sees the faint gray-blue cast of dawn through the living room window. Then—a few inches below windowsill—she makes out the shape of the cardboard boxes, along with his camera.

She swings her legs off the bed and sits up. Looking at his camera, she thinks of the photo albums she has saved, tucked beneath her bed. Frozen frames from each of her relationships, before they splintered or broke. All preserved on film—it occurs to her—except for Angelo Martinez, her first love from high school.

She remembers wistfully how innocent they were. And how they rushed. Nervous and eager, embracing on the living room couch, getting tangled in a pink Afghan before her parents returned from a movie.

But in her albums, there are no photos of Angelo, or of them as a couple. Nothing, beyond her memory of the physical act, which lasted only a few moments, ending with Angelo's sudden release. Still, he was gentle with her, and asked if she liked it. Quickly she answered, yes. But she was flustered by the rising sensations that deserted her when he finished so quickly. Even so, his tenderness lingers in her memory.

After a moment, the bathroom door swings open, and Chris returns with a towel around his waist.

"Elita?"

"Yes?" She's relieved that he's smiling.

"Does coffee sound good?"

"I'd love some."

He turns away from her, drops his towel and steps to the dresser in the closet, where he retrieves fresh underpants and puts them on, followed by a clean gray T-shirt, then yesterday's Levi's. In the nightstand drawer, she notices the socks, still lined up in a row, except for the pair she used as a blindfold.

As she watches Chris lace up his shoes, she feels a faint stirring of desire. But she also has the urge to look under his bed. It's silly, she knows, but maybe he has also saved pieces of his life that have cracked or shattered. Or, she wonders, has she already seen those souvenirs, among the Polaroids in his rosewood box? She realizes something simple, like a creased corner, could mean this one worked out, or this one didn't.

He stands up and comes to her side of the bed. Somehow he finds another Mary Chapin Carpenter CD, and puts it in the player. He keeps changing tracks until he finds "A Place in the World," which is one of her favorites.

Humming a little off tune, he runs his fingers through his hair, then finds his baseball cap, next to the clock radio. "Coffee's on the way," he says, walking to the kitchen.

She dresses slowly, intending to shower at her motel. There, she'll have a chance to fix in her mind everything she shared and felt with Chris. Inside her room, she'll close her eyes, letting her skin remember his touch. Her recollections will be the measure of what it meant and how she felt.

From the kitchen, she hears the grinding of coffee beans. She looks for her purse, then remembers it's on the couch. She gets it and returns to the bedroom.

Facing the tall pair of mirrors in the corner, she takes her brush from the purse and begins to stroke her hair, enjoying the way it tugs at her scalp. The face that stares back at her is almost, but not quite, happy. More satisfied than happy, she thinks.

She stops brushing and looks again. Closer. That's not it either, she realizes. It isn't satisfaction. What she sees is a sweet confusion, mixed with relief—as if wonderful things have occurred, but perhaps too quickly. Still, she's glad for everything that happened.

She looks once more at herself, and there's less confusion. More of an acceptance. Smiling, she decides not to apply any makeup.

Finished dressing, she slips her brush into her purse and walks into the kitchen.

Chris stands at the counter, pouring two cups of coffee. "Sugar or cream?" he asks.

"No." Tentatively, she comes to his backside and puts her arms around him. Feeling his warmth, she rests her cheek on his shoulder.

Carefully, he turns to face her, leaving their coffees on the counter. She leans into him, rising up to kiss him lightly.

"Will you remember me?" she asks. Then waits, feeling the soft rise and fall of his chest.

"Yes, Elita. I will."

She closes her eyes, letting sensations come to her, wrapped in memory. Him, sitting in his canvas chair, drinking coffee. Them, walking, arm-in-arm, past little shops. The whirring drone of a bottleneck guitar. The taste of Merlot wine. Persimmon-scented candles. Then luminous flashes of them in the mirror, making love.

"So will I," she says.

Terry Bennett

Filigree

Antioxidants & Other Stories

D oes it hurt?" Raymond asked. He sat by her side, holding her hand as she stretched out in the reclining chair.

Cindy bit her lip. "I shoulda finished the bottle."

Fidgeting, Raymond tapped the toe of his shoe, almost hidden beneath the black cuff of his oversized pants. "That bad, huh?"

She squirmed instead of answering.

Leaning over Cindy's prone figure, Mickey reached down with a beefy hand. It was covered with closely-spaced indigo tattoos of concentric circles, spreading outward from each knuckle and fingertip, giving his hand the appearance of a topographical map. Gently, he pressed the heel of his hand to her forehead, which flattened her copper-streaked bangs.

"Hold still, babe."

"Sorry Mickey." She half held her breath, tensing her shoulders as she stared at the cluster of six needle tips Mickey was using.

Mickey dipped the needles in ruby-red ink. "How's it feel?" he asked.

She made a face. "It aches. Really hurts."

"Hey, man," Raymond said, flexing one of his pipe stem arms. "Can't you ease up with that tattoo gun? Give her a smoother ride?"

Mickey raised the hand-held device. "It's called a *machine*, not a gun."

"Whatever, man."

Mickey wiped off the excess ink and toed his foot pedal, causing the set of needles to vibrate up and down with a soft chatter that tightened and worked into a hum. He bent over, guiding them to her flesh, where he added a rich streak of ruby-red within a curved line, thickening a single rose petal.

"Did you hear me?" Raymond said.

Mickey glanced at Raymond, then studied his work-in-progress. "*She* wanted it, Buddy. And you went along."

Raymond blushed hard, dark enough that his peach fuzz mustache seemed to disappear. "Not on her tits, I didn't."

Cindy jerked upright, forcing Mickey to pull back.

"Great," Cindy said, glaring at Raymond. "*Now* you tell me."

"But I'm here, right?" Raymond said with a pained look, holding up both hands. "I mean, I could be hanging with my homies."

Cindy shifted, looking from Raymond to Mickey. "Can you believe this?"

"Any more sudden movements," Mickey warned her, "and you're outta here, with a full rose on one and half a rose on the other."

"Shit." Cindy tugged at the hem of her suede skirt, keeping it mid-thigh. "I'm trying to hold still."

"All I meant," Raymond said, "is they're fine, jus' the way they are."

Mickey sat back and checked for the next pigment he would need.

She pointed at Raymond. "You're the one who keeps rappin' about 'making a statement.'"

"With my art, you mean?" Raymond bent forward, a silver scorpion dangling from one earlobe. "*That* kinda statement?"

"No." She hiccupped as she focused on him.

Raymond threw his shoulders back. "You sayin' my paintings ain't statements?"

"Well, yeah, they are. But this is different, Ray. I'm talking about *us*."

"Us?"

"You gotta quit moving around." Mickey laid his tattoo machine next to the gooseneck lamp he was using. He twisted the lamp into a new position. When he let go, it wobbled for a few seconds, casting a shimmering pool of light across Cindy's breasts, spilling twin shadows.

Mickey leaned sideways, getting a new angle, and inspected his work. "Okay, babe. I need a little lift now, to get at the undersides."

She squinted, looking past the glare of the gooseneck lamp. "You what?"

Mickey demonstrated. "Like this. Tuck your hands behind your head."

As she reached behind her neck, a trio of bracelets made a soft clinking noise, sliding down her wrist and forearm to her elbow.

"This is about *us*," she said, peering at Raymond. She raised one hand, shielding her eyes from the lamp.

Raymond ran his fingers through his hair. "Where are you goin' with this?"

She rolled her eyes. "Don't you know what day this is?"

Raymond thrust his chin forward. "Tuesday. It's fuckin' Tuesday, okay?"

She squeezed her eyes shut. "Jeez, you really don't remember."

Mickey blew out his breath and pulled back, cradling his tattoo machine. "Maybe I should take a break, so you two can thrash this out."

"It's our *anniversary*, Raymond. Three months of living together."

"Yeah?" Raymond inclined his head. "You hear that, Mick? The fuss she's making?"

"To you, it's Mickey."

Cindy looked from Raymond to her breasts. Each nipple formed the center of a rose in full bloom, seen from above, with her right breast finished and the left one halfway done. "Making a fuss?" she said. "That's what you call this?"

"Lighten up," warned Raymond.

She narrowed her eyes. "Wouldn't you call this a statement?"

Raymond blinked. "About us?"

"Man, it's *definitely* break time." Mickey wiped the excess ink off the needles, disengaged the needle bar that held them, and dropped it into the waste can.

Cindy sat up, cupping her breasts, facing Raymond. "Come on, Ray. Who'd you think this was for?"

Mickey laid the tattoo machine on its side and stood, shaking his head.

Raymond scooted his chair sideways, blocking the exit, keeping Mickey between him and Cindy. "Don't bail on me, man. She's getting weird."

Mickey reached into his sleeveless Levi's jacket, finding a cigarette. "Save it, Bud. I'm not in the counseling business."

Cindy reached out, hooking the pocket on Mickey's jacket. "Can't you keep going?"

"Yeah," said Raymond. "Get it over with."

Mickey leveled a blunt finger at Raymond. "This was going real smooth 'til you popped off."

Raymond took a step back.

Mickey sat down and stuck the cigarette between his lips without lighting it.

"Really," Cindy said. "Let's finish it."

Mickey nodded. "Commitment is an attitude I can dig."

"No way," Raymond said. "Don't be laying that on me."

"Hardly," Mickey said, without looking in his direction. "I was talkin' about the lady."

Cindy tilted her head sideways, until she could see past Mickey to Raymond. "Come on, Ray," she coaxed. "Sit by me." She patted her thigh.

"Not if you keep raggin' me with this anniversary shit."

"*Shit?*" She balled her hands into fists.

"Don't start," Raymond said, narrowing his eyes.

"You're the one—"

"*Hey,*" snapped Raymond. "I'm telling you, bitch. Keep it up and you'll be sorry."

Mickey peered over his shoulder, locking eyes with Raymond. "Care to step outta the booth?"

"She's *my* woman," Raymond said.

"And *my* customer."

Raymond pulled back, and Mickey reached past the autoclave, to a stainless steel tray. He picked up a new ink cap for his tattoo machine, switching from ruby-red to Kelly green, getting ready to color in the stem and leaves on the unfinished rose.

"You get off on that?" Raymond asked. "Stickin' her with that gun?"

"My job," said Mickey, "is all I'm trying to do. And you're getting in the way."

Raymond tensed and dipped into the pocket on his baggy pants.

Mickey laughed. "Pull a blade and you'll learn firsthand about getting stuck."

Raymond froze.

Mickey waited, inviting Raymond to make his move.

Cindy slapped the arm of the recliner. "Enough with the macho bullshit! My tits hurt, and I want you to finish."

When Mickey turned back to Cindy, Raymond clenched his jaw and edged his chair forward. "All I'm telling you, Cyn, is that—"

"Mickey?" Cindy asked. "Does it look okay?"

Mickey chuckled. "What do you mean, 'okay?' It looks great, babe. See for yourself." Holding his cigarette between two fingers, he gestured. "Look above the couch, or at any of the walls. This whole place is mirrors."

"With my contacts out, I can't see shit."

"It's a curly-cue sorta design," Raymond said as he reached past Mickey, squeezing her hand.

Mickey twisted around, nearly nose-to-nose with Raymond. "It's a filigreed rose, not some weak-ass curly-cue design. And I've had just about had it with your mouth." He raised a beefy hand and pointed. "Wait on the other side of that curtain, or take it outdoors. Your choice."

"Come on, Cyn. Tell this guy—"

"You heard him, Ray."

"Oh yeah...." Raymond said, drawing it out. "That's fine. Jus' fine." He dropped her hand and stood. Jerking back the curtain, he stepped into the waiting room.

"*Close it,*" Mickey ordered.

Raymond hesitated, then yanked the curtain shut.

Cindy used the back of her hand, wiping away tears. "Jeez. I could use another drink."

"Sorry, babe," Mickey patted her hand, "not on the premises."

"A drink would be good," Raymond said through the curtain. "Maybe a few, to stop your whining."

"Oh, really. Like *I'm* the problem."

"Come on," Mickey said in a soothing tone. "Settle down, so we can finish."

Cindy sniffled, smearing her mascara as she brushed away tears. "You're sure they look all right?"

"Let me put it this way," said Mickey. "We're close to having four masterpieces. Two of mine, on two of yours."

She seemed to think about it, then managed a shy smile. "I hope they're knockouts, on account of how bad they hurt—like someone smacked 'em, hard enough to bruise."

Mickey nodded. "I know, babe. But the pain won't last."

He opened the lid on the autoclave, removed a plastic bag and took out a needle bar with six needles attached. Carefully, he slipped the feeder end of the needle set into the metal tube, which he attached to his tattoo machine.

She sighed. "How about some ice? Wouldn't that help?"

Mickey shook his head. "Afterward, that'll keep the swelling down. But we can't use it right now."

"Ice would feel good."

Mickey pointed at her breasts. "If you hold it against your skin, too much water can make you scab. Then you'll lose some color."

"Never mind, then," Cindy said, staring at the ceiling. "I mean, we've come this far, haven't we?"

Mickey nodded.

"Anyway, it's really my feelings that hurt, more than my skin."

"What a surprise," said Raymond, "like you weren't gonna tell us."

Mickey rummaged around in a drawer and help up a small jar. "How about some Noxzema? Rubbing that in might help."

"Hey, man," Raymond said in a loud voice. "Don't be touching her."

"Listen, hardass," said Mickey. "She's hurting."

"I don't want him touching you, Cyn."

"Listen, pal. She's the one who rubs it in, not me."

"Never mind," said Cindy. "Let's keep going."

Mickey put away the Noxzema and picked up his tattoo machine. He dipped its set of needles into the cap of green ink.

Cindy snickered. "When it comes to ice-cubes, I heard something from this photographer. A guy who shoots centerfolds."

"Yeah?" Mickey paused, half-smiling. "What's that?" Gently, he touched the needles to her skin and depressed the foot pedal. The needles vibrated and began to hum.

Cindy bit her lip against the pain. "He rubs with an ice cube to make your nipples stand up."

Mickey laughed. "Like goose bumps, huh?"

Raymond drew the curtain back, scowling at Mickey. "Stop talking about tits."

"When you're in my parlor," Mickey said, "it's Art, with a capital 'A.' Not tits."

Raymond gripped the curtain. "Hey, man. Don't be dissing me about art. It's what I do."

"Spare me," Mickey urged. "You're clueless when it comes to art."

"Yeah?" sneered Raymond. "You think?"

"I'm telling you, pinhead—tattoos, etchings, nude photos...*whatever*. Long as it's done with class, all of it's art." Mickey set down his tattoo machine and flexed his hand, giving it a rest.

Raymond thumped his skinny chest. "Real art? You wanna see some *real art*? My stuff's hanging in a gallery, man, down on Seventh Street."

"Yeah? And mine's *walking* down Seventh Street, offering a feast for the eyes. Not to mention this good-looking babe, laid out in front of me."

Cindy rolled her eyes, then drew one finger across her neck, just below her chin. "If you don't mind, fellas. I'm up to here with you guys yakkin' about art."

Slowly, Mickey gazed from her neck to her breasts, then back to her neck. Grinning, he said, "*Almost* up to here."

Cindy lifted her head to look at her breasts, then burst out laughing. "Sure, I get it."

"Man, quit talking about her tits. It's like you're trying to turn her on."

Mickey lost his smile and fixed Raymond with a menacing look. "Back off, Chico, and let me work."

Raymond flinched when Mickey got up and jerked the curtain shut.

Behind the curtain, Raymond gripped the switchblade in his pocket, but didn't pull it out.

Mickey shook his head and picked up his tattoo machine.

Seeing the needles, Cindy looked away.

"I'm telling ya," Raymond said. "I don't like you talking 'bout her tits, man, 'cuz that's close to doin' it."

"Give me a break," Mickey said, guiding the humming tattoo machine across the rise of her breast, shading the thorns on the rose stem.

"I mean it, man," said Raymond.

"Hell, you think I haven't seen the nitty-gritty before? In this line of work?"

Cindy stuck her fingers in her ears.

Raymond jerked open the curtain, glaring at Cindy. "*You're* the one who started this."

Ignoring him, Mickey smiled at Cindy. "Give yourself some credit. It's a daring tattoo."

"Thanks." Cindy reached over and patted Mickey's knee.

"On account of *us*," Raymond said, jutting his chin at Mickey. "You and me, Cyn."

Cindy squeezed her eyes shut. "Hold it down, okay? I've got a headache from the booze."

"Ain't that right, Cyn?" Raymond said, raising his voice, thumping his skinny chest.

Mickey lost his smile. "Listen, Romeo. Zip your lip or I'm gonna tattoo your *ass*—with my foot, instead of this machine."

Raymond jerked the curtain closed. "*Fine*, Cyn. It's been three months, all right. But to hell with it. 'Cuz who needs to get hung up, you know? Even on someone special."

"Well I *am* special, Ray."

"Not if you're gonna be a drag," he said. "'Specially with my artwork needin' some attention. Otherwise, how am I gonna get the break I deserve?"

Cindy rolled her eyes. "Maybe *I'm* the one who needs a break, you know? From both of you."

Mickey, who'd been following their argument, raised his eyebrows. "What do you mean, 'both' of us?"

"Cyn, you're fulla crap," said Raymond.

"*Men*," she said, wearily. "That's what I mean."

Mickey gave her a sympathetic smile. "Maybe you're right." He lowered the needles to the rose stem.

"Really?" She licked her lips, trying to hold still.

"Not altogether." He toed the foot pedal, getting the needles to vibrate. "But I'll give you this much. You're better off not setting your sights too high."

"You're fulla shit," said Raymond.

She squeezed Mickey's knee. "Are you putting me on?"

Mickey winked. "Not a bit. Then there's a lot less pain."

She thought about it. "From not expecting too much?"

Mickey shrugged and kept working.

She sighed. "It's always men who ruin love."

Behind the curtain, Raymond said, "What about sex? I'm good enough when you wanna get laid."

Cindy eyed the curtain. "Love is more than sex, Raymond."

"What kinda crap is that?" Raymond said, peeking through the curtain. "Somethin' you read?"

"Oh yeah," Cindy said. "Like you're the expert, and Mister Dependable, to boot."

"Well I damn sure don't need no Dear Abby bitch telling me how to be."

Cindy flinched when the parlor door slammed, fanning the curtain, which lifted, then fell. Her lip began to tremble, and she squeezed her eyes shut.

Mickey shook his head. "What a loser."

Without opening her eyes, she bit her lip. Tears began to spill from the corners of her eyes.

"Hey," Mickey said. "Are you gonna be okay?"

She rolled over on her side, fishing with one arm for her big handbag on the floor.

"Let me," said Mickey. He scooped it up and handed it to her.

She propped herself up on one side and rooted inside the purse, finding a wad of tissues. Sniffling, she swiped at her nose, then dabbed her eyes, which smudged her eyeliner.

"Shit," she said.

"Take it easy," said Mickey. "You're gonna be all right."

She dug back into the purse, coming up with a pack of Winstons. She pulled one out, tapped it on the tabletop and slipped it between her lips.

"Not supposed to let you do that," Mickey said. "I've got alcohol in here and other flammables."

"Yeah, yeah," she said, pointing at the cigarette between his lips, glaring at him.

"Right." He said it with an air of resignation, then opened a drawer, retrieved a lighter and got her cigarette going.

She took a deep draw, pursed her lips, and blew smoke, shaking her head.

After a moment she stretched out on her side and offered him the cigarette.

He used it to light his own, then passed it back to her.

"Well," she said. "Here I am again, dumped by some wannabe who doesn't know dick." She sat up, hauled her purse onto her lap and pulled out her bra.

Mickey used his swivel stool to turn away. Dressing and undressing wasn't something he watched.

"Hey, Mickey?"

"Yeah?"

"Tell me what you really think. Take a look and tell me."

He swung around, seeing her in the glare of the lamp. She was cupping her breasts from underneath, to offer a better look at them.

"Like I said, Cindy. They're nice. Really nice."

"Even with one half-done?"

He offered a gentle smile. "Call it a work in progress."

"How long will they keep hurting?"

"A few days from when I finish. If you *want* to finish."

"When we started, I thought you said—"

"*Hey.* If I tell anyone they can quit, it's bad for business. 'Cuz most everybody gets the urge to stop, partway through. And if I agree, they expect part of their money back. But you got dumped, so I won't hold you to it...long as you don't tell anyone about me cuttin' you some slack."

She used the heel of her hand, wiping at the dried smear of mascara. "That many people wanna quit?"

He nodded. "On account of the pain. What they make of it."

She set her bra across her knees and looked back and forth, from her breasts to a blurry version of herself in the mirror—all she could see without her contacts.

After a moment, she let out a ragged sigh. "I think I should finish up. Do the whole thing."

"You're sure? Knowing it's gonna hurt?"

She nodded, blinking back tears.

"When I think about everything else," she whispered, "this ain't so bad."

Terry Bennett

Saving Grace

D octor Carlson settles into his high-backed chair. He smoothes his salt-and-pepper mustache and studies me. His eyes are gray and calm, but seem to glisten, as if freshly dotted with Visine to ease his fatigue.

He opens the notebook bearing my name and turns to the marker.

"A few years ago," he says, "you quit writing country-western songs to work the hotline."

From the couch, I nod. "That's right, at the Bereavement Center."

"Volunteering?"

I start to give him a look, then manage a smile. "It's not much of a paycheck, but I'm a counselor. Not a volunteer."

He jots something in his spiral notebook, then looks at me. "Isn't that quite a change?"

"How do you mean?"

"Going from country-western lyrics to grief counseling?"

I consider how alike they are, but say nothing.

He changes his grip on the pen. "How would you describe your new work?"

I look from Doctor Carlson to the stoneware pot that holds a squat gray cactus, with its shield of thorny pads.

My eyes continue on their usual circuit, taking in his bookcase, then two diplomas. Both are from UCLA, with *William Emit Carlson* scripted on them in gold leaf. Between them—hanging by its ribbon, framed under glass—is the Silver Star, awarded to him by the U.S. Marine Corps, citing his service in Vietnam. Seeing it, I'm grateful. I find it reassuring that he's seen casualties first hand.

"What are you feeling?" he asks.

I settle back into the couch, trying to feel nothing but leather upholstery.

"Thomas?" He maintains eye contact.

I long for indifference, or even the anger I took refuge in during the media frenzy, back when the camera crews were camped on my doorstep. Like the time they waylaid the kid delivering my pepperoni pizza and bribed him with a hundred bucks, then donned his uniform and barged in, shoving a microphone in my face.

Remembering the incident, I raise my hands to my temples and press hard with my fingertips. But it's too late. Another memory intrudes—of a jangling telephone.

"Thomas, what's going on?"

"The phone call," I confess, resentful now—as if the events it led to were his fault, instead of mine.

"What about the call?"

Pressure builds inside my head. "I still remember. Every word of it." I massage my temples. "It's been three years. *Three lousy years*, and I still can't put it behind me."

"The call?"

I draw a breath. "No. Everything that followed."

As he nods, I grit my teeth and try once more to decipher what happened.

* * *

It began with a harsh ringing that seemed to grow louder as I rolled over in bed. I blinked, searching for the phone, fumbling in the near darkness I had created using musty wool blankets to cover brittle window shades.

Finally I found the phone beneath the snare drum, which was vibrating as the phone rang.

"Come get your brother," warned Louie Chen. "He's pissing off a real hard-ass…this guy the size of King Kong."

I promised to hurry, despite the insistent throbbing that gripped my head.

I'd filled in on drums last night at the Lonesome Trail, playing for a thrown-together band that favored songs by Merle Haggard and George Jones. By itself, that would've been great, but I had to back-up this wannabe who sang off-key and mangled the lyrics. So I'd matched the lead guitarist, drink-for-drink, to relieve my ears.

Struggling now to get upright, I half-crawled into my Levi's. I sat on the floor and grunted, pulling on my scuffed-up Tony Lamas. Remembering that all my shirts were dirty, I put on the one I'd worn the night before, with the red yoke and pearl snap buttons.

I got the shakes just from getting dressed. My stomach clenched as I squinted into the glare of afternoon sunlight, slicing through the narrow gap below my improvised curtains. Shielding my eyes, I got up and stumbled to the bathroom. I avoided the mirror while pouring a tumbler of Early Times. Gingerly, I wet my toothbrush, worked my teeth, then downed four aspirin.

Usually I took my time retrieving my younger brother, Ryan. But Louie never called unless enough storm clouds had gathered for lightning to strike. Plus, it was my turn in the barrel. After all, Ryan had rescued me two weeks ago, when Heather handcuffed me to my truck and maced me. Trying not to trip, I donned wraparound sunglasses, put on a suede jacket with fringe on its sleeves, and grabbed my Stetson.

Ten minutes later—having run a pair of red lights—I arrived at Louie Chen's Bar. Downshifting, I slipped my beat-to-hell pickup between a Harley with bald tires and a white El Camino with a mashed fender. Across the parking lot, the door to Quik

Stop Liquors swung open and a man shuffled out, wearing muddy pants and a torn T-shirt. He raised his brown-bagged bottle and took a slug. Behind him, Karl Kopinski, the owner, stared as I climbed from my truck. I pointed to Louie's sign, reserving six parking spaces. Kopinski stuck his chin out and snapped his suspenders.

Ignoring Kopinski, I took a moment to consider Louie's clients. He catered to guys with tool belts and skinned knuckles, so I pitched my Stetson onto the front seat. No sense adding to Ryan's troubles, looking like John Wayne coming to the rescue.

As I made my way to the bar's entrance, I checked my pockets. I found three crumpled twenties and a pair of ones. Hopefully that would settle Ryan's tab. I also found a cocktail napkin, scrawled on with a red felt-tip. I realized it was a verse for one of my half-finished songs. Something about losing my head, then my heart and soul in a topless bar. No doubt inspired by visits to the Brass Bulldog, where my brother worked part-time as a bouncer.

I pushed through Louie Chen's double-door entrance, into the tunnel of the bar's darkened interior. The window blinds were always closed and most of the lights had burned out, so I stopped and removed my sunglasses. Traces of light reflected off hard hats, worn by men hunched over their drinks.

In the distance, a low growl rumbled and I froze, trying to locate Louie's dog.

From the gloom, Louie laughed. "Don't worry. Your ass is safe."

He stepped forward where I could see him, wearing his "Do I look like I give a shit," T-shirt and a canvas apron. He hooked a thumb over his shoulder. "Romeo's back there with your brother."

I nodded and looked past Louie's cousin, Nelson, who was slicing limes. At Louie's you never found cherries, olives or onions. Instead you found double-packs of aspirin and bottles of fire-breathing homemade sweet-and-sour sauce, reserved for Louie's Mandarin buffalo wings.

When my eyes adjusted, I spotted Ryan. He sat near the end of the bar, where Louie had parked his rust-pitted, three-wheeled barbecue. Below Ryan, curled up against the tarnished foot rail, lay the black and white hulk of Louie's ancient pit bull, Romeo.

I moved forward, taking in the overhead scorch marks where red-hot wiring had damaged the ceiling two years ago, causing a minor fire. Even with new wiring, the electricity often failed, so Louie kept two propane heaters on hand, plus a half-dozen kerosene lamps along the bar, and several orange candles with Chinese calligraphy that ran up their sides.

I neared Ryan and Romeo, who looked like a pair.

Romeo sported a bandage on a torn ear. His massive head rested on both paws as he stretched out on the floor, near scattered peanut shells and an ashtray full of beer. He drooled, breathing deeply, revealing a broken incisor.

Wearing sweat pants and a jersey, Ryan sat on a stool. In profile, he presented a compact bundle of muscle and sinew, hunched forward with his elbows on the bar. In the dim light, I couldn't see the scars that marked the folds of skin at the corners of his eyes. On the barstool to Ryan's left sat his battered leather gym bag. Zipped open, it held boxing gloves and a sparring helmet. On the floor next to his stool rested two full grocery bags with their tops taped shut.

Just past Ryan, a huge bearded man in grease-stained coveralls occupied the last stool, presenting the profile of a Neanderthal. I watched as he nudged my brother and said, "Give it a rest."

Immediately, I understood Louie's apprehension.

Looking straight ahead, Ryan studied the control buttons on the beat up portable CD player that Louie had bolted to the bar in place of a jukebox. Next to it, a galvanized bucket overflowed with CDs. Louie called it his "barter bucket," because—when he was in the mood—he would credit CDs against bar tabs that had gotten out of hand.

"Did you hear me, pal?" The big man nudged Ryan a little harder.

As I reached Ryan's side, I recognized the jackets on a few CDs he had lined up on the bar. Three were from my country-western collection. The other two were demo-CDs, showcasing

songs I'd written that hadn't drawn a flicker of interest from anyone in Nashville.

Ignoring me and the big man, Ryan pushed a button on the
CD player.

Seconds later, a mournful fiddle and pair of steel guitars
played a bittersweet eight-bar introduction. Then the plaintive
voice of Leon Russell started in with a mournful twang:

"Just because I ask my friends about her,
Just because I spoke her name somewhere..."

"Shit," growled the Neanderthal, drowning out Leon Russell. "That's the tenth time, buddy."

Leon Russell paused, then wailed: *"She thinks I still care..."*

"I said, give it a rest," muttered the big man.

"Hey, Ryan," I said, eager to distract him.

I took the second stool to his left, leaving his gym bag between us, and kept my distance from Romeo and the bearded behemoth. "How's it going, little brother?"

"Thomas," Ryan answered softly, keeping his eyes straight
ahead.

Only Ryan still called me Thomas since I'd taken the handle
of "Tommy Lee" in hopes of hawking the country-western songs I
wrote between truck-driving shifts and the occasional fill-in gig I
landed, whenever some drummer took sick or laid low, dodging
relatives or creditors.

Gingerly, I reached over and turned the volume down, re-
ducing Leon Russell to a murmur.

Ryan turned my way and narrowed his eyes.

I held up a hand. "Just so we can visit. Okay?"

The big man snorted and gave me a sullen look, which Ryan
paid no attention to.

I set one boot on the brass foot rail, sizing up Ryan's condition as Louie walked over.

"Beer or whiskey?" Louie asked, wiping down the bar.

"Both," I said. My stomach felt queasy from last night, and I
expected a little hair of the dog might help.

Louie put a shot glass in front of me. "Depth charge," he announced, then drew a draft beer. He set the mug of beer by the shot glass, which he topped off with whiskey. I saluted and dropped the shot glass into the mug. It sank, trailing an amber stream as foam welled up.

"Ryan," I said, "you know…." I stopped and took a long drink, bolstering myself.

"The thing is, Ryan…." I paused to belch. "Remember two weeks ago, when you broke off sparring and brought me that hacksaw?"

Ryan shrugged, but didn't answer.

I dipped into a bowl of unshelled peanuts. "Anyway, I'm still grateful."

"Ahhhhh," Louie said, with a rare display of sympathy. "More problems with Debbie?"

"No," I said, "*Heather*, not Debbie," hoping that Louie's mistake would draw Ryan out. But he didn't respond.

"Heather," I explained to Louie, "is the meter-maid who cuffed me to my truck."

Louie raised his eyebrows. "What for?"

"Because I kept double-parking inside her patrol area, so she couldn't ignore me. Now, *Debbie*…she was a month earlier. Remember? She dealt pan and low-ball at the Garden."

Louie wrung out his bar towel. "Thaaaat's right. Debbie gal, she dealt you out." He slapped his thigh, laughing at his own joke.

Ryan frowned. "Didn't she split?"

Grinning, Louie nodded. "She hired on at the Indian casino up by Red Bluff, once they promised to keep your brother away."

I indulged them with a smile and drank some beer. "See, little brother? Sure enough, she's gone. But I'm still walking and talking, you know? Getting on with my life. Just like *you* should. After all, what's one more between the two of us? Debbie, Heather…." I cracked open a peanut and waited for him to add to the list.

Louie looked from me to Ryan, whose eyes had clouded over.

"I swear," Ryan said, making a fist. "This one hurts something awful."

I wanted to say she'd hurt him no worse than the others.

Louie shook his head. "Two brothers, same curse."

Unfortunately, he was right. My brother and I had the same Achilles heel. A single glance from a woman who'd caught our eye, or the scent of her perfume, or just the sight of her walking down the street, and—what can I say? We'd fall...and I mean *hard*, pole-axed by love. We'd have it bad—*so bad* that we'd drop everything that should have mattered. Sticking to our jobs? No way. Watering the lawn or remembering to eat three meals a day? Not a chance. Restraint and good judgment were flat-out abandoned. Once under the spell, we would pursue women with round-the-clock phone calls, gifts, and visits—showing up on their doorsteps day and night. And although we never fell for, or competed for the same woman, my brother and I shared the exact same runaway compulsion.

At first—feeling flattered—the women usually agreed to a few dates. Some even went to bed quite willingly. But soon, our inability to curb our impulsive behavior created a downward spiral...one in which my brother and I were doomed to crash and burn. Inevitably, both of us pissed off every woman whose attention we sought.

The only saving grace—if you can call it that—was a matter of "timing." For some reason, my brother and me seemed to have alternating cycles. When one of us was getting dumped, the other had recovered enough from his last go-'round to offer a lifeline. Mostly soothing words, a sympathetic ear and a stiff whiskey. That was a good thing, especially since Ryan took his losses harder than me. At least *I* thought he did, although some friends would disagree—probably because Ryan complained less. But once he hit bottom, that boy embraced misery the way a drunk hugs a bottle.

Louie touched my beer mug. "Another?"

I nodded, then leaned toward Ryan. "You?"

He shook his head, and for the first time, I noticed that his hands were empty, without a drink that he'd drained or one in progress. I leaned back, checking his rear pocket for a hip flask, but didn't see one.

Further up the bar, a man raised his voice, saying, "Don't be telling me about love. You wouldn't know it if it bit you on the ass."

Ryan closed his eyes and shook his head. From my own experience, I could sense what he was feeling—the bitter realization that, having ticked off his latest dream woman, she would avoid him at all costs.

I said, "Hey, little brother, you're a survivor. Don't forget that."

Between the two of us, there wasn't much that we hadn't seen or suffered when it came to romance. With Ryan, women had taken out restraining orders, paid for billboards telling him to drop dead, and flat-out skipped town. One had even become a nun. Anything to escape his unrelenting pursuit. As for me, I'll admit to having suffered the most insults because I'd been at it longer, being four years older.

Ryan opened his eyes, and I flicked a peanut in his direction. "Care to tell me her name?"

Ryan set his jaw and boosted the volume on the CD player, just as Leon Russell pined:

"Let that silly notion bring her cheer."

The violin and pedal steel began a duet, echoing the singer's melancholy voice.

I couldn't help bobbing my head in time—preferring Russell's rendition to that of George Jones, or even Hank Williams, who had penned the song.

Neanderthal tapped Ryan on the elbow. "Hey, pal. Didn't I warn you?"

With Ryan wearing a jersey, I could see his shoulder muscles bunch. I'd seen the same thing in his boxing matches, just before he fired devastating punches. Even now, five years after his run as a middleweight, he remained a fearsome sparring partner, delivering savage body shots that all but paralyzed his opponents.

"Come on," I said to the big man. "Let me buy you a drink."

He gave me the once-over, staring at my cowboy boots, belt buckle and fringed jacket, then said, "You'd better save your quarters for the pony ride."

Ryan smiled and rolled his shoulders.

Quickly I stood, hoping my six-foot one-inch frame might draw his attention from Ryan. Being five inches shorter, Ryan looked like less of a threat, but that was hardly the case. I'd seen him hit the heavy bag hard enough to snap whatever chains it hung from.

"Sit down," Ryan told me.

"Come on, guys," I cajoled, looking from Ryan to the hulk. "Drinks for all of us."

The big man tipped his head to one side, then the other, cracking his neck. "Zip it, buddy."

"Hey. That's my brother," Ryan said, raising his voice half a notch.

Neanderthal smirked. "Think I can't handle the two of you?" With a casual, almost lazy motion, he backhanded the CD player, which shattered, scattering pieces in all directions.

Halfway up the bar, Louie hollered, "That's *enough.*"

"Yeah?" snarled the bearded man. He slapped both palms on the bar. "Maybe I'm just getting started."

"Don't push it," I urged, hoping it wasn't too late.

Neanderthal gave me a measured look. Slowly, he clenched a ham-sized fist. "Butt out, Slick, while you're still standing."

"*Romeo,*" yelled Louie.

Romeo's eyes flew open and he lurched to his feet. Growling fiercely, he swung his head back and forth, eyeing every leg that rested on the foot rail or hung off a bar stool.

Customers scrambled for altitude. I vaulted the bar, getting behind it, while others climbed their stools or stood on the bar.

"Easy now," Ryan said to Romeo, who had narrowed his eyes and flattened his ears.

Everyone had taken cover, except for my brother and the big man.

Ryan and the behemoth stood up slowly and held their ground, facing each other, despite Romeo's ragged growl.

"Last chance," said Ryan.

The bearded hulk flicked open a double-edged knife he had clenched in his fist. "If that mutt bites me, I'll skin him alive."

A wet rumble sounded, deep in Romeo's chest. His hackles rose and he snarled, baring teeth the size of two-penny nails.

As Neanderthal glanced at the dog, Ryan fired a blistering one-two-three left-right-hook combination, almost too fast to see.

The first punch—a stiff jab—broke the big man's nose; the right-cross landed just above his heart; and a sizzling hook dug into the man's ribs, hard enough that he folded over, dropping his knife.

Groaning, he staggered and managed to straighten up, taking a backward step that knocked over his stool. Ryan cranked another hook that caught him square on the side of his jaw.

The instant it hit, the big man's eyes fluttered and he went down hard. He landed on the fallen stool, snapping off one leg, which shot across the floor.

Romeo lunged, seizing the loose wooden leg. He whipped it back and forth, hammering the side of the bar, then spat it out. Snarling, bright-eyed, he swung about and lowered his head, lining up on the unconscious bully.

"Romeo *stop*," Louie shouted. "*Stop!*"

The dog froze, ears cocked, and gnashed his teeth, eager for his next command.

"*Kennel*," Louie yelled.

Romeo hesitated, then scuttled—still growling—to the other end of the bar. Using his head, he rammed a self-locking hinged door that swung inward, and pushed his way into the kennel beneath the bar. Once inside, he couldn't leave unless Louie pushed a foot pedal, releasing the latch.

"Jesus," I said, peering over the bar from Louie's side, unnerved by the punishing blows Ryan had landed.

Ryan stood calmly over the bearded hulk, who lay on his side, out cold, blood oozing from his nose.

Louie glanced from Ryan to me, then flipped open his cell phone.

"Come on," I pleaded. "The bastard pulled a knife. Ryan had no choice."

Louie gave me a hard look, then snapped his phone shut. "Ryan's got to leave. And pay damages."

"Deal." This was a bargain, compared to posting bail. Before Louie could reconsider, I vaulted the bar, back to Ryan's side, and slapped money on the bar. Lowering my voice, I told him, "Outside. *Now.* Wait in the parking lot."

Ryan scowled as if I'd caused the whole ruckus, then grabbed his gym bag and the pair of sealed grocery sacks he had left on the floor. On his way out, he kicked open the double-doors, hard enough that they kept flapping on their hinges once he cleared them.

Louie came around to my side of the bar, shaking his head. "Bad temper. Very bad."

He picked up the fallen knife as a half-dozen regulars reclaimed their seats. A few headed for the exit, complaining.

Louie flipped them off, hollering, "You needed the exercise." Then he bent over, grim-faced, and nudged the Neanderthal, who groaned, but didn't open his eyes.

"Sorry," I said to Louie.

Louie gave me an exasperated look. "I don't need this crap."

"Well, that makes two of us."

Louie seemed to calm down as he closed the man's folding knife. Slipping it into his back pocket, he said, "When's your brother going to quit?"

"Drinking?

"No. Being such a hot-head."

I snorted, trying to imagine that.

Louie frowned. "He's always been touchy, but now he seems worse."

"I suppose." I eyed the fallen giant and finished my drink.

"Both you guys are terrible, but Ryan's got no excuse. He could settle down."

"You think?"

"Sure. Him and that gal at the Brass Bulldog…." He snapped his fingers a few times. "You know…the nice one you talk about."

"You mean Brenda-Mae?"

Louie smiled, tracing a heart on his chest. "Maybe she's the one."

I shook my head. "Not a chance."

Brenda-Mae, a college student and featured dancer at the Brass Bulldog, had the hots for Ryan. But that didn't spark his interest. The way it worked, it had to be *him* falling…not the other way around. Even when I passed on to Ryan what she'd told me, about wanting to ring his chimes, he'd responded with a half-hearted smile, saying she deserved better. Then told me what I already knew—that he held onto friends much better than lovers.

Louie counted out the money I'd thrown on the bar. "You worried about Ryan?"

I shrugged, not sure how to answer. If this had been one of Ryan's watering holes, like the Body Shop, or the Brass Bulldog, it wouldn't have gone this far. People would have known that he boxed for a living and warned off the big man.

A tall silhouette filled the door, and I caught the gleam of metal handcuffs and a Sam-Browning belt.

I glared at Louie. "You said you wouldn't call."

"He didn't," the uniform answered, walking forward until I recognized Pete Swensen, the security guard from next door at New Valley Savings and Loan.

Swensen canted his head, studying the fallen man with an air of indifference. "Looks like he's breathing pretty regular."

"Pulled a knife," Louie said.

Swensen nodded. "S'what I heard." He raised his eyebrows expectantly, looking at Louie.

"No police," said Louie. "Everything's okay."

"Probably," said Swensen, taking a seat on the nearest stool. "But I'll stick around, 'til this fool can get to his feet."

I could see the relief in Louie's eyes. Swensen, before retiring, had put in twenty-five years as a state trooper. In his second-to-last year, he had single-handedly stopped four pistol-wielding bank robbers, dropping a pair of them with one shot apiece, then convinced the others to surrender. The way Louie told it, Swensen had hollered, "Hell, it's your call, fellas. Makes no difference to me."

I picked up the broken bar stool while Louie poured Swensen a coffee.

At our feet, the battered man blinked a few times and managed to sit up. Touching his ribs, he groaned.

"You run into something?" Swensen asked.

He spat a stream of pink saliva that caught in his beard. "Tripped," he grumbled.

Swensen sipped his coffee and nodded. "Happens."

Neanderthal winced, pressing one hand to his nose, then stared at the blood on his fingers. Slowly, he began looking around on the floor, running his hand beneath the brass foot rail.

Swensen stood up, inches from the man's fingers. "Better you don't find it. Or ask for it."

Neanderthal spat once more, gathered himself, and got to his feet, remaining hunched over. He left, clutching one hand to his ribs.

Swensen watched until he made it through the double-doors, then gave me a pained look. "What's with your brother, pulling out the stops like that?"

Too tired to argue, I said, "Who knows?"

"Well," Swensen said, tipping his cap back. "With a knife, it could've been worse."

He finished his coffee and pushed the cup away. "Where you parked, Tommy Lee? Next door at the Step-and-Stagger?"

"Yeah."

"Still driving the supreme machine?"

Louie grinned. "You mean the two-tone? Irene Ball Peen?"

Swensen nodded.

"Indeed I am," I admitted. "Nothing but the finest—bondo and primer."

Swensen laughed. "You made the five o'clock news with that one."

They meant my Ford-150, which had suffered greatly two months ago at the hands of Irene Holt. When I wouldn't back off, she had taken a ball peen hammer to my pickup, leaving over a hundred-and-fifty dents, evenly spaced, a hand's width apart from one to the next. They ran in a fairly straight line across the front of my hood, down one side, across the tailgate and up the other side. Hence, "Irene Ball Peen," and my heavy investment in bondo and primer.

"Come on," Swensen said. "I'll say hi to your brother."

"Are we square?" I asked Louie.

"Go on," he said, snapping a towel in my direction.

Swensen started to dig out pocket change.

"No, no," said Louie. "Tommy Lee paid for your coffee."

Swensen smiled.

I walked outside with Swensen, into the sunset's pink glow, which tinted the sidewalk and maple trees in front of Louie's.

In the parking lot a small crowd had gathered, not quite forming a circle around my brother. Stripped to his waist, he was jumping "rope." Except his version of a rope was an eight-and-a-half foot length of quarter-inch steel cable, secured at each end by wooden handles with ball bearings, so that the cable would rotate freely.

Karl Kopinski stood near the doorway of his liquor store. "Tommy Lee," he called out. "I warned your brother. He's on private property, interfering with my business." Kopinski thrust his chin at Swensen, daring him to disagree.

Deadpan, Swensen studied the scruffy onlookers. "I wouldn't call it interfering, exactly. Judging by all the brown bags, I'd say business is good."

"You think?" Kopinski began counting the bag holders with a twisted, arthritic finger.

"Relax," I said. "I'll get Ryan."

169

"Then again," said Kopinski, "later is fine." He limped off, herding a pair of newcomers into his liquor store.

I approached my brother at the back of the lot, where the L-shape formed by Quik Stop Liquors and Louie Chen's Bar sheltered him from the wind. The steel cable made a soft whirring blur as Ryan swung it with ease, jumping in place, barely lifting his feet on each revolution—just enough to clear the cable as it swept underneath.

By now his face had gone slack and his eyes had lost focus, but I wasn't surprised. I'd seen this before. The other times I'd watched him work out for an hour straight, doing push-ups, sit-ups, or jumping rope, he always seemed to enter a trance.

Now, as he jumped in place, perspiration dotted his forehead and chest, but his breathing remained slow and steady.

Swensen waved to Ryan and got no response.

Looking at Ryan, I told Swensen, "This could go on for quite a while."

"So?" Swensen scanned the paved lot and gestured at the onlookers. "At most, he's blocking two parking spaces, and both driveways are clear."

Peering through the small crowd, I saw that Ryan was surrounded by a powder-blue chalk line he must have drawn on the pavement. It almost formed a closed circle, about twelve feet across, except for a two-foot gap. At intervals, spaced out along the edge of the circle, were small piles...of what, I couldn't tell. So I stepped closer.

My stomach clenched as I recognized the objects. "What the hell," I demanded, "is *this*?"

* * *

I watch Doctor Carlson turn a page in his notebook. "These objects, you recognized them as gifts? From your brother to the women he pursued?"

"That's right. Bracelets, movie tickets, carnival dolls, boxes of chocolate...a collection of things Ryan had sent them as a sign of his love."

"But if these were gifts he had sent...."

I glare at him as he sits there, holding his pen. "You already know," I say, "how he got them back."

He waits.

"You must've heard," I say, "from the damn news stories. From the stupid claims they made."

He nods. "Except that was their version. What's yours?"

I sit up on the couch. "My version? As if I'm not sure what happened? Is that what you're suggesting?" In the back of my mind something flares brightly. Quickly, I smother it by gripping the couch, then forcing myself to focus on the couch's shape and texture.

Doctor Carlson sets his pen down. "Isn't this part of it?" His tone is neutral, but a sharp pain lances my gut.

"Part of what?"

"Why you're here, and still upset with the media...three years after the fact."

I swing my feet off the couch, planting both heels on the carpet. "Those bastards twisted everything." I recall a violent starburst of light and squeeze my eyes shut. *Hard.* Just for a second.

Doctor Carlson nods. "To an extent, the media distorted what happened, because their coverage was so skewed. But in earlier sessions, you've mentioned your own confusion." He pauses, flipping to the front of his spiral notebook. He quotes. "*Confusion, is what you said, from all the different interpretations.*"

"What they did," I insist, "was put their own spin on it— every one of them. Just to grab headlines or jack up their ratings."

He gives me a steady look. "But you did say that, didn't you?"

"Fuckin' vultures, is what they were, the way they kept at it."

"Please," he interrupts, raising one hand. "Your reaction— this anger of yours—is drawing us away from what happened. You're focusing on 'them'...on the 'collective,' instead of on you."

"And?"

"Thomas, please. I want to know what *you* experienced."

I take a deep breath and hold it for a few seconds.

He watches me carefully as I run my thumbs across the tips of my fingers, feeling the stiff white scar tissue. I wore mittens, early on, to protect each skin graft.

"Go back," he urges. "Go back and tell me about those objects...the returned gifts."

I stare at the scattering of freckles on the back of my hands, then at the thickened skin on my palms, and the tips of my fingers, turned grayish-white, like melted paraffin.

"Thomas?"

Too tired to argue, I lie back down, half-closing my eyes, and stare at the ceiling.

"What Ryan used to do—what we both used to do—was bombard them with gifts. Anything to show how much we cared." Embarrassed, I pause, not wanting to describe the juvenile gifts Ryan and I had chosen from our stunned haze of infatuation.

"What it came down to," I add, "was that we couldn't help ourselves. We'd pester them, non-stop, for their attention and affection."

He gives me this walking-on-eggshells look. "Nevertheless, you expected them to respond somehow? To this abundance of gifts?"

Chagrined, I let out my breath. "*Compulsive.* I know that's how we acted. But for me and my brother, once some gal caught our eye...that's all she wrote. Swear to God. It was like a riptide pulling us out to sea. Except we welcomed it, instead of fighting it. Couldn't wait for that current to sweep us away."

He nods. "And the particular gifts your brother set out on this chalked circle...how would you describe them?"

I grit my teeth and pick at the scar tissue on one of my fingers. "In a way, they were all the same."

"How's that?"

"Sooner or later, this avalanche of gifts would scare the ladies, or piss them off. So they'd either ditch our gifts, or send them back."

"I see."

I pick harder at my scar tissue. "I suppose *return to sender* was their message."

"And your brother had these gifts lined up, along this circle?"

"Just a sampling. But I understood, right away."

Doctor Carlson smoothes his mustache. "Understood what?"

"What they were, where they'd come from. And how upset these women were."

He says something I don't quite hear as I drift off, anticipating the distraught phone calls I'll be answering tonight, sitting in the cramped cubicle I've called my office for the past three years. It's cramped and chilly, with threadbare carpet. Even so, it's bearable because the walls are lined with photos of my wife and twin girls. The most recent snapshots are from the twins' first birthday—showing off my blue-eyed blonde haired imps, both tugging at their mother's dress.

Knowing they'll all hug me when I get home is what helps me carry on, fielding calls from others who have joined the club. New members to our society-of-the-bereaved, admitted for the usual price—the death of a loved one.

For some, it's a loss they saw coming, from a lingering illness. For others, it arrived when they least expected it—cutting them wide open. Either way, they're left behind, facing cruel questions while they struggle with their grief. So I do my best...trying to listen and console.

A steady, rhythmic noise brings me back, and I look up. Doctor Carlson is tapping the pen against his notebook.

I look from his pen to him, and think about snapping his pen in two.

Breaking my silence, he says, "Tell me, Thomas. What did your brother say about the gifts he'd laid out?"

One by one, I pop the knuckles of my left hand, then my right hand. "We've been over this."

He settles into his chair, waiting.

Finally, I say, "With me, it always came down to words. With Ryan, it was physical. And that day was no different. He said damned little."

Doctor Carlson closes his notebook and gives me this bleary look that suggests fatigue, or maybe disappointment. Then again, maybe he's just irritated, like I am. Tired of going back and grinding through what happened, until it feels more like recitation than something I witnessed.

Finally, he says, "You have me stumped."

"How's that?"

"What you've been recounting...is that what *really* happened, or just a safe way to describe it?"

My chest begins to tighten.

"After all," he adds, "it was three years ago. How clearly do you remember?"

I look away.

"I'm sorry," he adds. "Of course you remember." He rests his hands on his knees. "What I'm trying to get at is this. *How*, exactly, are you remembering it? Are you dealing with the real events—as they actually occurred?"

My chest ratchets tighter, until it's hard to breathe.

He gives me time to respond.

When I don't, he says, "What if you imagine yourself standing by the chalked circle, watching your brother jump rope?"

I don't answer.

"Will you at least try that?"

I close my eyes, fighting off anger, then fear. Slowly, I find myself going back.

* * *

The onlookers surrounding Ryan were drinkers from Louie's Bar and Quik Stop Liquors. I counted nine men and two women, mostly in their forties or older, each throwing a long shadow from the setting sun. I approached them and the chalked circle, catching the hum of Ryan's spinning steel cable. His bare chest gleamed as he bounced softly on his toes. But it was the piles of gifts that caught my attention.

Even with all the stories Ryan and I had swapped about our doomed love affairs, I never realized he had saved so many of the gifts sent back to him. A few, maybe…but this? I studied the collection, trying to recall who he had hoped to charm with a pair of CDs featuring Engelbert Humperdinck's love songs, or with a gold-plated bracelet that glittered from a Zirconium on each of its links. Each gift was pathetic. All reminders of how pitiful my brother and I could get, once we were spell-bitten.

Pete Swensen returned to my side, munching one of Louie's barbecued chicken wings. He held out a paper plate with a pair of wings, covered with Louie's red sweet-and-sour sauce, which reeked of jalapeno peppers drowned in pineapple syrup, loaded with sugar and garlic. "Care for a bite?"

When I imagined the fiery taste, my stomach skipped and rolled. "No thanks."

Swensen took another bite. "How are you doing with…." He paused, frowning, then motioned with the chicken wing. "You know…the one who gardens?"

"The landscaper? Natalie?"

"That's the one."

"She shredded my love letters for compost."

Chewing, Swensen raised his eyebrows. "My kind of gal. Very direct."

I couldn't disagree. Natalie had been a total rush. Intoxicating just to be around, doing even the simplest things, like sharing a cup of coffee or going for a walk. And the sex had been great—this crescendo of back and forth surges that all but curled my toes. But in the end, none of that had mattered, because she dumped me…like all of the others.

Not wanting to dwell on how it ended between us, I turned to Ryan and leaned in to catch his attention. "Hey! Shouldn't you be at Brogan's Gym?"

As he kept jumping rope, Ryan did this bit-by-bit pivot, inching around in my direction, until he met my gaze.

"Did you hear me? Shouldn't you be sparring at Brogan's?"

"Nope. This week I'm at PAL"

The Police Athletic League gym, with its leaky ceiling and makeshift lights, reminded me of Louie's Bar.

"Tournament?" I asked.

"Right, for the high school seniors." As the cable whipped through the air, he shifted the pattern of his footwork, bouncing only on his right foot—never missing a beat—then switched to his left foot. "The best kids are entering the Golden Gloves." He spoke without sounding the least bit out of breath. "They've been sparring with me. Tuning up for elimination bouts."

I smiled at the notion of him holding back, so the kids could hit him. "Want a ride?"

He shook his head, shifting his feet again, edging around as he kept jumping, slowly turning away from me. By now, the ring of onlookers had grown, picking up folks who were strolling by.

I saw a black and white patrol car slow down, then coast to a stop.

Swensen smiled and walked over, then knelt, getting eye-to-eye with the patrolman who rolled down his window.

"Nope," I heard Swensen say. "No complaints that I've heard of."

Across the parking lot, Kopinski peered through his half-opened door. I'm sure he hoped the cops would leave before any of his brown-baggers staggered or fell.

Swensen raised his plate, saying to the patrolman, "Come on, take the last one."

The cruiser pulled away and Swensen walked back, carrying an empty plate.

"Hell, Tommy Lee. This is starting to look like a swap meet." He nodded at the cheesy gifts stacked along the chalked circle.

I had to agree. They weren't the sort of keepsakes that tugged at a woman's heart.

A cool breeze ruffled my hair as the sunlight faded and dusk came on. It had to be five or six o'clock by now. I raised my jacket collar and gazed at Ryan, whose face, chest and arms were covered with a sheen of sweat. Even his drawstring pants were soaked through.

I needed to clean up for tonight's gig, unless the drummer I was spelling had finished his bout with bronchitis. I walked around the chalked circle until I faced my brother.

"Ryan, let's pull the plug on this." I gave him my best go-along-to-get-along smile. "What do you say?"

Ryan's eyes were focused on something in the distance, or nothing at all. His only response was the metronomic beat of the steel cable, nipping the pavement with each revolution. Miffed, I took in the growing ranks of Kopinski's brown-baggers. Maybe what I needed was a shot of whiskey.

A horn sounded, and a bright green Channel Eleven van pulled over, braking hard, barely missing a white Honda that cut across its path and skidded to a halt.

Recognizing the Honda, I groaned and joined Swensen.

"What?" he said.

"Here comes trouble."

Shirley Martin climbed out of her Honda wearing a khaki jumpsuit and work boots. She strode over, tucking her long red hair beneath the hard hat she wore at construction sites.

"Hello, Tommy Lee." She gave me a tight smile.

"Miss," said Swensen, touching the visor of his cap.

Ignoring Swensen, Shirley craned her neck, looking at Ryan.

"He's hard to forget," she said, sounding like she still held a grudge. "Mister Unstoppable, training with a jump rope."

"If it's such a fond memory," I grumbled, "why are you here?"

Keeping her eyes on Ryan, she shrugged. "Got a call from a girlfriend who drove by, telling me how weird this was. So I had to check it out." She stood on tiptoe, scanning the crowd, which had grown. "Look at that," she said, and pointed behind us.

Louie Chen was rolling his ancient Weber barbecue into the parking lot, with Romeo following, wagging his tail.

Shirley focused on Ryan, then nudged me. "Come on," she said. "Let's get closer."

Against my better judgment, I followed her as she slipped through the bystanders, maneuvering closer to the chalked circle.

"*Hey,*" she said, and clipped me with her elbow. "What's with your brother displaying our private history?" She glowered, gesturing at one of the piles Ryan had set out.

I started to ask what she meant. Then I recognized the vise grips I had sent her, asking her not to be such a ball buster with Ryan, once she started dumping him. But she must have figured the pliers were from Ryan, and sent them his way. Next to the vise grips were the presents Ryan had given her, knowing she was an electrical engineer. Atop a lava lamp, he'd placed a cassette tape featuring Debbie Boone's old single, "You Light Up My Life." At the base of the lamp, he'd fashioned a little nest from green-and-white strands of insulated wiring, then filled it with tiny candy hearts and tagged it with a note that said, "Be my lovebird!"

"Isn't that a bit personal?" Shirley yelled at Ryan, pointing at the stack.

Ryan gave her the same response I'd been getting. Silence. That and a thousand-yard stare, accompanied by the steady tattoo of his steel cable, rapping the pavement with each revolution.

"Ohmigod!" said Shirley, taking hold of my arm. "That's *Ellen's* stuff, isn't it?" She pointed out another stack of gifts.

I could see a black plastic derby, alongside a set of metal wickets that were duct-taped to a jar of honey. Without an attached love note, it took me a moment to figure it out. No doubt, this was Ryan's version of a "sticky wicket," and the plastic hat was his attempt at a proper British bowler. These were gifts he had sent to Ellen, a local croquet champion who liked to put on British airs, even though she admitted to being born and raised in Gladewater, Louisiana.

"How do you know Ellen?" I asked.

"Honey, pu-*lease,*" Shirley said, making a tsking noise. "I'm a card-carrying member of the Trahern Club."

When I blinked, dumbfounded, she gave me a look of pity. "I'm not kidding, Tommy Lee. It's a support group of women who have suffered the same fate—dating either of you Trahern brothers."

"Support group?"

"You know, sharing what we have in common—like the two of you resorting to your stupid ploys."

"Our what?"

"*Ploys.* Like your brother's reverse psychology—swearing he has to abstain from sex, because he's in training. Or you, carrying on, telling your latest heartthrob she's inspired you to write a love song."

Startled, I flashed on Natalie, shredding my love letters for compost, and realized I had recently penned a verse or two, using her name. One of the many songs I hadn't finished.

Rich black soil
Birthing flowers of grace,
With all that toil
Brightening her face.
Sweet Natalie, Sweet Natalie,
Won't you take the time...

Like most of my lyrics, I had started these on the tail end of a six-pack, convinced I was writing a hit...then abandoned them when I sobered up.

Behind me, a woman's voice said, "Oh this is good. *Really* good."

I turned and saw a perfectly coifed thirty-something brunette in a Kelly green double-breasted suit. When she raised the microphone with its Channel Eleven logo, I recognized her self-confident air, but couldn't recall her name. She anchored one of those bullshit shows they call a "news" magazine. Supposedly it featured lifestyles and regional news, but mostly it scraped bottom. Tabloid television, pure and simple.

"Could you repeat that?" she asked, thrusting her microphone at Shirley.

"Easy now," I said, and took hold of Shirley's elbow, turning her away from the microphone.

I whispered, "Can't you give Ryan a break? He's really down right now."

Behind us, angry voices sounded.

I did an about-face, joined by the anchorwoman and her cameraman.

Louie Chen and Karl Kopinski were arguing in front of Louie's barbecue, with Pete Swensen trying to referee as Romeo lowered his head and began growling, staying close to Louie.

"Hold on," Swensen told Kopinski, all the while keeping an eye on Romeo, whose ears were laid back. "Louie isn't stealing your customers."

"He *is*," Kopinski insisted.

"Then you tell me," said Swensen. "What's going to happen once they eat barbecued chicken? Especially Louie's chicken wings, loaded with enough spices to blow fire out your ass. Do I have to draw you a picture?" He pantomimed someone clutching his throat, then chugging a beer.

"Get a shot of them arguing," the anchorwoman told her cameraman. "Then we'll get the two brothers."

Off to my side, I heard Shirley say, "That's right, Ellen. Ryan Trahern, in the parking lot at Quik Stop Liquors."

When I faced her, she holstered her cell phone, looking smug.

Behind me, a hydraulic whine caught my attention. I watched as the van raised its microwave dish, setting up a direct feed to its TV studio.

By now the spectators around Ryan stood four or five deep, and I noticed more women were showing up. I started to exit the crowd when someone grabbed my arm. I turned, seeing the collapsed nose of Rafael Hermanez, a fighter from Brogan's Gym.

Puzzled, I asked, "Why are you here?"

He grinned, flashing teeth with gold caps. "Someone from PAL called, askin' for your brother. Then Brogan gets another call...some dude askin', is this some promotion Brogan cooked up—getting Ryan to go for some record, jumpin' rope. So Brogan sends me over, yelling, 'If any reporters show, talk up the gym.'"

Rafael paused, sneaking a look at Ryan. "So lay it on me, Tommy Lee. What's he doing?"

I shrugged. "Blowing off steam, I guess."

Rafael folded his arms, which rippled with muscle beneath his mahogany skin. "Izzat so? Over what?"

I scuffed the pavement with my Tony Lamas. "The usual."

Rafael gave me a sympathetic look, then a soft punch on the arm. "But not you, eh?"

I managed a weak smile. "His turn."

In the deepening dusk, he studied Ryan. "How long's he been at it?"

I squinted at my watch, barely able to read its face. "Nearly an hour and a half."

Rafael shoved a stick of gum into his mouth and nodded. "Got a good sweat goin'."

Several of the cars driving past had turned on their headlights. Their beams swept by, catching Ryan's gleaming torso and the glint of his spinning cable. He was breathing harder now, doing some fancy footwork. He bounced in place, doing a heel-toe motion. Then he raised a knee up high, jumping on one foot for a few beats, before switching to the other foot. With every maneuver, the steel cable sliced the air and popped the pavement, never missing a beat.

Rafael sniffed hard, facing the soft cherry glow of the barbecue that was crowded with Louie's sweet-and-sour chicken wings. "I'm gettin' some. Are you?"

Before I could answer, a harsh band of light cut across the parking lot. Raising my hand against the glare, I saw a cluster of lights by the Channel Eleven van.

Backlit, the woman with the microphone approached me, followed by her cameraman. "What's this about?" she asked. "Why are these women so fascinated with your brother?"

"Ask *him*," I said, certain that Ryan would ignore her. I looked toward Ryan, surprised by the crowd. Besides growing in size, it had rearranged itself, so that the women stood closest to Ryan, with the men further out. Somehow, it reminded me of junior high school dances, where boys and girls lined up on opposite sides of the room, with the dance floor looming between them.

"Sir? It's Thomas, isn't it?" asked the anchorwoman, stepping sideways, keeping in profile to the camera.

"Tommy Lee," I muttered and worked deeper into the crowd, trying to lose her. To make my drumming gig, I'd have to leave soon.

A wash of light bounced along behind me, illuminating those to either side, as I kept pressing ahead. Over my shoulder, I could see the compact floodlight, mounted on the camera.

Rafael must have seen how pissed I was, because he winked as I passed him. When I looked back, he was standing in front of Miss Microphone.

"Excuse me," she said.

"*No problema,*" he answered, chuckling as he stepped left then right, mirroring her every move. He kept blocking her path, the same way I'd seen him maneuver in the ring, cornering his opponent.

I grinned and turned sideways, squeezing through the crowd.

As I neared Ryan, the men were talking softly amongst themselves, and all of the women were quiet. Stone silent, in fact. But what really unnerved me was the innermost ring of women, spaced out along the chalked circle, holding hands—all women that Ryan had dated.

Behind me, I heard a scuffling noise, followed by a grunt. When I looked back, the floodlight on the camera had disappeared. A moment later the stand of floodlights by the van cut out.

I had to blink, adjusting to near darkness.

Louie's neon sign had burned out the year before last. Still, I could make out Ryan because of a distant street lamp, the first evening stars and the weak spill of light from Quik Stop Liquors.

Ahead of me, the women standing on the chalked circle were barely visible, but their perfumes—blending on the evening breeze—marked their presence like an exotic bouquet.

If it wasn't my own brother, half-naked at the center of it all, I might have stopped and enjoyed the moment. But the situation bothered me. Something seemed wrong, out of kilter in some fundamental way, especially with the men and women separating from each other.

"*Hey*," I called to Ryan. "You've put on your show, all right? Now you should leave."

He didn't answer, and I sensed the women turning to glare at me as I moved closer. I passed the last few men and reached the band of space between them and the women. Ahead, through the forest of legs, I saw a sliver of light as someone lit a candle and placed it on the chalked circle.

"Excuse me," I said. Turning sideways, I angled forward, joining the women who stood shoulder to shoulder.

More candles were lit and spaced out along the circle. They were orange with Chinese calligraphy running up their sides—New Year's candles from Louie's Bar.

Now I could see Ryan, bathed in sweat as he jumped in place with his back to me, splitting the air with his cable. He seemed at ease, but also out of place—the way things look in a dream. Also, the incessant buzz of his cable seemed unnaturally loud. For some reason that pissed me off, and I moved to my left, noting that the women holding hands hadn't closed the two-foot break in Ryan's chalked circle.

"Do you mind?" I asked, reaching the innermost ring of women, who all faced Ryan.

They parted, but I felt their resentment. Shirley Martin stood to my left with her red hair streaming to her shoulders, no longer wearing a hard hat. To my right stood Ellen, the croquet queen. Both of them—and the circle of women they held hands with—had their eyes fixed on Ryan, who seemed to be focused on something none of us could see.

It felt as if Ryan was waiting...like *everyone* was waiting, and that put me on edge.

"Ryan," I said, "this has gone far enough."

Silence—except for the nipping of his whirling cable hitting the pavement, and the barest scuffle from his feet as he bounced in place.

I chewed at my lip, trying to make sense of it.

"*Hombre*," a familiar voice whispered, just behind me.

I turned, seeing Rafael.

"Man, your brother, he's in tip-top shape. But this is pushin' it, you know? He's probably clocked two hours, whippin' that cable."

"So?"

"I'm tellin' you, man. Jumpin' rope two hours is like runnin' a marathon, all of it uphill."

With his warning, I felt the first glimmer of fear. Even Ryan had his limit.

Beyond the crowd, I heard the squawk of a police radio. Then Louie Chen's voice drifted over. "That's right, officer. A peaceful gathering. See for yourself."

"Not a problem," agreed the gruff voice of Karl Kopinski.

The muffled reply sounded friendly, but the hiss and crackle of the police radio continued.

One of their voices said, "Just to be safe."

Then the thrumming of Ryan's cable changed, growing louder as it moved faster.

Rafael called out, "Hey, Ryan. Take it home, dude. Call it a night."

Off to our side, another van with a satellite dish pulled over.

When I turned to look at Ryan, his eyes focused on mine. His expression was so intense that I flinched and stumbled, stepping back.

* * *

I feel a hand on my shoulder and look up from the couch. Doctor Carlson is kneeling beside me.

"Are you all right?" he asks.

"Hell no," I say, then roll my shoulders, dislodging his hand. "You think I'd be here if things were fine?"

He looks embarrassed, caught out in the open like that, on his knees—away from his chair and diplomas.

"Well…." He stands. "You've gotten this far before, Thomas. On two occasions."

Knowing what's coming, I don't answer.

He returns to his chair and retrieves his notebook and pen. "Are you willing to go further?"

I blink because my eyes are filling. I wipe at them with the heels of my hands.

"What was it about your brother's look that unnerved you?"

I shake my head softly.

Doctor Carlson sits back and waits, but I answer with silence.

He flips through his notebook, finds something and taps it with his finger. "The gifts," he says, looking up. "Why were they so important?"

I focus on the ceiling. "Who says they were?"

"Well, Thomas, it's you who keeps bringing them up. Then you back off." He turns to a fresh page in his notebook. "Have you noticed that?"

I pick at the scar tissue on my hand, wanting to skip over this.

"Afterwards," I finally admit, "the gifts offered clues."

"Of what sort?"

I stare at the ceiling as a tear wets my cheek. "It's just…." I take a deep breath. "It's just…." My voice fades as I hold still, resisting the urge to stand up and leave. But it's so damn hard, wanting to answer without the pain of remembering.

"Thomas?"

"The police," I say, then have to pause and take a breath. "They treated it like a crime scene. I guess, because of the confusion and panic, it wasn't clear what had happened."

"But—"

"*All right,*" I snap, cutting him off. "They knew *what* had happened. But how it happened, and what caused it…that much they had to investigate."

Carefully, he leans back and holds still.

"So the police sorted out the gifts," I say, hearing my voice rise in pitch. "Then they interviewed the women so they could match them up...you know, with the stuff Ryan had sent them."

When I don't continue, he says, "So...all of this sorting and matching...did that provide any answers? Any insights?"

I stifle an impulse to laugh, causing another tear to slide down my cheek. "Later," I say, "the police let me inspect their interview transcripts, inside a cinderblock room. For six hours straight, I read and re-read all of them."

I wipe away tears, recalling the room's bleak walls and stale air.

"What's odd," I recall, "is how different it was for each of the women. In their interviews, none of them used the same words, or offered the same description of what had happened. Yet they all agreed on one thing."

Doctor Carlson looks at me, waiting.

My mouth goes dry. I struggle to admit the strangeness of what I learned, because it's both an embarrassment and a great relief. "The particulars...." My voice turns hoarse, but I clear my throat. "The interviews profiled each woman and how my brother pursued her. In that way, each case was different. But every interview ended on the same note. With a change of heart. They all forgave him for his earlier behavior—each and every one of them."

He leans forward. "Did that surprise you?"

I laugh bitterly as a tear reaches my lips. I'm surprised by its salty taste and feel a sudden thirst—a longing for a draft beer in an iced mug, with a sinking shot glass of whiskey, trailing an amber bloom.

"Thomas?"

Startled, I feel the heat of my blush. *Don't give up*, I think. Not when you've come this far. I close my eyes, forcing myself to go back. Willing myself to recall an armload of transcripts and what I learned from them.

Looking at Doctor Carlson, I say, "Something changed for those women as they watched Ryan tough it out with that steel cable."

"Did you talk to any of them?"

I shake my head. "Only the police."

In a careful tone, he says, "Why not the women?"

"With the damn media hounding me like a pack of jackals? Following my every move?"

Doctor Carlson seems to think that over. "Let's go back to the interviews."

I take another breath, feeling lightheaded…just as I did that night, watching the play of light on Ryan from the candles that surrounded him, causing his shadow to shiver as he jumped in place.

"Thomas? Did the police say whether they were satisfied with their interviews?"

"Yes," I whisper. "They were. Except for the one woman who didn't come forward."

"Afterwards, you mean?"

I nod and clench my teeth, trying to resist the memory I feel rising to the surface. I suck in a lung-full of air and let it out. That doesn't help—or keep me from remembering.

I feel like I'm falling and squeeze my eyes shut.

* * *

Standing on the chalked circle, I was only a few feet from Ryan. He kept jumping in place, with the crowd shielding him from the wind. In the flickering candlelight, his skin glistened, and the cable took on a lower hum, dropping in pitch…the first sign that he couldn't maintain this pace…that he might be weakening—pushing his legs, lungs and heart to the limit.

I wanted to speak, but couldn't, as the silence pressed in on me. Overwhelmed, I faced my brother, watching for a shift in his eyes as the sweat poured off him, puddling on the pavement…fanned by the cable.

"*Tommy Lee?*" It was a harsh whisper, close to my shoulder. I turned and saw Rafael Hermanez, barely visible in the candlelight. "The rent-a-cop," he said, "Swensen?"

"Yeah?"

"He's on the phone talkin' to the police, askin' 'em to roll some EMT guys. Just in case."

My throat went dry. "You think he looks bad?"

"Not yet. But if he gets a chill, his muscles could cramp. And if he stops too quick, with his heart hammering like this—"

"Shit," I said. "The wind's picking up."

"That's why I talked to Louie."

Suddenly, my legs cast longer shadows, shooting past Rafael, and I looked behind me. On the chalked circle, someone had set out four of Louie's kerosene lamps. Their wicks burned brightly inside the curved glass covers.

Someone grunted, and I turned. Louie Chen knelt by my side, positioning the propane heater he had carried from his bar. It was the size of an office wastebasket. He set it near the gap in the chalked circle, forcing the women to edge around slightly. Bending over, Louie opened a valve. A soft hiss sounded, then Louie struck a match and there was the sudden whoosh of barely visible blue flame.

Louie smiled, looking from me to Ryan as the heater's coils began to glow, turning a soft reddish-orange. Romeo ambled to Louie's side, wagging his tail, then laid down, stretching out by the warmth of the heater.

"Ryan," I said, leaning forward, close to the buzz of his cable whipping past. "You've got to stop. You've gone too long. Whatever your point is—"

"*Point?*" Fiercely, he glared at me.

His wrathful stare was the same as our father's, and that startled me.

Usually, I remembered precious little of dad—who Ryan had come to resemble. But in that instant, in the look and the set of Ryan's shoulders, I glimpsed our father's fury.

As a mason, working with brick and stone, his frame had been packed with muscle, and he had the same crisp economy of movement that Ryan displayed as a boxer. That gave him a quiet sort of grace, but it soured—like the rest of him—when he drank. Then his grace seemed to fuel a simmering anger. And it only got worse when he tried to fix the rain-slick roof on our cottage and fell, crushing his left arm. After that, his temper began to rage, and turned on all of us.

* * *

"Is that what stopped you?" asks Doctor Carlson. "Ryan, reminding you of your father?"

"Yes," I answer, ashamed to admit it. "Soon after he ruined his arm, dad left us."

He leans back and doesn't blink as he watches me.

"Thomas?"

"What?"

"Is that what's stopping you? This link from Ryan to your father—of one loss to another?"

I'm confused as this connection glimmers for a second, then fades beneath my rising anger.

I sit upright, balling my hands into fists. "After dad left, we *had* to stick together. Within two years, mom died. Then Ryan and me had no one. Nothing but each other." I fight the impulse to cover my ears, not wanting to hear Doctor Carlson's next question.

"So you have old losses," he says gently. "And this new one."

I recall mom telling Ryan and me how our dad's leaving was for the best. We could get by, she assured us, on the welfare check. But her eyes told a different story. That we'd been flat-out abandoned.

"Losing mom," I say, "was much harder."

"Different than your father, who decided to leave," says Doctor Carlson.

I nod.

"Your mother had no choice."

After a long moment, I say, "Cancer is like that."

Before her illness, I remember mom caving in slowly. Once dad ran out on us, she worked two jobs to raise us, struggling the whole time. She fought hard, but it also seemed like a slow retreat on her part. As if she was waiting—hanging on, really—until her illness came. Then she got to lie down and rest.

"And your brother," says Doctor Carlson. "Did he have a choice? Or was it an accident?"

Panic gnaws at me and I close my eyes, suddenly skittish, as the weight of his question seems to press in on me.

* * *

I felt the warmth from the propane heater, fanned in my direction by the whirling steel cable. "*Enough*," I told Ryan. "Quit, or I'll make you."

The anger faded from his eyes, and he managed a weak smile. His way of laughing, I was sure, at the notion of me stopping him. But his smile couldn't hide the pain he was feeling. He wheezed now, taking each breath. His head hung lower, and his movements were more compact, so that he barely cleared the cable on each revolution.

Romeo edged closer to Ryan, whining softly, watching him.

"Please, Ryan," I said. "*Please*." And for a second, I thought he was going to stop.

Then he raised his head, looking past me.

When I turned, following his line of sight, I saw her some distance behind us, immersed in shadows. Slipping between the men, she headed our way, getting them to part as she moved forward. I strained for a better view and glimpsed her hair, golden, like sun-stroked wheat—but most of her was hidden by the men surrounding her.

I turned and looked at my brother, whose entire bearing had changed.

Sweat still drenched his body as he kept jumping, but his shoulders were upright—elevated by this surge of energy that flowed through him as the cable's hum grew louder. More than anything, his eyes had changed. They seemed to glitter in the candlelight. I turned again, following his gaze and saw that she had stopped, still bathed in shadows, not quite past the ring of men.

She didn't say anything, but the thrum of Ryan's cable shifted to a higher pitch.

When I glanced back, Ryan was double-timing as he jumped, running in place, pumping his knees nearly to his chest, like he did in training on the last thirty seconds of each three-minute round. But here, there was no bell. No round's end. No lull or break as he raced on, somewhere between frenzy and fury. His breath came heavy now—deep ragged pulls, causing his chest to heave.

The women surrounding the chalked circle stepped back, making room, as all of them faced the woman in the shadows.

I wanted to holler, *Ryan, for God's sake, stop.* But like the rest of the crowd, I succumbed to her spell as she took one more step.

I looked hard at my brother, whose eyes went wide for a second, as if startled by the hush that followed her—broken only by the rasp of his breath and the hum of the cable. And for that instant, he seemed almost suspended…in some shining state of grace, even though his frantic tempo hadn't slowed.

I twisted around, seeing something in the way that she stood, looking at him, and I had the feeling—in that split second—that a shift had occurred. Somehow, she had made it clear that she would go no further.

Turning back to my brother, I had the sense that he understood—more than anything, how final she wanted this to be.

His veins stood out on his chest, arms and forehead as the cable accelerated, whirling too fast to see. It made a staccato cracking, striking the pavement, fanning the candles so hard that their flames flickered.

Ryan turned to me, and his expression changed—filling with sadness, as the shadows around him seemed to tremble. Our eyes held for another second.

Then it happened.

He looked at her, set his jaw and leapt forward, whipping the steel cable so quickly that it disappeared in a hellish whine, slicing through the glass cover of a kerosene lamp.

In that terrible instant, I smelled the spilled kerosene.

Fanned by the churning steel cable, it was drawn into the slight vacuum that trailed, just behind its arc—surrounding Ryan with a kerosene mist that glistened in the candlelight.

As I cried out, the air seemed to vibrate, then seared with incandescence.

* * *

When I stop sobbing, Doctor Carlson gives me time to recover.

I ball my hands into fists, then clench harder, until my breathing slows.

I find myself hunched over, with my knees drawn to my chest.

Softly, Doctor Carlson says, "Are you able to continue?"

It takes me a minute to straighten out my legs and rearrange myself on the couch.

"Can you go on?" asks Doctor Carlson.

"Not about Ryan," I whisper. "Or what happened to him."

He raises one hand, as if to reassure me. "Then what followed," he says in a gentle voice. "Let's talk about that."

I take a breath and let it out. "About her, you mean?"

He shuts his notebook. "Maybe that would help. For instance...why do you think she didn't come forward? Afterwards, I mean."

A ragged tremor runs through my body. "I think what happened that night...I mean, what she saw—"

"Yes?"

I press both palms to my forehead. "I suppose it messed her up."

"Messed her up," Doctor Carlson says. "In what way?"

"*Shit*, how do I know? Probably she was afraid." I feel short of breath.

"Afraid," he says, "of what?"

"The horrible death she witnessed. Or maybe the media freaked her out, circling like vultures." My words, I realize, are rushed.

Gently, he taps the pen against his notebook.

"What?" I ask.

"*At the time*, you're saying, that's what you believed—about her not coming forward?"

"Yes."

"What about now? Has anything changed?"

I feel a knot in my chest, and my hands curl back into fists. "Why don't you spit out whatever you're getting at?"

Doctor Carlson squares his shoulders. "What I'm suggesting, Thomas, is that you no longer believe any of that kept her from coming forward."

"*Bullshit*," I say. "You may think you're 'dialed in' to me and what I believe, but you're not."

"Just look at the way you're sitting, so rigid, with your arms crossed."

"*So?*"

"I'm asking, because it might ease the pain you're feeling."

"Asking what?"

Speaking slowly, he says, "What if you've come to realize that *isn't* what held her back? Not your brother's death, or the media."

My insides twist, and the room seems to flatten out. I struggle to breathe. "Why does she even count?" I demand. "It's my brother we're talking about. *He's* the one who died."

"True. But is he the only one who suffered?"

I slap the couch with the flat of my hand. "So she didn't come forward. Who gives a shit? This is *not* about her."

"*Exactly.*" He keeps his eyes on mine.

All at once, I feel completely exposed, sitting on the couch. Exposed and trapped.

Doctor Carlson pauses, suddenly cautious, as if we are down to a single, fragile thread, running from me to him. My stomach churns. I think he's going to ask what I did when my brother caught fire.

Instead, I want him to ask what I think of *her*. And whether I've come to hate her.

In a voice so soft that I can barely hear it, he says, "Tell me, Thomas. Afterwards, when she didn't come forward, did the police try to find her?"

Feeling off balance, I nod.

"How did they do that?"

I draw a shaky breath. "First, they looked for something from my brother. You know...a note." At that instant, I realize I'm in too deep, with no way out.

"A final note," he suggests.

"Yes." I feel disloyal to my brother, admitting this. But now I can't seem to stop. "They checked the remains of his clothes," I add. "Then his car. Then his home." I take a deep breath, feeling dizzy.

"Go on."

I have the urge to roll off the couch, as if—somehow—that will allow me to escape. But I can't find the strength to move.

"Please, Thomas. Keep talking."

I lie back, too tired to argue.

"At his place," I say, "aside from the gifts and letters returned by the women he'd chased, all they found was ordinary stuff. Like a grocery list. His calendar and checkbook." My voice drops to a whisper. "Nothing unusual...except the collection of lyrics."

Doctor Carlson sets his notebook aside. "Please. Tell me about the lyrics."

My shoulders shake, and my chest begins to heave, but no tears come. "*My* lyrics," I choke out. "From all the songs I never finished. Ones I must've shared when we bar hopped, moaning and groaning about the women who'd dumped us."

He nods and waits.

When I don't speak, he says, "Did you know he had saved them?"

"No." I wipe my nose with the back of my hand. "Half the time, I didn't think he was listening. But it got to be a habit, me reciting whatever I was working on, half-singing, half-talking my way through the lyrics."

Doctor Carlson gets up and steps forward, holding out a box of tissues.

"A few of my verses," I say, grabbing a tissue, "...a few were so down and out, that the police thought they'd found a suicide note."

He pauses. "The police didn't realize the words were yours?"

"No, because Ryan had written my lyrics from memory. So everything was in his handwriting." I stop and blow my nose.

Doctor Carlson sits down. He gives me a minute, then says, "So there wasn't any note."

I shake my head and crumple the tissue I'm holding. "Still, the police kept trying. They wanted to figure out who she was...this mystery woman."

"Using the gifts?"

I pause, still light-headed, feeling like I'm half-floating instead of lying on the couch. "Doc," I say, "where are we going with this? How does any of this—"

"*Thomas*," he interrupts. "You're making progress."

"This? You call this progress?"

"I do. Just talking about it—anything that gets you further along. Whatever bits and pieces you remember."

"Like what?" I say, wanting to believe him.

"Well, like the police. You said they tried to find her, using the gifts?"

I shake my head. "Not at the beginning. They started off interviewing people who had been there—hoping to get a description of her. Except no one agreed what she looked like."

Doctor Carlson steeples his hands. "So that part, her physical description, was never resolved."

Of course, from the glimpses I got, I have my own version...my own recollection, which I sometimes alter when I play things back in my mind. As if that could change how it ended.

"Without a description," says Doctor Carlson, "what did the police do?"

"It gets even stranger. Pretty soon, folks who weren't there claimed they had been." I stare at my hands, clasping my knees, which I've drawn up to my chest. "On top of that, a few women—eager for the spotlight—insisted they were the mystery woman. So the police had to start over."

"How?"

"Working from television footage. They identified a lot of people who *had* been there and interviewed them. Despite that, no one could identify her. And no one remembered her saying a single word, or being spoken to—not by Ryan or anyone else." My knees start to hurt, so I release them and stretch my legs out.

"Finally," I say, "the cops considered the gifts around the chalked circle, shifting their attention to the one pile no one had claimed."

Doctor Carlson nods.

"But that led nowhere. Nothing had her name or address on it. Not even the postcards."

He raises his eyebrows. "So there *were* postcards. I'd heard…." He stops, probably recalling my cursing fits over the talk shows, with all the leaks and rumors they broadcast during the investigation.

"That's okay," I answer, not holding it against him that he watched the shows like everyone else. "These were postcards he had sent to her. That much they got right."

Doctor Carlson pauses, looking puzzled. "But you said there was no address on anything the police found at your brother's home."

"Hand-delivered, I guess. Then returned the same way."

"Ah." He smoothes one corner of his mustache. "Was her name on any of the postcards?"

"Not a one." I half-smile at the irony of it, the way she managed to stand Ryan on his head, to the point where his typically clumsy overtures began to verge on elegance. "He only addressed her as *the one who captures my heart*, or *soul mate*, or *the wings of my desire.*

There was no description of her. No mention of whatever they might've done together, or any places where they might've met."

"What *was* on the postcards?"

Picturing them, all turned over to the photographs they displayed, I recall beautiful green landscapes with open fields, lush with wildflowers, beneath magnificent clouds. "Ireland," I say, with a crushing sense of loss. "They were all postcards of Ireland."

"Was there writing of any sort?"

I nod. "On each of them he'd scrawled, it seems, different parts of a poem. Only fragments, though. Each postcard held less than a verse."

"A poem...." He tugs at the corner of his mustache. "A poem he was quoting, or something he had written?"

I look at my fingertips and palms, burned from grabbing at Ryan, then losing him to the blistering flames that drove me to my knees.

"His words, I think. At least I couldn't find any published poem that matched what he'd written."

Doctor Carlson purses his lips. "But...looking at the postcards, surely they must have suggested *something* about this woman." He lifts his eyebrows, looking hopeful.

Slowly, I shake my head. "Only the feelings he had for her. And that was the amazing part, because nothing about the postcards or gifts he sent her seemed to come from the brother I knew. Nothing resembled anything he had ever given to another woman. Everything was...too thoughtful, like the silver pendant—a Celtic talisman."

"Celtic?"

"Most every gift he sent her expressed a longing for Ireland. *Her* longing, I think, although it's clear he wanted to share her dream. Hell, he even purchased a pair of airline tickets. Open-ended, without any departure date."

"Then—"

I interrupt, shaking my head. "There weren't any names. Just two open tickets, to Ireland—back when you could buy such things from the airlines, without a name or address, or proving your identity."

Doctor Carlson leans back in his chair, quite intent as he studies me.

After a long silence, he asks, "Do you think he could have saved himself, once the fire started?"

His question cuts like a knife. To get past the pain, I draw a deep breath.

"No," I find myself admitting. "I don't think so." To my surprise, my voice is suddenly calm, as if it's someone else speaking.

Quietly, Doctor Carlson says, "Why not?"

The truth, I realize, is a form of a betrayal. At least it feels that way, sharing it with someone else.

"Thomas?"

"I don't believe he wanted to be saved." Saying that, I stare at my fingertips, examining their milky white scar tissue, as though it's something I haven't seen before.

"Either that," I add, "or what he did was an act of self-sacrifice."

"How?"

"Giving his life up to save someone else."

He sits there taking that in...not writing in his notebook. "Doesn't it matter a great deal," he says, "which of those it was? Suicide or self-sacrifice?"

I think of all the phone conversations I've had, inside my cubicle at the bereavement center—trying to help others grasp what can't be undone. I think about the changes I underwent...of being anxious to speak, until I learned to listen. Learned to embrace the stumbling words and halting sobs of men, women and children, ripped and torn by grief. Learned to let them recite the details, to see their loss clearly, then let it go. Whenever they could get that far.

I raise my eyes to Doctor Carlson. "I'd like to know. To be certain," I add, "that it was *his* choice—not something I could have saved him from." I keep my eyes open, wanting to see this room instead of the flames I remember, wrapping around my brother's legs, then racing upward to embrace his body.

Doctor Carlson looks away, giving me a moment.

I grab a tissue and wipe at my eyes and nose. The room seems too bright. When I sit up, a tremor runs through me.

"Thomas," he asks softly. "After the funeral, did you try to find her?"

I focus on Doctor Carlson's chin instead of his eyes.

"Did you?" he asks.

I take a ragged breath and release it slowly. "I considered making an appeal and asking her to come forward. You know, on television or radio. But the way the media kept hounding me and prying...then taking how my brother had lived and turning it into a spectacle—"

"So you didn't seek her out. For the sake of Ryan's privacy?"

I shake my head. "Because of his last wishes...at least, what I thought his last wishes were."

Doctor Carlson waits until I find the strength to finish.

"He died," I say, "over something he refused to continue, or wouldn't begin." I stare at my hands. "I doubt that I'll ever know which."

"His need to break his destructive cycle," says Doctor Carlson, "that much I can understand. But the price he paid—"

"No, you *don't* understand." I tremble as tears spill down my face. "All our lives, whoever we desired was out of reach because we were out of control. So maybe, for Ryan, it was less painful to end it. To escape whatever drew him into such misery."

Doctor Carlson waits.

Once my tears ease, he looks at me carefully. "Hasn't that left you with some questions?"

I stifle a bitter laugh. "*Questions?*" I squeeze my eyes shut, recalling the look on my brother's face as I reached for him through a wall of flames. For a split second, at least, his expression wasn't one of pain. For the longest time after it happened, I asked myself, was it resignation that showed in his eyes—in that last look he gave me? Or was it something else? Now, in my heart, as I lie on Doctor

Carlson's couch, clutching a wad of soggy tissues, it comes to me. Finally, I understand.

It was a look of *relief.*

As that sinks in, I am stunned, but certain. And I realize why he did it.

Doctor Carlson leans forward. Gently, he asks, "For you, Thomas, what's the most important question?"

I don't answer.

"Is it about her? Or your brother?" He lowers his voice. "Or you?"

His question sits like a weight on my chest.

"None of those," I answer quietly. "It's about making amends."

Satisfied, I stand up and start for the door.

He glances at his watch, then gives me a questioning look. "Shall we set a time for next week?"

I pause, taking a final look at Doctor Carlson, his diplomas, and the whole office. "No. Let's not."

I hear him get up as I open the door and step into the reception area. Then I grasp the next doorknob, opening the outer door.

Behind me, he says something, but I keep walking.

As I take the steps down to the sidewalk, I squint against the afternoon sun, hanging low in a pewter sky. The overcast sun is glaring, almost incandescent...but I don't look away.

It's four blocks to the parking lot, and I start walking, past scattered leaves that have fallen from the elms lining the street. The fall breeze picks up, cold against my face, and I think of my brother's ashes. I picture the spot where I placed them nearly three years ago. Out of respect.

They rest inside a simple mahogany box, big enough to hold a fifth of whiskey, which sits on a shelf overlooking Louie's bar. On top of the box, covered with a layer of dust, is a pair of open tickets booked to Ireland. They're paper-clipped together—along with a single postcard that shows a stone cottage, bleached from weather and age, surrounded by a glorious green meadow in Wicklow, Ireland.

But what no one else will ever see is the sheet of paper, surrounded by Ryan's ashes and bits of bone, that I sealed inside that mahogany box. On that paper is the one song I've written that truly sings. It reaches to the depths of my heart, which makes it a song I surely could sell. But it's one I never wish to hear…not from some hit singer on the radio, or any band working a nightclub.

It's my best and last song. My goodbye to Ryan.

And now it becomes something more. My thanks for his love. And for the searing flames that freed me from my own destruction.

Terry Bennett

Wishbone

I n wrestling, it's called *grappling*, when opponents seize each other, seeking an advantage. In boxing, it's called *looking for an opening*—the chance to deliver a knockout punch. In my family, it's called *conversation*.

"Don't do that," mother said.

"Do what?" I answered, removing a speck of mashed potatoes from my mustache.

"*That*," she said, pointing past the nose of my sister, Paula. "Ignoring the gravy your sister made."

I glanced at the small stoneware gravy boat. "But I don't like it. Never have."

Mother smiled, touching her lace collar. "Of course you do."

I turned to Paula, whose Sonoma State sweatshirt revealed a slip in stature, following last year's expulsion from Mills.

"If I skip the gravy, am I hurting your feelings?"

She inclined her head so that her shoulder-length hair tipped forward, hiding her smirk from mother. "Feelings?" she said. "Around here?"

Mother poked Paula in the shoulder. "What's *that* supposed to mean?"

"Mean?" Paula echoed.

"Yes," mother said, spooning cranberries onto Paula's plate. "You've had your share of opportunities, the way we've raised you."

Facing the living room, I caught the flicker of the television screen, and longed for the relief it offered. The Packers versus the Bears on a snow-swept field....

"Thomas," mother chided. "You're drifting away."

Offering what passed for a smile, I gave her one of my best moves. Silence. Shifting to my saintly expression, I bowed my head and addressed my plate, rearranging peas and pearl onions.

Paula couldn't stand it.

"Tommy dear," she began. The sweetness in her voice confirmed how much trouble I was in.

I leaned toward the gravy boat, hoping to distract mother with my boarding house reach, but Paula was faster.

"Why didn't you invite that young lady you're seeing?" Paula's emphasis was on "young", as opposed to the same-aged wife I had divorced in June, after the collapse of our twelve-year marriage.

With my arm half-extended, I turned to dad, desperate for an assist. Unless he spoke up, mother would skewer me with questions.

Dad blinked, touching his pocket protector, brushing a collection of worn mechanical pencils. "Son?" he said.

Sitting there, he looked like he had back when I'd seen him at work twenty years ago, when he had all but disappeared into the sheets of vellum on his drafting table, tracing the elevation, arc and radius of freeway interchanges, one after another, in an endless succession of engineering projects.

He blinked again, clearing his throat, then nodded at the turkey. "Wishbone?" he offered.

"Excuse me?" said mother.

Dad hesitated, looking from mother to me.

"What's her name?" Paula asked.

"Dad, that's a *great* idea." I set aside the gravy boat and picked up the turkey platter, centering it on the table.

"The candles!" mother said. "Be careful."

I rolled up my sleeves, then reached inside the bird, feeling its moist heat against my hand. I found the breastbone and gripped it.

With a twist, I pulled it free, holding it up, and looked at dad. "Are you ready?"

"Nonsense," mother said. "It has to dry."

Swallowing a laugh, Paula added, "Well, so much for that."

Mother turned on Paula, who drew back in her chair. "You find this amusing?"

I scrubbed the wishbone with my napkin, stripping off gristle and grease. "Come on, Dad. You and me."

I could sense him weighing the price he would pay for taking my side.

Come on, I thought. *You're* the one who offered. But something held him back.

"The wishbone's pretty slippery," I said. "Should we step away from the table?"

When I inclined my head toward the living room, something new entered his expression. A sudden awareness. Like the halfback who's been hammered all day, running to his left, then glimpses daylight—there for the taking—if he can reverse his field.

He stood. "You're right. Into the living room."

We were moving by the time mother recovered. "Stay away from that television," she ordered.

Dad and I squared off by his easy chair, which was tilted back in its reclining position. The length of its leather surface was so creased and worn that it carried the imprint of his body—like the weight of an invisible man.

Over my shoulder, I smiled at Paula, marooned with mother.

"Ready?" dad asked, gripping his end of the bone.

"Make a wish," I said. "Whatever you want."

"Well," he said, sounding hopeful. "Wouldn't *that* be something."

"*George*," mother said, drawing it out. Turning his name into a before-the-fact admonishment. "We're waiting."

Holding his end of the wishbone, dad closed his eyes and began moving his lips without speaking. Like someone praying.

His silence drew me in, filling me with curiosity. I wanted to know. Wanted to enter whatever he wished for. Shutting my eyes, I willed the wishbone to connect us, like a divining rod.

In that instant, I recalled a series of photographs from our family albums. Him standing tall in his Air Force uniform. Grinning. Books under his arm. Studying to become a combat pilot, before the training injury that ruined one eye. Then five years later, him in jeans and a windbreaker, thin and energetic—building this house. Hammer in hand, with a cigarette dangling from his mouth. Then twelve years later, in his new junior college sweatshirt, from the night courses he was taking. The two of us standing shoulder-to-shoulder, with me in my high school letter-jacket and both of us laughing. His last hurrah before extracting my university tuition from a job that was eating him alive, between a spiteful boss and squads of younger men overtaking him with college degrees.

When I opened my eyes, he was watching me.

"Ready when you are," I managed to say.

Still thinking of the photos, I adjusted my grip on the wishbone, hoping he would get the bigger piece, along with his wish.

"We're waiting," mother announced.

I glanced at Paula. She had the opportunity to escape, with dad and me to blame it on.

Returning my look, she placed her silverware on her plate, then stood, adding my plate to hers.

"Paula?" said mother.

"Just clearing the table." She strode toward the kitchen before mother could object.

Mother glared at me and dad. "Thank you so much for disrupting our dinner."

A smile tugged at the corner of dad's mouth. "The wishbone," he said.

Its greasy surface was difficult to grip, but we began to pull. Slowly. Steadily. Watching each other at first, then the wishbone as it bent.

It broke—taking me by surprise. But I was happy, coming up with the short end.

Dad grinned in triumph, and I clapped him on the shoulder…as close as I ever came to giving him a hug.

"So, Dad. What's it going to be? An exotic dancing girl, dressed in one-hundred beads—"

"—ninety-nine of which are perspiration," he answered, happy-go-lucky now, that phrase leaping to our minds from some long-forgotten story he had told me before the subdivisions arrived. When our home was still surrounded by young apricot orchards on an endless carpet of deep, rich soil.

"Sit down," mother insisted, "for dessert."

Dad eyed me, patting his shirt pocket the way he used to, before he gave up smoking. "You still smoke those cigars?"

"Not in *this* house," mother said.

Dad winked. Our freedom was at hand.

"Outside," I said. "I usually keep a few in my truck."

Paula reentered the dining room, scooping up dishes, then made a wide turn, heading for the kitchen.

"Don't be long," mother called after us.

As we stepped outside, I felt the heat of my mother's gaze on the back of my neck.

* * *

The half-dozen apricot trees that remained were bare except for a few withered yellow leaves that hung on, nearly lost in the purple dusk and dark cast of overhead clouds, heavy with moisture. Beyond the trees, the simple country road once fronting our home had become a four-lane highway, filled with cars whizzing past.

Climbing into my dilapidated pickup, dad said, "That was pretty slick, back there."

I grinned, then turned on the dome light, surprised to notice that his hair was thinning, with streaks of silver among the gray.

I reached across and opened the glove compartment. Debris spilled out. Old vehicle registrations. Notes to myself. A chewed up pencil, half its original size. A music cassette with that Credence Clearwater song that I loved—"Up Around the Bend."

But no cigars.

I turned out the dome light. "We could buy some at the all-night drugstore."

He started to speak. I expected him to say it didn't matter, but he stopped, looking back toward the house as he rubbed his Adam's apple.

"Let's do it," he said, sounding twenty years younger.

I started the engine, turned on the headlights and slipped into first gear, easing up to the mouth of the gravel driveway. "Coming right up. Two cigars."

"Big fat cigars," he said, giving me the double-eyebrow lift. His version of Groucho Marx, minus the glasses and the duck walk and the mustache.

"*Stinkin'* cigars," I said, upping the ante.

"*Horrendous* cigars," he countered, clearly in command of the situation.

Spotting a break in the traffic, I tromped the accelerator, spewing gravel as we shot into the gap, clearing second gear at forty miles an hour.

Both of us laughed, then settled into a silence as I signaled and cut over to the inside lane.

Above us, the stars were hidden beneath a canopy of dark clouds, while the crowded highway stretched out before us, outlined by opposing streams of light, one pearl-white and the other ruby-red. As I shifted again, accelerating, I began to regret how short our journey would be. Fifteen minutes, tops.

Dad touched my shoulder, bringing me back. "A penny for your thoughts."

That surprised me. It was something he used to say, but hadn't for years. No doubt because I hadn't done much listening since leaving home. But it felt different, coming from him now. It seemed more of a signal than a question. His way of letting me know that he was on the outside, waiting to be let in.

He hesitated, then squeezed my shoulder. "I often think of you."

Again, I didn't answer, but strong feelings welled up and my eyes began to sting. Slowly, the space between us filled with emotion. His and mine, as something passed between us. I couldn't say what exactly, but I could almost touch it.

A gust of wind rocked the car, and I tightened my grip on the steering wheel. Without meaning to, I found myself asking, "How do you keep on?"

Immediately, I felt bad and wished I could take it back. I hadn't meant to weigh him down. Not now. Not like this. But with my life so tangled in disappointments, I was desperate for answers.

Embarrassed, I drove a little faster, feeling the warm flush in my cheeks.

Instead of answering, he paused and looked beyond the traffic, which I realized was his way of taking in the question. Deciding what could be done with it.

Raindrops dotted the windshield and slid downward, shimmying against the wind, blurring the cars ahead of us. I turned the windshield wipers on low.

Finally, he said, "It's a long road. But you can't avoid it."

Tail lights flared as cars began to slow, approaching the intersection.

In my head, I repeated his answer, feeling a touch of panic. "I don't get it."

He nodded patiently.

Seeing the red light at the intersection, I downshifted, then stopped, waiting for his response.

Now I was able to accept the amount of time he took, addressing my question—unlike in high school, when my struggles with homework had drawn the same nod. Usually in mathematics, with me wanting the answers instead of his help—because, back then, I had to stifle my agitation, knowing I was going to hear it all.

First the theory, then the formula, followed by every factor that could possibly affect the answer.

Only somehow it felt different now, after so many years. Not like a lecture coming. More like a secret he was about to share.

The sparse raindrops became a drizzle as the light turned green and traffic started moving.

"Your dreams," he said. "The ones you hold too tightly?" He paused, touching his pocket protector. "They're the ones that get left behind. Almost like a piece of yourself, abandoned at the side of the road."

As I accelerated, I recalled *his* dream, of being a jet pilot. Someone whose trajectory would divide the sky.

"But," he added, "part of you has to go on." He looked at me expectantly.

"Which part?"

As I drove, I watched him from the corner of my eye, thinking it had to be the mind. But what if he meant the heart?

He shrugged, but it wasn't like he had given up. More like he had accepted something. A realization of some sort that I couldn't grasp.

Truly, I was grateful for his advice, but it confused me. And I found myself afraid to ask more questions. What if he couldn't answer?

I didn't want the sort of pain that came from expecting too much. Then it struck me, that it might be the same for him. Or maybe the way he saw things, it was *me* asking too much, instead of him saying too little.

"Dad, what I meant—"

He started to speak, then shook his head so slightly that I barely saw it.

I waited, biting my lip, so that I wouldn't interrupt his thoughts.

Several cars back, someone honked his horn as traffic slowed and raindrops began to fall harder, spattering the windshield, obscuring our view.

He took a breath and curled his fingers, then made a fist that trembled slightly as he raised it.

"Ignore the darkness," he said, "and stay on the road."

My mind raced. What did he mean, stay on the road? Thinking about it, I wondered how often he had come to a halt and abandoned himself, instead of pushing ahead. As if knowing that would lessen my own confusion.

I turned to him, trying to read his expression and the set of his shoulders. "Dad?" I said. "What happens if I do that?"

He lowered his fist, relaxing his hand. "You get another chance, like back in the living room."

Off to the side, I saw the drugstore and slowed down. Flipping the turn signal, I swung into the parking lot, then slipped my truck into an open space.

"All of us get lost," he said, "but you can find your way back."

He gazed across the parking lot, as if it were a vast distance, then nodded, almost to himself. "Only it doesn't happen the way you think."

I shut off the engine and faced him, half holding my breath as I tried to be still and listen. "Then how does it happen?"

He pursed his lips and shook his head. "That's hard to explain."

I waited.

After a moment, he gestured at the parking lot, ringed with puddles. "It happens…like this, in little moments that can pass you by. Like getting cigars, and being together."

I thought of all the moments I had missed, letting them slip past while I wallowed in self-pity, or blamed those closest to me for the life I was living.

We sat there a while longer, and I felt less anxious. Less apprehensive. Not like I'd been saved, or undone any of my mistakes. But at least I saw a difference. Something I could try for.

He sat there, letting me work it through. Giving me the time I needed. Finally, I gave him a little nod. He returned it, and we got out of the truck. Thunder rumbled softly as we crossed the glisten-ing asphalt, side by side. We were close enough that I could have thrown my arm across his shoulders. But I didn't. Instead, we kept walking, with neither of us saying a word. Just walking. Then, as I thought about it, I squared my shoulders and adjusted my pace, matching my stride to his.

Terry Bennett

Matinee

Brad? Did you hear me?"

"What?" I leaned across the kitchen table. Through the doorway, I could see the lower half of the bedcovers, steepled by Monica's legs.

"Bring me the entertainment section."

I took another bite of toast, set down the sports page and picked up "Out and About," which I'd been using as a place mat. Keeping it level, I reached over to the wastebasket with the plastic liner, then tilted the folds of paper and gave them a few sharp raps, knocking off the crumbs.

"Did you hear me?" she said, drawing it out.

I walked into the bedroom and reached out, offering her the pages.

"Wait." She put my pillow on top of hers, shoving them against the headboard. Then she sat back and began arranging her tangle of auburn hair.

"Sometime soon?" I said, my arm still extended.

She gave me a tight smile, took it from me, then flipped open the cinema insert, which she set on her lap.

As I started back to the kitchen, she said, "How about a movie?"

I stopped.

"Well?" She looked up.

Instead of answering, I walked back around the bed and raised the window shade. Clouds the color of ashes crowded the sky, while elm leaves tumbled across our lawn, coating it with scattered shades of brown that flickered and tossed.

"Matinee?" I said.

"Why? Because it's cheaper?"

I shrugged. "You're the one who splurges on popcorn."

She smiled. "Better popcorn than a shopping spree."

I was tempted to answer, but knew she wasn't being serious. For Monica, Sunday shopping was like Holy Communion— something to be observed without fail.

She turned the page. "Any show in particular?"

Running my fingers across my chin, I could feel stubble, but decided not to shave. I said, "What's playing at the Carlton?"

"Why?" She bent over, studying the listings.

"After the movie, we could cruise the bookstore."

She took a single sheet of newspaper and held it out, toward the light of the window.

"What's this?" She touched a red translucent smear on the newsprint.

"Strawberry jam, from my toast."

She made a "tsking" noise.

"Come on," I said.

She lowered the newspaper. "If it was the sports section, you'd be ticked."

I fought the urge to roll my eyes. "Fine."

She creased the movie section and opened it back up, holding it at arm's length.

"So," I said. "What movie are you thinking of?"

"Well, there's a new one with Jennifer Aniston that's supposed to be sweet." She flipped a page. "Here it is. *She's the One*, at the Emerald."

"Please," I said. "Let's skip the chick-flicks, okay? Save those for a night out with your lady friends."

She lowered the newspaper, pursing her lips. *"Chick*-flicks?"

"You know. The tear-jerkers."

"What's wrong with some honest emotion?"

"Come on. Those films are *anything* but honest. They're packed with false sentiment. That's why women who watch them are manipulated."

"What do you mean, manipulated?"

"Drowned in a deluge of saccharine emotions. As if that's going to solve everything in real life, let alone on the big screen."

"Saccharine? That's how you describe women's feelings?"

"You know what I'm talking about."

She held up a movie review with a photo of Jennifer Aniston. "This says *She's the One* is about family, Brad. Not just women."

"With a female lead? One who made her career starring as a clueless babe in a feel-good sit-com like *Friends?"*

She gave me an exasperated look and dropped the newspaper in her lap. "So what's left? Something starring Sylvester Stallone?"

I grinned. "Come on. You make it sound like I'm narrow-minded. Or worse yet, guilty of the worst male sin imaginable...*insensitivity."*

She thrust out her chin. "Aren't you?"

"Hell, no."

She responded with a triumphant smile. "Prove it, then. Pick a movie that's somewhere in the middle."

I thought about it. "Okay. Something with Mel Gibson. I know you like him. *And* his ass."

"Butt."

I rolled my eyes. "Whatever."

"Don't get smug. That doesn't mean I want to see him and Danny Glover shooting up half of Los Angeles in some raucous cop movie."

"Hey! Gibson's also done some serious stuff."

She crossed her arms. "For instance?"

"*Braveheart.*"

She laughed, shaking her head. "Talk about a monument to *machismo*—"

"Yeah? Well, what about that role he had with Julia What's-her-name?"

"Who?"

"Roberts. Julia Roberts."

Monica shook her head. "No way. They were never in anything together."

"Oh yeah?" I snapped my fingers. "They were in something about government schemes and brainwashing." I kept snapping my fingers, trying to think of the title. "Yeah, that's it." I said. "*Conspiracy Theory.*"

"Shit." She laughed, shaking her head. "You're right."

"*See?*"

She began to frown, looking at the newspaper. "So what's right for us?"

I shrugged, then sat on the edge of the bed. "Let me take a peek."

She raised her eyebrows, offering a coy smile. "Now you're talking." With one finger, she slipped a lacy strap off her shoulder, revealing the break in her tan line.

Turning away, I picked up the entertainment section, opening it to the motion picture listings.

"Brad?"

"How about *Passenger 57*, with Wesley Snipes?"

"Please, Brad. Don't."

Still looking at the newspaper, I heard her sigh, then felt the bed shift as she threw back the covers and got up, followed by the slap of her bare feet, crossing the oak floor as she walked to the bathroom.

I scanned the same movie advertisements she'd been studying. I didn't bother reading the self-serving blurbs they quoted, supposedly from enthralled movie critics whose sound-bite accolades reminded me of shish-kabob—tiny morsels of praise, skewered by ellipses and omissions.

When I lowered the newspaper, I could hear her peeing, leaving the door open the way she does. Then the flush of the toilet.

"Speaking of Julia Roberts," she called out, "how about *My Best Friend's Wedding?*"

"No way. That's double jeopardy. It would be like attending a wedding *and* a chick-flick. For Christ's sake, I've seen the previews."

Water ran in the sink for a few seconds, then she appeared in the doorway.

"Brad, forget about films as gender-wars, okay?"

It sounded like the start of a lecture, so I shrugged. "Whatever you say."

"Really, Brad. We don't need any more of the Mars-Venus thing."

"No kidding." Too late, I gave her a half-smile.

She folded her arms and frowned, resting one hip against the doorframe.

I waited.

"How about it?" she said. "Are you up for a movie or not?"

I met her gaze, then looked into the kitchen. I got off the bed, handed her the newspaper and walked back to my sports page and my half-eaten breakfast.

When I sat at the table, steam no longer rose from my coffee. I could see the thin, translucent film of grease that had congealed on the eggs I had fried, alongside my bacon.

"Brad," she said, "forget about movies that are *just* for guys, or for chicks."

"Yeah? Like how?" I leaned forward, looking through the doorway. "You mean, by forgetting who we are?"

"That's not what I'm saying."

I raised my palms. "Then what are you saying?"

"Why do you make things difficult, when it could be so simple, working out something?"

I turned a page in the sports section, to check the NFL standings. "For instance?"

"Instead of a chick-flick or a guy-flick, how about a movie that's like us?"

I lowered the sports section and just looked at her.

Her cheeks colored. She strode to the bed and snatched up the movie section.

While she rifled the pages, I used my fork, poking at a cold strip of bacon.

Checkout #5

W

illiam tipped the take-out carton upside down and poked inside it with his chopsticks. The last few noodles of tomato beef chow mein dislodged and landed on his plate, hitting two fortune cookies.

Below the kitchen table, William's miniature collie, Shorty, circled anxiously, the nails of his paws clicking on the linoleum.

"In a minute," William said softly.

After eating all but one of the noodles, he smiled and bent over, dangling the last noodle below the table. Shorty backed up toward the stove, then rushed forward. He gulped down the noodle as his wagging tail thumped the nearest packing box.

Similar boxes occupied most of the apartment, stacked from floor-to-ceiling. None of them were labeled, but as William glanced at the one touching his right knee, he knew what it held. It was jammed with the empty seed packets he had collected each spring from Grandpa Waller's vegetable gardens, until his death two years ago. Torn and crumpled, the seed packets pointed in all directions, but in his mind, William easily sorted them out in several ways—alphabetically, from artichokes to zucchini; or by brand, from Anaheim Chili Peppers to Straight-Eight Cucumbers; or by the season of planting, knowing, for example, that Gypsy Peppers belonged in a summer garden, while Acorn Squash should be planted in a winter garden. Whichever way he recalled them, William pictured every seed packet in perfect order, crisp and unspoiled.

Shorty nuzzled William's ankle and made a snuffling noise.

William leaned over, looking at his dog.

"All right," he said. "*You* choose."

He picked up the fortune cookies—one in each hand—and held them out at shoulder's width, above the dog's head. "This is the first sign," he said.

Shorty sat up and swung his muzzle back and forth between William's hands, waiting patiently.

William smiled. "All right. Then *I'll* decide."

He crushed the cookies and dropped them onto his plate. Two narrow slips of pink paper were visible in the crumbled remains. He picked out both fortunes and bent forward, brushing the cookie crumbs onto the mound of kibbles in Shorty's bowl.

The dog licked up the pulverized cookies, then began eating his dinner, crunching each mouthful.

With great anticipation, William examined the first fortune. It read, "In matters of the heart, no sign is too small." He ran a hand through his thinning hair and sighed, thinking of Deborah at the number five checkout counter, with her shining red hair, freckled skin and pale blue eyes. He'd been watching her since she hired on eight months ago.

He set that fortune aside and unfolded the second slip of paper. It read, "Stars shine brighter in the heavens."

William had been waiting for an omen, so he considered both fortunes carefully, deciding which was intended for him.

"Stars shine brighter in the heavens" sounded nice, but he didn't see how it applied to his life. He looked again at the first fortune. His eyes traced and retraced its letters and words. "In matters of the heart, no sign is too small." He began to feel a tightness in his chest that left him lightheaded. This must be the one, he thought. My fortune.

Hoping he had chosen correctly, he crossed the kitchen to the end table he had relocated from the living room. On it rested a tape dispenser, a pair of scissors and a stack of gold and blue coupons featuring a Hawaiian "getaway" vacation, tied in with discounts on Stouffer's microwave dinners—just like the ones that filled the freezer section of his refrigerator. One row was macaroni and beef, the other, meatloaf and gravy with mashed potatoes. Eight of each, to keep him in balance.

William stuck a piece of clear tape to the tip of his index finger, then precisely aligned the first fortune on his refrigerator, at eye level, just below his last fortune, which read, "He who hurries, risks all." He liked this one better. Much better. This is perfect, he thought, reading it aloud. "In matters of the heart, no sign is too small." Pressing firmly, he taped it in place.

Shorty woofed softly, and William said, "Just a second, boy." He knelt and taped Shorty's fortune at the dog's eye level, along with the others, adding to the dense mosaic of prior predictions.

"See?" he said, touching the fortune. "Stars shine brighter in the heavens."

Shorty darted between William and the refrigerator, licking William's chin.

"Like Sirius," he said, scratching behind his dog's ears. "Understand? That's *your* star, from the constellation Canis Major." As he named it, he imagined the night sky, strewn with stars. Stars, he realized, had been studied through the ages. He knew that because of all the reading he had done, standing between rows of bookshelves in the library, absorbing facts as fast as he could turn the pages.

Stars, for example, had been written about by many people. Astronomers named them and tried to figure out how they had formed. Astrologers used them as guides for decisions in everyday life. And the lyrics of many songwriters mentioned the beauty of stars, along with the hope they inspired.

That made him think of Deborah and what tomorrow might bring if he talked to her. He was eager, but also nervous—because whenever he approached her, words seemed to stick in his throat.

Would she understand? Would she like him if he revealed his true feelings? Or would she reject him, like the others?

* * *

The next morning, after his usual breakfast of blueberry Pop-Tarts and root beer, William stepped into the bathroom to brush his teeth. He opened the medicine cabinet.

Next to his toothbrush, he saw the Alka-Seltzer tablets. Their foil packets—pale blue, with silver borders—had yellowed since he had transferred them from his mother's home. Just looking at the Alka-Seltzer put a foul taste in his mouth. The foil packets reminded him of how often he had felt ill growing up with his mother, who had allowed him to turn up the sound on their television only during commercials. That was her rule, because she didn't want him interfering with her progress as an artist.

She would sit cross-legged in an easy chair, facing the flickering silence of the television screen, always wearing an assembly of sheer fabrics as she puffed on a filter-tip cigarette, with her hair piled high in a turban of towels. Silently, she worked with a stick of charcoal, rendering fierce likenesses of Jack Lord from *Hawaii Five-O*, or James Garner from *The Rockford Files*. Or she would sketch self-portraits from her own image, reflected in the glare of the television screen.

Her drawings would accumulate—one atop another without her turning a page in her art tablet—until he saw a twisted mass of limbs and torsos…often, it seemed, without clothes. But the figures often intertwined with her self-portraits, so that it became difficult to distinguish the particulars of their anatomy. That confused him, but held his interest, like the many layers of his mother's gauze-like gowns, which softened the outline and angles of her body.

While she sketched, if he said he was hungry, she'd say, "That's just your stomach acting up. Take an Alka-Seltzer."

Mostly, she wouldn't talk to him, or answer his questions, which he learned eventually not to ask.

As she drew, she would hum in a low quivering voice, her eyes riveted on the television. Usually it was a nondescript tune.

But once in a while she would sing "What a Wonderful World" in a throaty contralto, and her eyes would glisten as she gripped her charcoal stick, tracing and retracing the contours she had drawn.

William heard a soft bark and removed the toothbrush from his mouth. Over his shoulder, he could see his dog, Shorty, in the bathroom doorway. Turning back to the mirror, William saw himself holding a tube of Crest toothpaste. His mouth tasted fresh, but he couldn't remember brushing or rinsing.

* * *

William struggled to remain optimistic as he decided what to wear. Today might be a turning point, so he wanted to pick the right clothes. Something that would impress Deborah. Or at least make her notice him.

After donning fresh underwear and socks, he considered his three pair of shoes. The tennis shoes were durable, the Hush Puppies the most comfortable, and his wingtips looked new. He set aside the wingtips because their leather soles were too slick, then the tennis shoes, which seemed too casual.

With his Hush Puppies on, getting into his brown slacks was difficult. He managed though, even when a cuff hung up on the heel of his shoe. Then he slipped on the least wrinkled of his six white polo shirts and left his apartment.

He was still early as he carried his bag lunch and green canvas apron, walking to Vonnart's Supermarket. Ahead, he could see the vast asphalt parking lot and the glare of sunlight reflecting off the windows that ran across the front of Vonnart's.

He slowed his pace and asked himself...had he let his dog out before leaving for work?

Briefly, he closed his eyes and thought back. *Yes.* He remembered giving Shorty the crusts off the tuna sandwich he had made, just as Shorty came indoors after doing his business in the back yard. He recalled the exact route Shorty had taken, bustling down the narrowest pathway through the living room, between packing boxes full of newspaper horoscopes and the cases of smashed aluminum root beer cans he had saved.

William smiled as he walked. Given the current reimbursement rate at the recycling center, he estimated that the floor-to-ceiling roomful of cans he had smashed and saved amounted to one thousand three hundred and fifty-two dollar's worth of aluminum.

A horn blared.

William jumped, surprised to discover that he had stepped off the curb. He hopped back onto the sidewalk as a red Ford Fiesta sped past.

When he reached the edge of the parking lot, Evan Hendrix, the new day manager, stood in front of the automatic doors at Vonnart's entrance, buttoning his green vest. "Hey, Bill," he called out. "Today at least, you made it on time."

William forced a smile. Hendrix had only been there a few months, but was already making the rounds, talking to each employee about "efficiency" and "consistency."

Clutching his apron and bag lunch, William took an angle that passed by the checkout stands, instead of proceeding directly to the storeroom. He glanced at checkout number five, looking for Deborah, but a mammoth woman blocked his view as she stood to the left of her shopping cart, reaching into her purse.

"I know my checkbook's in here," she said.

William paused, waiting for Deborah's response. She didn't answer, but William recognized the soft clink of her bracelets hitting each other as she worked the barcode reader and the keypad to ring up the lady's groceries. He imagined Deborah's kind voice telling her, "Don't worry, you'll find it."

"Bill, now you're late." It was the voice of Hendrix, coming from the front of the store, where he stood with crossed arms.

Stiff-legged, William headed for the back of the store. Hendrix, he was sure, didn't appreciate his sense of order or attention to detail. At least not the way Mister Emerson, the previous day manager, had.

Upset, William pushed through the stockroom's double-doors into its vast interior, honeycombed with shelves that held cases of food in cans, or packs of foil and cellophane.

Syd Harper got up from his desk, flashing a buck-toothed smile.

"Billy, my man. Glad you're here." Syd slipped out of his apron, pulling it over his head. "Hendrix is driving me nuts, handing out memos, getting his six-ways-to-Sunday procedures in place."

"Why can't he leave things alone?" William jammed his sack lunch inside the mini-refrigerator, then put on his canvas apron.

Syd laughed. "Other way, Will." He made a circling motion with his index finger, pointing at William's chest.

William looked down and saw his apron was wrong side out, so that Vonnart's Market was stitched backwards, and his twenty-year pin hidden from sight. Quickly he reversed his apron, looking up as Syd handed him a computer printout known as the "Daily Price Book."

It typically ran two hundred pages on eleven-by-seventeen white paper and listed the prices for the nearly eight thousand items stocked in their store, given in alphabetical order, by brand. Just below the white title sheet were several yellow sheets. They carried the listings for any items that had changed in price after the data entry deadline.

William hefted the printout, then turned to the first yellow sheet.

"Expect a lot of price checks," Syd warned. "Seven hundred-something price changes didn't make it into the computer. So those ladies will be calling you." He grinned, pantomiming a cashier lifting a phone to hail William on the public address system.

William nodded with pride. Anyone else would handle price checks by going to the aisle and finding the price posted on the shelf, next to the item in question. But William skimmed all sixteen pages in less than a minute, committing each price change to memory. Then he set the price book on a wooden worktable, illuminated by overhead fluorescent lights.

The glare of the overhead lights caught the cover of the price book, which also served as a trial page, printed with numbers that ran from top-to-bottom and side-to-side in a dense, wave-like pattern, testing the printer before it churned out the daily price runs.

William tensed, squinting against the reflected light. After a moment, he realized the profusion of numbers on the trial page reminded him of his father's logbooks.

"I'm leaving," Syd called on his way out the door, but William barely heard him.

Memories leapt to his mind, from when his father had traveled up and down the counties of Yuba, Yolo, Placer and El Dorado. Using tabular entries and a cramped handwriting, his father had noted many factors in his logbook about the rivers and levies in those counties. His father had carried all of his logbooks in a sun-bleached leather satchel, with a worn strap that dug into his shoulder.

William picked up the Daily Price Book and closed his eyes, recalling his father's infrequent visits—one or two weekends per month. His mother would prepare dinner by thawing three portions, either of meatloaf with potatoes or of the macaroni and beef casseroles that she cooked once a month in great quantities, then stored in their freezer.

When dinner was served, William and his mother would sit in front of the television, eating off folding TV trays, while his father ate at his drafting table and used a gold-nibbed fountain pen to finalize his log book entries.

Despite William's questions, his father never explained the numbers. So William would get up at night, memorizing them while his father slept, until he began to grasp the pattern of the numbers, and how they measured water depth and current velocity, along with the height, width and slope of different segments of the levies. But the numbers always seemed to shimmer and drift as dawn approached. Finally, in his sophomore year of high school, William abandoned his father's numbers and took up his own, from the Daily Price Book at Vonnart's Supermarket.

A burst of chilled air shot through the air conditioner, spilling across William's shoulders. Shivering, he looked up from the

Price Book, surprised to discover that the minute hand had leapt forward on the wall clock. A half-hour had disappeared.

Quickly, he looked for the list of daily tasks and found it beneath Syd's apron on the work desk. He tried to focus on the list, but was distracted by the overlapping rings of coffee stains at the bottom of the page, where Syd must have set his cup of coffee. William noted how the rings barely touched each other at one tangent, like the pathways of separate orbits that would converge, but only at a single point in space and time. Orbits were celestial, and that made him think of Deborah with her wondrous smile. Was this a sign that their paths were to cross? Their lives to touch?

For that to happen, he knew she would have to take more notice of him. He set aside the daily task list and entered the employee's bathroom. Leaning forward, he examined his face in the mirror. Thankfully, he had remembered to shave. And he'd pulled off the tufts of toilet paper where he had nicked his Adam's apple. He wet his hands and smoothed back his hair. It was dull brown and cut short, unlike Deborah's, which had a vermilion brilliance and hung to her shoulders.

Discouraged by his reflection, he decided this wasn't the moment to approach her. First, he needed everything to be in order so that his mind would be clear…without anything to distract him.

He returned to the daily task list, and saw by the checkmarks that Syd had finished up on aisle six, restocking the canned sodas and colas. The next item to replenish was Skippy peanut butter. First, though, he had to see what kind of a job Syd had done.

He left the stockroom and turned the corner, heading for aisle six, passing Mrs. Westin in her faded pink housedress. She gripped her shopping cart like an aluminum walker, using it to keep her balance while she shopped.

"Morning, William," she said.

He turned, walking backwards, slowing his pace. "Can I give you a hand?"

She smiled. "Thank you, but not yet, William. I can still do for myself."

He waved and moved ahead. From the front of the store, he heard a woman laugh. It sounded like Margo, who ran the register on checkout number four.

In aisle six, he saw that Syd had replenished the sodas, but had failed to square up the individual cans, because their labels didn't face in exactly the same direction. Working quickly, he pulled the first four cases into the aisle, leaving them on the cardboard flats that remained from Syd cutting open the boxes.

William knelt and settled into a rhythm, working through each case, one row of cans at a time. When he was working on the fourth case, he felt someone watching and turned.

Evan Hendrix stood there, holding a clipboard, frowning.

"Bill," he said, "what are you doing?"

"Straightening up."

Hendrix tapped the clipboard. "Restocking comes first. *Efficiency*, remember?"

William nodded, refusing to look at him.

"Get on the peanut butter," said Hendrix. "Don't fuss with any displays unless you've finished restocking."

Clenching his jaw, William picked up the remaining flat of colas and set it on top of the others, fighting the urge to align each can by its label.

"Price check on register four," crooned a sweet but husky southern voice, amplified by the public address system.

William recognized Margo's voice. Happy for the diversion, he got to the white courtesy phone as Hendrix moved down the aisle.

"I'm ready," William said.

"Lipton's soup," said Margo. "The double-pack."

William saw Hendrix stop, scanning the aisle's soup section for Lipton's. William closed his eyes, rapidly running backward through the daily pricing sheets he pictured in his mind, going alphabetically until he found Lipton's soup, in singles, then the double-pack.

Gripping the phone, William said, "One dollar and twenty-nine cents," quoting from the page he visualized. "That's a week-long special."

"Thank you, Billy Boy," came Margo's husky drawl.

William hung up, pleased to see Hendrix examining him with narrowed eyes, holding a double-pack of Lipton's soup.

Before Hendrix could say anything, William started back to the stockroom, glancing up the aisle toward the registers. Margo gave him a wave and a smile.

William canted his head, trying to look past Margo for a view of register number five. He only caught a glimpse of Deborah's long red hair, because she had her back to him as she loaded a shopping cart with groceries she'd rung up.

William shook off his disappointment and returned to the stockroom. Carefully, he loaded four cases of Skippy peanut butter onto the hydraulic Pallet-Jack, then gripped its two mechanical arms. He steered through the double doors, toward aisle eight, where Hendrix would probably be waiting.

Hendrix stood there, all right, giving a pep talk to Buzz Avichi, the produce manager. William liked Avichi, who was an enthusiastic gardener and frequently contributed to his collection of seed packs.

When Hendrix glanced at William, Avichi stepped back and rolled his eyes, hooking a thumb at Hendrix. William stifled a laugh, looking down as he moved into the aisle. It took him only a few moments to restock the peanut butter, then another hour to straighten every item shelved on the west side of the aisle.

When he looked up, Hendrix stood there, tapping his wrist-watch. "You missed your first morning break," he said.

William looked at his shoes, instead of Hendrix.

"Add it to your lunch hour. I don't want any overtime or skipped breaks on your time card."

Keeping his head down, William steered the Pallet-Jack toward the stockroom. He passed Buzz Avichi, who whistled as he sprayed and misted the lettuce. Avichi grinned, giving him a mock salute. William returned the gesture, but felt out of sorts because Hendrix was picking on him.

Pushing through the storeroom's double-doors, William parked the Pallet-Jack, then picked up the clipboard with its checklist and attached manifests. As he thumbed his way past the top few sheets, something glossy fell out...that looked like a page from a magazine. William picked it up and it unfolded, showing a woman with no clothes on, lying back on the hood of a convertible. She had her hands clasped behind her neck and was winking at him.

Biting his lip, William turned the picture over and shoved it beneath Syd's apron on the worktable. Photos like that, he knew, were bad. And they made it difficult for him to swallow, seeing everything like that—all at once. It was hard enough just looking a girl in the eyes, and hoping she would smile instead of turning away.

He closed his eyes and thought back to his senior year in high school, when he had been paired in chemistry lab with Alice Sedaris. Slender and graceful, she had worn long skirts and thick-lensed glasses that magnified her perfect hazel eyes. More than once he had trembled when they touched hands, passing beakers back and forth, or sat side-by-side, recording their experiments in a shared notebook.

But Alice never responded to his smiles, or his offers to walk her home after school, except to say she was "otherwise occupied." Each rebuff made it more difficult to smile and nod, hiding the pain he felt. Finally, he obtained permission to change his seating assignment and work alone, rather than suffer another of Alice's rejections.

Now, as he sat between rows of boxes in the stockroom, dejected by thoughts of Alice Sedaris, he couldn't help recalling the next setback he'd suffered—two years later—at Vonnart's, when he had been flattered by the kind things Michelle had to say. With her copper-colored hair tucked beneath a UPS cap, Michelle's dull brown uniform couldn't hide how pretty she was. Often, on her daily deliveries, she lugged in packages, with him helping her. In return she usually said, "Thanks, handsome."

That left him imagining what it would be like to hold her hand, or to kiss her…wondering if she would taste like the peppermint gum he could smell on her breath. He never got to find out, because she transferred to another UPS route. It was an unexpected blow that left him dazed and deeply discouraged.

That same week, Mrs. Kravitz had moved into William's apartment building. At first, Mrs. Kravitz—whose pale complexion reminded him of his sixth grade English teacher—simply waved hello. Occasionally, she stopped to pet his miniature collie, calling him Tiny, instead of Shorty. Then one evening, she invited him in for chocolate chip cookies, suggesting that he sample them while she excused herself.

Moments later she emerged from the hall, wearing nothing but a flimsy nightgown that hung to her knees and started kissing him. He felt himself flooded with warmth as she pressed herself against him.

He wanted to speak, but felt short of breath.

He embraced her, just as she dropped her head to his chest and began to weep. Between soft, hiccupping sobs, she told him how her husband, Stan, had betrayed her with the young women who came to him for driving lessons. Not once, mind you, but on three separate occasions.

Two days later Mrs. Kravitz was gone, leaving him to wonder if he had done something wrong. It confused him, but not enough to abandon his search altogether, because he truly longed for someone to return his affection. But the disappointments and rejections he had suffered seemed more grueling with each occurrence, and that had made him more cautious. Guarded, even, to the point where he wouldn't reveal his yearning…not without some assurance that he would be accepted. So to protect himself, he endeavored to foretell the future. *His* future.

William glanced at the daily task list next to Syd's apron on the worktable. He realized there was a pattern to the list, no matter what angle he viewed it from. And this awareness he had for patterns—which were everywhere if you looked closely—was exactly what had helped him experiment with various means of predicting the future.

At the outset, he only made predictions to avoid further disappointments—to discover who he should avoid. Then he began to expand his forecasts. He made this extra effort because he took comfort in charting the larger course of his life, even when that produced the most abbreviated prognosis. At least it gave him *some* sense of direction. That, and the hope of avoiding further distress and embarrassment if he heeded *all* of the signs.

Accordingly, he had protected himself for the past several years, by indulging in horoscopes, numerology, and finally the I-Ching. And it had kept him safe. Until now. Until Deborah.

Standing in the stockroom, William glanced at the daily task list. He knew he ought to restock the next item, to keep Hendrix off his back. But his thoughts kept drifting to register number five, and the day he had first noticed Deborah.

It had been Wednesday, March twenty-third, four days after he had received his twenty-year pin. What he remembered most about that moment was the way she had taken out her barrettes and let down her radiant red hair. From that point on, he had observed her carefully. Soon, he learned to enjoy the ease with which she smiled and the slight lilt in her voice, which gave it an added sweetness. Also, he had seen the kindness with which she treated everyone. Not just the regular customers, or people who were polite to her, but *everyone*. Including him.

Of course, he hadn't divulged how strongly he was attracted to her. Or the way his heart beat faster when he saw her. In fact, he had barely spoken to her—and even then, only to answer when she addressed him. Usually for price checks.

But he had been planning for some time to strike up a longer conversation—to let her know how much he liked her.

Thinking now about the risk that involved made him nervous, so he reached into his left pocket and touched the three brass coins he used for casting the I-Ching. Feeling the shape and weight of the coins helped him alleviate his anxiety.

As he calmed down, he realized he was thirsty. But he had brought only one root beer with his lunch and didn't want to drink it now, so he left the stockroom.

Cutting across the back of the store to its far corner, he entered the break room, which had a vending machine that carried Old Granddad's, his favorite root beer. Noise filled the room, with employees chatting at three Formica tables as they ate and visited on the early lunch shift. As William dropped coins into the machine, he saw someone waving from the nearest table. It was Margo, wearing horn-rimmed glasses. His can of root beer rolled down the chute, landing with a clunk. He picked it up as Deborah walked in and sat next to Margo, who was rearranging the bobby pins that held her hair in a bun.

"Come look," Margo called to him. "Deborah has photos."

In a daze, he walked over and sat across from them, entranced by Deborah's smile as she looked his way.

"You're just in time," Deborah said, and opened a Kodak processing envelope, removing a stack of photographs. "These are from my sister's wedding."

Setting his root beer to the side, he wet his lips. Was this the time? Should he speak to her now?

Deborah began handing him snapshots, one at a time, as she gave him a running commentary about her sister, Lucinda, and her sister's new husband, Victor. He didn't say a word, but felt his skin tingle whenever her hand touched his. Also, he found himself sorting the photographs into two stacks—those containing Deborah and those that didn't.

Once he'd seen several snapshots, Deborah began scooping them up and passing them to Margo. Pretty soon Deborah was talking with Margo, who held all the pictures. Without the photographs, he felt invisible. As if he didn't exist.

All I have to do is speak up, he thought. Just tell her how much I like her. But not with Margo and the others sitting here.

"Victor's a nice enough guy," Deborah was saying, "but he and Lucinda are playing it so safe."

"Your sister says that?" asked Margo.

Deborah nodded. "Their whole life's mapped out for them, between Victor's job with Hewlett Packard, the fancy home they're saving for in Folsom and their plans to have two kids." She smiled. "Make that two kids and a dog."

Margo pursed her lips. "How does Victor compare to your Kevin?"

Deborah sighed. "At least Kevin's open to life. He's even thinking about joining the army." She started gathering up the photos.

William committed the snapshots to memory, quickly sorting them in his mind—putting all the ones of Deborah up front, pink-cheeked and smiling, in her powder-blue dress trimmed with white lace and accented with pearls.

Deborah added, "If Kevin enlists, it would be a chance to go overseas. To really travel."

William smiled. Losing Kevin to the army would be great. He had met Kevin last month at the company picnic. Deborah had introduced him after Kevin knocked in the winning run in the softball game. He was a broad-shouldered fellow with straw-colored hair whose face reflected a complete lack of concentration.

"Well," Margo said, "when you're young, like you two are, then it's easier, making big decisions like that."

"That's what we're thinking. And traveling could be a real adventure."

William felt the room tilt and gripped the edge of the table. How could she think of leaving—especially with someone like Kevin? Carefully, he stood and left the break room.

For the next hour he straightened up the stockroom, but had great difficulty concentrating. It was so unfair that Deborah might leave him.

The double-doors banged open behind him, startling him, and Hendrix briefly stuck his head in. "Lunch hour," he announced.

William didn't look up and didn't answer. He listened to the flap of the swinging doors, glad that Hendrix had left.

Dejected, William took his sack lunch and went outside, to one of the concrete benches that were on the strip of lawn at the edge of the parking lot. What he needed, he realized, was a plan. Some way to free Deborah from Kevin's influence and win her back.

As he sat and chewed his tuna sandwich, one possibility came to mind. Perhaps he could buy her a wonderful gift by selling all the crushed aluminum cans he had saved. But he needed more than a plan. He also needed a sign—some confirmation that this was a risk he should take, approaching her so boldly.

He reached into his pocket and pulled out the three brass Chinese coins, setting them on the concrete tabletop. Folding his hands, William began to narrow his focus. He wanted to formulate his question with great care, prior to tossing the coins.

He set aside the notion of buying a gift and concentrated strictly on Deborah. Filled with longing, he chose his question, posing it in a solemn voice as he stared at his folded hands.

"Are we right for each other?"

He picked up the three brass coins and tossed them six times, obtaining an answer which he recognized immediately. When he first began studying the I-Ching, it had only taken him a minute or so of tossing the coins to get a feel for how it worked. Converting the resulting patterns into the correct hexagrams is what yielded a reading. After that, memorizing all the hexagrams had been easy, because there were only sixty-four combinations to consider.

Now he frowned. From all the possible outcomes, his current reading equaled "mist" over "wind," with the "mist" clearly representing Deborah, and the "wind" being himself. What it indicated was a very nebulous relationship, and that discouraged him. He had hoped for something much stronger. Something more encouraging than last night's fortune cookie. This reading didn't seem to refine or strengthen last night's fortune. So he needed a clarification.

Two years ago, had he experienced a similar quandary, he would have sought resolution through the first number or series of numbers he saw. That's when he had studied every book he could find on numerology, committing them to memory as fast as he read them.

One year ago, the confirming sign would have come from an astrological reading. But he had soon tired of astrology. As a Virgo with Virgo rising and a Virgo moon, he had abandoned the Zodiac because of its vague and ambiguous predictions.

Currently, he favored the I-Ching, which he found better suited to his need for a sense of order and predictability. He especially liked its ability to adapt to situations that were changing. But this reading of "mist" over "wind" was too indecisive to help him.

He took a deep breath and released it. Letting his eyes half-close, he stood and walked further into the parking lot, barely listening to the clatter of two boys using skateboards to jump the concrete rails of the shopping cart return. He kept walking, passing a hopscotch game someone had chalked on the asphalt. Suddenly, he stopped and looked back.

The game's chalked outline, he realized, contained the shape of an I-Ching hexagram. *This*, he realized, could be the clarification he was seeking.

Within the hopscotch pattern, the single squares served as short lines and the side-by-side squares served as long lines, corresponding to the yin and yang of the I-Ching. Interpreted in that fashion, the entire pattern formed the thirty-fifth hexagram, "Chin," consisting of "fire over earth." Immediately that gave him a rush of hope, because he knew it signified rapid progress and a promising future.

All I have to do, he thought, is *speak* to her. Tell her how I long for her. He focused on the chalk lines of the hexagram, working up his nerve.

"Bill! Why aren't you inside the store?"

William turned, seeing Evan Hendrix, who stood at the pneumatic door, with the breeze tugging at his green tie.

"It's ten minutes past your lunch hour."

William grabbed the remains of his sack lunch, dropping a gob of tuna and mayonnaise on his pants. Flustered, he kept walking, trying to wipe it off with his lunch bag, but it left a dark, greasy stain.

He rushed past Hendrix, who called after him, saying, "Another shipment's arrived. Stock the special on aisle five—Hormel's chili."

William hurried into the stockroom, wishing he could ignore Hendrix and concentrate strictly on the I-Ching reading.

As he loaded the hydraulic Pallet-Jack with Hormel's chili, he realized he was holding his breath.

He exhaled and told himself, "Look for the right moment. Rapid progress is at hand." Clearly, that's what the chalked hexagram had foretold. "Fire over earth," he murmured to himself. "Fire over earth. It will happen if you seize the moment."

In his mind, he kept chanting *fire over earth* while he steered the Pallet-Jack through the double-doors, into the store's back aisle. Restocking was simple work. Work he could perform without thinking. But now he couldn't help smiling, because these items belonged on the aisle with a view of register five.

As he pushed the Pallet-Jack across the rear of the store, the vivid red and green stripes of a beach umbrella caught his attention. It rose above an end-aisle display of suntan lotion, with a poster that urged shoppers to "frolic in the sun," like the tanned young couple it showed. Wearing red bathing suits, they hugged each other on a brilliant ocean beach that was drenched in sunshine, with azure waves cresting behind them.

William slowed his stride, still gazing at the poster. Perhaps a wonderful trip was the way to win Deborah over. She had talked about traveling with Kevin, so maybe that was his answer.

"Excuse me."

Startled, William stopped short, pulling up on the Pallet-Jack. He had nearly collided with a rail-thin woman in navy blue sweats, whose shopping cart held Kellogg's Corn Flakes and bagels.

He guided the Pallet-Jack around her, trying to picture Deborah in a swimsuit, and felt warm, as if he was already on the beach. He thought of the money he could get by selling his aluminum cans and wondered how far they could travel.

A stooped woman in a wrinkled polka dot dress approached him, pushing a shopping cart that held a box of Tide. He recognized the widow Meredith and nodded as she passed by.

"Morning, Billy," she responded in a warbling voice.

Steering carefully, he passed the tall refrigerated cases along the back wall that displayed frozen microwave dinners. They held Lean Cuisine, Hungry Man, and Swanson's. Then Stouffer's, with a gold and blue mini-banner, touting their discount offer for a Hawaiian getaway vacation.

That's it, he thought. *Hawaii!* I'll ask Deborah to go to Hawaii.

Giddy with excitement, he sped up, pushing the Pallet-Jack past the end of aisle four and turning the corner, passing the cellophane packages of spaghetti, heading for the canned beans and chili.

"Price check on register five," came Deborah's voice, magnified by the public address system.

Stunned, he pulled back on the Pallet-Jack and slid to a halt. Was this the moment he had hoped for, when their orbits would meet? When their lives would touch? The perfect point in time, aligning hope, desire and action?

He leaned out from behind the Pallet-Jack and was rewarded with Deborah's smiling profile and the abundance of her crimson hair, fanned out on the shoulders of her green smock. Her fingers danced across the cash register keys as she chatted with an Asian woman, whose shopping cart was filled with fresh produce. Deborah paused to weigh each bag of vegetables as she rang them up.

Then Deborah saw him and smiled, waving him forward.

He felt a surge of excitement as he left the Pallet-Jack at the side of the aisle. His legs felt shaky. Overhead, the fluorescent lights seemed to flare at him. He drew a deep breath and strode forward. He shifted his eyes from Deborah to the woman she was helping. That way, he wouldn't get flustered or waver.

As he walked in their direction, he noticed the exact contents of the woman's shopping cart. Plastic bags filled with fresh broccoli, asparagus, green beans, bell peppers, bok choy, and snow peas. But as he lengthened his strides, staring at the vegetables, it wasn't today's price sheets that came to mind. It was the range of gestures he had witnessed that were specific to Deborah. The little half-wave she often made, smiling without showing her teeth— usually while greeting someone she knew. Or the dimples that deepened in her cheeks whenever she laughed. Or the way she pursed her lips before picking up the phone to use the PA system, calling for his assistance.

"Billy?" prompted Deborah, and his gaze locked onto her eyes. She was holding something up. "Price check?"

As he rapidly drew closer, she waved the object back and forth, and he saw it more clearly. Rectangular. A white box with fine gold striping and a large block of blue, with *Imperial* reversed out of the blue in white letters, alongside a red crown.

"Oh," he said, holding her gaze as he strode forward. "*Imperial Margarine.*"

Deborah nodded, giving him an expectant look.

Flustered, he realized she was waiting.

He closed his eyes as he kept walking, trying to visualize the price sheets. But he could only recall the way Deborah leaned over when she talked to little children perched in their mother's shopping carts.

"Billy? *Billy!*"

Startled, his eyes flew open and he found himself still walking at a rapid clip, bearing down on the customer's shopping cart, which Deborah had pulled to her side of the register.

Too late, he tried to stop, just as Deborah reached out to shove the cart aside.

He plowed straight into it, folding over at the waist. Falling toward the cart's crossbar handle, he made an effort to throw himself sideways.

Deborah lunged in his direction, trying to grab him, and they fell to the floor.

He hit first, flat on his back, thumping his head, a split-second before she landed on top of him.

Fire over earth, he thought, picturing the hopscotch outlined in chalk on the parking lot.

"Are you okay?" she asked, raising her head off his chest. She gave him an anxious look. "You really konked your head."

He was about to say, "I'm always thinking about you," when he saw *another* sign. One that he hadn't anticipated. There, in the spill of freckles across her face—directly beneath her left cheekbone—was the constellation of Canis Major, dominated by Sirius.

Suddenly, he realized his disastrous mistake. Last night, after the Chinese dinner, he had gotten the fortunes *reversed*. "The stars shine brighter in the heavens" wasn't his dog's fortune. It was *his*.

"Are you hurt?" Deborah asked, brushing his hair from his forehead.

In that instant, he understood. What he had longed for wasn't meant to be. Deborah was destined to be admired, but only from afar. Yet he was *so* close...*so* near to her now, that the idea of traveling with her to the sparkling beaches of Hawaii was overpowering. *Irresistible.*

She leaned closer, peering into his eyes. Then she glanced at her hand, where she had touched him. The tips of her fingers were red with blood.

William blinked rapidly, surprised by the circle of people surrounding them. Several bent over, staring at them, while others whispered to each other.

"Say something," Deborah urged, "so I know you're alright."

William struggled to speak. To tell her that they belonged together. But his lips felt numb. He couldn't focus as he tasted the sweetness of her breath on his face, then felt her hand, gently cradling his head.

"I've called an ambulance." It was the voice of Evan Hendrix, the day manager, but it seemed to be coming from Deborah, whose lips were pursed with concern.

Just beyond Deborah, in the sprawl of items spilled from the shopping cart, William saw the box of Imperial Margarine.

He wanted to say, *Hawaii*. To say, *we should go there*. But his view was obscured by precise rows of numbers that suddenly came to mind, almost like an intricate latticework he had to gaze through in order to see Deborah.

"Please talk to me," she pleaded. Still cradling his head, she stroked his cheek.

William began to weep softly. Images of an ocean, glowing in a sunset, shone through the sheet of numbers he visualized, highlighting a single line that he felt compelled to read aloud.

"Imperial Margarine," he whispered, wanting to stay in her arms. "Ninety-nine cents a box."

"That's right." Deborah said it gently, with her face silhouetted as the sun grew brighter and the ocean waves crashed behind her, then rushed to the beach, washing away the row of numbers for Imperial Margarine.

"*Us*," William choked out, raising his voice. "You and me."

"I'm right here," Deborah answered, suddenly visible for a few seconds, before the waves hissed and receded, leaving a fresh wall of numbers that pressed in on him, so dense that he could barely see.

Panicked, he called out, "Go with me, please. *Please!*"

"I will," she promised.

Other hands reached in, revealing two men in white uniforms at the edge of his vision. They lifted him onto something, then helped him lie down.

That didn't bother him because Deborah's hand was still on his, warm and soft. She said, "Everything's going to be okay, Billy. I promise."

The supermarket's pneumatic doors swooshed open and he caught a flash of sunshine. Then red hair as Deborah walked, keeping at his side, with a blue sky and clouds overhead. He had the sensation of rising as he was shoved inside a vehicle of some sort. Its doors closed abruptly, cutting off the sunlight. He jerked, trying to sit up.

"Don't struggle," Deborah urged. "I'm here. Right beside you."

He felt a rush of cool air as something pressed down over his mouth and nose, held in place by a strong hand.

He blinked, focusing on Deborah, sitting next to him. They were inside something with a metal ceiling.

Someone tightened a safety belt across his lap, and he knew. They were in an airplane, he realized. About to leave for Hawaii.

More seat belts were added, across his chest, then his thighs, and he could finally see Deborah without any numbers coming between them.

He felt tears of joy and saw that she too was crying. Thrilled to be together at last.

"It's all right," Deborah said in a soothing voice. "Everything's fine."

He began to feel lighter. Almost like he was drifting…filled with relief.

A soft tremor ran through his body as he let out his breath and closed his eyes.

He knew. *Hawaii would be wonderful.*

Terry Bennett

Trading Corners

S tanding on the sidewalk, Harlan Tucker shifted the scuffed gym bag to his right hand. Puddles remained from last night's drizzle, while across the street the first hint of dawn touched cinderblock buildings with flat gravel roofs. God bless, thought Tucker, grateful that even in January, LA's worst weather was rain, driven by a stiff wind.

He gripped the stairwell's pipe handrail. It chilled his hand as an overhead light cast his shadow. It ran in a long zigzag, down cracked concrete steps that were still damp. Tucker descended slowly, ignoring the ache in his bad hip. Still, he was pleased that the boxing rings were in the basement, free from the distractions he'd seen in other gyms, where gawkers wandered in off the street, annoying both fighters and trainers.

He opened the door to a deep gloom that carried the musty odor of sweat tinged with liniment. Except for a narrow crack of light beneath the closed locker room door, it was pitch black. Tucker turned toward the gym's farthest corner, where he couldn't see a thing. Still, he heard what he expected...a steady thrumming.

Light, Tucker knew, wasn't necessary for Skeet, who had taken his position facing the speed bag, and was so sure of his timing that he kept finding the swiveled bag in the darkness, driving it back and forth between his fists and the overhead platform, filling the gym with a sharp, syncopated reverberation.

Tucker smiled. Even in the dark, he knew that Skeet's fists were holding to a crisp rhythm, because the speed bag answered in kind. *Bop-a-ta, bop-a-ta, bop-a-ta.*

Tucker loved the sound of precision. And what he heard told him a lot about the skill of any boxer, be it the soft slapping of his jump rope, the rhythm of his speed bag, or even the crack of a boxer's power shots striking a heavy bag, swift and clean. All of it was music to Tucker's ears. And so much better, he thought, than the vicious gangster rap young fighters drowned themselves in. Even if its blasting, rambling, herky-jerky bullshit didn't dull their minds, Tucker figured it gave them bad ideas. Like the notion that they could take whatever they wanted, instead of earning it.

"Mornin'," Skeet called out, steady on the speed bag.

Tucker hesitated. "Same to you," he answered.

He located the switches and turned on a single light. From the high ceiling, a fluorescent light flickered, revealing Skeet's jump rope, coiled on the hardwood floor that ran along a wall of mirrors. That meant Skeet had finished ten minutes of rope work.

In the mirrors, Tucker glimpsed his own reflection. Mulatto skin that could pass for white, kinked silver hair, and a stoop that was getting pronounced, making his denim jumpsuit look too long in the legs.

Tucker faced the far corner and studied Skeet as he kept the speed bag moving. Flying off his fists, it marked the exact tempo and rhythm of his blows. The sound was right. But something else wasn't, and it took Tucker a few seconds to spot it.

Usually, when Skeet reached up with his fists and struck the speed bag, he was graceful. Smooth as silk. This morning though, Tucker noticed that Skeet's shoulders seemed stiff. Knowing Skeet, Tucker expected it could be from a touch of bursitis. Or it might be a trace of anger left over from yesterday.

Tucker turned on another light. Centered on the nearest bench, he saw the sweat-soaked scarf and stocking cap that Skeet had peeled off after his five-mile run. Tucker shifted his weight and massaged his sore hip, avoiding the lump of scar tissue.

As he watched Skeet work the speed bag, he took comfort in the rituals that had developed between them. He liked the exacting nature of their training routines and the dedication that boxing required. But beneath all of that, what counted most was the respect and trust that he and Skeet held for each other. That's why Tucker worried about the way yesterday had ended, with harsh words.

Tucker moved closer, limping past a row of heavy bags.

Sweat glistened on Skeet's face. His skin was obsidian black beneath the sheen of sweat. With his hands freshly wrapped, Skeet smiled as he worked, but his smile was tight. He moved in a slow circle, hitting the speed bag from all angles. Muscles and tendons rippled on his lean frame as his fists caught the bag with perfect strokes, keeping it in motion. It was too early in the workout for a timed round, so Tucker let Skeet find his own pace, warming up for what would follow.

Tucker leaned against the wall, wondering how to say what needed saying...how to get past Skeet's pride and his temper.

Skeet circled and drummed the speed bag, faster now, until his hands blurred, and rolling thunder echoed off the walls. He finished as Tucker turned on the last bank of fluorescents.

The spill of light drew Tucker's attention to the slight ridge high on Skeet's cheekbone. It was the only trace of the incision and stitches Skeet had had after the blow he had taken five weeks ago, when Hector Martinez had fractured his cheekbone. It was a heavy right cross from Martinez that had caught him.

From studying the video afterwards, Tucker knew that Skeet had seen it coming. So he could have slipped it, or backpedaled. Instead, he had tucked his chin and traded combinations—taking more shots than he'd landed.

"Here we go," said Tucker. From Skeet's equipment bag, he pulled out a pair of twelve-ounce gloves.

Skeet slipped them on and Tucker laced them up. Their eyes met. For a second, there was heat in Skeet's gaze. Then he shook his head and the tension seemed to disappear.

"S'all right, Tuck. You're entitled to speak your piece."

"It wasn't me I was lookin' out for."

Skeet half-smiled.

They moved to a tall heavy bag, suspended from an over-head beam. When Skeet nodded, Tucker set the wall timer for three-minute rounds, with only thirty-second rest periods.

The timer sounded three sharp bells, and the green light came on.

"Jus' footwork and shoulders," said Tucker.

Skeet began to dance around the bag, humming a faint melody that Tucker didn't recognize.

As Skeet moved, he twisted abruptly, rotating his shoulders and hips—as if snapping punches at the bag, but without lifting his arms. *Phantom* punches, Tucker called them. His way of reminding Skeet to drive each punch with his shoulders and hips, which is where the *real* power comes from. As Tucker liked to put it, the arms and fists might accelerate a punch, but they weren't the power. Just transportation, taking it from here to there.

"That'a way," Tucker urged. "Gimmie those rag-doll arms."

Watching Skeet work, he couldn't help thinking about the one thing all fighters had to suffer, sooner or later. The fall from grace. Or glory. Whatever you chose to call it. Every fighter lost it eventually. For some, once they hit their peak it took years to lose their edge. For others, if they took a terrible beating, one bout could do it. Even a single round.

As he tracked Skeet's movements, Tucker knew that Skeet had lasted longer than most because of what set him apart. His boxing was a cunning blend of grace and fierce precision that let him cut stronger men to ribbons, while avoiding their blows.

The short bell sounded next to Tucker, and the yellow light came on.

"Go hard," said Tucker.

Skeet kept on his toes and doubled his pace, twisting his shoulders left and right, firing phantom punches while he circled the bag.

With Skeet, it had taken a long while to begin the downward slide, but Tucker had seen the start of it.

Tucker rubbed his hip, thinking of his own pro career as a welterweight—first interrupted, then finished by Vietnam.

Six months into his hitch, on a humid morning, he had waded into elephant grass that stood six feet tall. Walking point, with his AR-16 port-at-arms, he heard a dull *whump* as the explosion knocked him off his feet.

The soldier who stepped on the land mine died, and Tucker was sent home with shrapnel buried in his hip. Months of recovery and rehab followed at the V.A. hospital, but Tucker knew his prize-fighting days were over. At first he was bitter, but his brother, Ben, convinced him to get on with his life. To do something, instead of feeling sorry for himself.

So Tucker mustered out of the Marines and made his way back to boxing as a trainer. First with amateurs, then with pros. It was strictly hand-me-down knowledge that he had first gleaned from his apprenticeship to Big Jim Duvall, who had migrated to Los Angeles after stints in Texas and Louisiana.

The long bell rang, bringing Tucker back as the timer's red light came on.

Skeet shook out his arms and smiled.

Tucker returned the smile, hoping that Skeet had put aside their quarrel. He held up the water bottle. "Drink. We'll get to rinse and spit later on."

Skeet swallowed as the bell rang three times, starting another round.

"Your choice," Tucker said. "Whatever you want."

In training sessions, Tucker usually called out specific punch combinations. But he didn't like too much structure following a fight. Allowing more flexibility afterwards helped a boxer unwind from all the precision and repetition that was demanded of him heading into a bout.

Skeet moved lightly on the balls of his feet, flicking jabs as he circled, adding the occasional right cross. Then he dropped lower in his stance, planting his feet, and fired body shots to the outside, left and right.

Beyond Skeet, Tucker took in the rows of fight posters that crowded the walls. The nearest one featured Bernard Hopkins and Felix Trinidad, two top-ranked middleweights who'd had the chance to fight Skeet years ago, when they'd all been welterweights. They had avoided Skeet, like most fighters had. If you asked, they'd insist it wasn't from fearing a knockout—and that was true. Skeet didn't have the same power they did. But he was slick enough to win on points, and make them look bad while he did it.

The yellow light came on with a short ring, and Skeet stepped up his speed and power, working inside combinations, followed by a chopping right. Grunting, he threw a left-right-hook combination that jolted the bag. The stop bell sounded with the red light, ending the round.

Skeet dropped his arms and stepped back, but didn't stand still. Instead, he backpedaled, circling the bag, keeping his eyes on Tucker.

Out of habit, Tucker used hand signals, rather than calling out the punches he wanted. Instead of saying, "Repeat your last combination," he used an upright index finger, making a quick circle.

Skeet nodded.

The start bell sounded.

Skeet delivered the same left-right-hook combination, and kept repeating it.

When the combination became fluid, almost too fast to see, Tucker caught Skeet's eye and gave him the next signal. Steepling his hands, Tucker gave them a quick tilt, left then right. That told Skeet to slip after he threw his combinations.

Skeet responded. Between sets of punches, Skeet rotated his shoulders as he dipped his knees, dropping lower to slip his head left, then right. Tucker smiled. It was basic. Part of the fundamentals. But it *worked*. Throw, then make 'em miss. That was the heart of it. Skeet glanced over, and Tucker tapped his index finger twice against his palm. Immediately, Skeet began to double his jab.

The hand signals were something Tucker had worked up while coaching amateurs. With amateurs, verbal instructions were only allowed between rounds, but a boxer often needed advice midway through a round. So Tucker used hand signals. If his boxer had the other fighter in a clinch, or if Tucker's fighter was sent to a neutral corner while his opponent took an eight count, Tucker's hands spoke to his boxer.

The sudden crack of Skeet's fists punching the heavy bag brought Tucker back. Once again, Skeet was hitting too hard.

Tucker put a hand sideways, chin high, and lowered it, to signal less force.

Skeet nodded and got up on his toes, throwing jabs and combinations that became smoother and faster as he quit loading up on each shot. But it didn't last.

Tucker frowned as Skeet dropped lower in his stance. That produced more power, but slowed his punches. Tucker shook his head. Immediately, Skeet lightened up, which boosted his speed as he struck the heavy bag.

Tucker realized this workout was going to be a tug of war between him and Skeet. Is this part of our argument, he wondered, or just Skeet shaking off the punishment he'd taken from Martinez?

Hiding his frustration, Tucker signaled for new combinations as the rounds progressed.

By the time Skeet had gone six rounds his sweat pants and shirt were drenched, but his breathing was good—deep and steady. Still, Tucker saw a tightness in Skeet's shoulders and brief pauses between shots. That's what Skeet had done trading punches with Martinez, going toe-to-toe, trying to concentrate his power—instead of doing a bob and weave to find a new angle, then throwing a quick counter-punch.

Tucker had pointed that out on the video a few days after the fight. And they had been discussing it ever since, with the words getting more heated each time. Last night's argument had been the worst.

Skeet had insisted his pro record of 65 wins, 4 losses and 3 draws spoke for itself. But in the last four fights, Tucker had seen

Skeet take a lot of punishment, with two of the four bouts ending as draws. So Tucker had started dropping hints that Skeet should plan ahead for his retirement. Skeet had taken offense, ignoring the wear and tear he'd suffered from eleven years as a pro, and before that, from forty bouts as an amateur.

Tucker had tried to talk it through, but Skeet had cut him off and walked away, telling him to save it for down the road. Then, when Tucker had raised his concerns again on the heels of Skeet's narrow victory over Martinez, Skeet had a meltdown. He got so angry that he yelled, "That's enough! It's *me* who has to decide. Not you."

Now the bell sounded, ending the round, and Skeet nailed the bag with a final one-two combination.

Tucker gave Skeet water and toweled off his face. "Good work," he said, then hooked a thumb at the ring. "Mitt drills. Three rounds."

Skeet shook his head. "One more on the heavy bag."

"Why? You've worked up a sweat."

"I want to dig in with power shots."

Tucker took a breath and let it out. "The way things went with Martinez, what you need is movement. Let the openings come, instead of trading shot-for-shot. *Boxing*, not punching, is what got you this far."

Skeet hesitated. "One more round. All power shots."

Tucker capped the water bottle and gave him a steady look. "What's with all the power shots?"

When Skeet answered with an elaborate shrug, Tucker knew that he was holding back.

"Better spill it, Skeet."

Skeet hesitated, then nodded. "All right. Here it is, straight up." Skeet gave the heavy bag a little shove, then shoved it again. "Some Russian fighter came through from another gym. Word's out that I'm getting a shot at Zakharov."

Tucker stopped the bag from swinging and shook his head. "If we had a dime for every rumor—"

"Really, Tuck. S'what he said."

Tucker shifted his stance, taking some weight off his bad hip. If that was true, it could be bad news. Tucker had seen Zakharov in action.

"This Russian, where'd he hear it?"

"Didn't say. But he knows Zakharov. Said he served with him in Chechnya."

Tucker knew Zakharov had driven a tank. He'd mentioned it in pre-fight interviews. Said he liked the way tanks could crush any resistance, making the enemy abandon all hope.

"Are you listening, Tuck? This could be our big break. The guy's ranked one notch below me."

Tucker turned it around, needing to see it the way Zakharov would. "So you're his stepping stone."

Skeet nodded. "Beating me would bump Zakharov up to fifth ranked—"

"Making him eligible to fight Bernard Hopkins, in Hopkins' mandatory title defense."

Skeet grinned, happy-go-lucky now, acting like it was money in the bank.

Tucker didn't want to spoil his good mood, but he still took it for the kind of rumor that boxers like to trade. Otherwise he would have heard it from Seth Porter, who had managed the gym and every fighter under its roof for the last thirty years.

Despite that, Tucker decided to humor Skeet. His cheek may have healed, but his confidence needed a boost. "Fine. Go with the power shots."

Skeet grinned and rolled his shoulders, getting ready.

"But," Tucker added, "only for this round."

The bell sounded, and Skeet hammered the bag with straight rights, then double-hooks, high and low. With each shot he grunted, putting everything into it.

When the round ended, Skeet's chest was heaving.

Tucker waved him into the ring for punch-mitt drills, to check his timing. Tucker climbed in after Skeet, then slipped on the pancake-flat, padded leather punch-mitts.

"Gimme a jab."

Skeet fired a stiff jab, and Tucker caught it, using one mitt to absorb the punch.

"Lighten up. Double your jab, then triple it."

This time Skeet flicked out his left. Each jab landed with a soft pop.

"Good," said Tucker. "That's what I want."

Skeet stayed loose, keeping his guard up, and threw smooth, quick jabs that conserved his strength.

Tucker concentrated, calling out combinations, then mirrored Skeet's movements, positioning the mitts to catch each punch that Skeet threw.

"Faster," Tucker said. "Jab, left-right, bob and weave, left upper-cut."

Skeet answered, pivoting his hips and shoulders with each punch—getting his body into it—instead of arm punching, like an amateur.

As soon as Skeet fired the left-right, Tucker countered, throwing a hook by sweeping his left arm and fist inward, toward Skeet's jaw.

Skeet got under it with a bob and weave. Immediately, Tucker braced one hand with the other, holding both mitts face down to catch the force of Skeet's counter-punch, a left uppercut.

Other boxers began drifting into the gym. These were the guys Tucker wondered about. Did they really think an eight-hour day would take them to the top?

They straggled in slowly, sassing each other. Mostly, they talked up whatever they had or hadn't done since yesterday as they walked to the locker room.

Tucker kept working Skeet, ignoring the young fighters who laced up their shoes and started their rope work, talking to each other in low voices. As Skeet popped the mitts and slipped Tucker's punches, the younger men began to jump rope, facing away from Skeet. But all of them followed his every movement in the wall of mirrors, watching a seasoned pro at work.

The long bell sounded with the red light.

Tucker said, "Last round coming up." He gave Skeet a drink, then saw the lanky form of Seth Porter coming down the stairs. Seth was wearing a suit and tie, and had arrived about an hour ahead of his usual schedule.

Seth waved Tucker over.

Tucker killed the timer and told Skeet, "Don't cool off."

He met Seth at the bottom of the stairs, wondering what was up. He saw that Seth's silver mustache was trimmed. Between that and the suit, he looked better, but Tucker couldn't help noticing the weight that Seth had lost. Weight he couldn't afford to lose.

Seth whispered, "Good news, bad news. Come to my office. Just you."

Tucker nodded and went back to the ring.

Skeet was jogging in place, talking to a young kid who was training for his first pro fight on an undercard. "In the first round, just breathe and move," Skeet cautioned. "But you got to jab, every time you move."

Distracted, Tucker peeled off the punch-mitts.

"What's up?" asked Skeet.

"With his brother passing away, Seth ain't the same. Wants to see me." Tucker shrugged. "Probably just wants a little time with someone who can remember better times, back in the day."

Skeet rolled his shoulders, working to stay warm.

"Skip the last round," said Tucker. "Do some light speed bag, three rounds. Finish up with crunches, two sets of a hundred."

Skeet nodded, watching the young fighter shadow box, flicking jabs.

As Tucker unlaced Skeet's gloves and pulled them off, Skeet asked, "What about this afternoon?"

"Have tuna salad for lunch and two helpings of fruit. Then a nap. Be here at three sharp to pump iron."

Skeet called out to the other fighters, "Crank up the boom-box if you want. Tuck's outta here."

As Tucker climbed the stairs, some half-assed jive rap music filled the gym, forcing boxers to raise their voices, hollering to each other as they skipped rope or shadow boxed.

Tucker reached Seth's cramped office, which smelled of cigars and the pastrami sandwich Seth always had for lunch. Seth gave him a weak smile. Tucker took a seat, facing thirty years of photographs that decorated the walls. Mostly black-and-whites, dulled with age. They showed Seth alongside each of the fighters he had managed, mostly before cable, satellite and closed circuit television.

Seth followed Tucker's gaze and shook his head. "That's when you worked for an honest dollar," he said, "before the likes of Don King, and all the hustlers who followed him. Back when a fighter's career mattered. Not just the money."

Tucker saw that many of the photos included Seth's half-brother John, whose two-packs a day had finally caught up with him. He'd fought it hard, going under the knife, then buying himself another six months with chemo.

Seth squared his shoulders. "How long we known each other, Tuck?"

"Twenty years." He pointed at a snapshot of a tall, raw-boned trainer wearing punch-mitts. "Since Big Jim Duvall took me on, teaching me corner work."

Seth nodded. "Well, there's no putting it off. Like I said, good news and bad news. Here's the good. Skeet might get a shot at Zakharov. The bad news is, I've sold my whole stable."

"Down to the last man?"

Seth nodded. "Every fighter's contract and the lease on this gym." He paused, turning to look at a photograph of his half-brother.

"Nothing's the same since John died. More work than fun, and me too tired to do my job—let alone what John used to handle, writing contracts and dealing with the commission."

Tucker nodded. "Then it's time to get out."

Seth picked up a pencil, frowned, and used his thumb to break it in half. "The thing is, once I decided to sell, I couldn't give it away, Tuck. I had to make it right for my family, you know? For thirty years, they put up with God knows what, because of this crazy business."

Tucker waited.

"That's why I sold to Jabbari."

In Tucker's opinion, Jabbari, who hailed from Jamaica, was the latest Don King wannabe. Not someone Tucker admired, or would trust. Still, he expected Jabbari would want him to stay on, since he and Skeet were a proven combination.

"Jabbari wants you here at two. That's all I know."

Tucker managed a smile and offered his hand. "I wish you the best, Seth. You and your family. You've been good for boxing."

They shook hands, then hugged across the desk.

When they separated, Seth wiped at the corner of his eyes. "Damn it all." He shook his head softly. "You gonna to break the news to Skeet, or should I?"

* * *

Tucker waited outside the gym, in his '68 Caddy, with his window rolled down. His hip hurt anytime he sat for too long, so he had his right leg up on the passenger seat, stretched out.

When Skeet came up the stairs, Tucker waved him over, motioning to the passenger side.

Skeet got in, and Tucker told him about the gym's sale to Jabbari and the possible fight with Zakharov. Skeet nodded and looked out the window, focusing on something in the distance.

Boxing is a hard business, run by a small community where everyone knows the major players. So Tucker didn't expect Skeet to be surprised about the gym changing hands, the fighter's contracts being sold, or the likes of Jabbari taking over.

Finally, Skeet said, "Seth cashed out. That's done. But this is my chance. This is the fight that can turn things around. When I whip Zakharov, that'll bump me into the top five."

Tucker held up a hand. "Don't be skippin' ahead to a title fight. It's Zakharov you're facing."

Skeet took a breath and let it out. "I got to think about this one, and all the next ones I can."

"What do you mean?"

Skeet scowled. "You know that damn franchise my cousin was so hot about? Well, that's where my savings went, six months ago. Then, last Thursday, he calls me. 'Stead of building three Chicken Delights, like he tol' me, he started construction on five, ran out of dough, and now the creditors are crawling up his ass."

Tucker closed his eyes for a second. "Can't you—"

"Forget it, Tuck. Your heart's in the right place, but I'm last in line. 'Unsecured' they call it. No strings on the money."

Tucker wondered what in hell Skeet had been thinking. The man damn near went to war, earning his money in the ring, then placed it in the hands of some cousin with a greasy dream? Might as well have put it on the line at Vegas and rolled the dice.

"Listen," Tucker said. "Losing your bankroll hurts, but that's behind you. And this purse for fighting Zakharov? Win-or-lose, it's enough to retire on."

Skeet poked him in the chest. "Man, I know you mean well, but don't be raggin' me 'bout hanging up my gloves. Not with Zakharov comin' at me."

Tucker rubbed his forehead, regretting what he'd said. He'd meant to offer comfort. Instead, he'd said the wrong thing. To a prizefighter, retiring seems like quitting. And you can't think about quitting with a fight in front of you.

"You're right, Skeet. Forget what I said. Just focus, you dig? Like a laser."

"My man," said Skeet. Sitting on the front seat, he grinned and gave a little bob and weave.

Tucker smiled, getting into it. "For starters, I'll call around and get tapes on Zakharov. Be here at three to lift weights."

* * *

Tucker went to Hector's Hawaiian-Taqueria, which was housed in a corrugated tin shack where the regulars sat shoulder to shoulder, wearing ball caps or hard hats, scuffed boots, and coveralls with loops for tools.

Tucker had his usual Corona beer and pair of Ono tacos, topped with grilled onions and mango-chutney. The din of conversation helped him relax as he put his thoughts in order. As he ate, he planned for his meeting with Jabbari. The man was a shark. He had a reputation for seeking out any sign of weakness, then using money or his bodyguards to get his way. With Jabbari, it all boiled down to money and power. But if Jabbari had followed Skeet's career, he'd see that better promotion could turn him into the moneymaker he used to be. Especially fighting someone like Zakharov. And if Jabbari understood that, he should also understand that it made sense to keep him on as Skeet's trainer, since the two of them had only lost two fights in seven years.

* * *

After lunch, Tucker entered the gym and found the stairway blocked by one of Jabbari's men. He was a huge black man with a pockmarked face, wearing a pale blue shirt the size of a tent.

"You Tucker?" he asked.

When Tucker nodded, the big man pointed toward Seth's office.

"Is Skeet downstairs?" asked Tucker. "You know who I mean? The boxer?"

Ignoring his question, Jabbari's thug kept pointing at the office. "Man's waitin'."

Tucker walked in to find Jabbari sitting at the desk, flanked by two heavyset black men in ill-fitting suits that belonged in a disco. Jabbari's skin was the color of soot. He wore a black silk suit, and gold rings on most of his fingers.

Frowning, Jabbari was reading what appeared to be a contract, running his finger along each line of print.

Both bodyguards glared at Tucker, as if daring him to make a move, until Jabbari raised his head with a bored look and waved them out of the office.

Jabbari motioned him to a chair.

As Tucker sat down, Jabbari asked, "How soon for Skeet? How long to get ready?"

"Depends. Who's the opponent?"

Jabbari gave a slow shrug. "Somebody wi' power, but not so much savvy."

Tucker waited, then said, "Like Zakharov?"

Jabbari's eyes showed surprise, but only for a second. "You hear dat? Where you hear?"

Tucker offered a shrug that matched Jabbari's.

"Well," said Jabbari. "'Tis true, I be havin' conversations with Bo Greene. He want to know if Skeet could put up a good fight 'gainst Zakharov. Somethin' fans talk about after."

Tucker gave a soft nod, then spoke with assurance. "Skeet would put on a show. Something they'd remember. He always does."

"You 'tink? Even wi' one fightah's career risin' an da odder one fadin'?"

"Skeet's record is solid."

"You get what I mean. Young an' strong, a puncher 'gainst da aging boxer—one known for fightin' pretty."

Tucker sat back in his chair, certain that Skeet's future was at stake. "Jabbari, this is the kind of match that draws money. Grace against power. 'Slick' Lewis and Zakharov the 'Red Hammer,' going at it."

"People pay, den get mad if it's over in one round."

Tucker shook his head. "Skeet will wear him down, instead of going head-to head."

"Still, Zakharov's strong."

"Even backin' up, Skeet's got a jab that slices and dices. Chasing Skeet, the Russian's going to tire. Skeet will help him along, going to the body. Then, when Zakharov's legs start to go, Skeet will step it up with combinations."

That drew a frown from Jabbari, followed by pursed lips. "Let me put dis anodder way. Don' wanna see Skeet get hurt. You 'tink he know enough to hold back? Protect hisself?"

Tucker had never heard of Jabbari taking the slightest interest in any boxer's health or welfare. Nothing beyond the money a fighter could generate. On top of that, anyone well versed in the fight game knew that Jabbari and Bo Greene had an unspoken agreement—a way to scratch each other's back. What the two of them did was help each other's rising stars by matching them up with fighters from each other's stables—fighters whose skills were starting to fade. Then, down the line, after one of their fighters nabbed a title, the favor was returned. The other promoter got first crack, having one of his fighters challenge the new champ.

"So, Tucker…if Zakharov traps Skeet in da corner, he'll cover up?"

Tucker showed no reaction, but got the message. Jabbari might as well have asked, will he take a dive? And Tucker knew. Knew that Skeet never would. Plus, Tucker didn't like the way Jabbari was treating him—like a dog that rolled over on command.

Jabbari leaned forward. "How 'bout it?"

Tucker held back his disgust. Unlike Jabbari, Tucker loved the fight game. Loved it to the point where he cared more about boxing than money, because, somehow, it nourished his soul.

Jabbari lowered his voice. "I'm countin' on you," he said, "you an' Skeet, to not disappoint me. 'Cuz disappointment make me mad. Make me do things."

Jabbari's voice was soft, but his gaze had hardened, and it made Tucker remember what had happened last year when a heavyweight was rumored to have crossed Jabbari, by refusing to take a dive. After his victory, he seemed to have gotten so drunk that he fell down a stairwell, more than once, breaking his neck.

Tucker chose his words carefully. "You're asking, can Skeet follow directions?"

Slowly, Jabbari nodded.

Jabbari had him cornered. Even if Skeet passed on the fight, Jabbari could blacklist him. No manager or promoter would touch him.

"Listen," Tucker said, trying to buy time. Wanting to get to Skeet before Jabbari could. "I don't think Skeet would have to be told how you want it to end. Not against Zakharov. Not the way Zakharov hits."

"You 'tink?"

"It comes down to this. If Skeet was in his prime, Zakharov would be the underdog. But that was four years ago."

Jabbari studied him carefully, like a man who wanted to be sure. "Tell me," he said. "Any 'ting you know dat would make it tougher for Skeet?"

Tucker felt a sour taste rising in his mouth. "Skeet's past his best years. He has to train non-stop to keep his edge. Any break in his routine...."

Jabbari smiled, and Tucker realized he had crossed the line. Jabbari felt that they'd reached agreement.

For an instant, Tucker wished he could take everything back. But it was too late. Skeet wouldn't walk, because he needed the money. And Jabbari had promised Skeet to Greene as a stepping-stone for Zakharov.

"Which would hurt most?" asked Jabbari. "Less time to get ready, or changin' his routine?"

Tucker forced himself not to look away. "Either one could cost Skeet the fight."

Jabbari steepled his hands, and his smile broadened.

One of Jabbari's men stuck his head into the room. "We're late for your plane."

Jabbari waved him away and turned to Tucker.

"Some 'ting else. You've got da good reputation, so I'd like your opinion."

"On what?"

"I'm adding fighters, so I'll need more trainers. Der are three trainers I might pick between. Tell me what you 'tink."

Tucker nodded, reminding himself not to get flattered. Jabbari had already tricked him once.

"How 'bout Kirby Daniels?"

"He's good, specially for honing a fighter who knows what he's doing. He's thin on patience, though. The man rants and raves if he has to lay down the fundamentals."

"An' Frankie Preston?"

"Solid. The man can work with fighters at any stage. He builds on what's there."

"How 'bout Tito Carvall?"

Tucker shrugged. "One of the best. But he breaks down every fighter and starts over. Insists on a new foundation. That's good for young boxers, but seasoned fighters hate him. Even the ones he helps."

Jabbari gave a slight nod. "For what it's worth, I 'tink you been straight wi' me." Slowly, he added, "I know we both concerned 'bout Skeet. Dat nothing happen to him."

Jabbari stood. The meeting was over.

* * *

Tucker approached Skeet where he lay on the weight bench, wearing baggy sweat pants and a hooded sweatshirt as he strained to finish his set. He was bench pressing a hundred pounds.

To Skeet's left, a balding heavyweight was flexing, admiring himself in a mirror that had cracked and been patched with duct tape. To Skeet's other side, a young kid with a buzz cut—probably a featherweight—was adjusting the load on the pull-down machine, removing a ten-pound plate.

"What's gonna happen?" the young kid asked the heavyweight.

The heavyweight turned to Tucker. "It won't be the same," he grumbled. "Not without Seth."

"Talkin' won't change it," said Tucker. "Better to keep working."

The young kid nodded, but didn't look convinced.

Skeet managed a smile. "Fourth set," he grunted. "Five reps each."

Skeet raised the barbell with trembling arms as the heavyweight spotted him, then set it in the rack.

Tucker inclined his head toward the stairs.

Skeet toweled off as they climbed the steps up to street level, where a high cloud cover painted the sky gray.

Tucker said, "There's no fight yet with Zakharov. Not officially. Jabbari and Bo Greene seem to be cookin' one up, but I don't trust either of them."

Skeet couldn't keep the excitement from his face. "Man, this is what I been waiting for. All those top-ranked guys, dodging me for so long. I'm due, baby. And this purse'll clear a hundred grand, win-or-lose. Got to."

"Maybe. Just don't spend it 'til we got a signed contract."

"Man...." He grinned. "This is the one, Tuck. Our chance for some glory." For a few quick seconds, he did the Ali-shuffle.

"Don't get ahead of yourself. We ain't sure it's Zakharov you'll fight. Not 'til we see it in writing."

"Yeah, yeah." Skeet gave him a pained look, too eager to calm down.

"Let's play it smart, is all I'm sayin'. Once your opponent and the date are picked, we'll tailor your training."

Skeet grinned as he twisted his shoulders from side to side. "I better get back. I gotta do squats."

Tucker nodded, knowing that Skeet was lining up on Zakharov, all the way.

Skeet jogged down the stairs, and Tucker followed more slowly, using the handrail. To his surprise, he caught up with Skeet outside of Seth's office.

Skeet stood, glaring at one of Jabbari's men, who was stripping photos off the walls and tossing them into a box.

"Hey, man," said Skeet. "That's history you're messin' with."

The big man didn't answer. He kept at it, taking down photos.

"Easy, now." Tucker put a hand on Skeet's shoulder. "We got to look ahead."

The big man turned to Tucker, showing a gold tooth and bloodshot eyes. "You. Tell the fighters this is Jabbari's place. From now on, they belong to him."

Tucker caught the set of Skeet's shoulders and pushed, getting him to move down the stairs.

"Glove up," he called after Skeet. "We'll take it out on the heavy bag."

* * *

The next morning, as usual, Tucker found Skeet inside the gym before sunup. He'd done his roadwork, finished his jump rope and was hitting the speed bag. Tucker selected twelve-ounce gloves from Skeet's gear, then motioned him over to the heavy bags. While Tucker put the gloves on Skeet and laced them up, Skeet dipped his knees and flexed his legs, then tipped his head from side to side, stretching his neck until it popped.

The differences were small, but Tucker could sense the impatience in Skeet—driven by his hunger for a match with Zakharov, and the doors that a victory would open.

"I know what you want, Skeet. And I understand how bad you want it."

"Then let's get to it."

Tucker saw how hard it was going to be, putting Skeet off, looking for the best way to warn him. "Don't get anxious, is all I'm sayin'. We gotta build this victory, step by step."

Skeet jogged in place, rolling his shoulders. "You're right. Strategize. Be the man with a plan."

Tucker nodded, still waiting for the right moment. "Against Zakharov, you gotta keep moving. Toe to toe would be suicide."

Skeet raised his gloves, then twisted his head and shoulders, slipping left and right. "He's never gone the distance."

Tucker shifted his weight, needing to ease the ache in his hip. "Usually he gets a knockout in two rounds. Four at most. S'why you'll need to backpedal and make him chase you. Keep him off with the jab."

Skeet flicked a jab at the bag. "What's his weak spot?"

"Don't worry. We'll find it. Once we've got tapes of his fights, we'll study 'em 'till we go blind."

Skeet grinned. "Now you're talkin'."

Tucker nodded, caught up in Skeet's good spirits. "We'll map it out and sharpen your combinations. But for *now*—"

"Yeah, yeah," Skeet grumbled with a smile. "I know what's comin'."

"In that case...." Tucker set the timer for three-minute rounds, with only thirty-seconds rest.

The bell rang and Skeet got some good head motion going. He shuffled to his left, then backpedaled around the heavy bag, sticking it with his jab, making it snap.

"That's good," said Tucker. "But when you jab, I want Zakharov thinking about it more than feeling it. So keep it fast and light."

A shadow fell across the floor, and Tucker turned, recognizing the thug in the pale blue shirt.

"Who let you in?" asked the big man, stepping closer.

"Seth," said Tucker. "He gave us keys a long time ago."

The big man motioned to Tucker. "Get the keys and come to the office."

Skeet turned toward the thug, taking the forty-five degree angle of a boxer's stance, and Tucker held up a hand. "Skeet, keep working the bag."

Skeet didn't move.

"It's me asking," said Tucker, "not him. Where's your key?"

Skeet kept his eyes on Jabbari's man. "Right front pocket of my sweats."

Tucker fished it out and followed the big man upstairs, into the office Seth had occupied. Now its walls were bare. Downstairs, Tucker heard the repeated crack of Skeet delivering sharp blows to the heavy bag.

Tucker dropped both keys on the desk. "Is that all?"

The big man cocked his head, regarding Tucker. "No. You got lucky just now. Specially with your friend's attitude." He reached into the drawer, pulled out two bricks of hundred dollar bills and set them in front of Tucker.

"That's nine grand. Your signing bonus."

Tucker stared at the money, leery of picking it up. "What does Jabbari expect for this?"

The thug shook his head, then added an airline ticket to the money. "It's Bo Greene you work for now."

Tucker examined the ticket. Southwest Airlines, one-way, Los Angeles to Sacramento.

The thug grinned at Tucker, showing crooked teeth that were stained tobacco brown. "You got two days. Greene wants you there by Friday."

Tucker thought about it. "What if I don't want the job, or get another offer?"

The man rolled his shoulders with a half-smile. "Don't get Jabbari or Greene pissed off. Either one of them. 'Less you want me earning the bonus."

Stone-faced, Tucker scooped up the money. He shoved it into the bib pocket on his denim jumpsuit, and started downstairs, moving slowly.

He knew Jabbari and Greene could put the word out, black-listing him. But Jabbari and Greene promoted fights mainly in the States. Maybe he'd head to Mexico. Working fights out of Tijuana was better than nothing. But where would that leave Skeet?

Descending, he gripped the handrail and fought off the pain in his hip. He could be in Mexico by nightfall, but Jabbari and Greene could still reach Skeet. So taking off was out. If he split, Skeet would pay for it, because Jabbari thought they had a deal.

Tucker started across the gym floor, watching Skeet as he worked the heavy bag, cracking it with double-hooks, low then high. Two other fighters were in the gym, both heavyweights, as was Frank Tanner, another trainer who had worked for Seth over the years. Often, Tucker and Tanner had worked the same corner in fights, with Tanner sometimes being the cutman.

Tucker stopped by Tanner, who was wrapping one of the big men's hands.

"Keep an eye on Skeet for me, okay? I gotta take care of some business for a few days."

Tanner nodded. "Sure. What routine do you have him on?"

"Another week of light work. Mitt drills for timing, but no sparring. Mix it up between shadow boxing and the heavy bag. Skeet knows the drill."

"Glad to help."

Tucker felt Skeet watching him and turned. He forced a smile. "Keep working," he called out. "I've got some business to tend to. See you tomorrow." He motioned with his hands like he was pushing something down, then tapped his stomach—his signal for Skeet to lower his stance and work the body with punches to the inside.

* * *

Tucker drove home to his stuccoed two-room apartment, that was situated directly beneath the booming flight path of LAX. As the dishes rattled from a departing jet, he found his sometimes-girlfriend, Parisha, sitting in the kitchen. She was frowning, and there were three empty Miller Lites on the table. Usually, the arguments started after her second beer or glass of wine.

Along the tile counter, he saw some apples she'd been peeling. They had turned brown, were sitting next to a pie tin that she'd lined and trimmed with a crust.

"What's this?" she demanded, handing him a slip of paper.

It was a note signed by his landlord, saying, "Your friends bought out your lease. Please vacate by Thursday."

Angry now, Tucker crumpled the paper and threw it on the floor. Just to spite Bo Greene, he thought about canceling his trip to Sacramento.

"You walkin' out on me?" Parisha demanded. She stooped and snatched up the scrap of paper.

"Listen," he said. "The gym's changed hands, and there's some shit I'm dealin' with. Don't give me no grief on top of it."

"That's what I am to you? *Grief?*"

He took a breath and let it out slowly. "This ain't about you, Parisha. You think it is, because you're halfway into a six-pack, but it ain't."

"Prove it."

"That's easy. Come with me."

She blinked, looking surprised, then puzzled. "Where? Where you goin'?"

"I haven't decided."

"What? For a weekend? For a little vacation?"

"It might be longer. Maybe a few months."

"Shit." She put her hands on her hips. "My life is here, Tuck, tied to my job and carin' for my Mama."

Tucker nodded, then turned and walked out.

She yelled after him, "What's with you, Tucker? What's your damn problem?"

* * *

Taking side streets to avoid the crush of the evening commute, Tucker drove through a light rain to a Russian bar he'd heard about. Two years ago it had opened as "New Siberia," then recently had changed hands, to a new Russian owner who had renamed it.

As Tucker walked to the entrance, the door sign read "The Ice Pick." Below it, someone had scrawled, "Way to go, Trotsky."

Tucker brushed water off his nylon jacket and stepped inside. Through a thick tobacco haze, he saw what looked like several Russian men lined up at the bar, wearing belted leather coats that made his jacket look cheap. Some of the men brooded and others talked, but they all puffed on cigarettes as they drank, ignoring the *no smoking* sign that was covered with graffiti.

Tucker sat at a small table. Instead of peanuts or beer nuts, it had a bowl of hard candy.

A waitress in fishnet stockings and a see-through blouse approached him, and he asked for two shots of their best.

"*Stolichnaya*," she said, "or *Ketel One*? It's a personal decision."

"Make it *Stoly*."

She left and he looked around, seeing that he wasn't the only black man there. That helped him relax, but he hadn't come to the bar for comfort. He had come because of Zakharov. The Russian was part of the mess he was in, not just Jabbari and Greene. So Tucker wanted to get a feel for Zakharov. At least for some part of his life, outside the ring.

He sat back and studied the other drinkers. Most of them seemed to have led hard lives. They stood as if they carried burdens, but weren't bending beneath the load. Tucker thought about Russian fighters and how they had come to America. For many years, along with the Cubans, Russian "amateur" boxers had earned many gold medals in the Olympics. Then the Berlin Wall had fallen in 1990, and Russian fighters saw the money they could earn boxing in the USA.

Quickly, they proved themselves to be tough bastards, like the current crop of fighters, which included the lightweight, Kostya Tszyu, and the heavyweight, Vitali Klitschko. Both of them were warriors.

Still waiting for his drinks, Tucker looked above the bar's entrance. He saw something like a banjo mounted on the wall, but its sound box was triangular in shape. Both the neck and face of it were inlaid with pearl and with something else that glittered.

The waitress arrived with his shots of *Stoly*, both chilled. She followed his gaze. "It's a *balalaika*," she said. "Its music is sweet, but sad."

He paid her, digging into his wallet, instead of his jacket's inside pocket, which held the plane ticket and the packs of Jabbari's hundred dollar bills. She frowned at his two-dollar tip and left.

Tucker killed the first shot, which felt cold going down, then became a hot ribbon, tracing the path it had taken. He blew out his breath, then sipped slowly from the second glass.

Tucker knew he had more than one problem. The first was getting blacklisted if he didn't train Zakharov. The second was getting beat to a pulp, or worse, if Zakharov lost against Skeet. He took a sip of vodka and tried to think it through. Jabbari and Greene couldn't afford an obvious dive. That meant Skeet might get off easy if an accidental head butt stopped the fight. If that happened, and Skeet was ahead on the cards, then afterward it was less likely Skeet would be punished. But if Skeet defeated the Russian soundly, there would be no escape from Jabbari's men.

Tucker tried to figure another way out, but it was tough. Jabbari and his men had been at this for a long while, so they'd watch for signs of anyone turning against them. Even if Skeet "injured" himself in training, Jabbari and Greene might postpone instead of canceling the fight, because Zakharov's opponent had to be someone of Skeet's ranking. Otherwise, winning wouldn't earn Zakharov a shot at the title.

Eventually, Tucker resigned himself. He had to train Zakharov to win and hope that Skeet would retire after the fight. That was the only safe path he could see through the minefield that he and Skeet faced.

With that decided, he looked around the smoke-filled bar, which was becoming more crowded. These people looked like they were among friends, mostly chatting or having friendly arguments. It made him dwell on how many of his friends and acquaintances he'd let go over the years, until now he felt close to only a handful of people. Admitting that underscored how small his world had gotten. Usually, reflecting on what he'd lost or given up in life didn't bother him. But tonight it did.

He took a sip of *Stoly* and thought about trying to make up with Parisha after her anger over the news that he had to leave town. But he knew better. Even if he got on her good side, he couldn't tell her what was going on—and she would want to know.

He couldn't trust her to keep her mouth shut about the fix being in, between Jabbari and Greene. After he left town, she might show up at Jabbari's gym, trying to get hold of him, and shoot her mouth off.

Tucker shook his head and drank the last of the vodka. It was tempting to ignore everything—to just go home and be with her. But he knew the odds weren't good. Probably, they'd just argue instead of making love.

He stared into his empty shot glass and wondered what it would feel like, leaving not just his friends, but the city. He'd grown up in LA, but his family was gone. His folks had died, and he was twice divorced with both ex-wives living in Texas—raising two kids he wasn't sure were his. And his lone brother, Ben, had moved to Dallas twenty years ago.

A bearded man to Tucker's left clapped another man on his shoulder, making him spill his drink. Both men laughed and signaled for refills.

Tucker expected he'd miss a few spots where he liked to eat and maybe a couple of the restored movie theatres he swung by whenever they ran a festival, showing films that starred some of the old guys—like Lee Marvin, James Garner, or Sydney Poitier. Mostly, though, he'd be leaving behind the dozen or so friends he knew through boxing. Really, that was about it. Except for Parisha.

He frowned, then waved to the waitress, indicating he wanted another shot of *Stoly*. He'd wait long enough for Parisha to be asleep, or to have left his apartment. Then he'd go home and pack.

* * *

Just before dawn, Tucker parked his old Caddy across from the Ace Hardware Store they'd rebuilt after the Rodney King riots in '92. He knew that Skeet passed it every day on his five mile run. Across the street, a city garbage truck eased forward, using mechanical arms to raise a Dumpster. Groaning, it finished the job and moved on.

Ahead, where the block ended, Skeet came into sight, running with ease. He was wearing sweats, topped off with a scarf and stocking cap. Tucker figured him to be on pace for an eight-minute mile.

When Skeet closed to within a hundred yards, Tucker got out and waved.

Skeet pulled up, jogging in place. "What's up?"

"Jabbari's given me the boot."

Skeet's face twisted in anger. "Fuck that. I'll tell Jabbari we're a team. I'll tell 'em—"

Tucker raised a hand, stopping him. "Don't, man. Don't lose your cool. Jabbari's lining up your fight with Zakharov."

"But you deserve to be there, man. To get your cut after all these years, thick and thin."

Tucker smiled at Skeet's loyalty. "It gets worse. I'm working for Bo Greene."

Skeet's eyebrows jacked up. "Training Zakharov?"

Tucker nodded. "If you want, I'll walk away. But that would hurt us both. We could get blacklisted."

Tucker watched Skeet's expression tighten as he figured it out. "So this way, with you knowing my every move, Greene figures Zakharov's got a sure thing."

"Pretty much." Tucker folded his arms and leaned against his Caddy.

Skeet cracked his knuckles. "Which means Jabbari has to know."

"He's in it, all the way."

Skeet thought it over. "With cornermen hiring out to top dollar," he said, "it won't be the first time a top trainer like you joined the other camp, goin' against a boxer he coached."

"That's what they're counting on."

Skeet shook his head. "Man, why they goin' to all this trouble? My fight with Zakharov's probably gonna be the undercard to some heavyweight bout. And everyone knows, heavyweights draw the high rollers and big bets. Besides, the odds 'tween me and Zakharov won't be one-sided. Neither one of us will be a long-shot, where they could score ten-to-one on a wager."

"Yeah, but this is Jabbari and Bo Greene, tradin' favors. Who knows what else is on the table?"

Frowning, Skeet said, "It still don't make sense. This Zakharov ain't got the personality. You savvy? This Roosky can't feed the cameras. He ain't no Sugar Ray, no Oscar Dela Hoya."

"Which tells me the deal could be bigger than Zakharov. Hell, for all we know, Bo Greene or Jabbari could be using the fight just to take in bets—to launder dirty money."

"So Zakharov's like me? Just a way for Jabbari and Greene to get ahead?"

"Damn straight. We just don't know the angle. It could be as simple as the Rooskies eager for one of their own to get some glory, and payin' to make it happen." Tucker pushed off his car and stepped closer. "It could be anything, Skeet. You follow? Doesn't have to make sense to us—long as Jabbari and Greene get somethin' they want."

Skeet looked away for a moment, then locked eyes with Tucker.

"Fine, Tuck. Train Zakharov. But get your money up front, 'cuz I intend to win. No matter what."

Tucker could see there was no chance of changing Skeet's mind, so he said it, straight out. "Then you better watch your back, Skeet, 'cuz Jabbari and Greene expect Zakharov to win."

"I got these," Skeet said, holding up both firsts, "so let 'em come."

For a second, Tucker felt like he couldn't breathe. Not with Skeet's pride blinding him to what lay ahead.

Slowly, Tucker extended his hand and they shook. Then gave each other a hug. Softly, Tucker said, "Just think on it, Skeet. That's all I'm askin'."

Skeet hugged him harder, saying, "It ain't over, Tuck. It just ain't."

Tucker stood back, fearing for his friend. Either way, Tucker thought, this'll be his last fight.

* * *

Thursday morning, Tucker flew into Sacramento, then caught a cab and set about looking for a place to stay within walking distance of Bo Greene's gym, on Del Paso Boulevard.

In that part of town there were few hotels to speak of, but lots of little shops, sandwiched between liquor stores and bars, with rows of small stucco homes tucked behind them, on either side of the boulevard.

By late afternoon, Tucker had found a rental—half of a tiny duplex, two blocks northwest of the gym. It took him thirty seconds to unpack. He had only two bags, one with clothes and one that held his punch-mitts and corner kit. The stacks of Jabbari's hundred dollar bills were hidden in the money belt he wore under his shirt and jacket.

The town struck him as small, with only a few tall buildings. He'd been there only five hours, but already he was missing how his day would have gone back home.

He would have started it over dark coffee and a plate of eggs with *chorizo*, while reading the LA Times at *Café Cubano*, which had a kitchen the size of a kiosk, with two picnic tables under a canvas awning. Then he would've done a morning workout with Skeet at the gym. Then lunch at Hector's, maybe having a grilled Ahi burger and rice. Then the afternoon with Skeet, as he went through the weights and his stretching routine. Come the evening, he'd spend a few hours with Parisha, maybe renting a video if they could agree on one, which was seldom.

Now his evenings would be more lonely, even if he and Parisha had argued three times for every one they made love.

* * *

The sun had almost set by the time Tucker took his bag and walked to Bo Greene's gym, still wearing his money belt. Sacramento in late January was cooler than LA, so he had to keep up a good pace, otherwise a chill would settle into his hip.

He found Greene's gym on a street corner, set up the opposite from how Seth had done it. This one had glass picture windows across its front and its north wall, with blinds that were only closed partway.

Peering through the front window, Tucker saw a small counter and cash register by the entrance, watched over by a large black man with Rasta hair, all twisted and snarled. At the back of the gym, two boxing rings were roped off on raised platforms.

Barbells and weight machines were up front, with floor-to-ceiling mirrors and large floor mats along the south wall for jumping rope and shadow boxing. Heavy bags hung from a beam in the center of the gym, and speed bags were in the northwest corner, squeezed in next to one of the rings.

As he stood on the sidewalk and looked to his left, Tucker got his first clue as to why Zakharov might prefer training in Sacramento over Los Angeles. There were two Ukrainian churches within sight, the nearest one occupying what had previously been a movie theater, with its ornamental marquee still in place. Instead of displaying a movie title, the red plastic letters on the marquee spelled out, "He has risen. Matthew 28:1–10."

From the glass doors that served as an entrance to the church, two heavyset, pale women stepped onto the sidewalk, chatting earnestly. Each wore a lacy handkerchief pinned on her head, and a dress that reached her ankles. Banners hung from lampposts near the church, proclaiming something about the "Pride of Del Paso Heights." Tucker looked from the banner to Bo Greene's gym and had his doubts.

Tucker felt the temperature dropping slightly as a few cars drove past with their headlights on. He patted his money belt, making sure that it didn't show. Then he entered the gym.

B.B. King was playing on the sound system, cranking out "Ask Me No Questions." The air carried a sweaty tang. Up front, the big counterman with the half-ass dreadlocks wore a Bob Marley T-shirt. Even sitting down, he was taller than Tucker. He gave Tucker a look like he didn't want to be bothered, then snapped his fingers. "Hey, you're early. I didn't expect you 'til tomorrow." He hooked a thumb toward the rear of the gym. "Zakharov's about to spar in the big ring. I'll introduce you."

Tucker made it around the counter, working to hide his limp. "Not yet. Let me watch for a bit."

The man shrugged. "Whatever you say."

Tucker walked to a wooden bench on the near side of the bigger boxing ring. As he sat down, the money belt pinched his waist.

Carrying that much money made him think of all the times he'd had none, working his way though two divorces and child support. Those were bitter times, when Skeet had dug into his winnings to tide him over, and never complained when it took Tucker the better part of three years to pay it back.

Tucker set his bag on the bench and unzipped it. He pretended to study its contents while two bare-chested men came out of the locker room, already gloved up, wearing boxing trunks, head gear and cups. One man was black. The other Tucker recognized as Zakharov. The black man looked light on his feet, with plenty of weight in his shoulders. Zakharov had skin whiter than toothpaste and displayed hard, flat muscles without much definition. Despite that, two things stood out. Zakharov had a scar that made it look as if someone had spooned out part of his left eyebrow. Also, his nose was splayed and bent to one side. Judging by the tilt of his nose, it had been broken more than once. Still, Zakharov walked with a swagger and was laughing about something.

Both men climbed into the ring, followed by a squat Mexican holding a water bottle and two mouthpieces. Neither boxer had a good sweat going, which Tucker didn't like.

The Mexican rinsed the mouthpieces and stuck one in each fighter's mouth. To the black man, he said, "Lots of movement and protect your ribs." To Zakharov, he said, "Cut off the ring."

The black boxer nodded. Zakharov's only response was to pound his gloves together.

Tucker studied the Russian and wondered if he could keep up with the moves Skeet had and the punches he could throw.

The boxers touched gloves as the Mexican moved to the wall timer and flipped a switch.

When the bell rang, the black man got up on his toes and did a little juke, then backpedaled.

Zakharov brought his gloves to his chin and moved forward, low in his stance. Every time the black man changed direction, so did Zakharov, advancing at an angle that let the black boxer retreat, but with less room to maneuver.

The black man started flicking jabs, even though Zakharov wasn't quite within range. Zakharov kept his gloves high and close together. He advanced, looking over their tops. Zakharov got closer, and his sparring partner's jabs caught his gloves, but didn't part them or find Zakharov's chin.

Tucker waited, sensing Zakharov's impatience.

Suddenly, Zakharov feinted, twisting low and to his left, as if to throw a hook. The black man covered up, dropping his elbows to his ribs, just as Zakharov threw an overhand right that struck his forehead, driving him back. As the black man bounced off the ropes, Zakharov clipped his chin with a hook. In the blink of an eye, Zakharov dropped his left shoulder, getting a lower angle, and dug to the ribs. That buckled the other man's knees, but with a grunt, he rallied, throwing a right cross that nailed Zakharov on the nose. Zakharov blinked and shook off the punch, then smiled as the black man made a quick pivot, getting away from him.

Moving no faster than before, Zakharov advanced, and in short order, cornered his sparring partner. The black man threw left-right combinations, but Zakharov managed a jerky bob and weave, evading his punches without backing up.

Zakharov feinted with his right and made his own pivot, anticipating how his opponent would try to escape. He did this just ahead of the black man, who made a sharp pivot, never expecting to come face to face with Zakharov, and the black man froze for the split second it took Zakharov to fire a jab, which was followed by a stiff right cross that snapped his head back.

Desperate now, firing on instinct, Zakharov's opponent countered with a right uppercut.

Zakharov took it on his chin and fired another hook, catching the other man's ear, spinning him in a half-circle, almost dropping him.

The bell rang, saving him from Zakharov.

Tucker bit his lip. Skeet was in for some hard times. Then he scolded himself, knowing what it would cost if Skeet won.

Quickly, the trainer gave water to Zakharov's sparring partner, who was leaning against the ropes, taking deep breaths. Over his shoulder, the trainer told Zakharov, "Skip the power shots. Show me your jab."

Zakharov grinned, but didn't answer. The trainer shook his head, then walked over and gave the Russian water.

The next two rounds were more of the same, with Zakharov not jabbing as much as using his outstretched left arm like a range finder, to measure his opponent's chin.

As the fourth round started, Tucker stood up, approached the trainer and said, "I'm Harlan Tucker, from Los Angeles."

The Mexican looked him over then reached down from the ring, offering his hand, and they shook. "Manny Gonzalez. Why didn't you speak up?"

"I wanted to see Zakharov at work."

When Manny nodded, Tucker added, "You okay with Bo Greene picking me to train Zakharov?"

Gonzalez glanced at Zakharov, as the Russian threw a wild hook that missed.

"I'll miss the money, but not workin' with Zakharov. I keep telling him he's gotta change for a fast fighter, the likes of Skeet Lewis. But he don't listen."

Tucker showed his respect, nodding, but wondered if Manny would give him everything he knew about Zakharov. Tucker realized Manny might hold out, or even try to trip him up if he was sore about getting bumped from the fight. And Tucker really couldn't blame him. He knew how often trainers sweated and worked year round with fighters, only to get shoved aside going into a televised match. Having to watch some other trainer make the sports page and get the big payday.

Manny hollered to the black man, "Stick and move!"

Tucker asked, "What's it like, working for Bo Greene?"

Manny took a long look at the counter man with the Rasta hair. "Greene doesn't come around much."

"He gives you a free hand?"

"Far as that goes, yeah. Get to pick my own team for the corner, long as it's folks with experience."

Tucker nodded, wanting Manny on his side. "You know," he said, "I might need some help getting Zakharov ready. Plus workin' the corner."

That brought a smile to Manny as he turned to watch the fighters. "Take it easy," Manny called to Zakharov. "I want you chasing him, not busting his ribs."

Tucker was glad to extend his respect to Manny, and to make use of Manny's experience with Zakharov. But getting on Manny's good side also galled Tucker. It reminded him that he was abandoning Skeet, who had stuck with him all these years, despite a rocky start.

As Zakharov caught his sparring partner with an awkward jab, Tucker thought back to when he had first worked the corner for Skeet.

At Seth Porter's request, Tucker had signed on to work the corner in a ten-rounder, but he hadn't been in the best state of mind. Three hours before the fight he'd had a screaming match with his second wife, which had led to his being drunk by the time he arrived at the Forum and found Skeet, who had gotten tired of waiting and wrapped his own hands.

Skeet won the fight, pulling it out on his own, but afterwards he had cut to the chase with Tucker. Getting toe to toe, Skeet said, "Even with you half in the bag, old man, I'm learning a lot. Stuff that could get me a championship belt. But next time, I might need everything you know. So you gotta make up your mind. Get a grip on the booze, or hit the road."

Embarrassed, Tucker had promised, "It won't happen again."

Now the bell rang, ending Zakharov's fourth round, and Manny waved the boxers over. He unlaced their gloves and pulled them off. "Zak," he said, "this is your new trainer, Harlan Tucker."

Zakharov pulled off his headgear, spat out his mouthpiece and turned to Tucker. Up close, Tucker saw Zakharov had pale blue eyes and a birthmark on his cheek where it looked like someone had rubbed it with rust.

Zakharov studied him, then extended his hand.

Tucker took it, expecting the soft grip most fighters used as a way of protecting their hands. Instead, Zakharov's grip was like a vise.

Tucker squeezed back just as hard, without setting his jaw, or showing any other sign of effort. After a moment, Zakharov let go, saying, "Pleased. Good to meet you."

Tucker said, "Finish your workout with Manny. You and me start tomorrow. Be here at eight."

Zakharov gave him a half-smile, then turned back to Manny, who pointed at the speed bags.

* * *

That night, sitting at a wobbly table in the kitchen of his duplex, Tucker stared at the peeling paint and thought about getting phone service hooked up. Then chose not to, knowing that he'd end up calling some of his friends, and miss being in LA. Or he'd phone Parisha and get an earful for walking out on her. The worst part, though, was wanting to call Skeet and see how he was doing, and to wish him well. But that wouldn't make things any easier. Not for either of them.

Tucker rubbed the spot where his hip had begun to throb from walking to and from the gym. He glanced at the takeout cartons of Kung Pao chicken and pan-fired noodles he had brought home. He ignored the rental television and just ate. The food wasn't good, so he threw out what he didn't finish and turned in, peeling back the covers on a sagging bed.

* * *

Tucker got to the gym at a quarter to eight. He found Manny waiting, sipping coffee and eating a tortilla he'd coated with butter and a sprinkling of sugar.

"Coffee?"

Tucker nodded. As Manny poured him a cup, Tucker asked, "What kind of diet is Zakharov on? How many calories? How many meals a day?"

Manny smiled. "All my other fighters listen up pretty good. I get them to cut out the fats and eat lean. They get just enough calories to build them up, instead of tearing them down when the work gets harder, closer to a fight."

"And Zakharov?"

"First time I tried that, he told me about fighting in Chechnya during sub-zero winters, where he ate everything and anything to survive. Rations, horses roasted over a fire…even a dead man's leg. Said he ate for strength, and didn't need me telling him how."

Tucker pictured Skeet, sitting down to a meal of fish, rice, green beans and fresh fruit. Skeet was careful, adjusting his diet to keep an exact balance, working for stamina as well as strength.

"If Zakharov's so bad at listening, how did he learn to box?"

Manny bit into his tortilla. "The Russian Army throws some boxing into their training. Plus, he'll try any drill I give him. But if he can't see what comes of it, that's it. Either he asks what's next, or goes back to what he knows best."

Tucker sipped his coffee. "What are his strengths and weaknesses?"

Manny smiled and swallowed some tortilla. "Strengths? There's no quit in him; he can cut off the ring; and his fists are like sledgehammers. The man can break bones with them. Also, he's not a bleeder like most Russians. That's the good news."

"And the bad?"

"No jab. Not enough head movement. Worse than a Mexican fighter about backing up. If reverse was a gear, Zak's never found it or used it. So his opponents are never surprised. He just sticks to his bread-and-butter punches. And he loads up too much. He could be quick, but isn't. When I ask for combinations, he puts two goddamn punches together. Three at the most."

"How about roadwork? Pumping iron?"

"He'll ride a stationery bike while he watches TV or videos. No running to speak of. With the weights, I try to put fighters through multiple sets on different exercises. Mostly, I want stamina. But he insists on power lifting. Just squats and bench presses."

The buzzer rang at the gym's entrance, and the beefy counter man with ragged dreadlocks came in, carrying his coffee and an open box of powdered sugar donuts.

Manny gave him a nod, then walked Tucker over to the weights, showing him brand new machines by Universal and Nautilus. Then an old bench, patched with duct tape, next to the free weights. "This is Zakharov's spot."

The door buzzer sounded, and two younger fighters came into the gym, one pushing a bicycle. Tucker checked the clock, and saw that Zakharov was twenty minutes late.

Tucker thought about Skeet. By now, he'd have run five miles, done six rounds on the speed bag and be halfway though his time on the heavy bag.

Manny shrugged. "What else you wanna know?"

"Has Greene set a date for the fight?"

"He wants to hook up with the Roy Jones, John Ruiz bout. Zakharov and Skeet will improve the undercard."

"Shit. That's only four weeks away."

Manny nodded. "Zak doesn't mind. Says a soldier's always ready."

Tucker wondered about Zakharov's condition, especially when it came to the endurance he would need against Skeet. "It's been what, four months since Zakharov's last fight?"

"Just about. He KO'd Garcia in round two."

"You been watching any tapes of Skeet's fights?"

"A few."

"Show me what you've got."

* * *

By the time Zakharov showed up, it was almost eleven. A blonde in a black turbo Saab dropped him off. She gave him a smoldering, curbside kiss, then drove off with a screech, leaving a patch of rubber.

Zakharov came in looking tired and red around the eyes.

Tucker realized that back in LA, he and Skeet would have wrapped up their morning workout by now.

To Manny, Tucker said, "I need a moment with Zakharov."

Tucker followed Zakharov into the locker room.

Zakharov sat on a bench, then opened a locker that held a large gym bag. He set the bag on the floor, bent over and unlaced one of his street shoes.

Tucker kicked the locker door shut, slamming it with a bang.

Zakharov didn't flinch. He finished unlacing his shoe, then started on the other one while he looked at Tucker. "What's with you?"

Tucker straddled the bench, facing the Russian. "Listen, Zakharov. We both been to war. You in Chechnya, me in 'Nam. And we both been in the ring. Now you might be a hardass and I know you've put down most of the fighters you've faced. That's right, knocked 'em cold. But this Skeet Lewis is somethin' else. And I know, 'cuz I trained the man for seven years."

Zakharov gave a small nod. "I appreciate dedication. But I've seen the tapes. He's lost strength. He's getting old."

Tucker gave him a hard, thin smile. "As a soldier, have you seen what happens in the field when there's bad intelligence, or piss-poor planning?"

Zakharov didn't answer, but his eyes said, yes, that he'd seen it firsthand.

"Listen, Zakharov. I don't mind confidence in a fighter. Even arrogance, if it gets him through. But I assume you understand the value of scoutin' the enemy. So I'm gonna tell you this once.

"You've only got three tapes of Skeet, but the man's had forty bouts as an amateur and seventy-two as a pro. Your first video is eight years old. He was just developing his style. Quicker then, but not as slick. Your second tape, he broke his right hand in the second round, then went the distance, winning it with his jab and hooks. Didn't tell no one after, 'cuz he didn't want it known he could be hurt. So you can't ignore his right hand, like that tape suggests. And your last tape…his sister died the week before, killed in a drive-by shooting. So, in that match? Skeet's hand had healed, but his heart wasn't in it.

"An' that means you got trouble…*real trouble*…if your fight plan's comin' from those tapes."

Zakharov seemed to give that some thought. "How many knockouts?"

Tucker sat back. "I know you think it's all about power. You're like that big cannon on the tanks you rode. Right?"

Zakharov nodded.

"But I'm sure you've seen what a machine gun can do. Shreddin' a man. Rippin' him to pieces."

"Yes."

"I've trained Skeet for seven years, and I know every one of his tricks. Every strength and weakness. I'm gonna show you two videos. Then you decide. I'll stay if you want my help."

* * *

"This is Skeet in his prime," Tucker said, rolling the first tape.

It showed Skeet training, working at his fight weight of 160 pounds, alongside stable-mate Ruben Vasquez, a cruiserweight with lightning speed who had won gold at the Olympics.

The first sixty seconds showed both men hitting heavy bags. Skeet was relaxed, getting his rhythm going, throwing crisp five-shot combinations. Vasquez was cracking single punches that sounded like pistol shots, causing the bag to jerk, shudder, and sometimes fold at the middle. Even as an amateur, Vasquez looked better than Zakharov, both in movement and power.

Zakharov paid close attention as the tape shifted to a sparring session between the two men.

"This is three weeks before Skeet's fight. I told him and Vasquez to step it up."

On the video, the bell rang and Vasquez moved in, throwing a solid jab. Skeet slipped left and right. He backpedaled against Vasquez's advance, then got under his punches with a bob and weave, firing a crisp double-hook to the ribs. Before Vasquez could recover, Skeet did a fast pivot and fired a right that wobbled Vasquez.

As the sparring continued for three more rounds, Vasquez got peppered with lightning shots that clearly stung him, followed by the occasional uppercut or right cross that staggered him.

When the headgear came off, Vasquez had a bloody lip and a glazed-over look.

The second tape showed Skeet one year ago, fighting a twelve-rounder against Hank McGuire, a rawboned Texan whose style was similar to Zakharov's, with a steady advance and powerful one-two combinations. Every punch McGuire threw did nothing but cut air, or caught Skeet on his gloves. Then, as McGuire tired in the later rounds, Skeet did some fancy footwork, getting angles that let him rip McGuire with uppercuts and hooks. The Texan began to cover up, but it was too late. Skeet dropped him with a body shot to the liver that left McGuire gasping for air.

When Tucker ejected the video, Zakharov nodded once. "Yes. I want your advice."

Tucker tapped the videotape. "Will you do what I say?"

Zakharov made a fist. "I am a soldier who would rather die than lose."

"Then we need to get started. The fight's in four weeks."

* * *

Tucker laced up Zakharov's gloves and led him to the heavy bag.

"I know you're tough," said Tucker, "but you've got to protect yourself in the ring." He paused. "These three spots, no amount of toughness can protect, 'cuz they're naturally soft." He tapped Zakharov just above his ear, then poked him in his solar plexus. "Those are good," he added, "but this one's my favorite." He reached to the front of Zakharov's rib cage, on Zakharov's right side, and dug his fingers in beneath the lowest rib, finding his liver.

Zakharov winced and nodded.

"You need to stand less square to your opponent and keep your guard up. No more dropping your hands. No more throwing wide punches that leave you open for a quick shot up the middle."

"Show me?"

Tucker did, setting his feet at a forty-five degree angle to the bag, then kept his elbows in and fists high. He threw a few punches from that position, falling back into the covered-up position after each shot or combination.

He motioned to Zakharov. "Do it slow to start."

For the first week, they went at it like that, piece by piece, working on the fundamentals. Getting a better stance. Throwing straight punches, some of them from the limit of Zakharov's reach, so that he learned to work from the outside, instead of always barreling in. The hardest thing, though, was teaching Zakharov that he could throw a jab without loading up, or getting on top of his opponent.

"When you're in the ring," Tucker said, "keep your eyes on Skeet. But if you clinch or one of you takes an eight-count, watch my hands. I'll use them to signal the punches I want."

They tried it, but Zakharov had trouble following the more involved signals. Also, as Tucker thought it through, he realized that Skeet would understand everything he signaled to Zakharov. So Tucker told the Russian, "Only look my way in a clinch, if Skeet is turned away from me."

Toward the end of the week, Tucker's efforts began to pay off. He got Zakharov to add a little head movement. Also, each session started and ended on the treadmill. Tucker didn't want to risk injuring him with sprints, but even jogging on the treadmill would help. Tucker hoped it would keep Zakharov from running out of gas, if Skeet took him the distance.

Zakharov cursed on the treadmill. In return for such drudgery, he demanded terrible disco music from the 70's. Crap like "Get Dancin'," by Disco Tex and the Sex O-Lettes. Tucker agreed, but only after the Russian promised more mileage.

With the fight only weeks away, Tucker wasn't looking for any miracles. Just enough changes to make Zakharov a slightly different fighter from the one Skeet would expect. If Skeet had to make adjustments, that could give Zakharov an edge for the first two rounds, maybe three. And that was when Zakharov had the most power.

Tucker also changed the Russian's diet. Less fats. On the booze, he cut him back from a fifth of Vodka to two shots a day. One for a wakeup call, the other when he went to bed.

In the second week, Tucker got Zakharov back to sparring. With Bo Greene's okay, he brought in a new pair of fighters. First up was "Charming Billy" Stearns, a British fighter who was smooth and evasive in the ring.

Once the headgear was on, Tucker said to Zakharov, "This will be a test, about you following orders."

To Zakharov's surprise, after he and "Charming Billy" gloved up, Tucker used several Ace bandages, tied end to end, to bind Zakharov's right arm against his body in the defensive position, with his right glove touching his chin.

Billy, however, had the use of both hands.

"For the next three rounds," Tucker told Zakharov, "all you've got is your left hand. I know you like the power shots, but Billy's jab is razor sharp."

Zakharov narrowed his eyes.

"Trust me," said Tucker. "If you throw a long hook, he'll see it comin' and move. If you expect to hook, get in close. But I'm warning you. With Billy, none of your power shots will land. Not unless you work your way in behind the jab."

Zakharov glanced at Billy. "He doesn't impress me."

"Match his jab with yours, or it'll be a long three rounds."

When the bell sounded, Charming Billy glided to his left, flicking the jab. He had a two-inch reach on the Russian, and picked a spot on his forehead to begin a tattoo.

Zakharov threw a slow, pawing jab, putting one out with every step, so mechanical that he looked like a robot.

"Mix it up," said Tucker. "Double up, then single jabs."

Zakharov responded, working to cut off the ring, landing the occasional jab and slowing down Billy's punches.

"That's it," Tucker called to Zakharov. "Keep going." The Russian was doing better than he'd expected, so he felt encouraged.

When Billy was almost cornered, Zakharov lunged, throwing a wild left hook. Billy got under it, then came up firing a straight right that caught Zakharov on the chin.

"Patience," urged Tucker. "With your hook, wait 'till you're on top of Billy."

The round ended before Zakharov could corner Charming Billy.

In the second round, Zakharov crowded Billy and threw a double left hook, nailing his ribs as the bell rang. Billy wheezed, catching his breath while Tucker gave him water, but didn't complain. Zakharov was sweating hard from being on the move and throwing so many punches.

In the third round, Zakharov repeated his success, then head-butted Billy to keep him in place. Billy braced himself in time for Zakharov's hook. Even so, it staggered Billy and sent him sideways along the ropes. After that, Billy backpedaled and didn't get cornered.

When Tucker stripped off Zakharov's gloves and unraveled the ace bandage that had pinned his right arm, he told him, "You're doing good. But you have to get better, understand? So there'll be more of this. Then, with two weeks left, we'll go to combinations."

Zakharov grunted and rubbed his left arm.

"Don't worry," said Tucker. "It should hurt when you start out. We'll ice it and give you a rubdown after the treadmill.

* * *

Early on, Tucker had tried getting Zakharov to jump rope, but he just plodded through it, with no variation in his footwork. Jumping rope didn't seem to bring out any grace or rhythm in the Russian, so Tucker had him stick to the treadmill. He set up a TV and VCR in front of it, with Zakharov watching tapes of Skeet's boxing matches while he ran. Tucker hoped the Russian would commit most of Skeet's moves to memory. With Skeet's speed, he knew there'd be times when Zakharov would have to anticipate him, especially on his counter-punches. Otherwise, he'd eat plenty of leather.

Gradually, Zakharov worked up to running three miles at the start of his workout, and three miles at the end, still cussing, but Tucker saw him smile now and then. Mostly that happened when a videotape showed an opponent landing a punch that caught Skeet off guard and gave him a jolt.

* * *

Bo Greene, surrounded by his bodyguards, arrived at the gym on the following Tuesday. He interrupted Tucker's training session to shoot footage of Zakharov to promote the fight. Greene's entourage used vapors from dry ice and colored lights to make it theatrical, instead of like a real gym, with Bo Greene taking on the role of director, calling out what he wanted.

Greene had only a one-minute conversation with Tucker, asking, "Is Zakharov ready? Is he gonna put down Skeet Lewis?"

Tucker started to review their progress in training, and saw Greene's eyes drift to the video cameraman, who was loading fresh tape in his camera. Tucker adjusted, giving Greene what he wanted to hear. "Zakharov's in his best fighting shape and wants to win."

"Got any tricks in your pocket?"

"There'll be moves and punches Skeet hasn't seen before—not from Zakharov."

Greene stepped in close. "That's good. Because I want a win. You follow?"

Tucker nodded.

Greene started to turn away, then pointed back at Tucker. "Whatever it takes."

Tucker resisted the urge to spit as Greene hustled the cameraman over to Zakharov, then gestured at the raised ring. "Shoot from a low angle," Greene insisted, "to make him look taller."

* * *

Bo Greene moved everyone to Vegas one week before the fight. They set up a ring and training area in an air-conditioned warehouse. For living quarters, Greene reserved a giant suite for Zakharov, Tucker and the fight crew, up on the penthouse floor of Mandalay Bay, where the bout with Ray Jones and John Ruiz was featured as the main event.

Tucker worked to polish Zakharov and build his confidence. It was difficult, because Greene and his entourage kept showing up at the training camp. They distracted Zakharov with members of the press, or the glamorous women Greene kept on each arm.

Seeing the look in Zakharov's eyes, Tucker told him to ignore them and hit the bag, but Zakharov disagreed. "No. I need sex. Get me a woman."

Tucker compromised, saying, "I'll get you one tonight, but not after that. And go light on the booze."

Zakharov nodded. "Blonde. Long legs. Pretty."

"All right."

That evening, Tucker caught up to one of Greene's flunkies with all the gel in his hair, sporting diamond earrings. The man noted the details of Zakharov's request and said, "No problem."

Tucker was just as much in need of a woman, but didn't want a call girl. Parisha was still in LA, so he lay down in his hotel bed, clutching a pillow, and remembered better times. Back when he and Parisha hadn't argued so much.

* * *

Zakharov was washed out the next day. Tucker didn't like it, but at least the first part of the day would be spent on the press conference and preliminary weigh-in, giving him time to recover. After that, it was forty-eight hours to the final weigh-in, with the fight the day after.

By the time Zakharov put on the sharkskin suit and tasseled loafers that Greene's handlers had provided, he and Tucker were late for the press conference. Wearing laminated ID badges, Tucker and Zakharov took the VIP elevator and followed signs to the ballroom set aside for the occasion.

As they walked toward the head table, Tucker's eyes went to Skeet, who looked regal in a black Armani suit, blinding white shirt, and a purple silk tie that smacked of royalty. Beaming, Jabbari stayed next to him, and put his arm around Skeet's shoulder as he cracked some joke about Russian caviar not being the real thing.

Tucker saw Bo Greene stand, then motion to Zakharov, indicating the empty seat beside him. Zakharov stuck his chin out and strode forward, giving Skeet a fierce stare.

That's when Tucker saw the trainer, Tito Carvall, on Jabbari's side of the table. Tucker groaned, knowing that the Cuban, Carvall, had been the worst trainer to pick for Skeet. Despite Carvall's outstanding record with younger fighters, his practice of breaking a fighter down and building a fresh foundation would put him at odds with Skeet, who had long ago perfected his own style.

Carvall moved now and stood behind Skeet, trying to get his share of the spotlight. Skeet ignored him, except when Carvall put his hand on Skeet's shoulder. Without looking at Carvall, Skeet shrugged off his hand.

Tucker saw that Carvall already had his second cornerman and cutman with him. Tucker recognized them as men Carvall had worked with before. That made Tucker glad that his own crew had been with him all week.

With the cameras covering him, Skeet didn't so much as glance in Tucker's direction, but Skeet gave him a signal that no one else would catch, or understand. Using his index finger, Skeet gave a quick double-tap against his open palm. It was one of Tucker's oldest hand signals, calling for the double-jab.

Tucker smiled, knowing this was Skeet's way of greeting him. Letting him know the connection was still there. Still, Tucker felt a terrible ache in his heart, over having to be in the wrong corner, going against his best friend. And the worst of it was knowing that he had only one chance to save Skeet. By making him lose.

Zakharov got up from his chair, raising a fist in Skeet's direction. "America is weak," he said. "*Americans* are weak. You're going to feel the Red Hammer!" Every word sounded stiff and unnatural, as if Bo Greene had rehearsed him.

On cue, Skeet stood, being more familiar with promotional hype. He gave Zakharov a little bob and weave. "No Ivan-come-lately's gonna touch me, let alone hurt me! You 'bout to get a whuppin' from Skeet they-call-me-Slick Lewis."

The press laughed, taking pictures of Skeet as Zakharov frowned, then took his seat.

The circus continued, with the usual pre-fight questions and both promoters trying to speak for their fighters. Each camp showed footage of their fighter in training. That gave Tucker a peek at Skeet's final sparring partner, Greggor Markov, another Russian.

Markov had a similar style to Zakharov, with a steady advance and punishing body shots. At least, Tucker thought, Zakharov's going to be a different man in the ring, with jabs and head movement. And—hopefully—enough stamina to wait for a good opening, instead of forcing it.

At Tucker's insistence, the footage of Zakharov that Greene's crew had shot had been edited. Cut down to two minutes. It only showed Zakharov doing pushups, crunches and running the treadmill. Tucker didn't want Skeet getting any preview of the Russian's more defensive stance, or the jab he was finally using to set up his power shots.

Finally, the commissioner's representative, wearing a maroon sports coat, motioned both fighters to a raised platform that held a scale. The real weigh-in was in two days, twenty-four hours before the fight, so this was more for the press, giving them a photo-op to go with all the bullshit at the microphones.

Glaring at each other, Skeet and Zakharov stripped down and flexed while cameras flashed. Skeet showed whipcord muscle that rippled, without an ounce of fat, and was measured as having a two-inch reach advantage. Zakharov had trimmed down overall, and gained more strength in his legs, but he looked pale and unimpressive next to Skeet. The only thing that stood out was the unrelenting chill in Zakharov's eyes as he sized up Skeet.

Both men weighed the same amount, both two pounds over their fight weight—something they could easily sweat off before their match.

Afterwards, dressed in his suit and heading from the press conference to the elevator, Zakharov complained to Tucker. "Skeet showed me no respect. He kept butting in—screwing up what Greene instructed me to say."

"Forget about that. Be a soldier and get ready for battle."

Inwardly, Tucker gave Skeet credit for winning the verbal sparring. That had gotten to Zakharov, leaving its mark on his pride.

* * *

In the last two days of training, Tucker had Zakharov back off on the sparring, doing just enough to keep his edge. Mostly, Tucker had him shadow box and do mitt drills, trying to give him a little more speed. Tucker also made a final effort to correct the two flaws in Zakharov that Skeet could turn to his advantage. These were things Tucker had focused on for the last three weeks, but drilled on at length in the final two days of training.

The first flaw was Zakharov's habit of leading with his head when he bobbed and weaved, setting up to throw the hook. Step by step, Tucker demonstrated to Zakharov how he lost some of his balance and torque, setting up for the hook, whenever he leaned his head forward, past the point where his raised gloves could guard it. Plus, that left him open to a counter-hook.

Zakharov agreed, but only corrected the habit when yelled at. He had done it for so long in bad form that it felt right to him. The best Tucker could hope for was that Skeet would choose to cover up against Zakharov's hooks, instead of trading with him.

The second flaw was more serious. It didn't show when Zakharov shadow boxed, or hit the heavy bag, but came out when he sparred. In the fight game, it was known as a "lazy" right. Any time Zakharov connected with a heavy right—be it from a straight right, or working off a combination—he dropped his right hand as he brought it back. For a split second, his right hand dipped as he drew it back, exposing his chin.

That was something Skeet would certainly counter with a hook. So Tucker tried to get Zakharov to pivot to a new angle when his right landed. But the idea didn't stick with the Russian, who only did it once in a while.

In the end, Zakharov couldn't remove his flaws, but learned to brace himself and cover up quickly, taking less punishment.

* * *

The official weigh-in took only five minutes. Both fighters made their weight, and neither camp stuck around to play it up with the press. Tucker didn't want Skeet getting Zakharov frustrated, or distracted, and Tito Carvall stayed close to Skeet, whispering into his ear. Skeet's only reaction was to twist his shoulders, bumping Carvall, so that he had to step back.

Tucker's main concern, as they made their way back to their hotel suite, was to have Zakharov eat a big meal, gaining the weight he'd lost for the weigh-in, and to rest.

Zakharov grumbled in the elevator after noticing in the casino, on the sports board, that Skeet was getting even odds. Tucker let him vent and noticed that Zakharov seemed relieved to get back to their suite and settle in with Tucker's crew.

Manny, who was hungry, insisted that they order dinner. He clowned around, holding a room service menu in each hand like punch-mitts as he called out each entrée. "When I name the one you want, gimme a jab," he said.

Tucker laughed, grateful that Manny had found a way to ease everyone's pre-fight jitters. Zakharov joined in, jabbing at everything Manny named. "More," he said, "more," snapping a jab each time. Conrad Volker got into it, too, crossing his eyes and crying, "Where's the strudel? Momma Volker always gave me strudel!"

Finally, Tucker got them to calm down and said Manny could phone room service, once he wrote out what he wanted for Zakharov: broiled chicken and rice, tomatoes, two hard-boiled eggs, and a pitcher of grapefruit juice.

Once the food arrived, Zakharov sat down to eat alone in an adjoining room, so he wouldn't have to watch the rest of them put away the kind of food he wanted, but couldn't have.

While Zakharov watched tapes of Skeet and ate, Tucker and his crew tried to second-guess what Skeet's battle plan would be. They did that over Caesar salad and racks of barbecued ribs, along with baked potatoes swimming in butter, sour cream and chives.

Then, for the next two hours, they polished Tucker's plan for Zakharov. Mostly, it came down to countering Skeet's speed and finesse with Zakharov's power and the Russian's ability to cut off the ring.

Tucker expected that Zakharov could gain a slight advantage by covering up and moving more than Skeet expected. But there was no telling if the Russian would follow his new training or revert to old habits. In Tucker's mind, the only thing that seemed to come out dead even in this match was each fighter's pride and will to win.

As Tucker passed out a few iced Heinekens from the mini-fridge, his crew started comparing Skeet and Zakharov to former fighters who had graced the ring. Tucker took that for what it was…just another way to overcome the pre-fight jitters. But he approved and joined in on the bull session.

Manny was old enough to bring up "Sugar Ray" Robinson going against Jake LaMotta, the "Raging Bull." That was his take on the history of fighters like Skeet and Zakharov squaring off. Tucker felt a better comparison was Thomas "Hit Man" Hearns against "Marvelous" Marvin Hagler. And so it went, back and forth between Tucker, Manny and Conrad, with each man adding something to the discussion.

Then, as they reached the wee hours, they chased the kind of thing that you can never pin down entirely. Not just who had been great, but what had made them great. What had made them stand apart from all the others, earning them a special place in the lore and legends of boxing.

It was the kind of talk Tucker loved, but in the back of his mind, he was still worrying over what might happen to Skeet if Zakharov didn't win. To Skeet and to himself. Still, all the talk helped, and as the neon lights of the strip began to fade with dawn's approach, Tucker finally grabbed a few hours sleep.

* * *

The day of the fight, which would begin at eight that evening, Tucker gave Zakharov steak and eggs for breakfast. After that, Tucker only let him walk the treadmill for a half-mile, then shadow box three rounds to stay loose, followed by two rounds of mitt drills.

"This is fucked," Zakharov complained. "No sex and no violence. You call this America?"

Tucker did his best to help Zakharov ride out the tension that was building as the hour of the fight approached. Zakharov kept trying to pace, agitated by the excess energy he had stored up since Tucker had cut back on his training. Repeatedly, Tucker made him sit down in an easy chair, and try to rest while he watched tapes of Skeet.

Tucker didn't tell Zakharov, but he expected the Russian would need every bit of his reserves if Skeet made it through the first five rounds.

Mostly, Tucker stayed calm and tried to make Zakharov feel the same way.

Later, Tucker had Zakharov eat a light lunch of tuna salad. Then, with their undercard bout set to start in four hours, Tucker gave him a shot of vodka and ordered him to take a nap.

Zakharov didn't argue, but looked him in the eye and said, "Trust me. This fight is mine. I will win."

Tucker nodded, but the Russian wanted to shake hands on it, as if that sealed it, giving him the victory. Having seen all manner of behavior heading into the final hours before a fight, Tucker knew better than to mess with a fighter's rituals. He shook the Russian's hand, which Zakharov thanked him for as a solemn show of faith. Then Zakharov went into his room and closed the door.

Immediately, Tucker waved to Manny Gonzalez and Conrad Volker, getting them to his side. "You guys," he said, "get fightside and check out the dressing room and the ring. Prep our boy's gear. For damn sure, I want to have extras of everything. Not just gloves, trunks, cups and mouthpieces, you hear? I mean all the way down to tape, swabs, buckets, water bottles, Vaseline, and adrenaline for the cuts. *All of it.*"

"Got it," said Manny. He and Conrad left, carrying a notepad, making a list.

Tucker checked the mini-fridge, making sure there was fruit juice for Zakharov when he woke up.

Then Tucker let out his breath and listened to the quiet for a moment. Fighting his own restlessness, he sat down and picked up a magazine. Slowly, he flipped through it without reading a thing, barely looking at the pages.

At about 4 P.M., Bo Greene came by with his entourage to wish Zakharov well. They were already well juiced, and so loud that other guests of the hotel opened their doors and looked into the hall.

"Go away," Tucker told Greene, looking him in the eye. "If you want Zakharov to win, let him rest. I'll get him there on time."

One of the bigger men started to reach for Tucker, but Greene batted his hand away. Softly, he said to Tucker, "You'd better be a man who keeps his promise." He turned and left, flanked by his bodyguards, trailing a string of punks, hookers and flunkies.

Tucker locked the door, then approached Zakharov's room. He cracked the door and saw that the Russian was still asleep. Good, thought Tucker. He's going to need his strength.

He shut the door, walked the length of the suite to a sitting area that had a television and turned it on, keeping the volume down to a whisper. It was closed circuit, and it didn't take him long to find the channel where the casino was promoting the fights that would begin in three hours.

Tucker peeled an orange and ate it, paying little attention to the video clips that were shown of Roy Jones and John Ruiz, hyping the main event, doing their "bad blood" rap, followed by clips of the knockouts both men had achieved.

A tuxedoed announcer came on, mentioning the undercard fight with Skeet Lewis and Vladimir Zakharov. He said it offered a classic match up of speed and grace versus power and grit.

The video footage of Zakharov was brief, because Tucker hadn't let the public or any media watch his workouts. He didn't want Skeet or any of his crew getting wind of the adjustments he'd gotten Zakharov to make. Mostly, the footage was of past fights, showing Zakharov's knockouts, then the promo clip for tonight's fight, giving a close-up of Zakharov, shaking a fist and saying in his thick accent, "My hands will do the talking. They will hammer my opponent." The last shot was of Bo Greene with his arm around Zakharov, standing by one of the international restaurants in the

Mandalay Bay that was called the Red Square. It displayed a statue of Lenin that Greene and Zakharov posed beside.

Next up was video footage of Tito Carvall talking to an interviewer, while Skeet hit the heavy bag in the distance.

"Zakharov has power," Carvall admitted, "but he depends too much on it. In the end, it's about precision."

Behind him, Skeet glared in his direction, interrupting his workout, then walked toward Carvall.

"The outcome," said Carvall, "depends on who can execute the basic moves with the best balance and speed."

Skeet was walking quickly now, and slipped between Carvall and the camera, bearing down on the interviewer. "Precision?" said Skeet. "That's *bullshit*. My whole career's been about that, and it hasn't got me the ranking I deserve." His voice was rising, nearly to a shout. "Well, this is *it*, man. This fight means everything to me. It's my career on the line. My damn life—you understand?" He thumped his chest with his glove, shifting his stance to keep Carvall behind him. "There's nuthin' I won't do, and nuthin' I won't risk to win this fight."

Wincing, Tucker clicked the remote, turning off the television.

Back in LA, Skeet had made it clear he wouldn't take a dive. But hearing how upset he was tore at Tucker's heart. Come fight night, instead of having a true friend at his side, Skeet was already at odds with his trainer. And worst of all, the anger Skeet expressed might cloud his judgement in the ring.

Tucker bit his lip and shook his head, reminding himself that Skeet's impatience and anger, besides helping Zakharov, might save Skeet's life. Closing his eyes, Tucker felt sick. For the first time in his life, the sport that he had always loved had been ruined for him. He was trapped, working for dishonest men that he hated—men who wouldn't hesitate to kill him or Skeet.

Tucker took an iced mineral water from the mini-fridge and held it against the back of his neck. Gradually, it began to ease the knot of tension he felt. But what it couldn't do was lessen the ache in his heart.

* * *

In their dressing room, Tucker watched a representative of the boxing commission sign off on the tape that wrapped Zakharov's hands. Next, the same man inspected the gloves and watched Tucker pull them onto the Russian's hands, as snug as he could, then lace them up. For a puncher like Zakharov, Tucker wanted the gloves tight. Then Tucker wrapped duct tape around the wrists of the glove. That prevented the criss-crossed lacing of the glove from being used like a rasp, dragging it across an opponent's face. Also, the tape kept the end of a lace from flicking out and cutting a fighter's eye.

Carefully, the commissioner's rep signed off on the gloves, making sure that his signature crossed onto the tape.

Tucker whispered to Zakharov, "In a little bit, we'll start all the Hollywood bullshit, with music and dry ice while you enter the ring. But I want you thinking about the fight. About starting with your jab and being patient. Don't get anxious. Don't let Skeet set a quick trap and lure you in."

Zakharov thumped his gloves together. "Victory. I will earn it."

Manny Gonzales entered the room, carrying sponges, water, an ice bag and a bucket. Conrad Volker carried his cutman gear and wore a headband that was loaded with cotton swabs—some dry, some covered with Vaseline. He also had a metal "end-swell" hanging from a chain on his neck. It was the style Volker preferred—a flat piece of polished metal the size of a fifty-cent piece, with a metal ring on the other side to slip over his index finger, allowing him to press the smoothed metal side against any spots where Zakharov might swell up from blows he received.

Manny, Conrad and Tucker all wore black silk jackets. Bright red letters stitched across their backs read, "Vladimir 'The Hammer' Zakharov," next to a red hammer and sickle. Their jackets matched the trunks Zakharov wore, visible beneath the loose pullover that kept him warm.

A phone rang in the room, and the commissioner's rep answered it, then hung up. "Fifteen minutes until your entrance," he said.

Tucker positioned Zakharov in front of a full-length mirror and had him jog in place, then shadow box. After ten minutes, Zakharov had a good sweat going and Tucker slipped on his punch-mitts. Working methodically, he took Zakharov through the easiest punches: his newly perfected jab, then a left-right combination, finished with a jab. Then Tucker started him in on hooks and uppercuts—stepping forward or backward slightly with the occasional pivot, so that Zakharov had to keep on his toes and move to hit the mitts.

The phone rang again. The commissioner's rep answered, then hung up. "They're ready."

Tucker ignored him. Too much was riding on this to go in without his fighter in the right frame of mind. He put Zakharov through another set of punches, telling him, "That's it. Harder! Give me more!"

The Russian snapped off punches that staggered Tucker, even as he braced himself and caught them on the padding of his mitts.

Tucker called out a final set of punches, and was satisfied that Zakharov's blows were swift and punishing.

"You're ready," Tucker told him.

Tucker's corner crew joined him. Flanked on all sides by security men, they lined up with Tucker in front and Zakharov resting both gloves on Tucker's shoulders, followed by Manny, then Conrad. Keeping bunched up, they left the room, turned into the dim hallway and followed it into a temporary tunnel-like structure that the casino's stage crew had assembled. Tucker smelled sawdust from fresh construction as they passed through the tunnel, going from the multi-story hotel wing onto the main floor of the casino, where they angled back toward its ballrooms.

* * *

Security men with walkie-talkies were stationed along the route. Static and muted voices from their radios filled the air. The guards announced Zakharov's progress to those further up the line. Then the amplified voice of the announcer echoed above the crowd, hyping Skeet "Slick" Lewis as the ultimate test for Vladimir "The Hammer" Zakharov.

Tucker and his crew reached a larger, curtained tunnel and saw a bearded member of the broadcast crew with a camera on his shoulder. He kept the lens aimed just past Tucker, and began to backpedal, staying ahead of them, trying for a shot of Zakharov.

Lights dimmed ahead of them, inside the ballroom, except for the roped-off canvas boxing ring, set on a raised platform, which was flooded with the glare of lights hanging above it.

A haze rose in front of them from the dry ice, pushed by a battery of electric fans, and Tucker called to Zakharov, "Close your eyes."

Tucker slowed a bit, but kept them moving as a bank of fireworks released huge bursts of crimson sparks, forming the shape of a hammer and sickle. The fireworks made everything around them flicker like a red strobe light as the music for Zakharov's entrance cut in with a deafening boom. It had a brassy, double-time disco beat that almost hid the melodyn but Tucker still recognized it as the old Beatles song, "Back in the USSR."

More cameras faced them as they emerged from the tunnel, and boxing fans crowded up against either side of the aisle that led to the ring. Tucker saw men in tailored suits with women on their arms sporting low-cut gowns and glittering jewels.

Tucker picked up the pace, not wanting Zakharov to lose the sweat he'd worked up. Sometimes fans reached out, but Tucker ignored them and pressed forward, ignoring the pain in his hip.

Everything seemed to move faster as they reached the edge of the ring, and Tucker climbed the steps with an effort, afraid for a moment of losing his balance with the weight of Zakharov's boxing gloves on his shoulders.

Then Manny used his foot and one hand to stretch a gap in the ropes for Zakharov to slip through. Tucker joined Zakharov in the ring, while Manny and Conrad stayed outside, taking up their position at the corner.

A beefy security guard walked Tucker and Zakharov over to a commissioner's rep with tinted glasses and a laminated badge, who stood holding a walkie-talkie.

Off to his right, in the front row, Tucker saw Bo Greene, with a woman on each arm, holding court to his entourage. Looking about, Tucker found Jabbari near Skeet's corner, surrounded by the same thugs Tucker had seen before.

Skeet was already in the ring with Tito Carvall. Skeet still had his robe on. Keeping his back to Carvall, Skeet was putting on a show with rapid-fire shadow boxing.

Tucker knew it was meant for Zakharov, not the crowd. He prayed for Skeet to miss with his punches, then rubbed Zakharov's shoulders and told him to jog in place.

"Keep moving," Tucker told Zakharov. "While we're waiting, go easy, but give me some punches."

Zakharov rolled his shoulders and started punching.

As the announcer called out each fighter's record, Zakharov faced Skeet across the ring. Zakharov aimed his punches at Skeet, as if he were standing within reach.

Overhead, on the big-screens suspended in each corner of the ballroom, a photograph of each fighter was displayed, side-by-side, listing their reach, height and weight.

The announcer held out the microphone to the referee, a bald man with a pate that gleamed as if it had been waxed and buffed. The referee called both fighters to the center of the ring.

Tucker took the loose pullover off Zakharov and kneaded his shoulders. Tito Carvall removed Skeet's robe and did the same. Both fighters listened to the referee, but their eyes remained locked on each other and neither man blinked.

Tucker was glad that Skeet had ignored him.

The referee finished and told both fighters to touch gloves. Zakharov snapped his down from above, hitting Skeet's with a thump.

Tucker pulled Zakharov back into the corner, slipped through the ropes and told him, "Start with your jab."

Deliberately, the referee pointed to each judge, getting a nod in return, then signaled the timer, who struck the bell, starting the fight.

Tucker watched Zakharov advance to the middle of the ring, where Skeet met him.

Immediately, Skeet feinted with his right, following with a double-jab that nailed the Russian's forehead.

By the time Zakharov answered with a straight right, Skeet had slipped and grazed him with a hook that Zakharov got under just in time, causing the crowd to yell.

Skeet circled, firing jabs that caught the air or the edge of Zakharov's forehead, making him hesitate.

"Jab back," Tucker yelled, and the Russian did.

It wasn't pretty, but Zakharov began sticking his jab out, which at least kept Skeet from adding combinations to the jabs he was throwing.

Skeet backpedaled and moved side to side, looking for a new angle, while Zakharov advanced, keeping his gloves high, trying to cut off the ring.

"More jabs," Tucker yelled, and Zakharov threw a jab now and then, with Skeet staying just outside his reach.

To Tucker's surprise, Skeet leapt forward, throwing a straight right that split the Russian's gloves, then made a quick pivot. Planting his feet, he threw a fierce hook that caught Zakharov high on the cheekbone, just below his eye.

The Russian grinned at Skeet and motioned for more, but Tucker knew the blow had hurt him.

Behind Tucker, Conrad said, "I'm icing the Endswell, getting it ready."

Skeet bobbed, weaved, then tried to double his hook, but the Russian answered with an overhand right that struck Skeet on the forehead, knocking him backward. Skeet caught his balance, but found himself on the ropes.

Zakharov ripped several shots to the body, while Tito Carvall yelled, "Move! Move! Get out of there!"

Skeet caught some of the punches on his elbows and escaped with a pivot.

Tucker glanced at the clock. Thirty seconds left in the round.

"Work off the jab," he called to Zakharov. From experience, Tucker knew that judges often decided who had won a round based on the final exchange of punches as time ran out.

Zakharov raised his gloves and started after Skeet, taking his time. Skeet kept his distance and Tucker watched him shake out his left arm. Had Zakharov injured him?

Zakharov seemed to sense something and moved faster, firing jabs, then a wild hook.

Skeet escaped with a bob and weave, delivering a solid upper cut to Zakharov's gut, then another to his chin, snapping his head back.

The timekeeper slapped a paddle-stick three times, signaling the last ten seconds of the round.

Zakharov shoved, then nailed Skeet with a straight right when he bounced off the ropes.

Skeet grimaced and clinched, tying up Zakharov, then stepped around, getting the Russian off balance.

The bell rang, saving Zakharov from a chopping right that Skeet would have fired.

Manny shoved the stool into place and readied a water bottle with a spray nozzle as Zakharov walked to the corner. Manny misted Zakharov as Tucker sat him down and asked, "How do you feel?"

Zakharov spat out his mouthpiece, but wasn't breathing hard. Just deep, even breaths. "He's hard to catch. Fast."

Tucker said, "Don't jump in, trying to nail him. Stay covered up. Make *him* take the chances. When he does, be ready to counter."

A cameraman leaned over, focused on Zakharov.

"If you press the fight," Tucker added, "Skeet will make you chase him. Hold back and he'll get frustrated. He'll come to you."

The ring girl pranced by in a sequined bikini, holding up the card for round two.

"Lead with the jab," Tucker said, "and be ready to counter."

Conrad reached over with the Endswell, finding the red spot on Zakharov's cheekbone where Skeet's hook had landed.

Zakharov grunted. "Counter where?"

"Stick to the body. His arms will get hit if he covers up. If he doesn't, find his gut."

Manny brushed a little Vaseline on Zakharov's face, then smoothed it out.

The timekeeper slapped the paddle stick, and the referee hollered, "Seconds out."

Zakharov stood as Manny cleared the stool. Tucker climbed out, and Manny wiped down the canvas where spray from the water bottle had wet the corner.

Zakharov pounded his gloves as the bell rang, then advanced.

* * *

Tucker felt the first round had been a draw, but knew Skeet had looked more in command, and might've won over the judges. Even with Zakharov landing better power shots, Skeet had thrown more punches. So Zakharov was probably down a point on the scorecards.

Tucker hollered, "Work the jab."

As Zakharov and Skeet approached each other, Tucker saw Bo Greene beaming from a front row seat, pointing up at Zakharov while someone from the media offered him a microphone.

Skeet flicked a jab, then followed it with a lightning fast combination, doubling up, left-right, left-right.

Four rapid punches, stitched together like that, carried the same force as a single, knockout punch.

Zakharov was driven back, even though he caught them all on his arms.

To Tucker's surprise, Skeet pressed his attack, slipping inside to risk a quick uppercut, followed by a hook.

Both landed, but didn't seem to affect Zakharov, who countered with a double-hook that hammered Skeet's ribs.

Skeet grunted and stayed hunched over as he backpedaled.

Tito Carvall stood and yelled to Skeet, "Take your time. Follow the game plan."

Zakharov raised his gloves, keeping his guard up as he moved forward.

"You hear me?" hollered Carvall. "Don't rush!"

Tucker found himself nodding. He figured Skeet wasn't going to survive unless he played it safe by taking the Russian into the later rounds.

Tucker bit his lip and prayed for Skeet to stay angry and challenge Zakharov head-on.

But Skeet began to move sideways, flicking jabs that caught Zakharov before he could square up to Skeet and counter. Then Skeet reversed his stance, switching to southpaw. Tucker had seen him do it before, flicking his right like a jab, trying to throw off the other fighter.

Zakharov ate the right twice, then countered with a wild hook that grazed Skeet's chin, throwing Skeet off balance.

As Skeet switched back to an orthodox stance, Zakharov landed a quick one-two, drawing blood from the corner of Skeet's mouth.

Skeet faked a jab and landed a left uppercut, then an overhand right, making no effort to escape, even as Carvall yelled, "Pivot, damn it. Move!"

Zakharov answered with a low blow, followed by a quick double-hook.

The referee stepped in, giving Zakharov a warning, but Skeet was weakened, and Zakharov went after him as soon as the referee stepped back. Firing jabs, Zakharov worked Skeet into the corner, then loaded up, firing a heavy left-right combination, not bothering to keep his hands high as he brought them back, into the on-guard position.

Tucker winced, expecting Skeet to counter. But Skeet had been staggered and clinched. His left eye looked puffy from Zakharov's repeated jabs, and blood was dripping from his mouth.

As the referee stepped in, separating them, Zakharov glanced at Tucker.

Out of habit, Tucker motioned to Zakharov with his hands, mimicking straight punches, inside to the gut.

Zakharaov nodded, but when the referee broke up their clinch, Tucker caught Skeet watching and realized his mistake.

As the Russian started forward, Skeet let his gloves drift outward, giving Zakharov what appeared to be a free shot at his midsection.

"Back up," Tucker yelled, but Zakharov threw a straight punch, aimed at Skeet's midsection. He missed as Skeet made a quick pivot and countered with a fierce hook to the jaw that staggered the Russian.

Across the ring, Tucker caught Jabbari glaring at Skeet, then at him.

Skeet moved in to follow up on the hook, thinking the Russian would retreat, but Zakharov advanced and their foreheads collided.

Tucker prayed that one of them would be cut bad enough to stop the fight, but no blood showed when they separated.

Zakharov quickly advanced, hammering each side of Skeet's ribs with left and right body shots, getting the crowd to its feet.

Skeet staggered, and his face twisted with pain.

Tucker prayed that he'd go down and stay there for the ten-count.

Instead, Skeet slipped to the inside and traded shots, firing a flurry of uppercuts at Zakharov's chin, connecting three times for every body shot the Russian landed.

The crowd went into a frenzy.

Both fighters suffered during the exchange, but Zakharov's blows did more damage.

He got in another left-right that slammed Skeet into the corner. Again, Zakharov briefly dropped his right as he finished punching. With his legs wobbling, Skeet didn't clinch or pivot to escape. He kept firing, finding the Russian's chin. That's when Tucker knew that Skeet didn't care if he got hurt, or how bad. He wasn't going to retreat.

Skeet managed an uppercut to Zakharov's solar plexus, forcing him to clinch.

With his chest heaving, Skeet turned to Carvall, who screamed, "Don't trade with him."

Still clinching, Skeet turned to Tucker. Skeet's left eye was almost swollen shut. His lip was split wide and blood dripped from his mouth.

Behind him, Tucker heard Manny call out, "Zak, he's ready to go. Work him upstairs. Take his head off!"

Skeet gave Tucker a pleading look.

Seeing the pain Skeet was in, Tucker felt his guts twist. Still, he shook his head, knowing what it would cost if Skeet won.

The referee tried to separate the fighters, but Skeet held on a second longer, staring at Tucker, and his lips moved, forming the word, *please.*

Ashamed, Tucker looked away, but felt movement near his waist and looked down.

Out of habit, his hands had answered Skeet's plea for help. They were signaling how to counter when the Russian threw a left-right, then dropped his guard.

Skeet let the referee separate them, and shuffled slowly to his left. He seemed to run out of gas, letting his hands drop from his chin, down to his waist.

Zakharov threw a left-right that Skeet managed to slip, then countered with an overhead right that caught the Russian flush on the chin.

It rocked Zakharov, and Skeet followed it with a crushing hook that nailed him on the temple.

The crowd yelled, feeding their bloodlust as the Russian's legs buckled and he went limp, toppling sideways onto the canvas, landing with a thump.

Skeet stood there with his chest heaving, barely able to raise his arms overhead.

Tears spilled from Skeet's eyes as the referee started the ten count, then waved it off, ending the fight when he saw the Russian was out cold.

The cornermen for both fighters came through the ropes.

Tucker got the mouthpiece out of Zakharov's mouth and saw he was breathing without any difficulty. He steadied Zakharov's head as the doctor raised the fallen man's eyelids and checked his pupils with a flashlight.

Security men in maroon blazers entered the ring, then the tuxedoed announcer and the promoters, who worked hard, pushing people aside to make their way to the cameras.

Tucker used scissors, cutting the tape and laces off Zakharov's gloves. As he pulled one glove off, Zakharov's eyes fluttered, and he began to mumble.

Glancing up, Tucker saw an exhausted Skeet, hoisted up on the shoulders of his cornermen.

When their eyes met, Skeet's eyes said, *Thank you*, and Tucker's said, *I'm sorry*.

Manny and Conrad helped with Zakharov, getting him to sit up.

Slowly, Tucker stood, watching the press hold out microphones as reporters jostled to get past him and closer to Skeet, hoping for a gritty quote—something that could carry a headline.

Cameramen stood on the ropes at the ring's corner poles, or reached up, holding their videocams overhead, trying to capture Skeet's bruised but smiling face as he rode the shoulders of his cornermen.

But for Tucker, what filled his mind were moments in his life that he had cherished. His mother, bathing him as a child while she hummed a lullaby. A furious sidewalk race with his brother, Ben, on their first bicycles. The girl next door, Martha-Rae, giving him his first kiss. And then watching Skeet in the ring, as he worked his magic.

And as those slivers of memory passed through him in a few heartbeats—there rose a single, shadowed vision of a steep concrete stairwell. And of the sudden downward ride it offered, from Skeet's victory, into darkness.

About the Author

Terry Bennett was born in California and attended UC Santa Barbara where he studied art before leaving for Alaska to work as a commercial fisherman. He returned to California and fought forest fires while serving as a mountain rescue team member, then began working with words, first as a trade magazine editor, then as a copywriter. During the 1990's, he won five Persephonie awards at the William Saroyan Writer's Conference, and has had "Antioxidants," the short story that opens this collection, published in the *Red Rock Review.*

The fonts used in the book are from the Garamond family

Terry Bennett

The Toby Press publishes fine writing,
available at bookstores everywhere. For more information, please
contact *The* Toby Press at www.tobypress.com